# ROAD

## TO RUIN

# ROAD
## TO RUIN

The First Magebike Courier Novel

## HANA LEE

SAGA PRESS

LONDON SYDNEY **NEW YORK** TORONTO NEW DELHI

SAGA PRESS
AN IMPRINT OF SIMON & SCHUSTER, LLC
1230 AVENUE OF THE AMERICAS, NEW YORK, NEW YORK 10020

First Saga Press trade paperback edition May 2024

SAGA PRESS and colophon are trademarks of Simon & Schuster, LLC.

Simon & Schuster: Celebrating 100 Years of Publishing in 2024

For information about special discounts for bulk purchases, please contact Simon & Schuster Special Sales at 1-866-506-1949 or business@simonandschuster.com.

The Simon & Schuster Speakers Bureau can bring authors to your live event. For more information or to book an event, contact the Simon & Schuster Speakers Bureau at 1-866-248-3049 or visit our website at www.simonspeakers.com.

Interior design by Wendy Blum

Manufactured in the United States of America

10 9 8 7 6 5 4 3 2 1

Library of Congress Cataloging-in-Publication Data has been applied for.

ISBN 978-1-6680-3561-0
ISBN 978-1-6680-3562-7 (ebook)

*For Shalin, the sun to my moon*

# PART ONE

## CHAPTER ONE

# ROCK AND A HARD PLACE

*Second Age of Storms, 51st Summer, Day 20*

The pteropter came shrieking out of the hot blue sky like mana lightning, hell-bent on ruining Jin's day. Time didn't do her the courtesy of slowing down. One second she was roaring down the wasteland highway on her magebike, and the next, a demented flying beast had its claws in her shoulder. Right down to the bone, like the leather was nothing.

Jin yelped and twisted, which was exactly the wrong thing to do. The handlebars jerked. The bike shuddered beneath her. Wings flapped in her face as she fought to regain control. Then the front wheel hit a rock or a pothole or some stupid shit like that, and the next thing Jin knew, she was sailing through the air.

She hit the ground headfirst, flipped a couple of times, and finally skidded to a rest on her side. *Not dead* was her first hazy thought. Then: *That depends. What about the bike?*

She didn't dare look. Instead she lay there, battered and breathless, imagining the worst: a shredded, smoking heap of metal in a pool of bright blue mana. A scrapped magebike in the middle of the wastes was a death sentence.

First things first: Were her bones broken? Was her skull intact? Could she move?

Thank Rasvel for her bonehelm, carved from a saurian's skull and tougher than steel. She'd rattled her head around good, but she could still think and she wasn't seeing double. Her throat itched for a mana-cig. Good sign, probably. She confirmed her limbs were working by reaching into her breast pocket for a pack, only to find it empty. Right—she was trying to quit.

Finally she made herself look. Relief made her dizzy. The magebike was all right; it lay on its side in the dust, still bike shaped, smoking slightly. The sight lent Jin the strength to push herself upright, then to her feet. Goddamn, her shoulder hurt.

Jin glared at the reason she'd crashed. The pteropter was thrashing weakly on the ground next to the magebike. Just a little one, small enough to fit in her bonehelm. Jin limped closer and it screeched, reedy and thin. One of its four leathery wings dragged in the dirt, white bone poking through a mess of violet saurian blood. Beady eyes glared from the triangular head, above a beak lined with sharp teeth.

"Don't look at *me*." Jin heaved her bike upright and braced the kickstand on the cracked, pitted surface of the highway. "I was minding my own business. You're the one who tried to kill me."

The pteropter made a miserable keening sound and fell silent. Jin snuck a glance. The little saurian wasn't dead; its three unhurt wings were twitching, like it wanted to take flight. Clearly that wasn't going to happen.

Jin looked back in the direction she'd come. Air shimmered above the highway, hot and dry. Gravelly sand undulated and heaved as far as the eye could see, an infinite expanse broken only by the skyward-reaching teeth of a rock outcropping or the lone many-armed figure of a cactus. The wasteland wasn't featureless and flat the way city dwellers described, but even Jin had to admit there wasn't much out here to look at.

Except *that*.

Above the western horizon churned the crackling fog of a mana storm. Kerina Sol, her starting point, would have already closed its dome in preparation. Gales of wind and blasts of lightning would batter the city's shield, testing the limits of the shieldcasters who closed ranks to keep it raised. Jin could imagine the faint blue hum of the shield even if she couldn't see it from this distance. Everyone in the city would be safe from the storm so long as the shieldcasters held; only outriders like Jin were in trouble.

Likely the little pteropter wouldn't survive once the storm came this way. Even if it did, the wasteland sun would bake it to death— if its own kind didn't peck it apart first.

"Not my problem." Jin took off her helm and checked it for cracks. The bone hadn't even chipped. She hesitated, grinding her teeth, and the pteropter had the nerve to let loose a sad chirp that tugged at her heartstrings. "I said, not my . . . Ugh."

It *was* her problem, the way sick cats and kids in rags had always been her problem. The wasteland was meant to be her guilt-free zone, a lawless desert where the only person Jin had to worry about was herself.

*Not fair.*

What could she even do to help, anyway? She didn't have any- where to pack an injured pteropter. Jin glanced at her tank satchel and saddlebags, which were stuffed with expensive—and, for the most part, illegal—goods, including one love letter signed in swooping royal cursive and sealed with rose-scented wax. Prince Kadrin probably wouldn't appreciate pteropter bloodstains on his latest romantic missive.

That left her bonehelm. Fuck.

Jin knelt beside the pteropter and held out her hand, slow and careful. *You are an idiot*, she reminded herself. *It's a miracle you've survived this long.* The pteropter eyed her hand and clacked its toothy beak. Jin winced in anticipation.

"Easy, now—*ow, ouch, goddamn fuck*—"

She lifted the pteropter—its beak clamped down on her gloved palm—and stuffed it into the helm. Then she tore off her jacket and wrapped it hastily around the helm, fashioning a bulky sling. Finally she hung the cursed parcel on her handlebars and stepped back, panting.

The parcel shrieked. A sharp beak poked out from one of the orbital openings on the bonehelm and emitted a scratchy hiss. Jin massaged her shoulder.

"I'm gonna call you Screech."

She straddled her magebike, worked her hands over the textured grips, and inhaled, long and slow. Power rose from the dwindling store of mana in her blood, a simmer in her veins. It pooled in her hands until the heat grew almost unbearable—then a spark crackled between her fingers and danced over her knuckles.

Jin braced herself for the magebike's familiar roar, the blissful rumble of the engine between her knees. Nothing happened. Trapped in Jin's helm, the pteropter let out another screech.

"No," Jin said. "No, no, no."

She burned more mana. Sparks flew. Her hands grew hot and slippery, but the magebike made no sound.

Jin swore, hopped off the bike, and scanned the exposed machinery under the engine block. The crash must have knocked something loose. Where had that smoke come from?

"Oh Rasvel, not the engine. Please not the engine."

Jin pressed her forehead against the warm leather saddle and breathed in, then out. Her throat ached for the cool smoke of a mana-cig. She kept them stashed in her saddlebags now, too far to reach for one on a whim.

The sky darkened. Out west, the mana storm had barreled over Kerina Sol without breaking stride and was bearing down on her position. Bolts of blue and violet lightning stabbed down through boiling black clouds; a clap of furious thunder followed each flash. Closer together now. Much too close.

Makela's grasping fingers, she'd wasted too much time on the pteropter. If she didn't get her bike going, she was toast.

Sweating, she bent over the engine. Jin was no mechanic, just a sparkrider, and she didn't fully understand the bike's internals. No one did, except the artificers who put the bikes together and kept them running. It was all based on Road Builder technology, science lost to the ages and rediscovered in bits and pieces by scavengers combing the wastes for old ruins.

Mana went in the magebike's fuel tank and sparks went down the ignition line; that was the extent of Jin's comprehension. The tank was still one-third full, and the ignition line was intact. So what now?

A distant roar caught her attention. Not the oncoming mana storm, and certainly not the magebike under her grease-stained hands. Jin tossed sweaty black hair out of her face and glanced north. Her blood froze.

Out in the haze rode a half-dozen bikes, shiny and chrome under the darkening sun. Tattered standards flew above the procession; bonehelms gleamed in the last remnants of daylight.

Wasteland raiders. Just her fucking luck.

They'd be on her in minutes. But what were they doing? Raiders went storm chasing, not storm fleeing. Sucking up the mana that pooled in a storm's wake was a tenuous way to survive in the wasteland; riding along a storm *front* was a good way to die. Sure, they were sparkriders like Jin, so they might survive a few minutes in the storm—longer than anybody without the Talent. But there was just no goddamn reason.

Jin bent back to the engine and racked her limited knowledge of its workings. Sparks went down the copper wire connecting the grip to a metal box under the engine, which she'd heard mechanics call the mana regulator. Jin touched the regulator, and part of the metal shell came off in her hand, jagged and sharp.

*Oh.* That was probably it.

Shit. A busted mana regulator was one of the few things on her bike she knew how to replace, if she had the part. But out here in the wastes, still most of a day's ride from her destination, she was fucked. Unless . . .

She could bypass the regulator. Send a spark straight down the intake. It was a stupid thing to do, just like riding without a helm. Even odds that the magebike would either cough back to life or blow to pieces and scramble Jin all over the highway like an egg.

What other options did she have? Sit here, let the raiders skin her and strip her bike for parts? Limping into the storm was probably a more merciful end.

"This is all your fault," Jin growled at the pteropter dangling from her magebike's handlebars. It warbled back, then tucked its beak under an uninjured wing and . . . went to sleep. How? *How?*

Jin swung her leg over her bike again. If she was going to die, at least she would die in a magebike engine explosion, which was honestly a pretty badass way to go. Her mother's face flashed through her head, and Jin winced. Eomma would never forgive her for dying out here in the wastes without leaving a husband or wife or even a hush-hush lover to grieve. Organizing Jin's poorly attended funeral was probably Eomma's worst nightmare.

The thought made Jin's throat itch for that mana-cig again. She reached awkwardly under the engine block for the intake. Bending over brought her to eye level with the leather satchel strapped to the fuel tank, and her heart skipped a beat.

The crash had damaged more than just the mana regulator. Something sharp had sliced open the satchel. Jin was looking at torn leather and empty space where a jewel-encrusted scroll tube should have been safely ensconced.

"Shit."

When it came to cargo, Jin had three rules: no drugs, no poisons, no explosives. Those rules were her mother's condition for taking any of the coin Jin made as a courier. They'd probably cost Jin thousands of mun over her career, which was frustrating, but she knew Eomma had her reasons. So Jin stuck to questionably legal but harmless goods: imported produce, herbal remedies and aphrodisiacs, the latest in sartorial fashions, and, on one memorable occasion, a live prizefighter rooster. It all added up to a decent but unreliable income stream.

The letter in that scroll tube was worth more than the rest of her cargo combined. Prince Kadrin and his stupid letters were the only reason Eomma had a bakery and Jin had a paid-off magebike. He was by far her best client.

Raiders roared in from the north. Mana lightning raged in the west. Jin hopped off her magebike yet again and scoured the road, heart hammering in her chest. The ancient highway was riddled with enough cracks to hide a legion of scroll tubes. The sunlight was fading fast. Jin's breath came in short, desperate gasps.

There—a ruby glint under the failing sun. The tube was wedged into a deep crack, covered in dust and sporting a dent in its gold-embossed cap. Jin yanked it free, cringing as tiny gems popped off and went pinging over the asphalt. Oh well, they were Talentcrafted anyway. Kadrin could have someone replace them with the wave of a hand.

Jin could smell the storm now: a nose-hair-sizzling chemical tang. The raiders were gaining on her, too. Indigo smoke boiled from magebike exhausts as the riders' eyes glowed hot orange, pulsing with the wax and wane of their Talent. Shit, Jin could see their eyes now—that wasn't good at all.

Jin had a perfect track record of never having come face-to-face with a wasteland raider, thank you very much. And fuck if she was breaking that streak today.

She stuffed the scroll tube down her jacket and leaped onto her magebike. "Time to go!" she announced to the sleeping saurian swinging from her handlebars.

She thought about muttering a quick prayer to Rasvel before she shot sparks down her intake and blew herself into little Jin-flavored bits, but decided against it. Better if the Giver of Blessings didn't watch her screw up. Jin had no intention of waking up Talentless in the next life.

Power rushed to her fingertips. The engine coughed and roared to life—and more importantly, *didn't* explode.

"Fuck yes!"

She'd been born to be a sparkrider. She'd known it ever since she crested a dune for the first time and went sailing through the air on wings of steel and smoke. Her body and her bike were one, her home was the highway, and all that other sentimental crap.

She'd never had to tear ass on a magebike to escape a mana storm and a howling gang of raiders, though. At least, not at the same time.

Jin kicked off and fed the engine. It responded at once with a satisfying snarl and charged forward. She threw a glance over her shoulder just as the lead raider hopped the highway shoulder, swerved, and skidded to a squealing halt.

Jin's heart leaped. The raiders weren't going to chase her. They must have thought she'd make easy prey, stranded on the highway, but a sparkrider on the run was a different beast. Especially a courier, light and swift, unburdened by a knight's steel and shield.

The lead raider took off her helm. Dirty-blonde hair stuck up in spikes from a tanned face that was already too distant for Jin to make out her features. The raider raised her hands.

Baffled, Jin kept stealing glances back even as she sped away. The other raiders peeled off into the wasteland, shrinking to little dots as the mana storm boiled closer. Jin still had no clue why they'd ventured so near the storm front; clearly they weren't eager to face lightning. But the blonde raider stayed put, straddling her magebike and staring after Jin.

What was she *doing*? Rolling thunder and shrieking wind eclipsed all other sound; the sky bled blue to black. The storm was almost upon the raider.

Jin kept going. The last time she glanced back—right before the storm bore down on the faraway shape of magebike and rider—the nape of her neck prickled fiercely. Somehow, despite the distance, she knew the woman was smiling.

A tiny voice in Jin's head asked, *Don't I know you?*

Darkness and crackling blue lightning closed over the raider, stealing her from sight. Jin swallowed down a lump of fear and confusion. She muttered a few choice curses, her voice drowned by the roar of her engine. Then she shrugged and rode hard for Kerina Rut.

*Second Age of Storms, 48th Spring*

*Dear Princess Yi-Nereen,*
*I don't know if you remember me. My name is Kadrin, and I hail from*
*Kerina Sol. Ten years ago, my father was sent as a diplomatic envoy to*
*your city, Kerina Rut. I only remember bits and pieces of the crossing; I*
*was nine years old and rode in a knight's sidecar. But I recall very well*
*the year we spent in Kerina Rut, especially the friend I made there: the*
*daughter of the Shield Lord, our host, who did so much to make us feel*
*at home.*

*After all this time, I have finally worked up the courage to write*
*her. Do you remember me half as fondly as I remember you? My*
*father's time in Kerina Rut was shorter than planned, and our sudden*
*departure must have taken you by surprise. I hope you will accept my*
*long overdue apology and farewell.*

*I shall end this letter now, in case I am a stranger to you after all.*
*But if you do recall the boy who collected colorful beetles and taught*
*you to wish on falling stars, it would bring me no greater pleasure than*
*to receive your reply.*

*Please take care,*
*Prince Kadrin, Third Heir to the House of Steel Heavens*

# CHAPTER TWO

# THE PRINCESS IN HER TOWER

*Second Age of Storms, 51st Summer, Day 20*

The shield of Kerina Rut rose like a flickering bubble over the walled city, translucent blue and visible from miles away. Jin sped toward it with the storm licking at her heels and thickening the air with dust. Ordinarily she'd have ridden out of the storm's way, waited for it to pass over Kerina Rut before circling back. But for once in her life, she wanted to burrow behind the safety of a Wall.

The raider she'd seen was dead now, had to be. Lost to the storm. And Jin hadn't known her. Didn't know any raiders. So why was her heart still rattling against her ribs like she'd seen a ghost?

The guards posted above the western gate spotted her well before Jin skidded to a stop below. Sheets of corrugated metal rose up before her, twelve spans high with no visible entrance. At the top, where the shimmering blue edge of the shield met the metal ramparts, two bearded faces stared down at Jin.

"Open the gate!" she shouted, but the approaching storm drowned her voice.

After an eternity, one of the faces withdrew. Metal groaned and shrieked as the Wall split apart in front of Jin, two panels unfurling just wide enough to admit her and her magebike. Jin sighed in relief and walked her bike inside. The Wall sealed itself shut behind her with another earsplitting screech, enveloping her in darkness.

She waited. Behind her came the muffled howl of the approaching storm. Flanked by sheets of metal, she felt like a rat stuck in a drainpipe. Were the guards debating whether to grant her passage into the city? She never faced obstacles like this when the gate was open. Couriers were the lifeblood of trade between the kerinas, and all but the rookie guards were smart enough to pretend they hadn't peeked into her saddlebags after she pressed a couple of mun into their palms.

A thin blue crack split the dark before her and swelled as the Wall peeled open. Jin tensed. The little pteropter in her dangling helm chirped.

"Shh," she said. Then she made herself yawn, opening the back of her throat: one of the techniques she'd practiced to make her voice sound lower, more masculine.

The guard who had opened the gate stood in the widening gap, palm raised and eyes burning silver. Not all the city guards were metalcrafters, but there had to be at least one manning the gate. Colorful plumes waved from his crested helm; he bore a lance upright against his shoulder. Jin eyed the iron loops hanging from his belt. She knew from experience how quickly a metalcrafter could liquefy a pair of cuffs and slap them on her wrists.

The glow faded from the guard's eyes as the discordant shriek of metal died away. "It's a holy day, Courier," he said sternly. "Make no trouble."

Jin didn't know why the guards of Kerina Rut constantly assumed she was there to make trouble. Perhaps they were naturally suspicious of her for being a courier instead of a knight. The spark-talent she'd been born with had put both options on the table.

Knights served the kerinas and the High Houses that ruled over them; couriers kept their own counsel and traded the comforts of a home base for a life on the road.

For Jin, the choice had been easy.

She resisted the urge to adjust the headscarf she wore, to make sure it was covering all but her eyes. "Understood," she said in a husky tenor.

She'd perfected the voice over the years, as well as all the other minutiae that went into her male courier disguise. It was trouble-some—she couldn't risk more than a few words at a time—but well worth it. In Kerina Rut, a woman of Talent was something between a priceless jewel and a caged bird, and Jin didn't care to be either.

The guard's eyes raked over her body, made androgynous by lay-ers of concealing fabric and leather. He nodded.

"Welcome to Kerina Rut, Courier."

Two hours later, Jin sat on a bench in the central courtyard of the Tower of Arrested Stars, feeding Screech a handful of giblets. The pteropter snapped viciously at the meat, devouring lump after lump in jerky gulps. Jin found herself smiling, then yelped as a sharp tooth caught her thumb.

Giggles floated across the courtyard. A couple of Tower hand-maidens were dawdling at the foot of the stairs, watching her. One of them, a young woman with dimples and plaited hair, had brought Jin the meat. Jin hadn't the faintest idea what was so fas-cinating about the sight of a courier feeding organs to a saurian, but she wished they'd go away. If only she could wait for Yi-Nereen somewhere private.

An ornate metal staircase spiraled around the courtyard's rim, leading up to the Tower's spire—into the dizzying heights beyond the kerina's dome. During storms, the Tower's spire pierced the shield and was exposed directly to mana lightning. Somehow, through another process Jin didn't understand, the shieldcasters of the Tower were able to harvest the lightning and use it to enhance their Talent. No other city in the wasteland had managed to replicate the feat; it was the reason Kerina Rut survived still, despite its so-called population crisis: rapidly dwindling numbers of Talented children, halved with every generation.

Every kerina had been touched by the population crisis in one way or another, but Jin happened to know that the shieldcasters of Kerina Rut had been hit particularly hard. She guessed there were fewer than a hundred remaining in the city, and they all lived in the Tower, under the watchful eye of the Shield Lord. None were watched more closely than the Shield Lord's eldest daughter, Yi-Nereen.

Looking up at the distant blue sky far above the courtyard made Jin's stomach lurch with vertigo. The whispering of the women nearby didn't help. She closed her eyes and dragged in a deep breath. After three years of letter deliveries, she was used to the sense of unease that permeated every minute she spent in Kerina Rut—but if it weren't for Kadrin and Yi-Nereen, she'd rather avoid the city entirely.

"Courier Jin?"

Jin opened her eyes. Before her stood a tall man dressed in dark robes, his hair in a long tail flowing down his back. His large hands were folded over his sword-cane's handle, a scorpion's tail cast in silver.

"Teul-Kim," Jin said gruffly, rising from the bench.

Yi-Nereen's bodyguard looked her calmly up and down. Jin's skin prickled in apprehension. She was sure her disguise had never fooled Teul-Kim, though his loyalty to the princess had been sufficient to guard her secret.

"Her Highness will see you now. Leave your belongings here, please."

Jin glanced at her satchel and saddlebags, which lay scattered around the bench. She'd left her magebike at a garage on the way to the Tower, though it made her nervous that she didn't yet have the mun to pay for its retrieval. "I'll take this," she said, tucking Screech's helm under her arm. The saurian cooed; it sounded much more agreeable with a full stomach, never mind the broken wing.

Teul-Kim raised an eyebrow but didn't object. He led Jin up the spiral steps encircling the Tower while she did her utmost not to look down. The Tower stood on a rocky island in the heart of the mana spring, like a forbidding guardian overlooking the kerina. Jin could have gazed down upon the entire city, still dancing in the brightly colored throes of holy day festivities—but she'd rather not, thanks. Her guts were already in knots just thinking about the drop.

The smell of fragrant incense and the soft sound of a harp enveloped Jin as she stepped into Yi-Nereen's bower. She should have been prepared, but somehow she never was. It was like stepping into the perfumed lair of an ethereal creature. It never failed to steal Jin's breath away.

Yi-Nereen rose from a heap of cushions as Teul-Kim announced Jin's arrival. She was tall, almost of a height with her bodyguard. A saurian-bone corset outlined her waist, and her skirts and sleeves were a profusion of translucent, gauzy black fabric. More bones—small ones, the teeth and finger bones of young pteropters—studded her glossy hair. Her eyes were light brown and outlined in striking black galena.

"You may go, Teul-Kim," she said.

Jin blinked. Teul-Kim had always been present during her audiences with Yi-Nereen. She had the vague awareness that it was illegal under the kerina's laws for her to be alone with the princess, at least while disguised as a man—though Yi-Nereen had known her identity as a woman from the start. Had something changed? But Teul-Kim bowed and left the parlor without comment, as did the handmaiden who had been quietly playing the harp in the corner.

This was the first time Jin had ever been completely alone with Yi-Nereen. She stared at the floor near her feet; it was cool marble, white with swirls of gray and amber. Even though she wasn't looking at Yi-Nereen anymore, the princess's image was still imprinted on her vision, a blazing silhouette. She could hardly—

"Courier Jin," Yi-Nereen said softly. "Are you hurt?"

Jin risked a glance. Yi-Nereen was bent over something beside her bed of cushions, her shawl of black lace floating around her like a misty shadow. She straightened, revealing a small basin in one hand and a cloth in the other.

"That really isn't necessary, Highness." Jin's heart thumped in her chest.

"Hold still," Yi-Nereen said, drawing alarmingly close. Rosewater and sandalwood perfume drifted over Jin as Yi-Nereen dabbed delicately at a cut on her cheek. Jin closed her eyes, willing herself not to move or say anything stupid. Part of her was convinced this was a dream.

In the helm under Jin's arm, Screech shifted and shrieked.

The hand on Jin's face froze. The air crackled with energy. Power moved through her like a feverish chill, and she opened her eyes to see Yi-Nereen's face only inches from her own, eyes blazing electric blue. A shield had bloomed around them like an iridescent bubble, just large enough to contain the two of them.

"It's only a saurian!" Jin tilted the helm for Yi-Nereen to see. "A little one. Sorry—I should have said something—"

Yi-Nereen blinked. The blue faded from her eyes, and the shield wavered and vanished. Jin shivered as the heat of Yi-Nereen's power left her. It was a peculiar sensation, cold and hollow. But she had little time to ponder it, because the next thing Yi-Nereen did was faint. Right into Jin's arms.

Jin dropped the helm. It went rolling across the floor, prompting further shrieks of outrage from Screech. She strained to stay upright, caught off-balance by Yi-Nereen's deadweight. Fuck, but the princess was a lot heavier than she looked.

"Help," Jin said. Then, louder: "Teul-Kim! Help!"

Several minutes later, Jin was seated uncomfortably on a wicker stool as Yi-Nereen's handmaidens fussed over their mistress, dabbing her brow with a cool cloth. Teul-Kim stood in a corner, arms crossed. He occasionally flashed Jin the same flat stare he'd given her as he lifted an unconscious Yi-Nereen from her arms: as if this were all her fault.

"Don't worry over me," Yi-Nereen kept insisting. Jin restrained a smile at the reversal in their positions. "I'm only tired from the storm. I should have known better than to summon another shield so soon."

A butler entered the room, carrying a large basin. Jin sat up, her skin humming. She knew what was in the basin before she saw it: glowing mana, part sloshing liquid and part heavy smoke. Her throat itched with the same longing she often felt for a mana-cig, but stronger. Her head pounded with a dull ache, a sure sign her reserves were running low. The basin moved past her toward Yi-Nereen, where the butler set it on an end table beside the princess.

"Thank you." Yi-Nereen waved her handmaidens away. "Leave us, please."

Teul-Kim was the last to leave, his stare lingering on Jin.

Jin fumbled for the jewel-encrusted scroll tube she'd stuck down the front of her jacket and said, "I have Prince Kadrin's letter for you, Highness."

Yi-Nereen's heavy-lidded gaze rested on the scroll tube. For a moment Jin thought she saw sadness in the princess's eyes, but then a faint smile graced her lips. "In a moment. You look parched. Will you join me?"

She gestured toward the basin. Jin couldn't help but raise her eyebrows. It was odd enough to see mana brought into the bower like iced fruit on a platter; Jin had only ever refilled her reservoir at the spring, like ordinary people.

"I'm not sure if I should . . ."

"There's plenty here for the both of us."

Jin was powerless to resist. She shuffled closer to the princess, hesitated a second longer, then stripped off her gloves and plunged her hands into the basin. Cold smoke licked around her fingers, a pulsing current that felt like immersing her hands in something living. Out of habit, Jin closed her eyes.

She realized too late that when Yi-Nereen had said *There's plenty here for the both of us*, she'd meant *at the same time*. The princess's hands settled over hers, warm and light. Usually, infusing mana drenched every sense—like smoking a hundred mana-cigs at once, like diving into water so cold it numbed instead of hurt. But for the first time, Jin found herself too distracted to notice.

Drops of mana splashed to the floor and sizzled into vapor as Jin withdrew her hands. "I don't need much," she lied. Then, stealing another glance at Yi-Nereen's face, she added, "You certainly need it more than I do."

That wasn't a lie. While Jin had been lazing around in the courtyard, feeding giblets to a saurian, Yi-Nereen had been on the Wall with her fellow shieldcasters, holding back the might of the storm from destroying the entire city. It was no wonder she'd fainted. There were dark hollows under her eyes, and her lips were cracked.

Jin's Talent had given her choices—courier or knight—but Yi-Nereen had never had such a luxury. There was only one path ordained for a shieldcaster, no matter which kerina they were born to: a lifetime of service in the Shield Corps.

Jin could take the rest of what she needed from the spring. As intoxicating as it was to be in Yi-Nereen's presence, she couldn't stay much longer. She had other deliveries to make.

Yi-Nereen's gaze had found the (mostly) jewel-encrusted scroll tube again. "When you're ready, I would very much like to hear from Kadrin."

The first time she'd delivered one of the prince's letters, Jin had discovered one of Kerina Rut's more backward laws: Talented women weren't permitted to read their own correspondence. The loophole, apparently, was to have them read aloud by a man. There was a certain barbaric simplicity to it that Jin couldn't help but appreciate; as long as the city upheld this single law, there was no need to enshrine the dozens of others that would prevent Talented women from starting businesses, organizing meetings, or gaining their independence from men, the High Houses, and the temple in any tangible way whatsoever.

All of this boiled down to putting Jin in the awkward position of acting as literal mouthpiece for Prince Kadrin's love letters—and worst of all, over time she'd come to like it. Now the prospect of reading them to Yi-Nereen kept her up at night out of equal parts dread and anticipation.

Jin unscrewed the tube's gilded cap and shook out the rolled parchment. Yi-Nereen watched, her face alight with a look of breathless excitement that made Jin flush. *It should be illegal to look at someone like that.* She remembered suddenly they were alone, and her stomach turned over. She glanced hastily down at the letter.

"Dearest Reena."

She summoned her memories of the Sol-blood prince: his genial smile, his voice, the excitable way he moved his hands when he spoke. She willed away her self-consciousness, her fumbling awkwardness, and let herself believe she *was* Kadrin. For a little while, she could pretend the spellbound look in Yi-Nereen's eyes was meant for her.

". . . Most days, Reena, it doesn't trouble me to be Talentless. Everyone around me struggles with that more than I do. The royals of Kerina Sol may crow about equality and acceptance, but it's an open secret they think a Talentless prince is a tragedy. I don't agree with that. I see it as an opportunity. For the refugees who come to our city, fleeing places where they're treated like dirt—for the ones who don't make it here, the ones who die in the wasteland trying to reach somewhere they can just *live*, never mind grow wealthy and powerful—a man in my position owes it to them to prove he can thrive without Talent. It's the only way anything will change.

"But there are nights when I do mourn it. Nights when I wish I were a sparkrider like our dear friend, who uses her Talent to carry my words to your ears and yours to mine."

Yi-Nereen's eyes were closed as she drank in the sound of Jin's voice. For the space of a heartbeat, Jin wondered if Yi-Nereen could even picture Kadrin's face after twelve years apart. Perhaps her imagination showed her Jin instead.

*Focus*, she told herself. *Keep reading*.

"I don't care to make flowers bloom with a thought or mold glass into beautiful shapes. All I want is the ability to cross the wastes and see you with my own eyes. But alas, it isn't so. I must rely on Jin. Which isn't so bad—I trust her, and more importantly, I like her. But there's so much out there I want to see. I keep hoping someday we will, together.

"Take care, Reena. I look forward to your reply."

Jin carefully folded the parchment and placed it on the end table beside the empty mana basin. She would burn the letter to ashes before she left, like always, so no one would discover it in Yi-Nereen's possession. It was unfair—she knew Kadrin kept every single one of the princess's letters and reread them often—but necessary, since the things Yi-Nereen and Kadrin wrote to each other didn't always abide by royal protocol.

Yi-Nereen sat still with her hands in her lap and her head tilted to the side, as if to catch the echo of Jin's last words. Jin resisted the urge to stare at her, to savor the opportunity to study her face, and glanced around the room.

"Um, Highness? I don't see any ink or parchment. Should I come back later for your reply?"

Yi-Nereen opened her eyes. Tears brimmed on her lashes. "No reply," she whispered. "Not this time. Not ever again."

Jin's gut clenched. "What? Why not?"

Thoughts spilled through her mind in a chaotic rush. Kadrin would be heartbroken. Yi-Nereen must be in some kind of trouble. And what about Jin's income? She felt a little stab of guilt at that last thought.

"I'm engaged to be married."

"Married?" Jin blinked and asked, stupidly, "To who?"

It was a sign of Yi-Nereen's flawless manners that she didn't react to Jin's idiocy beyond a faint smile. "My family doesn't know Prince Kadrin and I exchange letters. They believe I'm in correspondence with his sister, Princess Eliesen. You see, Jin . . ." Yi-Nereen's smile grew cold. "In Kerina Rut, I may not speak to a man before I'm married, but I may tell a woman I love her. I may write her silly poetry and spend time with her as a man does with his wife. As long as it stops on the day my husband claims me."

Jin nodded, her cheeks flaming with treacherous thoughts. "I—I've heard it's like that here."

"My father has chosen a match for me. Not a prince of the High Houses, but the son of a wealthy family. They will pay an enormous bride price for a woman strong in the Talent. Like many others in the city, their bloodline is failing." Yi-Nereen gazed at her trembling hands. "I am the most powerful shieldcaster in Kerina Rut. I can only imagine the price my father demanded."

Jin thought of Prince Kadrin, of his frown that appeared so rarely—when he saw a servant struggling with too many plates, or a cat toying with a wounded bird. The way his face lit up when he saw her. Not because of her, of course, but because of what she brought him: a new message from the woman he loved. She'd never see that smile again if Yi-Nereen stopped sending him letters.

Her breath caught. Jin would never see Yi-Nereen again, either.

"Is there anything I can do?"

To Jin's surprise, Yi-Nereen nodded, as if she'd been preparing for the question since Jin arrived.

"Yes," she said. "I want you to help me escape."

# Road to Ruin

*Second Age of Storms, 48th Spring*

*Dear Prince Kadrin,*
*Of course I remember you. How could I forget? The year you and your*
*family spent in Kerina Rut is the only time in my life I can recall with joy.*

*Rasvel's mercy, what am I saying? Courier, have you already writ-*
*ten that down? Please discard the letter and start again.*

*Ahem.*

*Dear Prince Kadrin, Third Heir to the House of Steel Heavens:*
*I regret to inform you that although I do recall your visit to Kerina*
*Rut with a certain measure of fondness, I cannot exchange any further*
*correspondence with you. It would be indecorous for a woman in my*
*position. As fervently as I may wish for different circumstances, they are*
*as they are. I hope you understand.*

*I do accept your apology, and I hope it is not too forward of me*
*to mention that my greatest concern following your sudden departure*
*was not for your goodbyes or explanations, but for your health. I was*
*alarmed to hear of your illness, and it brings me great comfort to know*
*you recovered.*

*Please refrain from sending any reply.*

*Regretfully yours,*
*Princess Yi-Nereen, First Daughter of the Tower of Arrested Stars*

# CHAPTER THREE

# THE MAN BY THE SPRING

*Second Age of Storms, 51st Summer, Day 20*

"Escape," Jin repeated. "From your betrothed?"

Yi-Nereen swept a hand toward the lavishly decorated chamber, her wrist trailing black lace studded with seed pearls. "From the Tower. From Kerina Rut. From all of this." Her voice lowered. "From a future as an invisible woman. I can stomach my duty on the Wall, protecting my people. But I won't give up my body twice over to continue a bloodline."

Jin was silent for a moment. The magnitude of Yi-Nereen's proposal—all the enormous risk it posed to both of them—was dawning on her. "It might not be so simple."

"And if I stay?" Yi-Nereen stood, drawing herself up to her full and impressive height. "If my first and second child are both Talentless, the priests will declare my womb cursed. My brothers and uncles will be honor bound to take my life. My children will be branded and cast out into the wastes to die."

"Oh," Jin said faintly. She felt sick to her stomach.

*Somehow it's even worse than Kerina Tez.*

She'd fled Kerina Tez four years ago with her mother. By now the city was half in its grave, buried by storms and riots. Was Kerina Rut headed the same way?

"If they *are* Talented, the cycle continues. My daughters will be used as broodmares, and my sons will be taught to control their sisters." Yi-Nereen's eyes darkened and flashed. "That is the sickness at the heart of Kerina Rut, Courier Jin. My city is rotting from the inside. I cannot save it—if I stay, I can only become its victim, its tool."

Jin swallowed. Holy Rasvel, the princess was beautiful when she stood like that, veiled in black and gleaming with anger. But Jin couldn't afford to go slack-jawed right now. She needed all her wits about her.

"You think Prince Kadrin can help you?"

"This isn't about Kadrin." Yi-Nereen's voice was still hard, but her expression softened as she said the name. "I will accept refuge with his family, if he invites it. Otherwise, there is Rasvel's Sanctuary. Kerina Sol's priests interpret the Giver's will very differently from ours. They do not turn away refugees."

"I know," Jin said. "I was one of those refugees."

She regretted the words as soon as they left her mouth. If Yi-Nereen's face had gentled at the mention of Kadrin, it was kitten soft now.

"Oh," the princess said. Was that pity in her voice? Jin looked away. "But you are sparktalented, and Tez-blood, and . . . I assumed."

Jin could hear Yi-Nereen's confusion echoing behind each word. Why would Jin, a Talented woman, have needed to avail herself of Rasvel's Sanctuary? She would have had an automatic position among the Knights of Tez. She could have lived a life nearly as luxurious as Yi-Nereen's. All Jin would have had to do was cut off ties with every Talentless in her life. Including Eomma . . . and Falka.

Yi-Nereen was still looking at her, wringing her hands. Jin could not recall ever being irritated by the princess before, but now she was. She didn't need anyone's sympathy. She had her magebike, her Talent, and eyes firmly fixed on the horizon. Not mired in the past.

"Doesn't matter," she said. "Do you have a plan?"

Yi-Nereen nodded. "Everything is arranged—except for transportation. That's where I need your help." She hesitated, as if she knew Jin wasn't going to like what she had to say next. "It must be tonight."

Jin stared at her. "Why?"

"This is my last day of freedom." Yi-Nereen smiled faintly. "It is good you arrived today, Courier. I feared you would not."

*I almost didn't.* If she hadn't run afoul of Screech and the raiders, if she'd ridden out of the storm's path and spent the night in the wastes, Jin wouldn't have made it in time. Then what would Yi-Nereen have done? Jin didn't want to consider the possibilities. Her heart was thumping with rising panic, and she felt light-headed.

She stood up. "My bike needs to be repaired before I can leave. I don't have the coin to pay a—"

Yi-Nereen withdrew a silk pouch from her sleeve and held it out. "I wouldn't ask for your help without offering anything in return."

Jin shivered under the princess's dark, intense gaze. She took the pouch and stared at it without opening it. From the weight in her hands, she guessed it was more than enough mun to pay for a new mana regulator. "I can't take this yet." She thrust the pouch back at Yi-Nereen. "I need time to think."

Helping Yi-Nereen would make her a fugitive, a criminal under the laws of Kerina Rut like her father. She was used to operating on the gray side of the law, but that was just that: gray. Not stark black and white, like kidnapping a princess. She'd never be able to do business in Kerina Rut again.

Scratch that—if she ever came within a mile of Kerina Rut, the Knight Legion would run her down.

"Keep it," Yi-Nereen said. "I know what I'm asking of you, and that it isn't fair." Her voice trembled with what Jin could swear was genuine remorse. "But I have no choice. If you'll help me, meet me at the spring tonight, beneath my grandfather's statue. If not . . ." She bit her lip, standing up straighter. "Safe travels, Courier."

Jin understood the princess's words for the dismissal they were. She bowed stiffly, the pouch clutched against her chest, and took her leave.

Back at the garage where she'd stashed her bike, Jin found a boy with braided hair and crescents tattooed on his cheekbones cleaning a drive chain. She lingered behind him, caught off guard by a sudden memory. As a fatherless child, she'd learned her trade at the knee of a hoary gunrunner named Lorne. Lorne's workshop in Kerina Tez had been much grimier than this one, filled to the brim with spare parts from bikes a decade older than Jin, but she'd spent many an afternoon there, watching him work and handing him tools. Until she'd left.

The boy jumped as Jin dropped the silk pouch on the table beside him.

"Need a regulator replaced," she said. "Today. Will your master artificer do it?"

"I'll ask." The boy rolled his shoulders and stood up, glancing down the row of bikes parked along the side of the garage. "Which one's yours?"

Jin pointed. "The hauler over there."

The boy's eyes widened. "Is that a Vann?"

Jin was under too much stress to smile, though the boy's mistake was a flattering one. Not even knights rode original Vann magebikes anymore. The Tez-blood artificer known as Tibius Vann—the man who'd built the first magebike—had vanished some thirty years ago, though fortunately he'd left his schematics behind. Artificers from every kerina had been swift to copy his designs, some more faithfully than others. Most of the Vanns had long since been stripped down for parts. Jin liked to pretend she'd bought her magebike out of fondness for its classic style, but really it had been the cheapest hauler she could find.

"I'll be back to pick it up later. Can I leave something else with you?"

The boy picked up the silk pouch and hefted it in his palm. "Sure. Keep it safe for you, no problem."

"Thanks." Jin set her bonehelm down on the table. Screech opened his beak wide in a warbling yawn. "Don't let him out."

"Is that—a *pteropter*?"

"Actually, yes."

The boy gawked at her, then turned on his heel. "Uh, wait here a minute, sir."

He disappeared through the swinging door to the back room, leaving the pouch behind on the table. Jin idly plucked at the pouch's neck and glanced inside. Her stomach dropped. She'd thought the pouch full of small change, one- or four-mun coins; she'd been wrong. Swallowing hard, she tipped the contents into her palm. Hundred-mun coins, every last one, adding up to a sum so inconceivable Jin had to whisper it to herself over and over, like a prayer. *Nine hundred mun.*

She felt sick to her stomach. Yi-Nereen had let her walk out of the Tower with a small fortune in her hands and no guarantee of coming back. Somehow she'd known the weight of Jin's guilt would be stronger than any vow she could have sworn.

As the backroom door swung open, Jin hastily stuffed all but one coin back into the pouch and slid the pouch into her breast pocket. The extra coin she slipped into the palm of her glove. The boy came trotting toward her, carrying a small wire cage.

"Used to keep a hen," he said. "Cat got her."

Together he and Jin wrangled Screech into the cage. By the time they were finished, the boy was sucking on a freshly bleeding thumb.

"Wicked little beast, eh? How'd you catch it?"

Jin rubbed her shoulder. "He attacked me."

"That how it broke the wing?" The boy crouched on the floor beside the cage, keeping his distance. "A saurian don't heal like a normal beast. Won't starve to death, even if it don't eat. And their meat is right sour, too—just as bad as a cactus. Bizarre little things."

*Bizarre indeed.* Jin sighed. She was an idiot to think of keeping the creature, but the boy's words stirred a grudging kinship in her. *Don't heal like a normal beast*—fuck, she could have described herself in those exact words not too long ago. She'd been a wreck after leaving Kerina Tez. Both times.

"I'll clean out your helm for you, Courier, sir. Wouldn't want to crack your skull on the way home." The boy grinned at Jin, showing off the gaps in his teeth.

She teased the hundred-mun coin out of her glove and tossed it to him. "Many thanks."

She left the garage and the boy behind, feeling curiously adrift, as if Screech's weight had been anchoring her to earth. Above her stretched clear white sky, stained blue in places where the heavens leaked through the clouds. It was a hot afternoon, and Kerina Rut buzzed like wasps on a plate of fruit. Jin sweated under her head-scarf as she made her way toward the mana spring.

She could leave Kerina Rut tonight, alone, instead of rendez-vousing with Yi-Nereen. But of course she wasn't going to. Three years before, she'd agreed to carry Kadrin's letters and become his mouthpiece, his courier. Now the whole affair was coming to its conclusion, and just as it had begun, Jin was the only way it could finish. She had to bring the two lovers together.

Never mind that she was painfully infatuated with both of them.

Long ago, a passing storm had ignited the land where Kerina Rut now stood, opening a fissure a half-mile wide: a wound in the wastes, from which mana gushed forth like blood. Jin stood at the edge of that old wound now, gazing upon the mana spring. Storms were deadly, but they also brought life. Cities could thrive only on the banks of mana springs, where mana flowed in an endless stream to sustain the Talented who lived there.

Every part of life in a kerina depended on Talent. The function of the Shield Corps was obvious, but the other two High Talents were no less vital. Bloomweavers sang orchards to life and swelled fruit with their magic. Raincallers filled aquifers and bathhouses and sewers. Even the Low Talents were necessary for all the luxu-ries of civilization: metalcrafters patrolled the streets, worked the smithies, and kept the Wall in good repair, while stoneshapers built houses and windmills and granaries.

In a way, even Jin served the kerinas with her sparktalent, though not as directly as a knight would have. Kerinas had different specialties and varying ratios of Talent, so their imports and exports were varied as well; it was Jin's job to facilitate communication and trade between the kerinas. The only people who didn't serve the common good—at least, according to the temple edicts—were Talentless and criminals, most of whom wound up exiled.

Exiles became raiders, or they became dead.

Jin shook away the memory of the blonde raider opening her arms to the storm. What had happened to her? It still made no sense.

The shore of the spring bulged outward in a promontory. No one stopped Jin as she walked to the cliff's edge and took hold of the winch attached to a line stretching down into the mana's depths; as far as Kerina Rut was concerned, the spring was an endless resource. She pulled up a bucket of blue, half liquid and half mist. After rolling up her sleeves, she plunged in her arms without ceremony and closed her eyes as the mana's chill crept into her flesh—this time without the warmth of a princess's hands to distract her.

The pain in her shoulder eased. That was one of the many reasons Jin counted herself lucky to be Talented; she would always heal faster than a Talentless, thanks to the rejuvenating power of mana. It couldn't quite mend a broken bone, but it could close a cut faster than stitches.

After, she sent the bucket rattling back down the line and retreated to a nearby gazebo to recover. Infusing always left her dazed, mana-drunk, as the power spread through her veins. No replacement for getting properly shit-faced, of course—Jin's tab at the Kerina Sol watering hole could attest to that—but at least it soothed her craving for a mana-cig, an expensive habit she was better off giving up.

A man stood in the gazebo, arms clasped behind his back, looking at a wall papered with notices. Jin glanced curiously over his shoulder. Some of the notices were for courier work, but most were something else entirely.

Missing posters. Sketched faces of men and women stared back at her from the wall. Sparkriders, all of them, knights and couriers both. There had to be a dozen faces.

Jin blinked as unease pierced the mana fogging her brain. She sat down on the low bench wrapped around the inside of the gazebo and reached into her breast pocket. Her fingers bumped against the silk pouch. Not the pack of mana-cigs she'd been instinctively looking for—thoughtless habit, she wasn't even craving one right now.

"Need a spark?"

Jin glanced up. The man who'd been looking at the posters had turned. He was slim and whip sharp, his black hair pulled back from an aquiline face and bound into a tail.

"Thanks, but no need." She took her empty hand out of her pocket and gave him a considering look, up and down. A sparkrider, given his offer. Was he a knight? Eomma had drilled it into her head as a child to avoid the Legion, and Jin hadn't forgotten her lessons. But this stranger seemed too lean and fine, like he'd buckle under the weight of full plate.

"All those missing sparkriders," she said, gesturing toward the posters. "What do you think happened?"

"Raiders, most likely." The stranger put a hand under his bone-plated vest and took out a pack of mana-cigs. He lit one with a lazy twitch of his fingers, eyes flaring orange. "They've been more active lately. You're a courier, aren't you? You have the look."

Jin nodded, eyeing his cig. "Yes."

The stranger smiled faintly, then turned his back to her. His outfit was ostensibly the sort a courier would wear, all leather and saurian bone, but it was impeccably tailored and far too clean for him to have spent time in the wastes.

"Take care when you head back out there. What's your next stop?"

Jin hesitated. She was about to make herself an outlaw; if the man was a knight, she'd better not tell him she was headed to Kerina Sol to avail herself and a certain princess of Rasvel's Sanctuary.

"Kerina Lav."

"I have a friend there," the man said, still studying the posters. "A jeweler in the Quarter Market, name of Rex. He's partial to Kerina Rut plums. Always willing to pay a good sum for a fresh picking."

"Thanks." It was a good tip, the kind a fellow courier might share out of wasteland camaraderie. But Jin's hackles were up anyway, for reasons she couldn't put her finger on. Her growing sense of disquiet was a sign the mana fog was dissipating. In a minute or two she'd be ready to leave.

Jin didn't feel like waiting a minute or two. She stood, swaying slightly. The man turned to her, and for a brief moment Jin thought she saw a flash of color in his eyes—not orange, but something else. She blinked, and the stranger was smiling at her with eyes that were an ordinary dark brown, like her own.

"Safe travels, Courier," he said.

"Likewise," Jin said, though she was sure now he was no courier.

She left the gazebo at a leisurely pace, but paranoia pulled her into a side alley to wait. She was about to chastise herself for being foolish when the stranger went strolling past, whistling tunelessly. Though he didn't look left or right, Jin shivered as he walked by. She was certain, somehow, he'd known she was there.

The missing posters swam in her memory. Now *that* was paranoia. Jin shook herself, stepped out of the alley, and watched the stranger's back as he ambled out of sight. He wore no weapon—unusual for a knight. But if he wasn't a knight or a courier, what was he? A sparkrider who'd squandered his Talent on some other profession?

Never mind. She had bigger things to worry about. Now she was fully infused, free to leave Kerina Rut as soon as the artificer finished with her bike. But of course she'd already made her decision. She was going to meet Yi-Nereen at the spring tonight and help her escape.

Hopefully it wouldn't be the last mistake she ever made.

*Second Age of Storms, 48th Spring*

*Dear Princess Yi-Nereen,*
*If you are reading these words, I beg your forgiveness. The inability*
*to follow instruction is a perennial failing of mine, or so I am told by*
*various tutors.*

*Nothing has ever vexed me so much as your last letter. Sending no*
*response was an abhorrent prospect to me, as was the idea of damaging*
*your reputation. In the end, I felt bound to reply. You may discard this*
*missive unread, as is your right, and in that case I have asked Courier*
*Jin to convey my deepest apologies.*

*Though it may be too bold of me to ask, what social condition*
*renders it indecorous for you to receive letters from a childhood friend?*
*If you have met with some grave misfortune in the past nine years, I*
*shall do everything within my power to render aid. I cannot forget the*
*hospitality and kindness you once showed me, a lonely child far from*
*home.*

*Your concern for my health, while received with gratitude, was*
*cause for confusion on my part. Did someone lead you to believe my*
*family left Kerina Rut because I was ill? It sounds like there was some*
*misunderstanding. As a child, I was always in good health.*

*Sincerely yours, or deeply sorry, whichever is more appropriate,*
*Prince Kadrin*

# CHAPTER FOUR

# FUGITIVES

*Second Age of Storms, 51st Summer, Day 20*

Night fell over Kerina Rut in a black velvet curtain studded with ruby stars. Long ago, so long the memory was faded and stained with time, Jin's father had taught her the names of those stars. She squinted at the twinkling ember of Rasvel's Anchor, the star pointing her back to Kerina Sol.

The highways laid by the Road Builders in times of old never changed, but they could be tricky. No such thing as a straight road, Lorne used to say, except the road to perdition. Storms might not touch the roads, but they changed the lay of the land around them. Jin had ridden through a valley once, only to find the same road a bridge across a canyon on the return trip. When she lost her bearings, she'd learned to follow the stars.

She waited in a dark harbor south of the gazebo, concealed by a grove of plum trees planted around a marble statue. Rain Lord Zon-Lai's unsmiling face gazed upon her, his stone brow creased as if he saw through her disguise. Wind rustled the foliage; the fruit's aroma sweetened the night air. After an hour's wait, Jin gave in and ate two plums, spitting the wrinkled stones into the spring.

A blue pinprick shone across the spring from the Tower: a boatman's hooded lantern. Jin stepped behind the statue and watched the small craft approach. There were two figures in the boat: a broad silhouette manning the oars and a veiled figure sitting astern.

As the boat drew closer, the broad figure—Teul-Kim, no doubt—abandoned the oars and splashed through the shallows, drawing the boat ashore behind him. Jin winced until she noticed the waders he wore: knee-high boots of solid leather. Clearly he didn't want to risk mana poisoning by exposing himself to the spring for even a few moments. A human body could handle only so much past the point of full infusion; the limit was different for everyone depending on the strength of their Talent, but to surpass it was a death sentence.

Yi-Nereen stepped gingerly onto the bank, clutching the strap of a satchel. In the dim blue light of the hooded lantern, Jin saw the princess had made . . . well, an *attempt* to disguise herself. She was wearing trousers, a tight leather vest ridged with bone, and a veil over her face and neck.

There was nothing wrong with the vest—it was strikingly similar to what the stranger Jin had met in the gazebo wore—except for the distracting way it accentuated Yi-Nereen's figure.

"Courier Jin?" Yi-Nereen called softly into the darkness.

It was Jin's last chance: stay quiet and still behind the statue, and Yi-Nereen would realize her plans had come to naught. The silk pouch was heavy in her breast pocket. Would she be able to look Kadrin in the face and tell him what she'd done? How much of that mun would she have to spend on drink and mana-cigs to forget her guilt?

Jin stepped out of hiding. "I'm here."

She couldn't see Yi-Nereen's expression under the veil. But she saw the princess's shoulders sag, and she heard the soft release of a caught breath. Jin's own body was drawn tight as a crossbow's string. She was really going to do this—become an outlaw, like her father.

"I deliver Princess Yi-Nereen into your custody, Courier," the broad man standing beside Yi-Nereen said. Yes, it was definitely Teul-Kim, though he sounded stiffer than usual. "She is in your hands now."

"Twenty years, and that's all you have to say?" Yi-Nereen's voice shook. "I expected threats. *If you let anything happen to her, I'll hunt you down and kill you.*" She laid a hand on her bodyguard's arm briefly, then stepped away. "But I suppose it's implied."

Teul-Kim bowed to the princess.

"We will meet again, Your Highness, under the shadow of a shield."

"When the storm has passed," Yi-Nereen said, finishing the shieldcaster's traditional farewell.

Teul-Kim climbed back into the boat, and Jin helped push the craft away from the shore. At the last moment, Teul-Kim leaned close and spoke into her ear. "Watch over her. And do not underestimate her."

Jin shivered, half from surprise and half from the low urgency in the man's voice. Then she backed away to stand with Yi-Nereen and watched the boat's dark shape disappear into the pale blue mist.

"I did my best to shield him," Yi-Nereen said quietly, her gaze fixed on that fading figure. "Earlier this evening, we pretended to argue. I sent him away for the night—very publicly, in front of all of my handmaidens. I hope my father won't have him executed for this." She glanced at Jin. "We should fetch your bike and head for the western gate. I've bribed a metalcrafter to leave a gap in the Wall behind a toolshed."

"Let's get moving, then." Jin's pulse had picked up again and her stomach was in knots. What was it Teul-Kim had tried to tell her?

She forgot about Yi-Nereen's flawed disguise until they were halfway to the garage. A man slouched on a stoop, probably still drunk on festival wine, slurred something incomprehensible at the two of them; Jin saw Yi-Nereen flinch.

"In here," Jin said, leading her into an alley. "You need to—uh, adjust. Take off the veil and trust the dark to hide your face. And open the vest, let it hang loose."

"Won't it draw attention?" Yi-Nereen's fingers hesitated on the buckles. "You can see my . . ."

"It's better than—"

The sound of heavy footfalls and clanking bone hushed her. Jin held up a hand to silence Yi-Nereen, which was unnecessary; the princess's lips were pressed together, and she flattened herself against the mud-streaked alley wall as if she could sink into the stone.

They waited for the patrol to pass. The guards were talking in low voices. Jin couldn't make out words, but her skin prickled. Their conversation didn't sound like the bored chatter of men keeping the streets clear of mischief after sundown. Their voices were tense, purposeful, like men on the hunt. As they moved past the alley mouth, bone-plated uniforms glinting in orange torchlight, Jin caught a snatch of conversation that sent a chill down her spine.

"—heading for the Wall. The west gate—"

Yi-Nereen raised a gloved hand to her mouth. Jin waited until the guards were long gone, their torchlight a distant pinprick bobbing in the night. Then she asked in a low voice, "Who else did you tell?"

Her blood ran hot. The plan had been spoiled before it had even begun. Yi-Nereen was a princess whose only crime so far was to leave the Tower without an escort; she'd get away with a slap on her lace-veiled wrist. But what would happen to Jin? Did Yi-Nereen even care?

"No one! No one but Teul-Kim knows. I trust him with my life. I trust him more than you."

Jin knew her sharp tone had practically begged for the retort, but still, it stung. "So how did the guards find out? You said everything was arranged."

"No one was supposed to know I was gone! I told my handmaidens my moon blood had come early, and I wasn't to be disturbed in my chambers on pain of death." Yi-Nereen's eyes widened, pale and robbed of color in the moonlight. "Oh. *Oh*. I know how this happened. Did you meet a man today, after we spoke? Thin, dark, about your height? A sparkrider—or so he seems."

Jin narrowed her eyes. "What do you mean, *or so he seems*?"

"Then you did meet him." Yi-Nereen's oathless vehemence took Jin by surprise; perhaps princesses never learned to curse. "He's my betrothed, Sou-Zell. He must have seen you at the Tower, followed you until he found the right moment to cross your path. This is *not* good. He knows it all—our plans, our destination—"

"You think I would just run my mouth to the first stranger I happen across—"

"He's a mindreader."

Jin was about to protest that it wasn't possible—then she remembered the moment the slender man in the gazebo had turned his back on her. He'd been concealing the color of his eyes as he used a Talent. *A mindreader?*

It was shocking enough that the man harbored one of the rarest Talents Jin had heard of. She knew there were a number of minor Talents, most of which hadn't even garnered names thanks to their lack of ubiquity; among them, mindreading was the most infamous. But she'd seen the man light a mana-cig with a spark. He was a sparkrider *and* a mindreader, then. One in a hundred born with two Talents instead of one.

She gaped at Yi-Nereen. "A Twinblessed? So he—"

"Heard your thoughts, yes. Mindreading is rare, but there have been a few other practitioners in his bloodline, though they were all generations back. And Twinblessed children tend to crop up in failing lines like his." Yi-Nereen laughed, the sound stark and miserable. "Isn't that perfect? His family arranged our betrothal to lend the strength of my Talent to their weak bloodline. Yet if he were a woman, all the princes in the city would be vying for his hand, hoping his gifts would reappear in the next generation. Everyone thinks it's a woman's fault if she bears Talentless children, and the father has nothing to do with it."

Jin shook her head. Now wasn't the time to discuss politics or the hereditary mechanism of Talent, neither of which she knew shit about. "How much does he know? Did he—could he see everything?"

Her skin crawled. She'd always fought to be free. To owe nothing to anyone, to keep safe all her hurt and longing. This was one of her worst fears: to have someone see into her brain, sifting through her darkest thoughts.

"It depends on what you discussed," Yi-Nereen said. "It's a surface read, nothing deeper. The stronger your emotions, the more he could have sensed. It's best to be calm around a mindreader. Completely calm."

"Well, I didn't *know* he was a mindreader. You could've mentioned that."

"What did you tell him?"

"He asked if I was a courier. Where I was going. Of course I lied, but . . ."

"But he would have heard the truth anyway." Yi-Nereen made a little sound of despair. "We can't change our plans—there's nowhere to go but Kerina Sol. Kadrin and Rasvel's Sanctuary are my only hope. But if we can't even leave the city, it's a moot point." She covered her face and spoke softly through her fingers. "All is lost. He'll have guards patrolling every inch of the Wall. We'll never make it through."

An idea came to Jin, borne on the wings of desperation. It was utterly stupid, because her ideas generally were. But that couldn't be helped.

"What if we went over it?"

"This is lunacy," Yi-Nereen said. "Sheer lunacy."

Jin knelt on the garage floor and checked her bike's mana regulator. She breathed a sigh of relief; the artificer had done his job. "It's this or give up and turn ourselves in. Which means the executioner's block for me, so no thanks."

"Have you ever done this before?"

"I've seen it done by knights in full armor. How hard could it be?"

"*Trained* knights," Yi-Nereen said, "who weren't riding double, with a pteropter in a cage strapped in with the saddlebags."

To her own surprise, Jin smirked. "Perhaps he could help. Pteropters can fly, you know."

"It has a *broken wing*—"

Yi-Nereen fell silent as Jin wheeled her magebike out of the garage and into the darkened streets of the Sub-Ring. Out here in the shadow of the Wall was the roughest district of Kerina Rut, populated by vagrants, travelers, and outcasts. Here, too, were heavily fortified knight compounds. Jin usually steered clear, but tonight one of those compounds was her target.

The streets were far from deserted. Jin navigated her magebike around a man sprawled in a gutter and stalked past a gaggle of chattering drunks without turning her head. Confidence was key; it marked her as a man to whom the idea of being assailed after dark was a distant, unconcerning prospect.

Screech jostled his cage and chirped. The little pteropter seemed even happier than the last time Jin had seen him, though his wing looked no better. Jin had found the cage on the floor next to her repaired and refueled magebike, with a note on top: *He bites, but he's cute. Thanks for letting me look after him.*

If Jin had half a brain, she would have taken her bike and left the cage. Clearly the garage boy was better suited to caring for a pet pteropter than she was. But then again, if she had half a brain, this night would be going very differently.

Around one last corner, beyond the hunched shadows of shanties and run-down shops, Jin beheld their sole hope of escaping the city. From the street beside a squat knight compound rose a long ramp, two paces wide and built on thick support pillars. The ramp ended just above the Wall's crown, a sheer drop into the wastes.

Yi-Nereen gripped her arm. "You say you've seen knights in full armor make the jump. Well, I've seen one fall. A squire, only sixteen years old. Crushed beneath his magebike on the other side of the Wall."

"I've been riding longer than a squire." Jin straddled her magebike and patted the back of the leather seat. Her blood was pumping with a heady mixture of apprehension and eagerness. Part of her had never matured past the all-consuming desire to get on a bike and do stupid tricks, and this one would be hard to beat. "You'll see."

Yi-Nereen drew back, peering at Jin's face in the gloom. Her eyes looked huge, ringed with black galena and wide with fear. "Courier Jin," she said faintly. "You aren't going to get me killed, are you?"

Some of Jin's glee faded. "Of course not," she muttered, looking away, feeling chastised. "You won't be hurt, Princess. I promise."

After a long pause, Yi-Nereen took Jin's hand and perched on the seat behind her. The air was redolent of incense, and it took everything Jin had not to focus on the warmth of the princess's arms around her waist, or Yi-Nereen's breath on her neck. *Focus, you nitwit.*

She burned mana, and the magebike roared to life beneath them. The last of Jin's fear melted away. Now she felt the same way she did in the wastes with a storm crackling in the distance, close enough to promise danger. Taut, ready, alive.

Above the ramp, torches flared on the walls. Shouts echoed in the night. Someone must have heard Jin's engine; no doubt they'd been told to look for a sparkrider escaping with the Shield Lord's daughter. Jin bit back a curse. Well, it didn't matter. They would get just one shot at this anyway.

"Hold on," she said.

Yi-Nereen's only reply was to tighten her grip, stealing the air from Jin's lungs in more ways than one.

Jin lifted her foot and they were off, snarling through the night, a beast turned loose from its cage. The ramp loomed at the end of the street. They'd need to hit the slope with enough speed to make it all the way. That was Jin's final thought before she poured the rest of her Talent into the engine and commanded it to *go.*

The bike shot up the ramp. Vibration, sound, air rushing by— then, in a single breathless moment, they were in the air.

Lights flashed on either side and men shouted commands, but Jin heard nothing. They were above the Wall, soaring through the sky. She was hardly even gripping the handlebars. She could let go, and she'd truly be flying.

Then, among the chaos, she heard a command that chilled her to the bone.

"Archers! Loose!"

"Shit" was all Jin had time to gasp.

The air crackled and turned blue as a shield bloomed around them. Jin felt Yi-Nereen's chin digging into her shoulder, her whole body trembling. Then the ground rushed toward the bike. Jin flexed her legs on the foot pegs and instinctively let the rest of her body go slack. "Hold on!"

The bike plowed into the earth and charged forward with a heady roar. The breath surged out of Jin's lungs like water flowing from a rent cask. Her whole body was numb, but she knew she hadn't been hurt. The shield—which had sputtered briefly out of existence when they hit the ground—was back in full force, which meant Yi-Nereen was still conscious.

White pinpricks dotted the shield, blazing briefly before fading away. Crossbow bolts. Jin couldn't hear their whistle; the engine's roar drowned them out. No time to regroup. They had to put distance between themselves and Kerina Rut before anyone could follow.

They had survived the jump. And soon, Jin told herself fiercely, they'd be safe in Kerina Sol. She fed more sparks to the engine, and her bike hummed in response, promising a long night's uninterrupted ride. It was time to leave Yi-Nereen's home behind.

*Second Age of Storms, 48th Spring*

*Dear Prince Kadrin,*
*With deepest regret, I must reiterate: I truly cannot accept any more*
*letters from you, for reasons within neither your power nor mine to*
*repair. It was only at the stubborn urging of your courier that I read*
*your last letter at all. It was highly inappropriate of me to do so, and it*
*cannot happen again.*

*The customs of Kerina Rut demand that an unmarried noble-*
*woman thoroughly rebuff the advances of any man who attempts to*
*circumvent courtship protocols, no matter how persistent. It was differ-*
*ent when we were children. I hope you understand.*

*Since you inquired, it would be unconscionably rude of me not to*
*answer: I was informed your father abdicated his diplomatic appoint-*
*ment two years early because his son fell ill and needed to be brought*
*home. I am deathly curious to know why I was told such a lie.*

*Alas, since I am sure you will respect my wish not to receive further*
*correspondence from you, I suppose I will never know the truth. If you*
*send another letter, I shall be forced to remind you yet again of my*
*position, in no uncertain terms.*

*Imploring you to understand exactly what I ask of you,*
*Princess Yi-Nereen, First Daughter of the Tower of Arrested Stars*

## CHAPTER FIVE

# THE COURIER'S TALE

*Second Age of Storms, 51st Summer, Day 21*

They rode for a couple hours in silence, the twinkling lights of Kerina Rut fading into the distance, until Jin realized she had a problem: Yi-Nereen couldn't stay awake. The princess's grip on her waist had gone slack, and her head kept slumping forward onto Jin's shoulder.

"Shit," Jin muttered, not for the first time that night.

She wanted to put more distance behind her before stopping. The city guard hadn't been much of a threat, thanks to Yi-Nereen's Talent, but if the Knights of Rut came after them . . .

Well, she should have known it wouldn't be a straight shot to Kerina Sol. Not with a sleepy, saddle-sore princess on the back of her bike.

A rocky outcropping loomed in the glow of her headlights. *Decent place to stop.* She killed the engine, and the sounds of the wasteland at night rushed in to fill the silence: insects chirping, wind gusting over the rocks, the *tick-tick-tick* of the magebike as it cooled.

"Princess?"

"Mm."

Jin eased the unresisting princess off the magebike and propped her against a smooth rock. The satchel Yi-Nereen had been carrying slipped from her shoulder; Jin caught it and placed it on the ground next to the bike. Yi-Nereen's lashes fluttered in the moonlight, a sigh escaping her lips. Jin leaned closer to hear.

"Just a moment . . . Be better soon . . ."

Yi-Nereen was powerful, but her Talent obviously took a lot out of her. Jin recalled the little pinpricks of light bursting against the shield, each of them a deadly crossbow bolt, and shivered. The guards had been shooting to kill. Had Yi-Nereen's family already condemned her to death? Even after three years of reading Yi-Nereen's letters, Jin hadn't realized how little love the royals of Kerina Rut had for their own kin. The princess clearly hadn't wanted to expose the whole ugly truth to Kadrin. Jin could sympathize.

"Well," Jin said. "It's plain we can't keep going. We'll rest here until you're ready to move on, Princess."

A chirp rang out in reply, but it didn't come from Yi-Nereen; the princess's eyes had already drifted shut, and her head lolled against the boulder. Jin straightened and turned back to her bike. Screech's beak poked between the bars of his cage. His beady black eyes were fixed on Jin, watching her every move.

"Hungry little bastard."

She was unpacking her rations from the saddlebags when Yi-Nereen stirred and said faintly, "Courier? Is that food?"

"Yeah." Jin dumped a handful of shredded jerky into Screech's cage and squatted beside Yi-Nereen. The princess leaned against the rock as if she lacked the energy to move a muscle, but she eyed the round metal tin in Jin's hand with undisguised eagerness. "Thought you fell asleep." Jin opened the tin, then hesitated. "Ever had road cakes before, Princess?"

"Cake?" Yi-Nereen squinted at the tin. "There's cake in there?"

Jin opened the tin and offered one of the thin, flat biscuits inside to Yi-Nereen. "My mother makes these for sparkriders, for long trips in the wastes."

Yi-Nereen took a bite and chewed, her expression blank. Her gaze was distant and fixed on something past Jin. After a short silence—during which Jin fidgeted and took a too-large bite—Yi-Nereen swallowed and asked, "What's that?"

Jin glanced back. The heavens above were soot black, but to the north the horizon grew pale. "Still hours before dawn. Must be a storm."

"Are we in danger?" Yi-Nereen's voice was tight.

Jin sighed. Yi-Nereen had more than one reason to be exhausted, she reminded herself. Fear could hollow out a person like nothing else, and the princess had faced plenty of terror tonight. First the guards and the jump over the Wall, and now the barren wilderness.

Most people never left the shelter of a kerina's dome. Jin might be used to the wasteland and its dangers, but Yi-Nereen wasn't.

"We'll keep an eye on it. If it's headed for us, we'll be polite and get on out of its way."

Yi-Nereen nodded. Locks of hair had sprung free of her coif and coiled about her temples. She finished her road cake in small, delicate bites. Jin had never seen the princess eat before; she didn't know if her reticence was down to etiquette or if the food wasn't up to snuff. It seemed inelegant to ask. In fact, everything Jin could think of saying or doing seemed impossibly coarse. She settled for placing the tin on the ground, where Yi-Nereen could get herself a second helping if she wanted, and looking away.

The storm in the north grew slowly, from a distant pale glow to a swirling mass of dark clouds lit from within by azure lightning. "It's headed west, toward the Barrens," Jin remarked as soon as she was sure. "We're well out of its way."

Yi-Nereen breathed a quiet sigh of relief, though when Jin glanced over, her gaze was fixed on the storm. "What are the Barrens?"

"Nowhere we want to go," Jin said. "Have you ever seen a map of the wastes, Princess? You'll have noticed the big patch in the west without any roads? Well, there *are* roads leading into the Barrens— but no courier or knight has lived to map them."

"Why not?"

"Rovex," Jin said. "They attack and chase off anyone who enters the Barrens. There are so many there, some couriers think it's where they breed. Maybe even where saurians come from in general."

She noticed Yi-Nereen's wide eyes and decided to change the subject.

"So, is anyone going to come after us? The Knights of Rut?"

Yi-Nereen shook her head. "It takes a quorum of the High Houses to dispatch the Legion. I think my father will find it difficult to convince Knight-Commander Ren-Vetaar to send any riders as a personal favor; the Tower has fallen behind on its dues recently. The other royals won't see the benefit of diverting resources to retrieve one errant Shield Daughter, unless—"

"Okay, okay." Jin held up her hands. "You can just say no. I hate politics."

Yi-Nereen must have been planning her escape for a long time. Years, maybe. And who could blame her? On one hand, a shithole of a city where she'd be forced into an unhappy marriage—and on the other, safe haven with a prince who was clearly besotted with her.

"What about your fiancé?" Jin asked. "He's a sparkrider. Will he come after us himself?"

"I doubt it. His sparktalent is weak, which is why he never

joined the Legion. Most Twinblessed are weaker in both their Talents than you or I in our one. Besides, by now the other Houses will know I've fled, which means our betrothal is over. I won't be of use to him now."

Jin popped the last of her cake in her mouth. "Sounds like we're free and clear." So why did Yi-Nereen look so dismal? "Kadrin is in for the biggest surprise of his life."

She hoped to get a smile out of the princess, but Yi-Nereen stared past her in silence. Then she asked quietly, "Is Kerina Sol as Kadrin describes in his letters? A place where anyone is treated the same, no matter their Talent? It sounds . . . impossible."

Jin considered herself fortunate her mouth was full—it gave her time to think. What could she tell Yi-Nereen? Kerina Sol was no fairy tale. It hadn't suffered from the population crisis in the same way the other cities had; as far as Jin knew, the High Houses were still producing enough Talented children to safeguard future generations. But it had been affected in its own way. The practice of Rasvel's Sanctuary had made Kerina Sol a beacon for Talentless cast out by other cities across the wastes, and all the good intentions in the world couldn't eliminate the simple problem of not having enough beds or food for everyone.

When she and Eomma had first arrived, they'd lived in ghettos with other refugees. They'd slept on the floor of a common house, a shack no bigger than one of Kadrin's outhouses and crammed full of people who had nowhere else to go. Without a working mage-bike, Jin had spent months doing odd jobs and hard labor to save up enough for the first month's rent on a derelict bakery. And she'd been one of the luckier ones: young, able-bodied, and sound of mind. Others hadn't been so fortunate.

But Yi-Nereen wouldn't face what Jin had gone through. Kadrin would welcome her with open arms, and she'd take up a life just as luxurious as the one she'd left behind. Jin didn't know how to feel about that. Relieved? Annoyed?

"It's real," she said at last. "You'll see it for yourself."

Yi-Nereen toyed with the edges of her veil. Through the sheer black chiffon, Jin saw her brows furrowed in a pensive line. "How far is the journey?"

Jin was glad to change the subject. "I usually make the crossing in a day."

"Why travel by day? Wouldn't it be cooler after nightfall?"

"Easier to see storms coming in the daylight." *And raiders.* But best not to spook Yi-Nereen. "The roads aren't in the best of shape, either. Hard to spot potholes at night."

"Potholes." Yi-Nereen smiled, and Jin looked away. It was dangerous, that smile, like sunlight in her eyes on a tricky curve. "Sometimes the life of a courier seems so romantic, and then you remind me of all the ways in which it isn't."

Jin hesitated. "Still wouldn't trade it for anything."

Wind blew over the highway and the boulder where Yi-Nereen sat, ruffling her veil and making Jin shiver, though her riding leathers kept out most of the cold. Above, dark shapes flitted across the moon's glowing orb—a pack of pteropters, flying high over the wastes. Screech stirred in his cage and made a mournful warbling sound. Yi-Nereen raised her face to watch the saurians, and Jin watched the princess.

"I don't sleep very well." Yi-Nereen's face was still turned toward the stars. "One of my handmaidens often sings to me at night. I don't suppose you sing, Courier Jin?"

"Can't say I do."

Yi-Nereen settled her shoulders against the stone, drawing her knees up to her chest. "Then tell me a courier story. I like hearing tales, especially when they're true."

"Don't know if you'll like this one." Jin rubbed her nose. Her throat itched for a mana-cig, but for once she found the craving easy to ignore. "It's about running away from home."

"Ah," Yi-Nereen said, "then it must have a happy ending."

Jin sighed. "I'll let you decide."

There was an old courier expression: cities had hundreds of laws, but the mana wastes knew only one—survive at any cost. Gao-Jin understood the gist of the saying, but he'd never fully agreed. The mana wastes had plenty of laws.

Bring twice as much food and water as you think you'll need. Travel light as you can. Never fall asleep unless you can see the whole horizon. Watch where pteropters fly, steer clear of chandru, and ride like hell if you see a rovex. Mana, water, then food, in that order. If your magebike dies, you die. If your spark dies, you die.

The difference between the wasteland and the cities, Gao-Jin reasoned, was that cities needed men to enforce the law. The wastes needed no enforcer. So if you had to live by the rules of one and not the other, better to be an outlaw in civilization than dead in the desert.

He made his home in the wasteland, but his heart lived in Ke-rina Tez. A woman dwelled there who baked the sweetest road cakes he'd ever tasted. Her hair was silk and charcoal, her laugh warmer than the sun and quicker than lightning, her hands firm and gentle. Evemi, his wasteland flower. One day, Gao-Jin swore, he'd pluck her from the weeds and take her somewhere lush and green, a foreign land untouched by storms.

He'd have no place there. Without the storms, without mana, his Talent would dwindle and fade—and so would he. So taking Evemi away from the wastes would be his last delivery, the last moment before their roads diverged forever. Maybe that was why he waited.

He didn't know time was running out until it was gone. Sometimes it was months between deliveries to Kerina Tez, long months between precious days in Evemi's bakery and passionate nights locked in her arms. So it was that one day he walked into the bakery and heard an infant's wail before Evemi's voice. *His* child. He'd last seen Evemi six months before and hadn't even known she was pregnant.

In that moment, marked forever by the smell of fresh bread and a child's cry, Gao-Jin knew he'd never take Evemi to the green place.

"She's like you," Evemi crooned, stroking the infant's forehead. "Talented. The priests already tested her."

The test was simple and reliable: lower the child into a basin of mana and watch the color of their eyes. If it changed, the child was Talented, and their name would be written in the Tezaros, the register of Kerina Tez's full citizens. Otherwise, the baby was returned to its parents like a shameful castoff, for them to do with as they pleased. Sometimes that involved another basin at home, full of water instead of mana.

Gao-Jin held his infant daughter and wept. If only she'd failed the test. He knew what the priests of Kerina Tez would never accept: Talent wasn't a gift, but a curse. It sentenced her to a life in the wastes, a life among storms. At least, Gao-Jin vowed, he could teach her to make the best of it.

So he did. He built a sidecar for his magebike and took his daughter into the wastes before she could walk, teaching her the wonders of her prison. He showed her saurians and chasms split by storms, shattered remnants of ancient highways and plants twisted into new shapes by wild magic. He made the rumble of the mage-bike's engine into her lullaby and rocked her to sleep under crimson stars. Evemi was his wasteland flower, impossible and pure, but Jin-Lu was like him—born to a broken world, the same corruption flowing through her veins.

But the laws of men were changing. Gao-Jin watched Kerina Tez grow colder toward its Talentless, rewriting its laws, stealing their freedoms one by one. Evemi lost her bakery; a metaltalented savant claimed the building for his sculptures. The Legion grew more insistent; they wanted sparktalented children. Knights were dying in the wastes, falling prey to bandits and errant storms, and not enough children with the spark were being born to replace them.

"We need to leave," Evemi told Gao-Jin, her voice trembling. "I've had enough of this. We can't stay here. The priests—they'll take her from me."

So Gao-Jin made arrangements. One last delivery, to earn enough mun to pay Evemi's debts and build a new life in Kerina Sol. He'd never smuggled drugs before, but scraping together the coin from smaller jobs would take too much time. He needed a windfall.

His daughter was seven years old. Old enough to watch Gao-Jin, blindfolded and bound, be led into the square by temple guards, guided onto a scaffold, and bent over so his cheek rested against smooth, bloodstained stone. Old enough to remember the voice of the priest who read his sentence, though the list of charges blurred together into meaningless, damning noise. Old enough to recognize the prince who'd posed as Gao-Jin's supplier and watched his execution with a smile.

The blindfold stayed on. Gao-Jin died without seeing his daughter's face, or Evemi's. But Jin-Lu watched and never forgot. Her father had made the wasteland beautiful and refused to live by the laws of men, and now he was dead. She would use what he had taught her to take her mother and flee Kerina Tez, no matter what it took.

"It took thirteen years," Jin said softly. "And I spent most of those years dodging the Legion. I learned my trade from an old courier named Lorne. Riding was the easy part; I've always been good at it. The hard part was scraping together enough mun for a bike of my own. Eomma was scared of riding—that's why she never went anywhere with my father—but I couldn't afford a sidecar, so she rode out of Kerina Tez with her arms so tight around my stomach I thought I'd puke." Jin smiled. "A bit like you, Princess."

She glanced to the side. Yi-Nereen's head had slumped onto the boulder; her veil fluttered to the steady rhythm of her breath. Jin shrugged off her jacket and draped it over the princess.

Her throat clenched. For a moment, she saw someone else sleeping in Yi-Nereen's place. Emotion pushed against her ribs, a beast trying to claw its way out. All she could do was breathe, in and out, squeezing her hands in time with each inhale.

Her escape from Kerina Tez hadn't been without sacrifice. She'd left the rest of the story untold. Yi-Nereen didn't need to know the real reason Jin had been unable to refuse her back in Kerina Rut. Her secret shame, the stain on her past. Falka.

Delivering Yi-Nereen safely into Kadrin's arms would make it all right. Then, maybe, Jin would finally be freed of her guilt.

The next sound Jin heard was god-awful squawking, like a pigeon stuck in a tailpipe. She opened her eyes—apparently she'd dozed off—to see Screech noisily beaking at the bars of his cage, making enough of a ruckus to wake the dead.

Beside her, Yi-Nereen mumbled something in her sleep. Jin rubbed her eyes and yawned. How long had she slept? It must be near dawn, so why was the sky so dark?

Realization struck her cold, and a quick glance north confirmed her suspicions. "Oh, shit."

The storm had changed direction. Black clouds boiled across the horizon, filled with flickering blue light. Thunder shook the wastes. The storm rushed toward them at a speed Jin had only ever witnessed once—the day before, on the crossing between Kerina Sol and Kerina Rut.

"Princess. Wake up. *We need to move.*"

*Second Age of Storms, 48th Spring*

*Dear Princess Yi-Nereen,*
*After careful perusal of your last letter, I believe I understand your refusal to communicate with me. However, due to stupidity and an astonishing lack of grace, I persist in writing you nonetheless. Please don't blame Courier Jin. She deserves praise for her patience in explaining exactly what you wished of me.*

*Since I have bullied my way into gaining your attention, I owe you the truth about my family's departure from Kerina Rut nine years ago. It was indeed my fault, but I wasn't ill. The truth is, I'm Talentless.*

*My father brought me to Kerina Rut under false pretenses, purporting that I was a raintalented savant like the First and Second Heirs to my House. Who knows what he hoped to gain from such a lie; I've never had the courage to ask. When the truth got out that I wasn't, he was concerned about retaliation. I don't remember it, but I believe there were death threats.*

*I await your reply, in which I expect to find out precisely how much offense I have incurred. Since I am oblivious by nature, it may take a lot of letters to drive the lesson home, and long letters at that. Please employ whatever insults you can think of. I expect to be granted no quarter.*

*With utmost sincerity,*
*Prince Kadrin*

## CHAPTER SIX

# THE STORM GIVES CHASE

*Second Age of Storms, 51st Summer, Day 21*

They fled before the storm. Sharp and single-focused, Jin's whole body sang with danger. Yi-Nereen clutched her tight from behind. The princess might have been shouting in Jin's ear, but the wind's baleful shriek drowned her out. At any rate, it didn't matter.

No clever words could save them now. Their only hope was to outrace the storm.

Of all the wasteland's threats, mana storms were the most frequent but the least dangerous, as long as you knew what you were doing. *A storm isn't smart,* Lorne had told her. *It isn't hunting you, and it won't veer off course to follow you. It doesn't even know you exist. All you need to remember is this: when you see a storm, get the hell out of its way, and you'll live to see another day.*

Jin had learned to skirt a storm's edge, taking her bike off-road and into the wastes at a slant. Fleeing in a straight line was for fools who didn't understand the wasteland. But this storm was hell-bent on making a fool out of Jin, and a dead one at that. Because it *was* following her.

It made no fucking sense, but there wasn't time to think about it.

To make a bad situation worse, she wasn't alone. *Don't ever ride*

*full burn when you've got a passenger. You'll blow through your tank
before you know it, and an empty tank in the waste means one thing. I
don't need to fuckin' say it, do I?*

"No, Lorne," Jin ground out, her voice inaudible. "You didn't
need to say it."

Because they were going to die.

Lightning stabbed to her right and a rock lit up like a tree aflame,
a spiderweb of veins pulsing blue. Dark clouds churned overhead.
Jin felt the raw power of the storm at her back, a hand about to close
and squeeze her until she burst. She felt a premonition of her fate in
Yi-Nereen's clutching arms, Yi-Nereen's breath hot on her neck—
like a phantom of death perched on the back of Jin's magebike.

The wall of dust before them swirled and parted. Lightning
flashed. Jin's heart stuttered in her chest.

They weren't alone in the storm. She'd seen the unmistakable
shape of another magebike and rider, silhouetted in blue. For one
harried moment, she doubted it was real. Maybe that last bolt had
incinerated her without pain or fanfare, and the figure she saw was
Rasvel, Giver of Blessings . . . or was it her father?

Lightning flashed again. The other sparkrider had drawn closer,
so close Jin could make out the orange glow of their eyes inside the
saurian-bone helm. One gloved hand lifted and sliced forward, a
clear message: *Follow.*

Yi-Nereen shouted something incomprehensible in Jin's ear. It
didn't matter what she was trying to say; Jin had made up her mind.

The other sparkrider veered away, and Jin followed. She could
hardly see—her headlight was caked over in dust and the air was
nearly black—but she felt the ground slope beneath her, falling
away in a steep decline. Wind and debris howled around her as the
storm closed the last few inches of distance.

Faint dark shapes loomed on either side of the magebike. Canyon walls. The other sparkrider was leading her down a chasm hewn into the earth.

She'd heard stories from stranded couriers who'd waited out storms in cracks like these. Stories of mangled, rusted magebikes and skeletal remains found deep underground. Saurians lived beneath the earth, more vicious than the ones who roamed the wastes—or so the tales went.

The wind died away. The storm's howl grew quiet in the dark, and Jin realized the earth had closed over their heads. They weren't safe—the storm could wreck this tunnel, crush them in a collapse—but few situations were safer in this case. She slowed and cut her engine.

"Thank Rasvel." Yi-Nereen's voice in her ear was nearly a sob. "I thought we were going to die. Who is that?"

Jin stared at the back of the other sparkrider, who'd stopped ten paces ahead. "I have no idea."

The other rider's headlight flickered out. Darkness filled the tunnel. Hair standing on end, Jin stepped down from her bike and snapped her fingers. A trio of sparks floated up from her fingertips, hanging lazily in the air. The tiny motes of light showed her Yi-Nereen's face, her eyes wide behind the veil—but no one else.

"Where did they go?" Yi-Nereen whispered.

"I don't—shit!"

The other sparkrider materialized from the darkness, close enough for Jin to reach out and touch them. The faint, dancing light of her sparks illuminated a slim figure wearing a rough-spun sleeveless jacket and a blunt-nosed bonehelm. *Not a courier*, Jin's brain screamed at her. *Definitely not a knight.*

Jin staggered backward. She groped for her utility knife. Had she really been stupid enough to follow a raider into a tunnel? Fuck, fuck, *fuck*—

The sparkrider raised their hands. "*Wirja!*"

Jin froze. "What?"

"*Wirja*," the sparkrider said again, and pulled off their bone-helm. Jin gaped; the person standing before her was a boy no older than fifteen, dark-haired and gangly. His lip and left ear were pierced with bone; he wore a bracelet of polished beads on one wrist. He smiled at her hesitantly and spoke—and Jin didn't understand a word.

"What language is that?" Yi-Nereen demanded from behind her. "What's he saying?"

"I have no fucking clue," Jin said, before she could think better of it. Then she bit her cheek and added in a more pacifying tone, "I'm just as lost as you are, Princess."

"Reena." Yi-Nereen's voice was tight. "We're past titles, I think."

*Reena.* That was what Kadrin had come to call her in his letters. And Jin whispered it in the night sometimes, just to know how it felt on her tongue.

"I've heard raiders lose their minds after a while," Jin said. "Some of the plants in the wastes won't kill you; they'll just eat your brain from the inside out. Maybe he's addled?"

She doubted the words even as she said them. The boy didn't sound like he was speaking gibberish; there was logic and rhythm to his speech. It had to be another language. But that didn't make sense. Dirilish had been the common tongue of the wastes for hundreds of years.

Jin stared the boy down. He was still smiling at her, a little helplessly.

"*Faolin*," he said, thumping his chest. "*Se Faolin.*"

"I think that's his name," Yi-Nereen said, and before Jin could stop her, she'd taken a step forward. She laid a hand on her own chest. "Yi-Nereen."

"Careful," Jin said.

"I don't see any weapons. He's just a child, Jin. Maybe he has a family around here somewhere." Yi-Nereen glanced around in the darkness, her brows furrowed. "Don't people live in the wastes? I've heard tales, but I didn't know if they were true. Wastelanders— that's what my nursemaid called them. She said we all used to live as nomads before we built the kerinas, in the old days when the storms weren't so bad."

"I've heard the same tales, but I've never met anyone like that out here." Not once in all her years on the road.

Jin gripped the handle of her knife, though it was hard to maintain a healthy degree of suspicion with the sparkrider kid grinning at her like that. Maybe Yi-Nereen was right and he wasn't a raider. Kerinas could be cruel, but they didn't exile children to the wastes. Not Talented ones, anyway.

Wastelanders, though? How would they survive? You needed three things to live in the wastes: food, water, and shelter from the storms. Bloom, Rain, and Shield: the High Talents necessary for life. The boy couldn't possibly possess all three. He was a sparkrider, sure, so he could outrace the storms. But what did he eat?

"He saved us," Yi-Nereen said. Now she and the boy were both looking expectantly at Jin. "The least you could do is tell him your name."

Jin couldn't argue with that. "Jin," she said, touching her collarbones self-consciously. "Jin-Lu."

Faolin repeated her name, bouncing a little on the balls of his feet. Then he raised his hands, spoke a string of words, and turned away to take exaggerated steps into the darkness. Jin and Yi-Nereen exchanged glances.

"Should we follow him?" Yi-Nereen asked.

Jin could still hear the wind howling above, the storm lashing against the earth. "Can't hurt, I suppose." She hesitated. "Sorry I snapped at you earlier. We did almost die."

Yi-Nereen exhaled, long and slow. The galena around her eyes had smudged into shadowed pools of black. Grit clung to the fine mesh of her veil. "It's been quite an adventure." Her voice softened. "I never had the chance to thank you."

Jin looked away. "We should go."

They hurried after Faolin. Jin's sparks bobbed along overhead, fed by a steady trickle of Talent. She pushed her magebike over uneven ground, muscles straining with the effort. The kid walked fast. *What's the rush?* Jin wanted to ask, but of course that wouldn't do any good.

"You didn't finish it," Yi-Nereen said.

Jin grunted as she muscled her bike around a bend. "What?"

"The story. What happened when you reached Kerina Sol? How did you come to meet Kadrin?"

"Later," Jin said. "When we're safe."

She was too out of breath to tell any more stories now. What could she say about Kadrin, anyway? That his father, the Rain Lord of Kerina Sol, was nauseatingly wealthy, and his gardens overflowed with water-fed flowers? That when she'd answered Kadrin's job posting, his majordomo had taken one look at Jin's grubby riding leathers and tried to turn her away from the front door? That Kadrin himself was strong and handsome, with eyes that reminded Jin of precious wood cultivated in timber orchards by bloomweavers— no, she probably shouldn't mention that part.

Nor did she want to dwell on the year she'd spent in the slum quarter of Kerina Sol before she started working for Kadrin, trapped in a city that wasn't nearly as friendly and welcoming to refugees as Jin and her mother had been led to believe. She and Eomma had lived like animals, starved and surrounded by filth.

And all the while, she'd been desperate to return to Kerina Tez, because she'd left someone important there. Someone she loved. Someone she'd never see again.

The tunnel sloped upward. Light bled through the darkness. Jin dismissed her sparks as she and Faolin wheeled their magebikes around a bend and into the glow of dawn.

*Second Age of Storms, 48th Spring*

*Dear Prince Kadrin,*
*It's safe. My mother isn't reading these letters. Now we may dispense with*
*this ruse.*

*If your courier ever returns to you empty-handed, know it was not*
*my choice. I shall write you as much and for as long as I can, until*
*someone stops me. May our correspondence continue until the springs*
*all run dry and the stars fall from the heavens.*

*When it comes to the past, I have only this to say: you have nothing*
*to apologize for, Kadrin. In a childhood filled with shadow and silence,*
*you were my only brightness. After so long in the dark, receiving your*
*letter was like a glimpse of the sun.*

*By the by, after all these years, have you found yourself engaged or*
*married? I ask only so I may convey my best wishes to your other half,*
*though I suspect she does not require them, having already demon-*
*strated her good fortune.*

*Finally, please take better care of your courier. She is in sore need of*
*a new pair of riding gloves. Yes, Courier Jin, I am serious. Write that*
*down.*

*Until next time,*
*Princess Yi-Nereen*

## CHAPTER SEVEN

# A GREEN PLACE

*Second Age of Storms, 51st Summer, Day 21*

A canyon opened up before them, like something out of a fairy tale. Jin had seen grass only in the gardens of the wealthy, but here it covered the ground in a lush green carpet. Vines dangled from rock walls and ledges. She felt the same raw disbelief she'd felt the first time she laid eyes on Kadrin's home, the House of Steel Heavens. But that place had been created and painstakingly maintained through an arrogance of Talent, and this was a random canyon in the middle of the wastes. The air was fragrant with a familiar smell: baking bread.

Jin stiffened. She'd thought the canyon deserted, but now she saw its inhabitants: faces peering from fissures in the rock, looking at her and Yi-Nereen. People, young and old, expressions ranging from curious to hostile. There were dozens of them, and more every second. She was thoroughly outnumbered.

"It's green." Yi-Nereen's voice was faint with wonder; she didn't sound frightened at all. "Do you think they're all bloomweavers?"

Jin glanced around at the vegetation. All the plants that grew in the wastes were toxic, except for the ones bloomweavers could conjure from mana and the memory of a seed. But the grass and the vines didn't look bloomwoven, though she couldn't put her finger on why. They also lacked the eerie, twisted look of waste-land flora.

"Don't know," she said in a low voice. "I'm more worried about whether they're going to kill us."

Faolin glanced at her and raised his palm. *Wait*, the gesture said clearly enough.

Though her instincts told her to hop on her bike and speed back into the tunnel they'd just emerged from, Jin stayed put. Coming toward them across the grass was an aged man with white hair, flanked on either side by women. One of the women greeted Faolin with obvious relief, kissing his cheeks and forehead. She looked the right age to be his mother.

"Hello," Jin said, since she felt she ought to say something. "I'm a courier. My name is Jin."

The old man hardly spared her a glance. His wrinkles were so deep Jin could get lost in them. Shit, he might be the oldest person she'd ever seen. He spoke to Faolin in the same incomprehensible language, his voice slow and ponderous. Jin frowned; so Faolin wasn't addled after all. None of these people spoke Dirilish.

Faolin, she noticed, spoke to the old man with his head bowed, never meeting his eyes. *He's royal around here, then, or whatever the equivalent is.* As he talked, Faolin kept gesturing toward her mage-bike. No, not her bike. At Screech.

"They seem interested in your pteropter," Yi-Nereen said quietly. She was standing close enough for Jin to feel her warmth, which was distracting.

Jin was about to reply when all four of the wastelanders—Faolin, the old man, and the two women—turned as one to look at her and Yi-Nereen. Jin's skin prickled fiercely as she studied their expressions. Two of them didn't look friendly at all: the old man and one of the women. Faolin's mother started to speak, but the old man cut her off with a sharp retort.

"Maybe we should go." Jin's hand crept toward her knife. She realized she was standing between Yi-Nereen and the wastelanders, though she didn't know when she'd moved. "Get on the bike, Princess."

Thunder rumbled in the distance. Jin glanced at the sky. So did everyone else. Faolin's mother whispered something that might have been a prayer, her hands clasped around the saurian-bone amulet she wore. Above the soaring canyon walls, the sky should have been paling as the sun continued to rise—but instead it was growing darker.

Jin stepped forward and grabbed Faolin's arm. "Storm's coming this way. Your people need to get back in those caves."

The boy hesitated. Even if he didn't understand her, the urgency in her voice was obvious. He pointed at the sky, gestured eastward, shook his head. Jin understood his confusion. The storm was meant to be moving east, away from them.

How could she explain? Even if they spoke the same language, he wouldn't believe her. Storms didn't chase people.

"The storm is coming!" Jin raised her arms over her head, imitating a dome. "Where are your shieldcasters? Reena, show him what I mean. Show him your Talent."

"I can't," Yi-Nereen said. "Not unless there's a mana spring somewhere near."

Jin looked at her. "Shit."

Faolin had turned away and begun arguing with the old man again. Though he kept his eyes lowered, his voice was deep and serious. Jin thought he was trying to sound older, like a fully grown man. Did he have any authority here? Was he trying to convince the old man to let them stay?

Thunder rolled through the canyon again, and the faces that had been watching the exchange from gaps in the rock began to disappear, one by one. The wastelanders were taking refuge in their caves. Were the caves their only shelter? That wasn't a good sign. Every courier knew not to rely on stone or earth in a storm. Lightning could blast hills to rubble and bring fresh mana springs bubbling up from below. The ancient highways were the only part of the wasteland immune to change; everything else was impermanent.

Well, the fate of these wastelanders wasn't Jin's problem. She was about to grab Yi-Nereen and hop on her bike when Faolin turned suddenly and clapped a hand on her shoulder.

"*Vai*," he said. Behind him, the old man had crossed his arms. He gave Jin and Yi-Nereen one last distrusting scowl, then turned and shuffled toward a gap in the canyon wall, supported by one of the women.

"*Vai*," Faolin repeated, his voice insistent. He tugged Jin's sleeve. His mother hovered behind him, her eyes darting between her son and Jin.

Jin flinched as thunder boomed across the heavens. The sky above flickered. They were out of time. She stared into Faolin's dark eyes, her heart hammering in her chest. Maybe trusting him was a mistake. Maybe the canyon would fall to pieces in the storm. But leaving was no choice, either. She was running on fumes, and if the storm kept chasing them, they wouldn't have a chance.

"Jin?" Yi-Nereen's voice shook. "Are we staying or going?"

Jin swallowed. "Staying."

They followed Faolin into the mouth of the nearest cave. The narrow tunnel twisted right and flared into a wider chamber. Jin's first thought was *They aren't nomads.* She was standing in something more akin to a cozy hut than a cave. Herbs hung in aromatic bundles from racks driven into the pitted ceiling; alcoves in the stone walls had been smoothed and heaped with blankets. The air was fragrant with candle smoke and warm with body heat. Four children stared back at Jin from the alcoves as she leaned her magebike against a wall. The youngest gripped a carved wooden rovex.

"*Sevina?*" Faolin's mother glanced around the room, her voice rising in panic. "*Sevina!*"

She began ransacking the chamber, lifting blankets and opening baskets. Faolin hurried to help. Jin and Yi-Nereen exchanged looks.

"She's missing a child," Yi-Nereen said in a hushed voice. "Do you think . . . ?"

Wind howled outside. The storm had come upon the canyon. Jin screwed her eyes shut. She *sensed* it somehow, through the stone—a ravenous beast intent on its prey. "It's too late." Her chest was tight. "Maybe another family took the kid inside."

"And if they didn't?" Yi-Nereen's voice grew determined. "Jin, they must get mana from somewhere. If I had just a little more . . ."

"Mana?" Faolin asked.

Jin opened her eyes. The boy had halted in his frantic search and was staring at Yi-Nereen. Did he know the word? For a moment no one moved. Then Faolin snatched a woven basket from a shelf. Blue light spilled from under its lid. Jin pushed through the crowded room, her hackles rising.

Inside the basket were small glass bottles packed in moss, tied with ribbons and filled to the brim with liquid smoke. Mana. Jin cradled a bottle in her hand, feeling the icy warmth of its contents through the glass. How? Mana went inert just hours after being harvested from a spring, losing its glow and its potency—yet she was certain this was the real stuff. Her blood hungered for it; sweat beaded her skin. Riding full burn in a storm had nearly run her dry,

"Is that mana?" Yi-Nereen asked, shocked. "Preserved mana?"

"One way to find out." Jin turned and thrust the bottle into Yi-Nereen's hands.

Yi-Nereen hesitated, her hands trembling. Jin was about to offer to go first when the princess abruptly made up her mind. She pried the cork out of the bottle and drained its contents with a shudder.

Jin winced sympathetically. Of all the ways to infuse, actually *drinking* mana was fastest, but by far the least pleasant. The stuff tasted like bitter medicine. Of course, inert mana didn't taste like anything . . . so if Yi-Nereen's reaction was anything to judge by, these bottles were still potent. Somehow.

Yi-Nereen closed her eyes, curled her fingers—and a shield flared around her. Faolin gasped and grabbed Jin's sleeve again. His voice was rough with excitement. Jin caught the words *mana* and *Sevina*.

"It's real." Yi-Nereen opened her eyes. "We need to find that child. Quickly."

Faolin didn't need convincing. "*Vai!*" He tugged Jin and Yi-Nereen toward the mouth of the cave. His mother stared after them, wringing her hands.

Outside, the canyon was choked with darkness. Dust clouds roiled in the air, whipped into a frenzy. Thin tendrils of blue light snaked down from the sky, and the earth sang where they touched down, a high keening vibration that hurt Jin's ears. Teasers, Lorne had called those tendrils. They were vanguards to the real lightning, bolts that could reduce a person to ash in a single strike.

Yi-Nereen's shield flickered back into view around them. The wind's roar dulled inside the dome, and swirling dust settled to the earth. Jin dragged in a precious breath of clean air. They were safe, until Yi-Nereen's mana stores ran dry again.

"Stay close," Yi-Nereen said. "Jin, hold on to me."

There wasn't time to react before Yi-Nereen's hand was sliding into Jin's, warm fingers interlacing, her skin softer than silk. For a moment Jin heard nothing over the rush of her own blood in her ears.

Then a sharp jerk on her arm pulled her back to reality. Faolin was dragging Yi-Nereen by her other hand, shouting and gesturing toward some unseen point in the swirling darkness. Blue light flickered around them. Jin had never felt so helpless before. She'd never relied on anyone to keep her safe in the wasteland except herself. Wasn't she meant to protect Yi-Nereen, not the other way around?

Something huge and dark loomed out of the storm. A boulder, shaped like a kneeling chandru. At the base, huddled into a dip, was a child. She raised her tearstained face from her arms, wide eyes blinking in the glow of Yi-Nereen's shield.

Faolin fell to his knees, his voice sharp and trembling even as he gathered the girl into his arms. Jin's heart ached. She knew that tone. It was the way her mother chided when she fussed over Jin's bruises. It meant the danger had passed and everything was going to be all right.

Then the sky exploded into furious blue. Jin's hair stood on end. A mammoth bolt struck the ground so near to the boulder that the child screamed and Yi-Nereen's shield flickered. Close, much too close. Could the shield withstand a direct hit?

"Faolin!" Jin hauled the boy to his feet and—because she didn't know what else to do—swept the little girl into her arms. The child clung to her neck, pressing her wet face against Jin's cheek. Which way back to the cave? She couldn't see a damn thing. "Yi-Nereen, we—"

A thin trickle of blood ran from Yi-Nereen's nostril, over her lip. Her face was ashen. "I can't hold out much longer," she gasped. "Not alone."

Jin's mind went blank. She reached out, fumbling, and found Yi-Nereen's hand again. "I'm here," she said roughly. "Tell me what to do. How to help."

Yi-Nereen pressed her lips together. Her shield guttered like a candle in the wind, straining to hold back the storm. A fresh trickle of blood ran down her chin. "Do you trust me, Jin?"

*Out in the wastes, it's every sparkrider for themselves,* rasped Lorne's voice in the dusty corners of Jin's memory. *The wasteland doesn't know mercy or compassion. Just make sure you and your mage-bike make it home. That's all that matters.*

Jin thought of Kadrin. The warmth of his grin when he counted coins into her hand, as if making sure Jin was paid her due was a pleasure unto itself. The adoration writ plainly across his face as he listened to her read Yi-Nereen's letters, his cheek pillowed into his palm, lounging on a divan as sunlight streamed through the arched windows of the House of Steel Heavens.

Trust was something only people like him could afford. People who'd never known anything but love, warmth, and safety.

Yet Yi-Nereen had trusted Jin with not just her life, but her future. Now, Jin realized, all she wanted to do was surrender. Lower her walls and let the princess in.

She met Yi-Nereen's blazing blue eyes. "Yes," Jin whispered.

Yi-Nereen nodded. She took the child gently from Jin's arms and handed her to Faolin. Then she threw back her veil, reached up to cradle Jin's face in her palms, and drew her close.

Jin shuddered. Yi-Nereen's lips burned as they cooled her, like the icy fire of liquid mana. She didn't know if the shield was still there. The storm was rushing in, pouring into Jin's body and filling her with lightning. She *was* the storm. And she didn't care anymore whether it destroyed her.

Was it her traitorous imagination, or were Yi-Nereen's fingers winding through her hair, her body pressing hungrily into every curve of Jin's? It was . . . it was more than just a kiss. The heat of Yi-Nereen's mouth drew something from Jin, something vital. Weakness raced through Jin's limbs. Her veins burned as if they flowed with poison. Yet she clung to Yi-Nereen, one hand twisted in the princess's black hair and the other on the small of her back, holding her close—until sensation fled and Jin's strength failed her.

Then she spun away into darkness, hollow and cold, light as air.

# PART TWO

## CHAPTER EIGHT

# THE BOUNTY HUNTER

*Second Age of Storms, 51st Summer, Day 21*

Forty years ago, in a fit of genius, an artificer in Kerina Tez had invented the magebike. Ever since, the sparktalented men of Kerina Rut had chosen one of two paths: the path of the courier or the path of the knight.

Sou-Zell had chosen neither.

Instead he had channeled his considerable energy and ambition toward more rewarding pursuits: expertise in various forms of martial arts, the collection of a dizzying array of political secrets, and the careful grooming of a web of contacts through equal parts bribery and blackmail. All augmented by his open secret, his second Talent: mindreading.

Today, as he walked through the Academy District's shaded avenues, past gaggles of students laden with scroll cases and tenured researchers with their heads bent together in heated debate, Sou-Zell wasted no energy on the thoughts of those around him. He might find himself sucked into hours of discussion about inter-kerina politics or the ethics of branding the Talentless, and then he would miss his appointment.

He carried a stiletto and a pouch of blackpowder in his sleeve, in case this meeting went sideways. Every now and then, one of

Sou-Zell's contacts—sometimes people he'd exchanged favors with for years—would attempt to betray him. It happened with alarming regularity these days. His family's reputation was eroding as quickly as sand walls in a storm.

His marriage to Yi-Nereen was supposed to fix everything. But last night, on the very eve of their nuptials, he'd failed to stop her from leaving the city. She would face terrible punishment if she returned, perhaps even death—unless Sou-Zell could convince the Tower she hadn't fled at all, but had been kidnapped. If Sou-Zell could bring her back unharmed and contrite—along with the head of her abductor—then the union of their houses could proceed as planned, and Sou-Zell's house would be saved from ruin.

Everything could be put right again at the low, low cost of one dead courier.

He entered a courtyard paved in pale, seamless marble. Lush green ivy cascaded down the walls, shading dark recesses from view. Some of the alcoves were already occupied; Sou-Zell heard whispers and saw shadows moving behind the verdure.

The courtyard was a favorite haunt for students seeking privacy or meeting lovers in secret. Though he hadn't formally attended Kerina Rut's Grand Academy, Sou-Zell had spent his share of time here in his youth, poring over books and scrolls from the academy's archives. Archives to which he hadn't been granted access, though that hadn't stopped him. He'd never been tempted to use the alcoves for senseless dalliances; they seemed to him a waste of time.

He made his way toward the farthest alcove and ducked under the trailing ivy. Dried flower petals were scattered across the stone bench within—no doubt the remnants of some romantic tryst. Sou-Zell swept them away.

He didn't have long to wait. In fact, the bounty hunter had

probably been hidden nearby, waiting for *him* to arrive. The ivy twitched aside mere moments later, and a hooded figure stepped in. Air swirled in the newcomer's wake, sending petals dancing over the alcove's stone floor.

"You're late," said the bounty hunter.

Sou-Zell winced. He'd known he was meeting a woman, yet it was still a shock to hear a distinctly feminine voice alone in such close quarters. It was worse still when the bounty hunter pulled back her hood, revealing tousled blonde hair and full, arrogant lips. She appeared naturally much fairer of skin than Sou-Zell and most of the Rut-blood, but the sun had darkened her face to nearly the same shade as his. The acrid tang of storm dust clung to her and her clothes; she must have been fresh from the wastes when Sou-Zell's servant had found her in the city.

"You're mistaken," Sou-Zell said, recovering his composure. "I'm right on time."

The hunter shrugged. "True. But most of these meetings start with one party accusing the other of being late. Far be it from me to defy tradition."

Sou-Zell felt his nostrils flare. She dared speak to him of defying tradition?

"Enough," he said. "We're here to discuss business."

"I've already received the details from your servant. So we're not here to discuss business; we're here to haggle. Chasing a fugitive across the wastes isn't easy work, especially when she has a head start. Which means I only get more expensive the longer you pussyfoot around, Lord Sparkrider."

The sarcasm with which she imbued the title was obscene. And it made little sense to Sou-Zell. Unless his contact had lied, *she* was a sparkrider, too.

"Fine," Sou-Zell said. "I'll pay double whatever my servant promised you. A thousand mun, wasn't it?"

The man he'd sent had been instructed to make the bounty hunter the lowest possible offer that might entice her to a meeting, to ensure Sou-Zell would appear generous later. All part of the game, albeit one he despised.

The woman raised an eyebrow. "You must really want her back."

"It isn't about what I want."

Sou-Zell stopped. He reminded himself he was speaking to a woman, and an outsider. She wasn't even Rut-blood; by the looks of her, she was from a northern spring, likely Kerina Tez prior to the city's fall. Somewhere the men didn't value their women and let them gallivant about on magebikes far from home, meeting strangers in secret.

"Of course not." The woman sneered. "Advance me half, and I'll bring your princess home in three days, along with the courier's head in a saurian-leather bag. I'll even throw in the bag. A souvenir."

Sou-Zell put a hand inside his sleeve, where his coin purse rested alongside the pouch of blackpowder. "Princess Yi-Nereen is not to be harmed. Touch her and speak to her as little as possible, and bring her directly to me when you return."

The woman's sneer turned septic. "Afraid I'll corrupt your precious Rut-blood maiden? Teach her the men in this city are just walking cocks and she can find less pompous ones elsewhere? Now that you mention it, the prospect is tempting." She stroked her chin in mock thoughtfulness. "Hmm, I could even take your coin and disappear. After all, it's far too late for you to hire someone else."

Sou-Zell closed his hand around the blackpowder pouch. It would be so easy to draw it forth, burst it over the face of the insolent woman in front of him, and set the contents ablaze with a snap of his fingers. He'd practiced the routine many times—on dummies.

Instead he smiled thinly and burned the larger of his twin pools of Talent. Faint purple light illuminated the alcove as Sou-Zell reached for the woman's mind, probing for her thoughts. He would find whatever lay behind her sharp tongue and bitter hazel eyes. If she meant to do as she threatened, he would kill her.

But he felt nothing. Heard nothing. Her mind was empty as a dry well, without a flicker of thought or emotion. It was like she wasn't even alive.

"You lied," Sou-Zell breathed. "You aren't a sparkrider. You're Talentless."

The woman grinned like a desert fox. "Oh, you think so? All because your special Talent doesn't work on me? You don't know everything, Lord Sparkrider. Far from it."

She raised her hand, and her eyes blazed orange. Sparks danced between her knuckles, skittering across the callouses on her palm—callouses Sou-Zell recognized, the imprint of a magebike's handle-bars through leather riding gloves.

But it wasn't possible. Only the Talentless were immune to his mindreading, as they were to all other Talents. Immune because they lacked the vital essence of humanity, the magic that flowed through pure veins. A soul.

"My name is Falka," the woman said. "I'll take your job and your coin. I don't think any more negotiation is necessary. Do you, Sou-Zell?"

Sou-Zell ground his teeth. "No."

He drew out his coin purse and handed it over. Precious gems worth one thousand mun, half the sum he'd just agreed to pay this accursed woman. The coffers of Sou-Zell's House would be nearly empty after this, despite the careful lies he'd planted to suggest otherwise.

When Yi-Nereen returned, Sou-Zell would have to convince the Tower of Arrested Stars that giving away a disgraced princess's hand in marriage for free was better than killing her. Would Yi-Nereen ever appreciate his efforts? By fleeing their betrothal, she had ensured Sou-Zell himself would become her only hope of survival. Now she needed him as much as he needed her.

In the end, Sou-Zell reflected with a certain degree of ironic amusement, his marriage would become yet another exchange of favors owed. He hoped it would be the last.

"Now," Falka said, "I just need to know where your princess and the courier are headed."

Though the glow of Talent had faded from her eyes, they held a strange, ravenous gleam. For an uncomfortable moment, he had the feeling he'd given her all she wanted and more. He dismissed the thought as illogical, pure paranoia fueled by the inexplicable failure of his Talent. Whatever this woman was, she was correct; it was too late for him to procure the services of another bounty hunter.

He had already placed his bet.

*Second Age of Storms, 49th Summer*

*Dear Kadrin,*

*I apologize for the delay since my last letter. It shall please you to know that I have finally received all sixteen of the inquiries you sent over the past two months.*

*No, it will not be necessary to hire an expedition of knights to breach Kerina Rut's walls, nor to train Courier Jin in espionage and infiltration. The royals have brought the epidemic under control and ended the quarantine. I was glad to see Courier Jin's face again after so long an absence.*

*The only injury I suffered in the meantime was terrible boredom. It transpires that I have grown quite dependent on your letters over the past year. Without another means of entertainment, I was forced to devote more attention than usual to my studies.*

*At present, I'm learning about mana storms and pre-magebike wasteland travel. I suspect our friend, Courier Jin, possesses some knowledge on this topic. (She's been asking so many questions. Send help.) Truth be told, I was entertaining a fantasy of hiring a palanquin to bear me to Kerina Sol, like the princesses of old. But Courier Jin informs me the mana storms have grown much too frequent and deadly in the past fifty years to risk a crossing on foot, even with shieldcasters.*

*It was only a fantasy anyway. My family would never permit it.*

*Wishing you good health,*
*Your friend Reena*

## CHAPTER NINE

# REUNIONS

*Second Age of Storms, 51st Summer, Day 21*

J in dreamed. This was a familiar dream, a poem she knew by
heart.

She's twelve years old, cornered in an alley by a trio of knight's
squires. Their leader, the biggest of the lot, is called Demond. His
friends are holding her down while Demond kicks her in the side.
His face is a mess of blood and snot—Jin broke his nose moments
ago with a well-aimed punch.

In the dream, she can't remember why Demond hates her so
much, but he does, and he hates her mother even more. *Talentless
whore,* he calls Eomma, *with a filthy street rat for a daughter.*

They've quarreled for months, exchanging barbs and bruises,
but the game changes today. Demond snatches a brick from a half-
built wall and lifts it over Jin's head. She's pinned, can't escape.

He'll kill her, she realizes. Maybe he won't mean to, but he will.

Then he stumbles forward, whimpering, clutching his side.
Behind him stands a girl. She's older than Jin, with tangled dirty-
blonde hair and a red scarf tied over her face. All Jin can see is her
eyes, the coldest eyes she's ever seen in another child's face: light
brown flecked with gold and green.

She's buried a knife in Demond's side.

Demond slumps to the ground, his friends flee, and Jin looks up at her rescuer again. Here, the dream fogs over, blurs memory with illusion. She doesn't know the girl, not yet, but her lips trace a name anyway.

"Falka?"

The girl kneels to retrieve her knife, and Jin spots a raised white Talentless brand on the nape of her neck, same as the one she sees every night when she brushes her mother's hair. Then Falka stands, blood on her hands.

"I saved you, Jin," she says. "I love you. *Don't ever leave me.*"

Jin's dreaming brain knows this is wrong—this isn't a conversation they'll have yet, not for years. This is the first time they've met. Eight years before time runs out, before Jin leaves the girl she loves in Kerina Tez without a goodbye. Before Falka vanishes without a trace.

"I won't," Jin promises, though she knows she will. "We'll leave together."

Maybe this time the words will be enough to make Falka stay. Maybe this time, she'll still be there when Jin comes back for her.

It's a vain hope. Falka's fading now, right before Jin's eyes. Shadows swallow the alley and the girl along with it, calling her back to whatever void she inhabits when she isn't haunting Jin's dreams. Piece by piece, until all that's left is a whisper in the dark.

*Don't ever leave me.*

Jin reluctantly returned to consciousness, clinging to a ghost she couldn't quite remember. She had the sensation of lying somewhere soft, swinging gently back and forth. Children chattered nearby.

But every moment or two, a deep shudder ran through whatever she rested upon, like a giant was punching the ground.

Jin opened her eyes. Inches away, a face stared back at her—but it wasn't human. Two black eyes fringed with long lashes gazed at her from above a large, rounded muzzle. The creature's face was covered in small blue feathers. It lowed softly, bathing her in warm, foul breath.

It was a chandru. A fucking chandru, standing over her.

Jin swore and rolled to the side. Out of a hammock, as she discovered.

She hit the ground with a grunt and lay there, dazed. The chandru craned its freakishly long neck, staring at her from a lofty height, and huffed. The fall had knocked the wind from Jin's lungs. She couldn't move.

*So this is how I die.*

Somewhere nearby, a child laughed. Jin worked up the strength to turn her head. She was still in the wastelanders' canyon, stretched out on a bed of grass under a rocky overhang. The chandru stood looking at her, swaying slowly in place. It was smaller than the ones she'd seen roving the wastes—a juvenile, maybe, though it could still crush her skull with one step. The leathery sail rising from its back was ridged like a fan and splotched in blue and green.

Behind the chandru's stout legs lurked a gaggle of children. They were pointing at her, giggling and chattering in Faolin's unfamiliar language.

Damn it, she wasn't going to die on her back with kids laughing at her. That was out of the question.

Jin sat up and groaned. Her whole body ached, like she'd been down with a fever. What had Yi-Nereen done to her? The memory burned like whiskey in her throat. Yi-Nereen's lips on hers, drawing the life out of her. The storm raging around them. She'd survived, somehow. But where was Yi-Nereen?

"Jin!"

Faolin trotted toward her from behind the chandru. He patted the saurian on its broad shoulder, and it lowed again, swinging its head down to nuzzle his cheek. Jin stared at him, bewildered.

Chandru weren't as dangerous as their sharp-toothed cousins, the rovex, but every courier knew to steer clear of them. Their sheer size meant any interaction could end in broken bones and ruptured organs. Not a pretty way to die.

Faolin held out his hand and helped Jin struggle to her feet. He was grinning, obviously pleased to see her awake, but there was a hint of unease to his smile. Jin wished she could ask him how long she'd slept, but she had a more important question.

"Yi-Nereen," she said, waggling her fingers in front of her face to evoke a veil. "Where is Yi-Nereen?"

Faolin's smile faded. He looked her up and down. Then he snapped his fingers, and a spark flickered between his thumb and forefinger, crackling and hissing.

"*Se imbyr.*" His dark eyes found Jin's. "Jin *se imbyr?*"

"What? Why?"

Bemused, Jin burned mana and conjured her own spark. She'd guessed right; Faolin's smile returned in full force.

He grabbed her sleeve. "*Vai.*"

Jin knew that word by now. "All right, all right. I'm coming."

Jin liked holding the reins on her own life. Needless to say, she wasn't pleased to find herself in a wasteland canyon surrounded by strangers, separated from her bike, with a teenager leading her around by the sleeve. She was also fiendishly hungry.

Still, relief surged through her at the sight of Yi-Nereen lounging in a hammock sheltered between two rocks. Sunlight streamed down on the princess, catching gold in her hair. She held a wet calligraphy brush in one hand and a scroll pinned to a wooden board in the other. Her lips were pursed in concentration.

Jin moved closer, the grass cushioning her footfalls. "What are you writing?"

Yi-Nereen yelped. "Jin!" Her surprise gave way to a warm look of relief that melted Jin's bones into slurry. "You're awake."

*I truly believed we were going to die*, read the only line Jin caught before Yi-Nereen turned the board upside down. A faint flush colored Yi-Nereen's cheeks as she collected herself, eyes roving over Jin in a way that made Jin shiver. What an awkward silence this was—even if she didn't entirely mind the way Yi-Nereen was looking at her.

What was she supposed to say? *Thanks for the kiss. Did you mean to almost kill me?*

"I'm writing a letter to Kadrin," Yi-Nereen said at last. "It's silly, but I want to put one in his hand myself. No more intermediaries, just . . . us."

The warm sensation of Yi-Nereen's regard faded. Jin felt as if someone had punched a hole through her chest. A wry voice in her brain said, *Of course*, while another whimpered like a kicked puppy. *Stupid, stupid Jin.* The whole point had been to bring Kadrin and Yi-Nereen together, to begin the rest of their lives in bliss. Obviously that future wouldn't include Jin. Had she somehow hoped otherwise?

She dragged a hand over her face. "What happened after I passed out?"

"The storm only lasted a few more minutes," Yi-Nereen said. "It was gone as quickly as it came. I've seen my share of storms, but only from inside a kerina. Not in the wastes. Was that normal?"

"No," Jin said. "Storms don't change direction like that."

She could do this. She could spend forever talking about storms, about life in the wastes, as long as neither of them mentioned the kiss again. Sure, that meant Jin would never find out what Yi-Nereen had done to her, but that was a sacrifice she was willing to make.

"I knew it wasn't my imagination." Yi-Nereen shuddered. "It *chased* us."

As the princess stared pensively at her hands, Jin turned to Faolin. Now that she'd found the most important item on her list—*princess, check*—she needed to locate the second.

"Where's my bike?"

Faolin looked at her blankly. Jin sighed. She put her hands out as if she were gripping handlebars and made a *vroom* sound with her mouth. Never in her life had she felt so ridiculous, but it got the message across.

Faolin's face lit up, and he took her by the sleeve again. "*Vai.*"

The wastelanders had a garage, and it was in a sorry state. Three magebikes leaned against the wall of a small, cramped cave. One bike was so rusted Jin could tell no one had ridden it in years, and no one probably ever would again, unless two-thirds of the parts were replaced. Another she recognized as Faolin's bike, though she'd only seen it briefly; Jin had a better memory for bikes than faces. The third was Jin's.

Jin's relief at seeing her bike was immediate and uncomplicated, unlike what she'd felt when she saw Yi-Nereen. Even if the garage was small and dingy, it still smelled like grease and exhaust: familiar, comforting smells. She glanced at Faolin and, after receiving his encouraging nod, trailed her fingers across the handlebars of his bike. The boy must have already scrubbed it clean after the storm; not a speck of corrosive storm dust clung to the metal. A quick glance confirmed that he'd cleaned hers, too.

"Beautiful," Jin muttered. Faolin's bike looked almost identical to hers, though smaller: a courser, not a hauler, made for speed rather than ferrying cargo across the wastes. Another replica in the classic Vann style, right down to the . . .

Jin froze. Etched into the steering cylinder was a maker's mark, a pair of glyphs inside a hexagon. *Tibius Vann.*

Sweat rolled down Jin's neck. Faolin's bike wasn't a replica—it was an original. And she was prepared to bet her life that it wasn't thirty years old, like the last bikes the master artificer had crafted before vanishing without a trace. What did that mean? How was the bike *here*?

Faolin's people spoke a language that bore no similarity to any dialect of Dirilish Jin had ever heard. They must have lived in isolation for centuries. But magebikes had been invented only forty years ago, in Jin's father's lifetime. Had Faolin stolen his bike from a dead courier? Raiders did that—they killed couriers on the highway, desecrated their corpses, and stole their bikes or stripped them for parts.

Jin stared at Faolin, trying to reconcile the smiling boy with one of the crazed marauders she'd only ever seen from a distance. Were there no other sparkriders in the canyon? No one was riding that second bike around, that was for sure. It belonged on a scrap heap.

Too many questions, and she had no way to ask. Jin put shaky hands on her own bike to calm herself. She glanced at the saddlebags slung over the rear fender—everything was still there. Including Screech's empty cage.

Jin grabbed Faolin's arm and pointed at the cage. "Where's my pteropter?"

Faolin blinked at her. Behind him, Yi-Nereen said, "It was gone when we came back after the storm. I've asked, but no one understood what I was saying. Or at least they pretended not to." For the first time, Jin noticed dark shadows under the princess's eyes, as if she hadn't slept. Yi-Nereen glanced at the cage and added softly, "I hope they didn't hurt it."

"There's a young chandru wandering around out there. Like cattle." Jin's grip tightened on the rough cloth of Faolin's shirtsleeve. The boy's eyes widened, but he made no move to escape. "Do you eat saurians? Is that how you survive out here? Did you eat Screech?"

"Jin!" Yi-Nereen moved to take Jin's arm, but Jin flinched away from her. "I don't know what happened to your pteropter, but Faolin and his people saved our lives."

"We saved one of their kids," Jin said, "so I think we're square."

She turned her back on Faolin and strode out of the garage. Her chest burned, and a muscle in her jaw kept twitching, but the anger rushing through her was almost pleasurable in its familiarity. She understood anger well. It had lived inside her since the day she watched her father's execution. Anger was the feeling of being robbed, of having something she cared for ripped away . . . even if it was just an annoying little pteropter who'd once tried to kill her.

This anger had nothing to do with Yi-Nereen or the letter she'd been writing to Kadrin. It certainly wasn't betrayal or shame—shame at remembering her place.

*Forget the kiss. It doesn't matter.*

She smelled fragrant sandalwood before she heard Yi-Nereen's soft footsteps. "No reason to stay any longer," Jin said without turning her head or waiting for the princess to speak. "Kerina Sol awaits."

"Actually, there is a reason to stay for a short while," Yi-Nereen said. "Think about it, Jin. I've never heard of these wastelander people before now, and neither have you. We might be the first people from the kerinas to make contact with them in recorded history. Don't you want to know more about them? Find out how they've survived out here?"

In Jin's experience, anything unexpected you found in the wastes was likely to be dangerous. But a grudging part of her could see Yi-Nereen's point. Besides, they were guests of the wastelanders, and even *she* knew one couldn't rush off without thanking one's hosts. She was about to say so when Yi-Nereen said, "Besides, Jin . . ."

"What?"

"I need to thank you. For trusting me. For letting me do what I did to you."

Jin turned reluctantly to face Yi-Nereen. The princess's head hung low, her veil covering her eyes. The gems on her headdress glistened in the sun. Jin's breath caught, like it often did when she looked at Yi-Nereen.

She'd survived on stolen glances for three years, kept her longing in a cage and never let herself imagine more. Kissing Yi-Nereen had broken the lock, freeing the beast, and that would spell ruin if Jin wasn't careful.

"It's not something we've made public. The siphoning—it's how the shieldcasters of the Tower have managed to survive. Our blood has weakened over the generations, and more of our children are born Talentless; there aren't enough of us to hold out against the storms anymore. Not on our own." Yi-Nereen's voice was hesitant. "My grandfather discovered the technique. We can siphon mana from others using our Talent. A shield protects, but it can also take. An exchange."

"I thought your shieldcasters used the mana lightning somehow. Harnessed it. That's what everyone says."

"It's a lie," Yi-Nereen said. "One that is easier to stomach than the truth."

"You took my mana?" Jin shook her head. She was beyond bewildered at this point. Ever since she'd watched that raider walk willingly into a storm, impossible things had begun happening all around her. It wasn't a comfort to be the only one who didn't understand. "Even if that were possible, I didn't have any for you to take. I was dry."

"Dry of all *you* could access." Yi-Nereen was watching her carefully now, through her veil. "There is always mana in your blood, even if you can't use it to fuel your Talent. You would die without it. If someone takes it from you, draws out all you have . . ." She bit her lip. "I came close. Faolin used the rest of his mana bottles to infuse you while you were unconscious. If he hadn't had any on hand, I think you would have died."

Jin was silent. Again, she was at a complete loss. The secret Yi-Nereen had just revealed to her was obviously more consequential than the kiss—which hadn't even *been* a kiss, Jin reminded herself. Just a desperate act to save their lives. She should let it go.

But the beast inside her was very keen on *not* letting it go.

"If you hadn't done it, we would have *all* died," Jin said. "There wasn't any other way. Right?"

Now it was her turn to scrutinize Yi-Nereen's expression. But she was still wearing the veil, which wasn't fair. Through the black gauze, Jin thought she glimpsed the princess run her tongue over parted lips, as if she were remembering the kiss, too.

"I could have taken what I needed from Faolin," Yi-Nereen said. "In the moment, you seemed the better choice."

Jin swallowed hard. She felt like she was riding the edge of a precipice, a fingerbreadth from a long fall. Yi-Nereen had a way of making her feel like that under normal circumstances, but this was something new and thrilling.

"I suppose it would have been hard to explain what you needed. How did you tell him he had to use the bottles?"

"That's the oddest part." Yi-Nereen glanced over her shoulder. "I didn't have to. He already knew what to do."

Faolin emerged from the garage. He smiled at them both, though the expression was strained. That was understandable; Jin *had* shouted in his face a few minutes ago. She wasn't angry anymore, just hollow. Whatever the wastelanders had done to Screech, there was nothing she could do about it. It had been stupid to give the pteropter a name, anyway. Nothing she found in the wastes would last.

Faolin raised his hands and mimed eating, then quirked his eyebrows. Jin's stomach growled.

"Oh yes," she said. "Yes, please."

"Whatever they feed us," Yi-Nereen said, "I do hope it isn't saurian." Her mouth curled into a smirk at Jin's shocked expression. "What?"

"Nothing," Jin said. "I just didn't know you had a sense of humor. Or that it was twisted."

"I couldn't have survived a childhood in the Tower if it wasn't." Was Jin imagining the playful lilt to Yi-Nereen's voice? The princess couldn't possibly be so cruel as to *flirt* with her. "You'll find there's much you don't know about me, Jin."

"You don't say."

As Faolin walked off, Yi-Nereen followed him. She brushed past Jin and said in a low voice that curled like smoke in Jin's lungs: "I'm glad I chose you."

So Yi-Nereen wasn't entirely the person she'd comported herself as in her letters to Kadrin. *This* was the real Yi-Nereen, or at least another layer of her. Jin's traitorous mind thrilled at the thought and wondered if Yi-Nereen could have siphoned her mana by a different means if she'd wanted, or if it *had* to be a kiss.

*Don't*, she told herself.

But she knew it was already too late.

*Second Age of Storms, 49th Summer*

*Dear Reena,*
*At breakfast today, Eliesen demanded to know why I was grinning like a fool "after haunting the house for weeks like a tortoise with a stomachache." (It's true, he's been unbearable.) I'm so pleased to hear from you that I won't even scold you for making me think you were dead from plague.*

*On to matters of importance! Don't even think about trying to cross the wasteland on foot, Reena. If anyone is going to go walking into a mana storm, it had better be me. Idiocy is much more my style than yours, and my death wouldn't be a total loss, anyway. Jin tells me you would look quite fetching in funeral attire. (He made me write that. Actually came over and checked. Sorry.)*

*In all seriousness, leave the wasteland crossings to Jin. At least wait until someone invents a magebike that anyone can ride without needing sparktalent. I'm told artificers in every kerina are racing to be the first to complete a prototype that doesn't explode at first glance. Perhaps one day I can become the first Talentless courier!*

*I'm enclosing a prototype of my own, by the way. I've been trying my hand at growing flowers from seed. Father said it was ridiculous to playact at being a bloomweaver, and if I tell Mother, I'm sure she'll cry, but in the meantime I'm enjoying myself immensely. Let me know what you think.*

*Rejoicing that you aren't dead,*
*Your friend Kadrin*

## CHAPTER TEN

# WASTELANDERS

*Second Age of Storms, 51st Summer, Day 21*

To Jin's relief, the meal the wastelanders had prepared was vegetarian. They wouldn't eat saurian anyway, she reminded herself. Like everything that grew in the wastes, it wasn't fit for human consumption.

The fare was simple—fruits, vegetables, and grains—but all the people who lived in the canyon came to partake. Faolin's mother fawned over Jin and Yi-Nereen, smoothing out a blanket on the grass for them to sit on and filling their bowls with steaming spiced porridge. Farther off, among other families who'd gathered around blankets of their own, Jin spotted the old man who'd argued with Faolin about letting them stay. He glanced at her and Yi-Nereen occasionally, scowling, but kept his distance. So did everyone else, Jin realized. No one but Faolin and his mother seemed willing to come within ten paces of them.

"Tough crowd," Jin said. "We saved one of their kids and they still don't like us?"

Yi-Nereen swallowed a mouthful of porridge and bit down thoughtfully on her spoon. "Have you seen anyone here besides Faolin using Talent?"

Jin frowned. "You don't think—"

"I think they're all Talentless." Yi-Nereen said the words casually, but the trembling of her hands gave away her excitement. "Somehow they've survived out here for Rasvel knows how long, without shieldcasters or raincallers. They grow their own food—it isn't bloomwoven; I saw them carrying seedlings. And I've seen several elders. Seventy or eighty years old. Have you ever heard of a Talented living that long?"

Jin stared into her bowl. "That doesn't prove anything."

Disquiet buzzed in her belly. Yi-Nereen had a point, though Jin was loath to accept it. A shorter life span was the price they both had to pay for their Talent. Nobody liked to talk about it, but that was the ugly truth. At around fifty or sixty, their bodies would start rejecting mana, and they'd have a choice to make: keep infusing something their blood now renounced as poison, with all the painful side effects, or stop and wither away from mana thirst.

Talentless didn't face that fate. They went on until their bodies succumbed to old age, long past the point of becoming unable to contribute to society. Grayleeches, some called them. Jin had never resented the Talentless—her mother was one, after all—but she could see why others did. Now, sitting uncomfortably before the borderline hostile stares of the wastelanders, she felt as if she'd stepped through a mirror, into a world where *she* was the burden.

"Faolin is Talented," Jin pointed out. She glanced at the boy, who was grinning and putting on some kind of pantomime to get one of his younger siblings to eat her porridge. He looked ridiculous. Jin's heart softened, to her alarm.

"Yes, he is," Yi-Nereen said. "And that only proves my point. I've been watching him. He's popular with the children, but some of the adults act like he has the pox."

"Well, screw them," Jin said hotly, before she could think better of it.

Yi-Nereen didn't seem to notice her outburst. "I need to find a way to communicate with these people. If they can survive in the wastes, so can we—without the kerinas. Without Talent."

"I thought you wanted to go to Kerina Sol to see Kadrin."

"Of course I do." Yi-Nereen flushed slightly. Her hands were in her lap, twisting her skirt. "Jin, I . . . I wasn't entirely honest with you when I asked for your help. I wanted to escape my marriage, yes, but that wasn't the only reason I fled the Tower. There is something else of interest to me in Kerina Sol, besides Kadrin."

Jin had thought she was past being surprised by the princess, but clearly she wasn't. "What's that?"

Yi-Nereen bit her lip, as if she were unsure how to begin. "You know of Kerina Rut's population crisis, don't you, Jin? The dwindling numbers of Talented, fewer births with every generation."

"It's all anyone talks about there," Jin said.

"Because Kerina Rut is dying," Yi-Nereen said. "Water and food can be rationed, but the storms are growing stronger. Soon the Shield Corps won't have the numbers to protect the city—not everyone in my family can siphon, only my father, my brothers, and myself. And the crisis isn't restricted to Kerina Rut. It's happening everywhere, in every kerina, all over the wastes. Everywhere except Kerina Sol."

This wasn't news to Jin. It was the wastes' biggest mystery: that Kerina Sol, the only city to accept Talentless refugees, had somehow managed to sustain its numbers of Talented. And now that Jin thought of it, Yi-Nereen and Kadrin had often discussed the topic in their letters. Yi-Nereen was determined to find a solution; Jin had always privately thought she was unlikely to succeed where the priests of the temple had all failed.

"I remember now," Jin said. "You asked Kadrin to send you records from the temple in Kerina Sol, years ago. For your research."

"Yes. Now I must return the favor."

Yi-Nereen patted the satchel sitting on the ground beside her. Jin hadn't once seen it out of her reach, not since they'd left Kerina Rut.

"If the Houses of High Talent had caught wind of my conclusions, they would have surely taken steps to silence me. My only choice was to take what I'd learned to Kerina Sol and pray the royals there would listen. Or so I thought."

Jin squinted at her. "I'm having trouble keeping up, Princess. You're saying you've found a solution to the population crisis, and you needed to take it to Kerina Sol, but now you don't?"

"Coming here, finding these people . . . it's changed everything." Yi-Nereen's voice thrummed with excitement. "I thought we needed to reverse the crisis, ensure more Talented were born. What if that isn't the answer? Everyone in this canyon is Talentless, yet they've managed to survive—and thrive."

Jin looked dubiously to their left at one of the wastelander families. Children squabbled over a plate of sugared biscuits, all except one: an older boy who sat to the side, content to watch his siblings bicker. Old burn scars puckered his face and neck, and one of his sleeves hung empty. Maybe he'd been caught outside in a storm. Lucky to still be alive, if he had.

"This is no paradise," Jin said. "Any passing storm could destroy the canyon. Most of these people would die."

"There's no such thing as paradise, Jin." Yi-Nereen put her bowl aside. Her eyes were fixed on the same family Jin had been watching. Something about her expression made Jin twitch, though she couldn't put her finger on what. "Kerinas keep everyone safe inside a shield. But at what cost? No one has any power over their lives, not even the shieldcasters; everyone is trapped in the role chosen for them at birth. On the other hand, if we found other ways to survive the storms, we wouldn't need Talent at all."

It was the look of a researcher surveying a test subject, Jin realized. That was what had her on edge. She wished she could bite her tongue and simply nod. What use was her arguing with royalty? But something—perhaps her wounded pride—opened her mouth and said, "You don't know what it's like out here, Princess. You've only been outside your kerina for a day. Maybe it's too soon to draw any conclusions."

Yi-Nereen looked surprised; then she smiled so disarmingly Jin had to look away. "You're right. There is much to learn, and we've come to just the right place. I think I'll begin by asking for a tour."

She climbed to her feet and approached the family they'd been observing. Jin didn't hear what Yi-Nereen said, but she saw the princess gesturing toward the caves. Most of the family exchanged guarded looks, but the scarred boy nodded cautiously, wolfed down the last of his food, and stood. He and Yi-Nereen made an interesting pair, Jin thought sourly, watching them walk away. Yi-Nereen, tall and elegant in her black veil and tailored trousers, moving with grace, and the wastelander boy who limped alongside her.

She was a princess. Of course she would make sweeping judgments and casually decide the fate of thousands. *Don't underestimate her*, Teul-Kim had said. Jin might be ferrying her across the wastes, but Yi-Nereen was the one in charge. If the princess wanted to stay in the canyon, here they would stay. Jin couldn't very well leave her behind, could she?

A soft thump beside her announced Faolin. The boy sprawled in the grass, close enough that his shoulder bumped Jin's. He flashed her a smile and said something inflected like a question, angling his head toward her empty bowl.

"Oh, the food?" Jin nodded. "It's great. Thanks."

Faolin rubbed his stomach, beaming. Jin couldn't help but smile back. Despite all the mysteries of the canyon and Faolin himself, her gut told her to trust him. If Yi-Nereen was right, he was the only Talented in this canyon. What a lonely life that must be. Had he ever met another sparkrider before? He must have seen others in the wastes, but if he'd lived this long, he'd learned to keep his distance.

"Why did you save us?" Jin asked, though she knew the boy wouldn't answer. "Your leader wasn't happy that you brought us here. It's dangerous, isn't it? Now we know your people live in this canyon. We could cause trouble for you."

Faolin shrugged. At least *that* gesture was universal.

"What were you doing out in that storm, anyway?" Jin voiced the question, but she was asking herself more than Faolin, who couldn't answer her. It was quite the enigma: If he wasn't a courier, knight, or raider, why would he risk the wastes on a magebike? He had everything he needed here in this canyon: food, water, shelter. There was no reason for him to leave . . . unless he was looking for something out there.

Come to think of it, there was one word Jin knew they had in common. Maybe he could answer one of her questions after all.

"Faolin, where did your bottles of mana come from?"

The boy cocked his head. "Mana?" He made sparks dance over his knuckles, showing Jin.

"Yes, but *where*?"

Jin looked away with a sigh, and her gaze fell on Yi-Nereen's satchel, which lay abandoned in the grass. A brilliant idea struck her, followed instantly by irritation she hadn't thought of it sooner.

Jin pulled the satchel closer and reached inside. Her fingers brushed against the wooden board; for a moment the urge to pull it out and read Yi-Nereen's unfinished letter overwhelmed her. *No. That's as bad as mindreading.* She swallowed and kept rummaging until she found what she was searching for: the princess's calligraphy brush, pot of ink, and extra parchment.

"I'm going to draw a map. Starting with us, here." She drew a squiggly canyon and an *X*. Faolin leaned on his palm and watched the brush move over the parchment, his brows drawn together. "Here's a compass. Do you know what a compass is?" She sketched a compass rose and marked each of the cardinal directions before realizing the glyphs would be useless. "There. Can you show me where your mana spring is?"

Faolin took the brush and let it hover above the parchment. He hesitated, looking at Jin through his lashes.

"Go on," Jin said encouragingly.

The boy took a deep breath and began to draw. Jin stared at the parchment, puzzled. She'd expected some measure of distance, landmarks, or even just an arrow to indicate direction. Instead, Faolin was drawing *people*. Stick figures, sure, but definitely people.

He drew three figures, side by side. One tall, two short. Beneath the trio, a collection of shapes that Jin's mind readily translated into something familiar: a magebike. Three lines connecting each of the three figures to the bike.

Jin nodded. "Sparkriders," she said, tapping the lines. Her fingertip came away wet with ink. "Three of them." She frowned. "Even though there were only two bikes in your garage."

Faolin nodded. He pointed at one of the smaller figures and thumped his own chest.

"That's you."

A shadow flitted across the boy's face. Slowly, deliberately, he painted a thick line across the taller figure—then looked searchingly at Jin. Jin gave a small, commiserating smile.

"One of them died." Faolin's father, perhaps? Or a grandparent, if his Talent had skipped a generation as it sometimes did. Whoever they were, they were gone now.

Jin indicated the third, unidentified figure, the same size as Faolin's own. The boy already had a man's height, so the size differences likely meant that he and the unidentified person were both descendants of the taller one. Siblings, perhaps? Or cousins.

"Is that your sibling?"

Faolin drew a wide circle around the third figure. *"Amrys."*

"Amrys," Jin repeated. Was that his sibling's name, or just the word for brother or sister? Rasvel's mercy, this was difficult.

Faolin tapped the third figure insistently. *"Amrys. Se Amrys."*

"I get it," Jin said. "This person, whoever they are, is called Amrys. Why don't you introduce me?" She looked around. Faolin's siblings were nearby, playing a game involving colored stones under their mother's watchful eye. Among them was the child Jin and Yi-Nereen had saved from the storm, giggling with her siblings as if she remembered nothing. "Is that her?"

Faolin shook his head. His face was tight with pain and frustration. He wrapped his arms around himself and tucked his head between his knees. Jin knew then: whoever Amrys was, they were gone.

But not dead. If they had been, Faolin would have crossed out their figure.

"They disappeared in the wastes, didn't they?" Jin cleared her throat, grateful for once Faolin couldn't understand her. She didn't have the right words to say. Losing a parent was one thing, but a sibling . . . Well, Jin was glad she didn't have any to lose. "I'm sorry."

So Faolin was the only sparkrider left among his people. The only Talented person at all. What kind of life did that mean for him? She thought of the way he'd spoken to the elderly leader when they'd arrived, with authority she wouldn't expect from someone his age. It struck her as cruel, the way Talent could make an adult out of someone before they were ready and steal half a life from them. She shivered.

Now she was positive she knew why Faolin had been out in the wastes during the storm. He'd been keeping an eye on it, making sure it wouldn't get too close to his people. Did they even appreciate what he was doing for them?

Faolin raised his head from his knees and looked at her, eyebrows knit together, lips slightly parted. Jin studied his expression. He looked *hopeful*. And he'd come and sat next to her for a reason, had drawn those figures for a reason. There was a question in his dark brown eyes. For a moment, he looked strikingly similar to Yi-Nereen; his expression was the same as the one she'd worn when she asked Jin to help her escape Kerina Rut.

He wanted her help to find Amrys.

# Hana Lee

Dear Kadrin,

Are you telling me you managed to cultivate blush-on-the-vine without a bloomweaver's aid? From seed? The specimen you sent was beautiful, even if it was already dead by the time it reached Kerina Rut. The wasteland isn't kind to flowers.

You knew it was my favorite, didn't you? I don't recall mentioning that before. Perhaps it slipped my mind. (She doesn't remember telling me.) Blush-on-the-vine can sprout almost anywhere, but it takes a skilled bloomweaver to make it flower. You must have a way with plants—I'm impressed.

Here in Kerina Rut, men and women who are courting aren't allowed to speak to one another for the first three months. All they are permitted to do is send each other flowers. So all of the flowers carry meanings, which change depending on the number of flowers and how they are arranged and the expression of the messenger who delivers them. In this way, a single bouquet may contain an entire poetic confession.

Fortuitously, one of my handmaidens is bloomtalented. I've commissioned a bouquet from her, which I will instruct Jin to deliver along with this letter. I know the Sol-bloods court one another freely, without need for intrigue. Do your flowers have a language? What will my flowers tell you? I'm curious to find out.

With fondness,
Your friend Reena

## CHAPTER ELEVEN

# BACK ON THE ROAD

*Second Age of Storms, 51st Summer, Day 22*

The next day dawned with a chill that forced Jin to spend the early hours curled up in a ball with her blanket tucked over her head. Typical wasteland weather: brutally hot afternoons leading up to a storm and cool mornings in its wake. Faolin roused her with a steaming bowl of oats—bless him—and together they ventured out of the cave, Jin's breath a fog in the air before her.

In the canyon, the grass glistened with crystalline dewdrops under the generous light of a clear dawn. Standing in the middle of the grass was Yi-Nereen, face tilted toward the sun like she was a flower in bloom. She wasn't dressed in men's clothes anymore, but in a flowing black caftan edged with silver thread. Her hair was done in a simple braid, free of the bone pins and jewels that had adorned it in Kerina Rut, though she still wore skeletal bracelets. Yi-Nereen was never far from her bones.

Jin hesitated, half-hidden in the canyon wall's icy shadow. Merely approaching Yi-Nereen felt like sacrilege. She was more otherworldly now, barefoot in the ruddy glow of the rising sun, than she had been lounging on pillows in her perfumed bower, attended by handmaidens.

The spell held no sway over Faolin, who marched straight up

to Yi-Nereen and offered her a mug of tea. Feeling foolish, Jin slouched over and mumbled, "Morning," without making eye contact. Instead she craned her neck to follow the princess's gaze toward the sky, where the small black shape of a pteropter circled in the cloudless blue. "What are you looking at?"

"I thought . . ." Yi-Nereen shook her head. "Never mind." She rubbed her eyes, which were free of galena. Jin had never seen Yi-Nereen's face bare of makeup before, and the sight made it all the more difficult to remind herself of the vast gulf between their stations. "Did you sleep well, Jin?"

*Not in the slightest.* Although she and Yi-Nereen had been separated by half a cave and three of Faolin's snoring siblings, Jin had spent hours tortured by the notion that they were sleeping in the same room, breathing the same air.

"Fair enough," she lied. "You?"

Yi-Nereen only smiled and looked away, a tiny gesture that had Jin's heart in shambles. "You said you would explain your plan in the morning. So, where are we going?"

Jin had spent the previous evening wringing information from Faolin in frustrating drips. The boy's eagerness to provide details was counterproductive; the more he spoke, the less she understood. She thought she'd been able to grasp the basics in the end, at least.

"An unmapped mana spring nearby. Faolin's sister Amrys went missing there a few weeks ago. I thought we could ride out, fill up, and search for any signs of her."

Yi-Nereen frowned. "She went missing in the wastes weeks ago? Jin, the girl must be dead." She glanced at Faolin, who was listening intently to their conversation, and her face softened. "The most we might find is a body."

"I know," Jin said, lowering her voice even though there was no point. "But there's more. Faolin's seen other riders around the spring. Raiders, sounds like. They could've taken her."

Yi-Nereen's sigh was heavy with pity. "If raiders took her, do you think she's any more likely to be alive?"

"Maybe, though she'd wish she weren't."

Raiders were the greatest threat in the wastes, not storms or saurians. A storm wouldn't chase you and a saurian wouldn't eat you, but a raider was liable to do both. Exiled from the kerinas, raiders had few choices for sustenance: wasteland plants that killed fast or slow, or flesh from the only game to be found out here. If that flesh was already infused with mana, so much the better.

Jin knew a few couriers who kept a dose of poison on their person whenever they entered the wastes. She might have done the same, but what did she care what happened to her body after death? Lorne had said it best: *Everyone's gotta eat.*

"Not to mention," Yi-Nereen said, "even if she is alive, the two of us are hardly equipped to perform a rescue."

"I *know* that." Jin's patience was running thin. "You don't have to come. You can stay here in the canyon and study these people until I come back."

Yi-Nereen gave her a long, cool look. "Of course I'll come. Is that what you think of me, Jin? I don't want to *study* these people—I wish to learn from them, so we can help everyone. That includes Faolin and his sister."

"Sure." It was an acknowledgment, but not agreement and certainly not an apology. Jin had no idea if Yi-Nereen meant what she'd just said. She'd seen the way the princess had looked at the wastelanders yesterday. And they clearly didn't want to share their secrets with Yi-Nereen; they wanted the pair of them gone. But Yi-Nereen was a royal, and she wasn't used to having her whims denied.

"I only want to understand the risks," Yi-Nereen said, "and to make sure you understand them as well. It's imperative that my findings reach Kerina Sol, which will necessitate that both of us survive this excursion."

Jin glanced at Faolin. He was toeing the grass, trying to hide his impatience. Something loosened in her chest now when she looked at him, which annoyed her. *Don't get attached, Jin. It won't end well.*

But what if that was the whole story of his life? He was a kid trying his hardest to protect his people, who treated him like a pariah for it. He'd lost his sister, possibly the only person in this hidden society who knew what that was like. And here Jin was, distancing herself from him for her own selfish reasons. No, she wouldn't do that anymore. For fuck's sake, she owed him her life.

"He's their only sparkrider," she said. "If I don't help him, he might never get another fighting chance. I'm going."

Yi-Nereen looked at her sidelong. "How does a courier stay in business with such a charitable heart?"

Now it was Jin's turn to frown. "What's that supposed to mean?"

"It means I doubt Faolin or any of his people are in a position to compensate you for the danger you're putting yourself in."

"You mean the way you compensated me?" Jin put her hand in her breast pocket, closed her fist around the silk pouch that still held eight hundred mun. "Do you think I got you out of Kerina Rut for the money?"

A pause as a flush tinged Yi-Nereen's cheeks. "Well, why else?"

Heat smoldered in Jin's chest, even as her feet burned with cold from standing in the wet grass. The morning dew wasn't all that beautiful, she decided. It looked lovely from a distance, but only as a fantasy, not quite real enough to touch. Reality was disappointing.

"Let's not keep Faolin waiting," she said. "I'll get my bike."

When they emerged from the tunnel into a familiar gray-brown landscape of sand and rock, Jin began to doubt that the canyon and all it contained had been real. It seemed a storybook place now, green and magical. A place where humans and saurians lived side by side.

Anxiety soon drowned those thoughts. Jin remembered fleeing the storm, crashing blindly through the wastes, veering left and right in a vain attempt to throw the howling wind off their trail. Now she didn't have a clue where they were. She had to find higher ground and get her bearings, locate the nearest roadway. But Faolin had already taken off on his magebike, kicking up a plume of dust. Jin followed.

Her discomfort faded as she picked up speed. Pleasure filled the space behind, pulsing to the rhythm of her sparks. Jin was always glad to set out from a kerina, trading the cramped, complicated world where people walked on two legs for something far simpler. Out here was sky and dirt and precious little in between. What more did she need?

Home wasn't a place for Jin. It was a feeling, *this* feeling.

Up ahead, Faolin had a good lead on her. He and his magebike were little figures enveloped in dust, flashing when they caught the sun. Jin felt a grin creep across her face as she bent low over the handlebars. Her irritation with Yi-Nereen seemed unimportant now, just another burden to leave behind.

Without turning her head, she shouted, "Shall we catch up with him, Princess?"

She didn't wait for Yi-Nereen's reply. With a surge of her Talent, the bike shot forward. The engine roared, just as eager as Jin herself.

She felt Yi-Nereen's arms around her waist, tight as a corset—or so Jin imagined, as she'd never worn one before. Moments later they were gliding alongside Faolin, matching his speed.

Faolin glanced sideways. He edged forward, then backward. Jin couldn't see his face under his bonehelm, but she could picture his ever-present grin. The invitation required no words.

"Looks like the kid wants to race."

"Well," Yi-Nereen said breathlessly, "I wouldn't wish to disappoint him."

Jin and her magebike both growled in fierce approval. She burned mana. Sparks skittered over her knuckles and the bike leaped forward. Faolin didn't miss a beat. He whooped and charged after her.

Wind battered Jin's helm and riding leathers. The world flew by on either side, a blur of tan. Yi-Nereen was laughing, a riotous sound pitched with equal parts fear and delight. Jin was incandescent. Here was the only language sparkriders needed to understand each other: speed.

Her disadvantage in the race was that Faolin knew the land. He must have ridden off-road for most of his life. She glanced right and saw that the boy had climbed a ridge and was skimming wildly over the dunes, gaining speed on each ascent and nearly soaring to the next. Jin was so enthralled she forgot Yi-Nereen was perched on the back of her bike. She cut a steep turn around a boulder, leaning so sharply her ankle almost touched the ground—Yi-Nereen shrieked in her ear, and the two of them nearly lost their balance.

Jin slowed deliberately until Faolin fell back to join her.

"You win," Jin called to him. "I'll want a rematch—the princess can ride with *you* next time."

She expected a reprimand from Yi-Nereen; the stunt with the

boulder could have cost them dearly. But Yi-Nereen rested her chin on Jin's shoulder and said, "I've never had so much fun. That was glorious." A moment passed—then she said in a tone of quiet wonder, "*You* were glorious."

Faolin pointed at the sky. Jin darted a glance upward, her heart thumping. A pteropter had swooped down from the heavens and was keeping pace with their magebikes, flying low enough for Jin to see the pattern of feathers on its underbelly.

Yi-Nereen gasped. "Is that your pteropter?"

"What? There's no way—"

The pteropter let loose an earsplitting screech. Jin's heart leaped. It wasn't possible—the pteropter flying overhead had four wings whole and unharmed—but it was Screech. She'd recognize that caterwauling shriek even if it came from a teapot.

She had to look away from the sky as she cut a wide curve around a man-size cactus jutting out of a crack, its upturned arms bristling with venomous spines. When she glanced up again, the pteropter had veered away. Jin coasted to a stop and put down her feet as the engine idled, watching the dark shape dwindle into the western skies.

Was her memory playing tricks on her, or was Screech bigger than the last time she'd seen him?

"That reminds me," Yi-Nereen said. "I came up with a theory about Faolin and his people. I wasn't sure, but . . . your pteropter makes for compelling evidence."

"Evidence for what?"

"I think they're herders. They care for the saurians, nurse them when they're injured. Somehow the saurians help them survive. Water—I couldn't figure out how they got their hands on water. If they get it from the saurians . . ."

Jin snorted. "You think they milk the chandru? Like goats?"

Yi-Nereen huffed, her breath hot on Jin's neck. "Just because it sounds ridiculous—"

The roar of an approaching magebike cut her off. Faolin had circled back to fetch them, clearly impatient.

"Later," Jin said. She touched off and followed Faolin up the ridge of a hill. Yi-Nereen's theory *did* sound ridiculous, but Jin couldn't deny the evidence before her eyes: Screech's wing had shown no signs of healing until they'd brought him to the waste-landers. And Faolin's people *had* seemed interested in the pteropter when they'd first arrived.

No ordinary animal would heal that quickly, even with treat-ment. Jin had a disturbing mental image of Screech disassembled on a bench like a bike undergoing repairs. But he was certainly no machine; he'd taken meat from her hand and eaten with gusto.

At the hill's crown, she parked beside Faolin and gazed down. Below, the ground sloped into a wide, shallow valley, like a smooth bowl cut into the earth. At the bottom of the bowl sat something entirely unexpected: a stone temple, like Jin might find in any ke-rina.

Except this one was ten times larger, and all but destroyed. Crumbling walls, fallen pillars, and caved-in wings, all in such mas-sive proportions Jin wondered if the distance was tricking her eyes somehow. No human hands could have built the structure, besides a small army of stoneshapers with a spring's worth of mana.

Yi-Nereen let go of Jin's waist and hopped down from the bike. The two small steps she took forward were stuttering and full of wonder. "Are . . . are those Road Builder ruins?"

"Must be," Jin said. She ran her tongue over her lower lip, try-ing to mask her awe. The wastes were littered with ruins, but she'd never seen anything so large or well-preserved. The temple before them dwarfed any stray monoliths she'd glimpsed from the highway or inscrutable tablets she'd sold to relic traders over the years. "I thought he was taking us to a mana spring."

Faolin was beaming, obviously enjoying her and Yi-Nereen's reactions. He nudged Jin in the shoulder and pointed at the bikes.

"Yeah," Jin said. This time she consciously bit down the urge to keep her distance, and she smiled back. "We'll race again once we find your sister. All three of us."

The boy nodded eagerly, like he understood what she'd said. Then he gestured at the valley floor. Tread marks led down the side of the bowl toward the temple. Jin recalled another detail she'd gleaned from their stilted conversation: Faolin and his sister weren't the only sparkriders to visit this place. Her skin prickled.

"Perhaps there's a spring in the ruins," Yi-Nereen said doubtfully.

Jin fingered the utility knife in her belt sheath, wishing she'd brought something more substantial.

"Let's hope so," she said.

*Second Age of Storms, 49th Summer*

*Dear Reena,*

*How cruel of you to send me a message I can't decode! The flowers are lovely, but they've driven me insane. (He's fine. Don't worry.) Honeythorn, cloud-of-heaven, and erasmuth. Though the flowers have wilted, I've written down their names. Someday I shall solve this mystery, or else my tombstone will read, "KADRIN THE CLUELESS, BEWILDERED BY FLOWERS."*

*Alas, I have no coded messages to send you in return. Instead I'm enclosing a copy of the census records you asked for. I wasn't confident I could get my hands on them, but it turns out my sister knows an acolyte with access to the temple archives. Given how eager the acolyte was to help, I have a sneaking suspicion that their relationship isn't quite as innocent as Eliesen has led our parents to believe. Good for her.*

*These census records contain every marriage and birth recorded in Kerina Sol over the past two decades. Our kerinas are at peace, so sending them to you probably isn't treason. You'll have to explain to me again why you want them. I keep all of your letters in a secret, secure location (it's a box under his bed), but somehow I've managed to misplace a few, probably from rereading them too often.*

*I like sharing secrets with you, Reena. It feels clandestine and exciting, doesn't it, to have something only you and I share? I suppose Jin knows, too. Just the three of us, then. Can't say I mind.*

*Your partner in crime,*
*Kadrin*

## CHAPTER TWELVE

# TROUBLE FINDS THE CANYON

*Second Age of Storms, 51st Summer, Day 22*

Falka held the empty bottle to her nose and inhaled. Traces of mana vapor chilled her sinuses, sent a shiver down her spine—she still wasn't used to handling the stuff raw. She fingered the blue ribbon tied around the bottle's stem.

"Cute," she said.

Then she dropped the bottle. It shattered on the stone at her feet, and each of her hostages flinched—except the old man Falka held by the collar of his vest, keeping him upright as he knelt on the ground. He had ceased his feeble struggling and hung limply in her grasp.

"Pity we don't speak the same tongue," Falka said. "I'm good at getting people to see reason, once they understand their options. But it seems words won't suffice here."

No one else in the canyon reacted to her voice—not the small group of hostages Falka had ordered her freebooters to take as soon as they'd arrived, nor the rest of the saurian herders, who had mostly hidden in their caves while Falka's band searched the settlement. The canyon, so picturesque when they had arrived, was in shambles now. Baskets and sacks lay strewn across the grass amid heaps of smashed vegetables and spilled grain. The marauders had stuffed their saddlebags with food and discarded all they couldn't carry. The herders had clearly had a good harvest; Falka doubted many would die of starvation in the coming weeks.

Two of Falka's people, Tusker and Mei-Lee, amused themselves by shaving a child's head while she screamed and her mother wept. Falka watched them from the corner of her eye. Their sadism didn't please her, but at least this game was bloodless, unlike their usual entertainment of cutting open lizards' bellies and stringing them over cactus arms by their guts. The two were among the most waste-addled of her freebooters, and they had to direct their energies somewhere.

Falka bent down and plucked a shard of glass from the ground.

"One more time. I'm looking for two women." She held up two fingers. "A sparkrider and a shieldcaster. I know they were here; this is the only place between Kerina Rut and Kerina Sol where they could have sheltered from the storm. So where did they go? Ziyal, show them the map again."

Ziyal, a snub-nosed Lav-blood with a pierced lip, shook the map in front of the herders. Paper didn't last in the wastes, so the map was embroidered into Falka's blanket. Ziyal had stitched it herself and given it to Falka as a thank-you for taking her on as a freeboo-ter. That was one reason why Ziyal was Falka's favorite.

"They're dumb as chandru." Ziyal wrinkled her nose. "Can't un-derstand a thing you're saying."

Falka sighed. "They aren't dumb. They've survived out here without any help from the kerinas for generations. They've even learned to grow their own food without any bloomweavers. Not only that, but they taught Tibius everything he knows about sauri-ans." She raised her voice, knowing the herders wouldn't understand but wanting Tusker and Mei-Lee to hear her over the screams of their victim. "That's why we aren't going to harm them. None of them bleeds. Got it?"

Ziyal rolled her eyes. "If Tibius owes them so much, why'd he give us the spark and leave them in the desert to rot?"

"Careful, Ziyal," Falka said. "What's been given can be taken away."

Ziyal touched the back of her neck, where Falka knew a Talentless brand hid beneath her headscarf. Each of her freebooters had one, though some had carved or burned them away. Falka covered hers only to protect her skin from the sun; indoors, she kept it bare in a show of defiance. There was nothing shameful about being Talentless. One day, she would make sure everyone in the kerinas understood that.

She ignored Ziyal's petulant expression and crouched beside the old man, touching his throat gently with the shard of glass she held. "Tell me what I want to hear," she said, her voice soft. "Or you'll leave these frightened people without a leader. Those are the choices."

The old man's breath came in fearful pants, but he said nothing. Falka frowned at him. He was scared, but not desperate. He clearly believed her threats were genuine—so if he were willing to cooperate, he would be making himself clear. He wasn't, which meant the language barrier wasn't the problem. He was just being a stubborn old fool.

"Why?" she asked. "The women I seek are strangers to you. Why protect them?"

"Maybe they aren't alone," Ziyal said. "One of these herders could have gone with them. There was fresh storm dust in that garage, and this bike hasn't ridden since the gods were suckling babes." She aimed a kick at the rusted beater they'd dragged from the garage.

A second sparkrider among the herders? Why hadn't Tibius mentioned that after they'd taken the girl? Falka blinked to cover her unease and gave Ziyal an approving smile.

"So you're protecting one of your own," Falka told the old man. "A noble patriarch. Well, that means I'll have to—"

The ground shook. Falka jerked, startled, and her shard of glass nicked the old man's cheek. She heard a low bellow, so deep it rattled her bones, and Mei-Lee's shrill cry of "Saurian!"

The chandru had come out of nowhere. It thundered across the canyon, half a ton of leathery bulk with a spined sail rising above its humped back, moving faster than it had any right to. A small one, Falka thought, nowhere near the size of the behemoths she'd seen roaming the wastes. But it was still fucking huge and headed straight for her.

Tusker wasn't fast enough to get out of its way. He rolled screaming under the chandru's armored feet and lay silent in its wake. To Falka's chagrin, her first thought was *About time.*

She threw out her hands and burned mana. Sparks streamed in a hot shower from her palms and skittered off the chandru's hide like grains of sand. The beast didn't even slow down. Of course, she should have expected that. Fucking stupid instinct, to throw sparks at a lightning eater. The chandru bore down on her, and she leaped sideways—no time to gather herself for anything more than a clumsy slide over the grass.

"Falka!" Ziyal shouted, but Falka was already on her feet and facing the chandru, breathing hard, the shard of glass still clutched in her hand and wet with the old man's blood. She tossed it aside with a dismissive grunt and drew her real weapon from its sheath on her belt: a broad saber, cast all in one steelform by a metalcrafter, its curved blade one with the hilt and grip.

The chandru snorted and swept its long tail over the ground, narrowly avoiding several of Falka's hostages—all of whom were scrambling to put distance between themselves and the enraged beast. Falka glared into the saurian's flat, reptilian eyes. She felt grudging respect for the creature. None of the herders had so much as swung a fist while her freebooters looted their caves and rounded up their children. It seemed only their pet chandru was willing to defend its home.

If Tibius were here, perhaps he could have gotten the beast under control. Falka would just have to solve this problem in her own way.

"Come on," she said, waving her saber. "Test me."

Bellowing, the chandru started toward her. Falka didn't wait for it to close the distance. She darted forward, cutting off the chandru's charge, and slashed at its side. Her saber scored the beast's hide, slicing through the thick skin. Blue blood spattered the grass. Falka was vaguely aware of the old man attempting to stagger to his feet, roused by the chandru's pained cry, only for Ziyal to force him back down. She whirled and prepared to slash again.

Something smacked into her legs and sent her tumbling ass over teakettle. The beast's tail. Her saber flew from her hands as she hit the ground headfirst. The world flashed white with the impact and shifted out of focus. She couldn't feel her limbs. Damn it, she wasn't about to get trampled to death in front of her freebooters. Not before she'd caught up to Jin and seen the look on her face when she realized—

The chandru screamed. Falka raised herself up on her elbows, panting. There was the chandru, slumped on the ground, lowing in agony. Ziyal stood over the beast's hunched shape, her spear buried in its chest.

Well, Falka had to give it to her. Spears were better suited to killing saurians than swords.

"Blasted lightning eater." Ziyal spat on the beast's bloodstained side without much feeling. "Should I finish it off? These herders will just put it back together in the next storm if I don't."

Falka coughed. "Don't bother. It'd be a waste."

She staggered to her feet; the canyon shifted and wobbled around her, and bile welled up in her throat. It had been an unlucky fall. Falka ground her teeth, forced her nausea down. She couldn't show weakness in front of her own freebooters, either. Most, like Ziyal, wouldn't risk losing their Talent just to take Falka down a few pegs. But a few of them, like Mei-Lee—who was prodding at Tusker's limp body with her foot, a mesmerized grin on her face—were feral enough to tear her apart, Talent or no Talent.

The old man was still kneeling, though no one held him now. His eyes were fixed on the moaning chandru; tears ran down his cheeks.

"Why waste your tears?" Falka demanded hoarsely. "They don't feel pain. They just make that noise to let you know they're damaged."

She cast one final scornful look at the old man and turned her back on him. The rest of her hostages hadn't gotten far. They were huddled against the canyon wall. Nine children between the ages of four and ten; they cringed and clung to one another as Falka approached.

"Hush, brats," she snapped. "This'll be over soon."

She snatched the smallest—a curly-haired girl no more than four years old—and held her saber to the child's neck.

Someone screamed. A woman pushed her way through the

herders watching from the cave entrances and fell to her knees in the grass before Falka, anguished words spilling from her mouth.

"Don't *tell* me," Falka said. Her head was ringing, her freebooters were getting impatient, and her hostage was sobbing all over her hands. She'd already spilled blood without meaning to. "Use the map. It's right over there."

The map lay discarded on the grass near Tusker's crumpled body. The herder woman snatched up the blanket, spat upon the corpse, and returned to Falka to point at a spot between the stitched lines with shaking fingers.

*The temple. Of course.*

"Finally," Falka said.

She pushed the child into her mother's arms, hollow of satisfaction. Even without Tibius's injunctions, Falka wouldn't have cut the girl. She was the toughest of her freebooters, the fastest rider, the best negotiator—but her damned soft streak might be her undoing someday.

She wanted to excise every last squirming soft part of herself, toss them by the roadside where they belonged. She wanted to be hard and dry as boiled saurian leather, tough enough to withstand anything. She never wanted to hear a dead man's voice echo in her skull again.

If she couldn't leave her past behind, at least she could drag it into the light and destroy it. She could hunt down the person who'd hurt her the most, make them suffer as she had.

It was time to find Jin-Lu.

*Second Age of Storms, 49th Summer*

*Dear Kadrin,*
*It was sweet of you to send along the records, although I hope you paid*
*our courier well for her trouble; six hundred yards of parchment must*
*have been a burden to carry across the wastes. (They were.) Sadly, I'm*
*afraid these records aren't complete. The project I've taken up is an in-*
*vestigation into the heritability of Talent, how it's passed down through*
*families. So I need records that list the Talent of each parent, if they*
*have one, and what Talent was identified in their children.*

*Never mind that anyway; don't trouble yourself. The project was*
*ill-conceived. The archivists of the High Houses are much more quali-*
*fied to solve Kerina Rut's population crisis; I don't know why I thought*
*my contributions might be of value.*

*It's only that I can't quite come to grips with something. So far, all of*
*the High Houses' attempts to deal with the problem have come in the form*
*of more restrictions on the Talentless and harsher penalties for women who*
*bear Talentless children. However you feel about the ethics, in theory those*
*tactics should be effective. We've plenty of evidence to prove Talent is passed*
*along family lines. So why aren't these methods working? Fewer Talented*
*are born every year, regardless of parentage, as if to spite our efforts.*

*Not only that, but Kerina Rut isn't the first to try weeding out their*
*Talentless through systematic exclusion. Kerina Tez, our sister to the*
*north, tried the very same, and the latest reports from that city are night-*
*marish. I fear the situation in Kerina Rut is only a few years behind.*

*I've gone on a depressing tangent, haven't I? My apologies, Kadrin.*
*I shall try to think of more pleasant topics for my next letter.*

*Thinking of you even in my darkest moments,*
*Reena*

## CHAPTER THIRTEEN

# TEMPLE OF BONES

*Second Age of Storms, 51st Summer, Day 22*

Jin and Faolin stashed their bikes in a niche between two pillars that had toppled into each other, creating a spiderweb of cracks. They picked their way through fallen stones with Faolin in the lead, until they stood before a statue in the center of a vast, dusty courtyard, where silence pressed down on Jin's shoulders like heavy hands.

The statue depicted a veiled woman. Bony, elongated fingers carved from cold stone reached toward Yi-Nereen as she stepped closer. "This looks just like the carvings of Makela in my family's shrine."

Jin gazed up at the faceless statue and shivered. When she was young, the priesthood of Tez had declared images of the Talent Thief to be false idolatry. They'd shattered sculptures, burned scrolls, slashed paintings. She'd heard of an unfortunate artist who'd had his fingers fed to starving dogs—and all for nothing, in the end. Refusing to acknowledge Makela hadn't prevented her curse from destroying Kerina Tez.

"So where—" she began to ask, but Faolin stepped toward the statue before she could finish. He paused for a moment, then reached up and grasped the statue's outstretched hands. Jin felt a chill; somehow the gesture seemed sacrilegious, profane. A moment later, stone shifted against stone, and a slab at the statue's base slowly ground back into a hidden recess, revealing a ramp sloping down into darkness.

Jin gaped. She glanced at Yi-Nereen, expecting the princess to look as surprised as Jin felt.

Instead, Yi-Nereen was beaming. "Wondrous."

"Strange," Jin muttered.

Doubt gnawed at her. The part of her that had been taught never to trust a stranger in the wastes rebelled against descending into the dark passage. Faolin could have been lying about his missing sister; this could be a trap. The gut instinct that told her to trust him could be wrong. What kind of mana spring lay under Road Builder ruins?

But she wasn't overburdened with options. She needed more mana to get to Kerina Sol, and she'd promised Faolin she would help. It was too late to back out now.

She followed Faolin down the ramp. Sparks danced around the boy's head, shedding fitful orange light against the passage's smooth-cut walls. The tunnel was spacious, wide and tall enough to accommodate their magebikes—if they'd brought them. Indeed, when Jin bent to examine the floor, she found more tire marks in the dust. Why, then, had Faolin insisted they leave their bikes aboveground? A disquieting thought struck her: perhaps he was worried about disturbing something below the ruins.

"A temple to Makela," Yi-Nereen said. Her voice echoed in an unfamiliar way. She was close enough for Jin to reach out and touch, and part of her wanted to do it—to draw Yi-Nereen as near to her as possible. "I've never heard of such a thing. Who would worship the Talent Thief?"

Jin blinked, and the impulse she'd felt to touch Yi-Nereen vanished. "Talentless, obviously."

"Truly?" Yi-Nereen sounded skeptical. "I thought even the Talentless would fear her. Resent her, even. She stole their . . ."

"Their what?" A familiar heat crept into Jin's blood. She didn't *want* to become angry with Yi-Nereen, not again, so she forced her voice to remain level. "You can't really believe the Talentless don't have souls."

"Of course not," Yi-Nereen said, a little too hastily for Jin's liking. "I only meant, surely Talentless couldn't have built this temple. Not without stoneshapers."

"Because nothing can be accomplished without Talent?" Jin said. "There's no such thing as a Talentless mason, or gardener, or baker."

She heard the edge to her voice and cursed herself for her short temper. *Stop it, this isn't helping.* The confusion in Yi-Nereen's silence was palpable, and Jin's self-hatred grew with each passing moment. Faolin was studiously quiet, though he couldn't have missed the tension.

"One doesn't need Talent to be capable," Yi-Nereen said after a while, sounding uncertain. "I don't look down on them, Jin. People like Kadrin and your mother—"

"Don't compare Kadrin to my mother," Jin said. "Kadrin's a prince. My mother is branded. Right here." She touched the back of her neck. "Every Talented in Kerina Tez had the right to do whatever they wished to her, take whatever she had. She wasn't human, not to them. I've seen the same brands on *your* Talentless, Princess."

Jin's hands were trembling. She quickened her steps, passed Faolin, and moved ahead into the dark. Her sparks danced around her head, mimicking her scattered thoughts. She shouldn't have said any of that to Yi-Nereen. They weren't friends; she was Jin's employer. What was the point? Once she delivered Yi-Nereen to Kerina Sol, she'd never have reason to see her again. She and Kadrin would be happy together, and Jin would go back to her old life.

All three of them were from different worlds, but at least Yi-Nereen and Kadrin had been born in the same dimension. Jin was just a deadbeat courier with no prospects. Who was she to think she belonged with either of them?

And yet . . . that *kiss*. The wind, the storm, Yi-Nereen's lips on hers. The memory made her shiver. She'd never forget that moment.

But it had all been a transaction. Not a kiss. A *siphoning*.

She was nearing the bottom of the ramp. Ahead, the passage opened into dark, empty space. Jin cast a few sparks before her, trying to discern how large that space might be, but the little orange motes flickered out when they left arm's reach.

Faolin pattered down to join her. In the erratic light of her sparks, Jin saw him touch something on the wall: a smooth, bulbous protrusion, like a sconce. She felt the familiar prickle that meant another sparkrider was burning mana nearby. Electricity skittered from Faolin's hand into the sconce, but—were her eyes deceiving her? No. The motes were blue, not orange. *That's not right.*

Light flared inside the sconce, a steady blue glow that leaped to another sconce a few yards along the wall, then another. Jin sucked in her breath, caught utterly off guard. The chamber flared to life around her, vast, empty, and filled with ghostly azure light. It was an amphitheater, or at least Jin guessed so from the benches cut into the stone floor. Neglect hung heavy in the air.

How many people had once worshipped at this underground

temple? Thousands, perhaps. Now there was nothing left but ruins, sitting at the bottom of a crater like old bones under the sun.

Jin inched toward the wall, unnerved. Movement caught her eye: a large iridescent beetle scurrying into an alcove just above head height. Swallowing, Jin stepped toward the alcove. Either it had been intentionally carved slightly too high for its contents to be viewed easily . . . or the Road Builders had been unnaturally tall, like Makela herself. Jin shook away the disturbing thought and stood on her tiptoes to peer inside.

A skull stared back at her. In the blue light, the bone had a grayish hue. Dried vines wove in and out of the eye sockets, brittle enough to crumble to dust if touched. Piles of ash-like detritus around the skull suggested long-rotted flowers. After a moment's horrified shock, Jin stepped back. Her heart was pounding.

"There are bones in here," she said, whirling on Faolin. "Where *are* we?"

"Bones?" Yi-Nereen's voice rose with excitement, not fear. She swept past Jin and gazed upon the skull with wide eyes. "Road Builder remains? They can't be. No one has ever found those before." She raised her hand reverentially as if to touch—and out of the corner of her eye, Jin saw Faolin flinch.

"Don't." Jin grabbed Yi-Nereen's wrist.

Yi-Nereen released a shaky breath. "You're right, of course." She lowered her hand, but her eyes still shone. "I thought the canyon was incredible, but this . . ."

Jin wrapped her arms around herself, frowning. "I wouldn't call blue light and old bones *incredible*."

More alcoves lined both sides of the amphitheater, high along the walls near the ceiling. Each was cut in such a way as to hide its contents unless you were standing right in front of it. Did every single one contain a skull, separated from its owner and placed here for display? Jin didn't feel like checking. What a damned creepy place. She couldn't wait to leave.

The sconce Faolin had touched still glowed a steady blue, like all the others. Jin reached warily for it. It was smooth, slightly warm to the touch, and had the texture of brushed steel. Faolin had activated it with his Talent somehow. Could any sparkrider do it, or was he special?

Faolin was still watching Yi-Nereen, who had fished some parchment out of her pack and was trying to open a sealed bottle of ink with her teeth. He caught Jin's eye and smiled, though he looked uneasy.

"*Vai,*" he said, taking her by the sleeve. Jin resisted the urge to pull away.

"Come on," she said to Yi-Nereen. "Mana first, sketching later."

Yi-Nereen looked longingly at the skull. "I can stay here while you—"

"*No.*" The word came out more sharply than Jin had intended. "We're not splitting up."

*I shouldn't have brought her along.* The thought pulsed through her as Faolin led the way into a corridor lined with glowing sconces. It was one thing to risk her own life to help someone she'd just met. But she hadn't signed up to guard a princess while they toured a haunted underground temple.

She couldn't get the skull out of her mind's eye—those staring, empty sockets. Bones without a soul to inhabit them: it was profane, unnatural. The kerinas gave their dead back to the mana springs, where they dissolved completely, bones and all. Jin had given over her share of dead that way, starting with her father.

*And I would've done the same for Falka, if she'd left a body behind.*

At least there were no alcoves in this hallway. Instead, rows of cuneiform adorned the walls, the same as the runes that decorated kerina temples: the language of the Road Builders. Here and there, the incomprehensible runes were broken by recognizable motifs etched into the stone: a leafless tree, a coiled snake, a lidless eye. Jin liked the drawings about as much as the skulls. But Faolin trailed his hand along them as if they were all familiar friends, mumbling to himself in a sort of breathless singsong whisper.

"Wait." Yi-Nereen stopped in the middle of the corridor. "Faolin? Can you read these?"

Jin groaned internally. Faolin looked at Yi-Nereen, then at the rune she was touching, his brow furrowed. "*Se akram*," he said. "Makela *vidam akram*."

"No one alive can read this text," Yi-Nereen said. "No one even remembers who the Road Builders were. All we know is that they built the highways and worshipped our gods." She turned to Jin. "That little settlement in the canyon . . . somehow Faolin's people have preserved hundreds of years of linguistic history, kept it secret from the rest of us. Jin, they might *be* the Road Builders. What's left of them."

"First they're wastelanders with pet saurians, and now you think they're Road Builders?"

"I can't be sure. I always thought the Road Builders looked different from us—they were closer to the gods, after all. But what if they didn't all die out, and instead they changed and kept themselves hidden? It's been centuries. They might not even remember who they are."

"So leave them alone," Jin said. "Unless you still think you know what's best for them."

Yi-Nereen stared at her. "What?"

Jin shook her head. Anger was pulsing through her again, and this time she didn't even know why. She couldn't articulate what she felt; if she opened her mouth, she didn't know what would come out, but she thought she might regret it.

Yi-Nereen was still staring at her, long enough to make Jin's skin crawl. "Are you still angry about what I said before?" she asked. "About your mother?"

"I don't know," Jin said. "Maybe."

Right now she was more concerned about the skulls and the drawings and Faolin's unsettling ability to read the Road Builder glyphs on the wall. Every inch of her was screaming that they weren't meant to be here, that they should leave immediately. *What's dead should stay buried.* But of course the comment about her mother had bothered her. She didn't want to hear Yi-Nereen blathering about how capable the Talentless were when Jin had seen them beaten and spat upon in her streets. The princess had looked down on it all from her gilded tower, dreaming of ways to save them by making sure fewer of them were born.

"My mother died in childbed two years ago," Yi-Nereen said. Jin looked at her sharply, wondering if the princess was a mindreader after all. The flickering blue light of the sconces gave her calm face an unnatural cast, as if she were a corpse herself. "The baby didn't live, either. Her seventh stillborn. When we talk about our numbers dwindling, it isn't in the abstract."

Jin remembered then what Yi-Nereen had said to her in the Tower: *I won't give up my body twice over to continue a bloodline.* Was that the fate Yi-Nereen had foreseen for herself: confined to the birthing bed until it killed her, just like her mother?

She was on the verge of apologizing when she thought of the Talentless women in Kerina Tez, who had been stolen away under cover of darkness and made forcibly sterile—and why she and her mother had fled the city with a single night's warning. The memory closed her throat. "Let's just find the mana."

Yi-Nereen looked like she was about to say something, but she simply nodded. "*Vey* mana," she said to Faolin. The boy glanced at Jin and pointed toward a doorway at the end of the corridor. Jin forced a smile in thanks. So Yi-Nereen had learned a few words of the wastelanders' language—or the Road Builders' language, if her theory was correct. *Give her a few weeks down here with Faolin, and she'll be fluent.* The thought wasn't a comfort.

The doorway led to a storage room stacked high with moldered crates. At some point centuries ago, Jin thought, the space would have been filled with the reek of decay; but by now, whatever could rot had long since done so.

"This isn't a mana spring," she said to Faolin.

The boy reached for an iron bar leaning against the wall. Jin tensed—she couldn't help it—but Faolin stepped toward a crate and began prying off its lid. Wood creaked and blue light spilled from the growing crack as Faolin levered the bar back and forth.

The lid popped free. Jin stared down at small bottles tied with ribbon and packed in straw, identical to the ones she'd seen in Faolin's cave. Bottles filled with glowing blue mana.

"I knew it," Yi-Nereen said from the doorway. "That mana must be centuries old—yet it's perfectly preserved. Mana from the time of the Road Builders. Do you know what that means, Jin? Before the storms, before the springs, there was already—"

"Mana," Jin said.

She plucked a bottle from the straw and rolled it between her palms, savoring the coolness of the glass. Finally, something down here that felt right. She popped the cork and drank. The mana hit her tongue and throat with the force of strong liquor, icy hot and merciless. She swallowed, coughed. In that moment, it struck her that she hadn't craved a mana-cig since waking up yesterday. Since she'd infused bottled mana for the first time.

When she turned around, Yi-Nereen was watching her. "How do you feel?"

"It's the same as the stuff back in the canyon," Jin said. "This must be where they get it. Put some in your bag—for the road. Who knows if we'll need it."

She turned away, but not before she caught the disappointed look on Yi-Nereen's face, like she'd been expecting some big revelation. Too bad. Jin didn't care about uncovering all the secrets of the Road Builder ruins, or saving all the Talentless in Kerina Rut, or whatever Yi-Nereen was trying to do. She'd learned long ago that you couldn't change the world, or even understand how it worked. All you could do was survive and make sure the people you cared about survived, too.

Jin's problem had always been that she couldn't control who she cared about.

"Faolin," she said. The boy turned to her at the sound of his name. Smiling, of course. The kid never stopped grinning, just like a puppy. "Thanks. You've kept up your end of the bargain. Now I'll help you look for Amrys."

There was just one issue with that. She had no fucking clue where to start.

*Second Age of Storms, 49th Summer*

*Dear Reena,*
*Shall I tell you another secret, Reena? It's embarrassing, but . . . read-*
*ing troubles me. It always has. The letters seem to move on the page,*
*and the words flow out of my head before I can grasp their meaning.*
*I always ask Jin to read your letters aloud when she delivers them, so I*
*can be sure I won't miss a thing.*

*My deepest apologies for the incomplete records. I'll see about get-*
*ting better ones, but it may be a while. Eliesen is on the outs with that*
*acolyte she's been wooing. Love is such a fickle beast, isn't it? I told her*
*they should try writing letters, but she slammed her door on me. Sisters.*

*So you're trying to solve Kerina Rut's population crisis? I think*
*that's admirable, and by no means a waste of time. Who says you're*
*any less qualified than some dour archivist who's spent his life writing*
*reports on royal bowel movements? You actually care about Kerina Rut*
*and its citizens. All of them.*

*Keep at it, Reena. I'll give you all the aid I can. I haven't a frac-*
*tion of your intellect, but between your brains and my charm (ha), I*
*know we can change the world.*

*Don't forget to take care of yourself, too. Constantly being called*
*to serve in the Shield Corps must be exhausting. I can hardly imagine*
*what it's like, having no responsibilities myself. I spend all my waking*
*hours staving off boredom through silly hobbies and keeping out from*
*under the feet of people who have real work to do in my House. Oh,*
*and rereading your letters, of course. So you may be as morbid as you*
*like; no words from your lips shall bring me anything but happiness.*

*At your service, always and completely,*
*Kadrin*

## CHAPTER FOURTEEN

# A SCHOLAR AND HER SCRIBE

*Second Age of Storms, 51st Summer, Day 22*

*B*ack to the room full of skulls, Jin thought, glaring up at the alcoves with their hidden horrors. *Wonderful.*

Faolin had led them back to the amphitheater. Jin had thought all the walls bare at first, but she'd been wrong. Up close, she realized the entire wall opposite the entrance was an engraved mural cloaked in dust, its once-vibrant colors lost to time and neglect. A short flight of steps led up to a dais beneath the mural.

Faolin tugged Jin onto the dais, but she resisted. "This can't be right," she said. "I want to know where you last saw Amrys. Did you see the raiders take her from here?"

"*Wirja*," Faolin insisted, gesturing toward the mural.

"He said that when we first met," Yi-Nereen said. "*Wirja*. I think it means . . . 'wait'? 'Have patience'?"

"I *am* patient," Jin said. "Fine, I'll look at the damn mural."

The dust caking the carved lines and the inconstant light of the blue sconces made it almost impossible to tell what the mural depicted. Jin summoned a few sparks and rubbed away dust with her sleeves amid muttered curses. The mural was in three panels divided by thin lines, she realized. The first panel, all the way to the left, depicted a man and a woman embracing. Faolin hovered at her shoulder, buzzing with barely disguised anticipation.

"Let me breathe, will you?"

Jin massaged her temples with a sigh. She imagined the skulls gazing down at her from their alcoves, the eyes of the dead watching her. What was she doing here, anyway? If this mural held some clue that would help her find Faolin's sister, she was the last person who was likely to discover it.

"Princess?" Gods, how Jin hated asking for help. "What do you make of this?"

Yi-Nereen hesitated. Then she stepped forward, rolling up both sleeves of her caftan—Jin had to look away, face burning; *what* was it about that motion that flustered her so?—and bent to examine the portion Jin had wiped clean. Jin didn't move, though she could smell the scented oils Yi-Nereen had put in her hair. *One more day and we'll be in Kerina Sol*, she reminded herself. *Focus.*

"This man is a bloomweaver." Yi-Nereen pointed at the masculine figure, who held a staff encircled in vines. "They're commonly depicted holding plants or wearing garlands. The woman, though, she isn't holding anything. In carvings, that usually denotes a Talentless."

"What about that?" Jin tapped the part of the carving that resembled a third figure looming over the embracing couple, faceless and indistinct, hands outstretched with fingers longer than the couple themselves. "It's supposed to be Makela, right?"

"I think so. It might be part of a creation myth. A union between a bloomweaver and a Talentless. Some Rasvelites think that's how the kerinas came to be. Although the drawings I've seen always depict Rasvel blessing the couple, not Makela."

"How do you know all this?"

For a moment, Jin didn't care about the skulls or the aura of foreboding that clung to the temple halls like a second layer of dust. All that mattered was Yi-Nereen, talking as if she'd been a scholar all her life, with Jin as her scribe. The thought made Jin's heart hurt, just a little, for how much she wished it could be true.

Yi-Nereen's lip quirked. "I had tutors. Wealthy men prefer educated wives."

And there it was—the reminder that Yi-Nereen had always been intended for someone else.

Jin busied herself wiping dust from the middle panel of the mural. "There's the couple again," she said, trying to sound as if she cared. "And that's definitely Rasvel."

On the wall, the man and woman stood hand in hand. Beside them stood a figure Jin was familiar with from depictions of Rasvel, which were reproduced on everything from vases at market stalls to lovingly rendered paintings hanging at the Kerina Sol temple: a smiling bald man with glowing, pupil-less eyes. He was reaching toward the woman's belly.

"The Giver of Blessings," Yi-Nereen said. "The woman must be with child. That's odd."

"Why?"

Yi-Nereen frowned at the wall. "It's backward. I've heard this tale before. On the day of their marriage, a bloomweaver and a Talentless woman are blessed by Rasvel, who promises they'll have a Talented child. Makela tries to steal the child's Talent during the pregnancy, but Rasvel's blessing is too strong; her curse backfires. The child is born with Talent different from the mother's and father's. A miracle."

"So Rasvel and Makela should be switched?"

"Perhaps." Yi-Nereen looked thoughtful. "What about the final panel?"

Jin's sleeves were caked in dust, so she resorted to taking off her jacket and beating the wall like a rug. When the resulting cloud settled, she and Yi-Nereen drew closer to look at the same time, and their elbows touched. Jin jerked back as if she'd been stung. She'd ridden across the wastes with Yi-Nereen's arms around her, but the accidental touch felt different somehow, stolen.

"I was right," Yi-Nereen said.

In the third panel, the man and the woman were hunched figures, stooped from age. Between them stood a young man with his arms stretched to either side, surrounded by an etched dome.

"He's shieldtalented," Jin blurted out, before Yi-Nereen could. "Right?"

The smile Yi-Nereen flashed her was enough to make Jin's heart flutter. "Correct. Even though neither of his parents were. It's rare, but not unheard of."

"The sparkrider who taught me to ride was born to a pair of raincallers." Jin frowned. "He figured his mother had cuckolded her husband. Power flows in a straight line, and all that."

"No, Jin." Yi-Nereen's voice rose with excitement. "This mural, this temple, it all supports the theory I was building about the Talentless in Kerina Rut. Don't you see? Talent is passed from parent to child, yes, but not always. Kerinas aren't large enough to sustain themselves that way. Eventually brothers would have to marry sisters to continue the bloodline."

"The priests don't allow those kinds of matches."

"No, but neither do they allow mingling of the High Talents and the Talentless. It dilutes the bloodlines, or so they claim." Yi-Nereen's eyes flashed. "If I'm right, Jin, their meddling has only made matters worse. I've written a treatise on the subject that would have earned me exile if anyone in Kerina Rut had discovered it." She patted her satchel. "With my research and what we've found in the canyon and this temple . . . One moment, I need to take down some notes. This will surely convince the High Houses of Sol."

Jin bit her lip. *That damned treatise again.* "You do that," she said. "All I want to know is this: What does this mural have to do with Faolin's sister?"

Faolin perked up, hearing his name. He stepped back onto the dais and gestured toward the mural, arching his eyebrows.

"I don't know what you want me to do," Jin said, frustration creeping into her voice. "It's a creation myth, but it's backward. How does that help?"

Faolin's face fell. He shifted his weight from foot to foot, shoulders sagging. Clearly this wasn't the outcome he'd hoped for. Feeling guilty, Jin reached out and touched his shoulder. "Hey. It's okay. We'll keep looking."

The boy looked at her hand in surprise, and Jin wondered with a pang if it was uncommon for someone to offer him reassurances. The faint shadow of his former smile appeared on his face. He briefly laid his fingers over hers, then gently shrugged her off and moved toward the left side of the mural. Jin watched him run his hands over the etched stone. Yi-Nereen was busy digging through her satchel for her inkwell. It looked like Faolin was searching for something, too.

Then she heard it—a soft *click.*

Yi-Nereen's head snapped up. "What was that?"

"Some kind of switch." Jin's heart was racing now, though she wasn't sure why. The air in the amphitheater felt almost too thick to breathe. She hadn't seen any obvious place for Faolin to touch, no shifting panel or button-shaped depression. Now he was moving to the second panel. There was another *click*.

The hair on Jin's arms was tingling. She didn't know what was happening, and she didn't like it. Down here she felt the same way she did in the kerinas: lumbering and slow without her magebike. It just made matters worse that she had Yi-Nereen and Faolin down here with her. People had a way of worming under her skin, making her feel like she had to protect them.

After she'd left Kerina Tez, she'd sworn off taking responsibility for anyone but Eomma ever again. It never ended well. Not with her father, whose last request had been for Jin to look after his magebike, which had been stolen only a few days after his death. Not with the Talentless street orphans in Kerina Tez who'd treated her like an older sister—she'd left them behind in the crumbling city, their chances of survival next to nil. And certainly not with Falka.

"Wait," Jin said, but Faolin had already stepped toward the third panel. "Wait, before you—"

*Click.* This time the soft mechanical noise was followed by a deeper rumbling sound. Faolin stepped away from the wall as it began to move. The two halves of the wall slid slowly apart, splitting the central panel in half so the bloomweaver stood alone on one side, his wife and Rasvel on the other.

Jin took an instinctive step back. She put an arm out to catch Yi-Nereen as the princess moved eagerly forward.

"*The Talent Thief comes by night, cloaked in secrets,*" Yi-Nereen said, hardly seeming to notice Jin's hand gripping her sleeve. "This truly is her temple."

The two halves of the wall ground to a halt, revealing a pitch-dark chamber beyond. Jin snapped her fingers. Orange light flickered in the dark. A chill rooted her in place. "Rasvel have mercy."

More bones. She was looking at a room heaped with full skeletons, brittle and yellowed with age. The skulls in the wall alcoves had been arranged intentionally, even artfully, but there was no art in the way these skeletons were strewn across the floor, only the hand of ancient suffering. Those bones were the remains of perhaps two dozen people who had died where they lay now. The air wafting forth from the room was stale.

"Look," Yi-Nereen said in a hushed voice, pointing. Across the sepulchral chamber was another doorway leading into darkness. "Where do you think it leads?"

"*That's* what you're wondering?"

Faolin stood beside the entrance, his head bowed. Now he looked up and met Jin's gaze. "Amrys," he said.

Jin pulled back her sparks; they danced in a tight circle around her head. She didn't want to look at these bones anymore. "She went in there?" Her stomach churned. "Or someone took her in there. Well, I can see why you didn't want to look for her yourself." *Or perhaps he did, and whatever he saw warranted backup.*

Yi-Nereen shielded her face with her sleeve, but the light in her eyes was undimmed. "She certainly isn't among these skeletons. They're ancient."

Jin's shirt was plastered to her back with sweat, and not just from the heat down here. Her heart quailed at the thought of setting one foot into that room full of corpses. Not simply alone, but in the company of a boy she couldn't understand and a princess too emboldened by the thrill of discovery to heed any danger. Jin couldn't think of a better recipe for disaster.

*No. I'm not doing this.*

She had promised to help Faolin, but her promise hadn't included dragging Yi-Nereen into danger alongside her. So she wouldn't, simple as that. Jin would bring Yi-Nereen kicking and screaming back to the canyon if she had to; then she would come back here with Faolin alone, hopefully armed with some kind of weapon.

Jin took a deep breath and turned to face them both: Faolin, who was looking at her with wide, expectant eyes, and Yi-Nereen, who was scrawling notes on a parchment against the wall, her tongue pressed between her teeth.

"We're leaving."

Yi-Nereen's brush froze. "What?"

Jin winced. This wasn't going to be easy, and Yi-Nereen would probably hate her for the rest of time. The thought almost made her give in, but she forced herself to hold fast.

"You heard me," she said. "I won't be responsible for your death, Princess. I promised to bring you safely to Kadrin, so that's what I'm going to do."

"What about Faolin?" Yi-Nereen gestured toward the boy, who hovered near the wall, visibly uncertain, glancing between them both. "You promised to help him."

It was clear as day Yi-Nereen cared about her research, not Faolin's sister, and her pretending otherwise made Jin's blood boil.

"That's none of your business," she said. "Whether I come back to help him later has nothing to do with you."

Yi-Nereen pursed her lips. "Let's entertain that proposal for a moment." Her voice was haughty and cold; she sounded more like a royal than ever. "You're refusing my help, going into the dark to face Rasvel-knows-what in the company of a boy whose language you don't understand? This is the worst idea you've had yet, Jin."

Jin laughed incredulously. "You think I'll be safer if—"

"All the sparkriders I've met are exactly like you." Yi-Nereen's anger wasn't shrill. Her voice had deepened into molten metal. It was frightening, unexpected, and . . . well, attractive. "Swaggering, tough, and convinced the only person they can rely on is themselves. Aren't you forgetting something? *Your* sparks didn't save you when the guards of Kerina Rut bombarded us with arrows. Your bike didn't save you in the canyon when the storm hit. You needed me then, and you'll need me in there." She pointed into the dark, hand shaking. "And I—I need you; you know I do. So let's stop this foolishness. Please."

Her face was flushed, her eyes bright and gleaming with unshed tears. Jin felt like clothes on a wire, flapping helplessly in the wind. What could she say to that? It had almost sounded like a confession . . . and that kiss in the storm had felt like a real kiss, too.

*It doesn't matter.* Even if there was something more there than a hopeless one-sided infatuation, it could never happen. Jin couldn't do that to Kadrin.

"You hired me to take you to Kerina Sol," Jin said. "That's all."

Yi-Nereen's lip trembled, but she held her head high. "What you said back in the canyon, I thought . . ." She shook her head. "Never mind. I was mistaken."

Jin couldn't bear to look at her any longer. The coin pouch in her breast pocket seemed to weigh a hundred pounds. It didn't matter what Yi-Nereen believed, even if part of Jin wanted to hurl the pouch at her feet and deny everything she'd said. Coming here with Yi-Nereen had been a mistake.

"Come on," she told Faolin, who stared at her uncomprehendingly. "We're leaving." He looked at the chamber beyond the mural, then at Jin, his head tilted. "I'll come back," Jin said, though she knew he wouldn't understand. Perhaps by the time they reached the canyon, she'd think of a way to tell him. "I promise."

She picked up her jacket from where it lay on the floor and turned her back on the room full of bones. With a heavy heart, under the condemning gaze of the skulls hidden in the walls and the disappointed stares of two living souls, she made her way to the amphitheater's exit. She heard Yi-Nereen say something in a low, comforting voice to Faolin.

They climbed the ramp toward the surface in silence. Jin's chest burned with shame, no matter how she tried to banish it with reason. Once Yi-Nereen was safely in Kerina Sol under Kadrin's protection, the princess could hire a company of knights to take her back to the ruins if she wished. She didn't need Jin for that. It was better for both of them to end this journey as soon as possible, even if—*especially* if—Yi-Nereen was capable of returning a fraction of Jin's feelings.

In a mere two days, Jin would be back to keep her promise to Faolin. His sister had already been missing for weeks; what difference could two more days make? Her thoughts wandered back to his drawing, the tall figure he'd crossed out—the mysterious third sparkrider among the wastelanders. Maybe it hadn't been one of Faolin's people, but another courier like Jin herself. They could still be out there, roaming the wasteland without a care for the boy they'd left behind.

*But I'll come back.*

Daylight streamed down the end of the ramp. Jin breathed in deep, savoring the clean scent of the surface. She could hear wind murmuring through the ruins above, like voices. After the oppressive silence of the underground temple, she would have welcomed even a storm.

Raising a hand to shield her eyes from the sun, she stepped out of the darkness—and froze.

It hadn't been the wind. The voices were real.

Sunlight glinted off the chrome shells of a dozen magebikes encircling the tunnel's mouth and the statue of Makela. Riders in tattered black leather and bonehelms leaned against their bikes, armed with an array of weaponry: spears, cutlasses, crossbows with quarrels fletched in saurian feathers.

Jin whipped around, still half-blinded by light, and screamed down the ramp. "Go back! Reena, Faolin, *run*—"

Someone grabbed her from behind. Jin kicked, wrenched away from her assailant and into the arms of another. She sank her teeth into a forearm, heard a strangled curse, tasted sweat and blood. Then someone tangled a fist in her hair and yanked her head back.

She stared up at a face that struck a chord in her memory even though it was upside-down. A thin nose and prominent cheekbones strewn with freckles, a mouth turned downward at the edges in a permanent pout. Brown eyes without a trace of warmth, flecked with golden green.

"Falka," Jin choked out.

Jin's ex-girlfriend—her childhood friend and first love, a specter of sweet regret and broken promises—smiled at her, sharp as shattered glass.

"Found you," Falka said.

# Road to Ruin

*Second Age of Storms, 49th Summer*

*Dear Kadrin,*

*Since you have given me permission to be morbid, morbid I shall be. My mind has been filled with darkness of late. The Tower feels like a prison I shall never escape, my mother and father my jailers, the Shield Corps a penance for a crime I cannot remember. If I am not exhausted, I am restless; if I am not restless, I am listless. Yet I am conscious at all times that what little freedom I possess could be taken from me at any moment. I have such dread for the future, Kadrin. These letters are my only solace—and if anyone finds out who I have been writing to this whole time, I shall not be allowed access to parchment nor ink nor courier ever again.*

*I pray this shadow will pass. My circumstances are unlikely to change for the better, but perhaps I will learn to see them differently. I despise myself for burdening you with all of this unpleasantness; it is far from what you deserve.*

*It pained me to read your last letter, and not because of your sister's troubled love life—though she has my condolences. I cannot stand to hear you talk about yourself as if you're worthless. Not when you are the only reason I—*

*Don't write that down, Courier. Simply write "You are not," and let us leave it at that.*

*Yours for as long as you can bear it,*
*Reena*

# CHAPTER FIFTEEN

# LOVE AND OTHER GHOSTS

*Second Age of Storms, 51st Summer, Day 22*

*It isn't possible.* The thought hammered through Jin's head despite the evidence of her eyes: Falka in a raider's leathers, faded red scarf looped around her neck, fingerless gloves chalky with road dust. Falka was Talentless—she couldn't spark a magebike. Falka was a girl from the streets of Kerina Tez—she couldn't be a raider. Falka was *dead*—she couldn't be standing over Jin, alive and well.

"Nothing to say, after all this time?" Falka caressed Jin's cheek and let go of her hair. "Come up now, Highness. There's no use hiding down there. I know these ruins like the back of my hand, and this is the only way in or out."

Jin collapsed to all fours and watched, trembling, as Yi-Nereen and Faolin emerged from the tunnel. Yi-Nereen kept herself between the raiders and Faolin—*Stupid,* Jin wanted to scream at her, *don't you care about your own safety?*

Beneath her veil, Yi-Nereen's brown eyes scanned the circle of armed raiders and fell on Jin. "Jin, are you all right?"

Falka crossed her arms and looked Yi-Nereen over from head to toe with a smirk. "So this is your new girlfriend, Jin? She's tall. And a powerful shieldcaster, from what I hear. Look at you—apparently your tastes have evolved."

Two of the raiders flanked Jin, brutal-looking women with spears pointed at her neck. No chance of escape. But Jin didn't care about that, not anymore. "Falka, how—what happened to you?"

"You want to talk about old times?" Falka laughed, a bitter sound that made Jin flinch. "We'll have plenty of time to reminisce. But not now. I didn't come all this way for *you*." She eyed Faolin, who stood just behind Yi-Nereen, gripping her arm. "I'm here for the shieldcaster princess. The kid will make a nice bonus. He's sparktalented, isn't he? Like his sister."

A flicker of fierce protectiveness pierced the fog in Jin's mind. But before she could say anything, Yi-Nereen spoke in a low voice. "Jin, who is this woman? You know her?"

Falka lunged at Yi-Nereen like a striking viper and seized her by the chin, exposing the smooth column of her throat. "Don't speak, my dear," she said into Yi-Nereen's ear. "Not to her, not ever again."

A spark danced over Falka's knuckles and hissed against Yi-Nereen's skin. For a moment Jin was entranced, dumbfounded by the impossibility of what she was seeing. Then Yi-Nereen yelped in pain. The sound brought Jin to her feet, stumbling forward until the raiders caught her. Faolin shouted a protest and grabbed Falka's wrist. Falka glanced at him, lip curled. She tore her wrist from his grasp with ease, unsheathed a gleaming saber, and held it to his chest.

"Don't hurt them!" The raw desperation in Jin's own voice startled her. "Falka, stop. They aren't part of this."

"I've already told you, the princess is the reason I'm here." Falka let go of Yi-Nereen and smiled, as if admiring the tiny burn she'd left on the princess's jaw. "I've been paid a small fortune to drag her back to Kerina Rut. That arrogant fiancé of hers can't seem to let her go. Not that I blame him. *I* know what it's like when a girl breaks her promises and disappears without a goodbye."

"I never had a chance," Jin said hoarsely. "I came back, but you were gone. I looked for you. I thought you were *dead*."

Memories overwhelmed her. Pacing across Lorne's workshop with Eomma's temple summons crumpled in her hand while the old man entreated her to get out of Kerina Tez as soon as was humanly possible. *The priests have been gathering up Talentless women all over the city, calling them in for special prayers. Most of them haven't come back.*

*I can't leave without Falka*, Jin had said. But in the end, she'd had no choice. She could take only one person with her, and it had to be her mother. She couldn't find Falka to say goodbye, but Lorne had promised to give her Jin's final message: *I'm coming back for you.*

It hadn't been enough. When Jin returned to Kerina Tez the next spring, both Lorne and Falka were gone. Lorne had died of a burst blood vessel in his brain, and his apprentices had given him to the mana spring, but no one could tell Jin what had happened to Falka. It wasn't just her who'd vanished—so had Demond, Jin's childhood nemesis, who'd barely survived his stabbing nine years before. He'd been forced to give up his squire training and become an acolyte at the temple.

Jin had put two and two together and understood the worst had come to pass. She'd been too late. At least—and it was a cold comfort—Demond was gone, too. It was just like Falka to drag her murderer screaming into the afterlife alongside her.

"Dead? Hardly." Falka turned a circle in the dust. "Better than before, even. This Talent of yours is quite the lovely curse. I can go anywhere I please now, storms be damned—as long as I never leave this godforsaken wasteland. I'm a parasite now, addicted to its blood. Just like you."

"I—I don't understand." How had Falka become sparktalented?

It wasn't possible. Talent didn't work like that, didn't lie dormant in a person only to manifest after decades.

"That's the thing, Jin." Falka cocked her head to the side. Her smile had lost its razor edge for a moment. The sight transported Jin into the past, to windy days together atop the Wall, looking out over the wastes. Falka's warmth in her arms, the weight of responsibility, its bittersweet taste in her mouth. "You never did."

"Let Reena go," Jin said. "You must know what Kerina Rut is like. It's as much of a shithole as Tez, in its own way. You'd be sending her back to die."

She scrabbled in her breast pocket with a shaking hand and drew out the silk pouch Yi-Nereen had given her; it slipped from her fingers and thumped into the dirt.

"If this is about coin, I'll pay you. Eight hundred mun to let her go."

The softness vanished from Falka's face, replaced by her familiar mocking sneer.

"If only this were about coin," she said. "If only it were so easy to make the past go away. You know, Jin, the princess's fiancé asked for something else besides his bride. Your head."

"*No.*" The soft gasp came from behind Falka. "I won't allow it."

Jin looked past Falka and met Yi-Nereen's eyes for the briefest of moments. A chill rushed through her; she was suddenly certain that Yi-Nereen was going to do something stupid, and there was nothing she could do to stop her.

A translucent blue wall bloomed in front of her. Buzzing filled the air and a familiar electric tingle raced across Jin's skin. Her mouth went dry. A split second shot by in stunned silence as Jin's brain sorted out what had just happened. Yi-Nereen had summoned a shield around herself, Faolin, Falka, and most of the raiders—and she'd left Jin outside it, along with the two women holding her.

One of the women released Jin and lunged forward, battering the shield with her fists. "Falka!"

*No.* Yi-Nereen had sealed herself and Faolin into a shield with half a dozen armed bandits and Jin's pissed-off ex-girlfriend. Rasvel's mercy, why would she do that? Falka would tear her apart. Then her shield would come down and they'd be back where they started, except the princess would be—

Something was wrong. Falka was stumbling around inside Yi-Nereen's shield like a bat in a closet. Why didn't she simply rush at the princess and overpower her?

Jin sucked in a breath. She saw it now: a deeper blue separating Yi-Nereen and Faolin from Falka and the raiders, an uncanny double shimmer to the air.

Yi-Nereen had done something Jin didn't even know was possible. She had summoned *two* shields at the same time, one inside the other, sealing herself and Faolin away from their enemies. It was a staggering display of power. How long could she keep it up?

"Get out of here, Jin!" The shield distorted Yi-Nereen's voice, but Jin could still make out the words, could still see Yi-Nereen's blurry figure on the other side. "Now! Get help. You can't protect me."

*Fuck no*, cried every inch of Jin, *I'm not leaving you.* She'd lost too many goddamn people in her life. She wouldn't abandon Yi-Nereen, not now, not when she was so close to bringing her and Kadrin together.

But what could she *do*? Convince Falka to see reason? Fight a half dozen battle-scarred raiders with her own bare hands? She was helpless. Useless. Just like always.

One of the raiders—a Rut-blood woman with a shaved head and eyes blackened with galena—still held Jin by the arm. The other was pounding on Yi-Nereen's shield. Jin sucked in a breath; her world narrowed. She was a kid again, weak but scrappy, and her tormentors were distracted. *Seize the opportunity. Take it and run.*

She twisted to the side, burned mana, and shot a shower of sparks into the Rut-blood woman's face. The woman screamed and stumbled back, dropping the weapon she held: a polearm ending in three spiky prongs, clearly intended for unseating sparkriders.

Jin snatched up the weapon just as the other raider whipped around to face her. This woman had a pierced lip and the copper-hued hair of a Lav-blood. Her eyes were wild with rage.

Jin didn't hesitate. *Cities have hundreds of laws, but the mana wastes know only one: survive, at any cost.*

She lunged forward. The trident slid into the raider's chest, impaled her like meat on a spit against Yi-Nereen's shield. The shield flickered where the triple points of the weapon dug in, but held. The raider coughed blood.

Inside the shield, Falka screamed a name. *"Ziyal!"*

No time to stop, to realize what she'd done. Not yet. A few paces away, the raider she'd blinded was doubled over in the dirt, cursing and clutching her eyes. Jin let go of the trident, left it embedded in the chest of the woman called Ziyal and turned away. Her gaze fell on one of the raiders' bikes. Her own was too far; she didn't have enough time. Yi-Nereen's shield could come down at any moment.

"What a *fucking* surprise," Falka said through the shield. Jin glanced back. Falka's eyes burned into hers from over the shoulder of the pinned, dying raider. "Jin-Lu, the brave courier, steals a magebike and rides to safety. You will never—" Her voice thinned and broke, but her stare was steady and white-hot.

"You will *never* stop running."

Jin straddled the raider's magebike. The handlebars were wrapped in something that looked disturbingly like human leather, and the bike's weight felt all kinds of wrong between her knees. Still, it was a bike, and that was all that mattered. She flexed her hands on the grips and looked at Falka.

"I'll come back," she said.

"Don't you dare—"

"I wasn't talking to you."

Jin breathed out, long and slow, and let her Talent burn. It scorched her insides and poured out of her fingers. The magebike roared to life. It was angry, this bike. It was battered and furious and it hated her, but she would make it obey.

She could hardly see Yi-Nereen through the dual walls of shimmering blue. But the shields were holding. They would have to hold as long as Yi-Nereen could stand it. Because Jin *was* coming back, and she wouldn't come alone.

No more broken promises.

Jin kicked off and tore away in a cloud of dust. The ruins blurred around her, transformed into familiar wasteland, vast and desolate. Unshed tears stung her eyes. Bile rose in her throat. She wanted to pull over and sob, vomit, anything to shed the burden of what she felt. But instead she burned mana, more and more, not just to feed the magebike's engine but to scour herself from the inside out. Her hands blistered on the grips, but still she rode.

Alone, she rode for Kerina Sol.

*Second Age of Storms, 49th Summer*

*Dear Reena,*
*You could never be a burden to me. Don't you remember how this all started? It was I who stepped readily into your life again, without knowing what it would be like or what kind of woman you had become. All I knew was I could never forget you, not if I lived for centuries. There is a bond between us stronger than any storm.*

*Someday, when the skies are fair and men are true, we shall meet again. A knight said that to me once. Hold that in your heart, Reena, and never forget it. It's my promise to you. For now I lack the power to fulfill it, but fortunately I'm not alone; I have my trusty courier at my side, and soon she shall be at yours. Let's meet in this world of ink and parchment, over and over again until we can conquer the leagues between us.*

*All my love,*
*Kadrin*

## CHAPTER SIXTEEN

# THE LAST BREATH

*Second Age of Storms, 51st Summer, Day 22*

F alka's throat ached. She'd been screaming, but she couldn't remember what. The last hour of her life was a crimson fog.

Jin-Lu, roaring out of sight, dust plumes settling in her wake.

The thrum of the princess's shield as Falka beat and slashed, to
no avail.

Mei-Lee whimpering on the other side, clutching her burned
eyes.

"Falka . . ."

Someone was saying her name, garbled and distorted. *Is this
happening now? Or is it a memory?* She felt like the dream world, or
wherever she went during her fugues, was trying to claw her back.
Words danced in the echoing cavern of her mind: *Disorientation.
Memory loss. Personality change.* Tibius Vann's words, before he'd
stolen her sanity and replaced it with Talent.

She'd survived his gods-damned procedure, and she'd swear up
and down to her freebooters that it had made her stronger, given
her what she'd always longed for: freedom. But a part of Falka knew
she had never been the same since. There were too many nights
she couldn't remember, mornings she'd woken with blood on her
hands. That was the price, Tibius had said, of dealing in souls.

"Falka."

She grasped for the present, pulled it closer. She was standing between two shimmering walls of force, caught between two shields. Princess Yi-Nereen was inside the inner dome. But the voice speaking Falka's name came from outside. It came from a blurry figure slumped against the wall of force, pinned by—it was hard for Falka to see from this angle—a trident.

She recognized that trident. It was Tusker's. But he was dead, wasn't he? He'd died earlier, trampled by the chandru in the canyon. Mei-Lee had taken his trident. But before Jin rode away, she'd grabbed it from Mei-Lee and . . .

*Ziyal.*

Clarity came gasping back. That was Ziyal pinned to the shield, her body pierced in triplicate. The earth at Falka's feet was soaked in blood that had seeped under the shield where it met the ground. That wet, choked voice from beyond the wall was Ziyal's.

Falka turned. The Rut-blood princess knelt only inches away, so close yet untouchable. Her eyes were closed; she wore an expression of deep concentration.

"Take down your fucking shield," Falka said. "Let me out of here so I can help her. Jin-Lu is long gone."

Yi-Nereen opened her eyes. For a moment she and Falka locked gazes; hatred shivered through Falka's blood. Then Yi-Nereen nodded. Falka's skin prickled with the rush of dissipating power as the outer shield collapsed—the inner remained intact. There was a *thump* behind her.

Ziyal lay on the ground, curled around the trident in her chest. Blood pounded in Falka's ears as she knelt.

"Let me see. Let me fucking see."

Ziyal hissed through clenched teeth, but she didn't resist as Falka pried her fingers away from the wound. One of the trident's blades had pierced her under the collarbone; the other two were in her ribs. The air was rank with blood-stench; a slippery layer coated everything—the dirt, Ziyal's chest, Falka's hands. Damn it all, the smell was making her dizzy, but she sank her nails into consciousness and held on.

She'd just lost Tusker. Fucker that he was, he was still one of hers. She wasn't going to lose Ziyal, too.

"Bandages," she barked at the freebooters who had crept cautiously around the shield to see what was happening. "Alcohol. Now!"

"Falka." Ziyal reached for her, dragged a bloody handprint down her shirt. Her eyes were bright and gleaming, her face drained of color. "Don't . . ." The word became a rattling sigh.

Someone pressed a bundle of cloth into Falka's hands.

"Hold on," Falka said. "I'm going to pull this out now. It'll hurt. Ziyal?"

*No,* said a tiny voice in her head, the voice of a child. *Don't leave me. Everyone leaves me.*

"*Ziyal. Ziyal!*"

Exhaustion soaked Yi-Nereen to her core. She knew the feeling well. Ever since childhood, this had been her lot in life: to stand on the Wall in a storm, flanked by her kin, her body nothing more than a conduit for her Talent. From her splayed fingers stretched a shimmering dome, an extension of her flesh. She felt the slashing blades and beating fists of the raiders as hot bursts of pain.

She would not yield. She never had.

Her eyes were closed, but she heard the cries of the raiders' leader. Falka, Jin had called her. They were awful cries, raw with grief and rage. Part of Yi-Nereen shuddered at the sound, but another part—her colder self—was removed, indifferent. *Raiders' lives are short. The life of any Talented is short. What a waste, to spend it on pain.*

The initial assault on her shield had already drained too much of her mana. It would take Jin more than a day to reach Kerina Sol and return, even if she found Kadrin and mustered aid right away. Yi-Nereen estimated she would last perhaps two more hours, if she didn't collapse from exhaustion first.

When she'd dropped the outer shield, she'd seen a window of opportunity flash by. Falka and her raiders had been distracted with the dying woman; they'd moved away from the inner shield. Though it was difficult and required great concentration, Yi-Nereen could walk without letting the barrier drop. If she'd coordinated with Faolin, the two of them could have stolen an unoccupied bike and followed Jin. But Faolin hadn't understood Yi-Nereen's urgent whispers and meaningful jerks of her head, not quickly enough.

Now the raiders surrounded them again. Yi-Nereen's barrier prevented them from drawing closer, but she would have to let it down momentarily to run to one of the magebikes—and after what Jin had done, the raiders would surely be swift to react.

It was hopeless. But Jin had gotten away. If that was the last and only good deed Yi-Nereen accomplished in her short life, at least it would give her succor in death.

"I'm sorry," she said to Faolin. The boy crouched at her side, clinging close and making himself as small as possible. "I couldn't save either of us."

She knew what fate awaited her: Falka would drag her back to

Sou-Zell, and either he or Yi-Nereen's family would punish her. Most likely the punishment would be death, and if it was not, Yi-Nereen would take matters into her own hands. She would not die the way her mother had.

But what did Falka have planned for Faolin? *The kid will make a nice bonus.* She wouldn't simply let him go.

Something nudged her elbow. Yi-Nereen opened her eyes and sucked in a breath. Faolin was holding a small glowing bottle; his hands were cupped around it like he was offering her a gift.

"Mana," he said.

Yi-Nereen looked down. Between them lay her open satchel, filled with bottles of preserved mana. The memory came rushing back; Jin had told her to stuff the bag with mana. *For the road.*

"Oh, Jin," Yi-Nereen breathed, her chest light. "I could kiss you again."

Jin was still two hours from Kerina Sol when she felt the bike shudder. "Piece of raider shit," she said, her voice lost in the wind. "Behave. We're almost there."

Her eyes stung; the wind had scoured her face numb. Once again she found herself roaring down the highway without a bone-helm, but not because it was swinging from her handlebars with a wounded pteropter inside. She'd left it at the temple with her mage-bike. And Faolin. And Yi-Nereen.

Her body still screamed at her to turn around. She was going the wrong way, riding away from people who needed her. Fleeing again. Why, why was this her life?

She'd made a stupid mistake, just like her father—she'd let someone in. More than once. It was clearly ingrained in her bones to screw up. Falling in love with Falka was almost excusable: she'd been a child, and Falka had saved her. But letting two royals steal their way into her heart over a bunch of stupid letters? That was a mistake only Jin could make. *Foolish Jin, who falls in love at the drop of a hat.*

She shouldn't have let it go on this long, should have told Kadrin to kick rocks and find another courier as soon as she started catching feelings. Before butterflies started churning in her stomach when she walked down the shaded avenue toward the House of Steel Heavens. Before she started seeing Yi-Nereen's lips and galena-lined eyes in her dreams. Before it was too damn late.

The magebike shuddered again. Then, without warning, the engine seized. Jin pushed sparks and got nothing in response, just the silence of a dead bike coasting on fumes.

*"Fuck."*

This wasn't happening. Not when every second mattered, when all she could do for Yi-Nereen was ride like the wind for Kerina Sol.

"You piece of *shit*—"

Then she hit something. A pothole, a rock, something she hadn't seen because her eyes were blurry with tears. The world lurched out of gear for one sickening second that stretched into infinity. She fought for control of the bike, evened out the handlebars, and brought it to a screeching, skidding halt.

Then it was just her, panting, straddling a dead bike under the vast blue of the wasteland sky. Stillness.

The bike wouldn't start again no matter what she did. It wasn't *her* bike, just a decrepit machine some asshole raider had tricked out with custom parts and ridden to the verge of death. She should have taken the risk and run for her own bike back at the temple.

Up in the cloudless sky, a dark shape circled and screeched. Jin shielded her eyes against the sun.

"What the fuck are *you* looking at?" she screamed at the wheeling pteropter. Her throat ached. Her hands were blistered. "You think I'm going to die out here? Go hassle someone else!"

She kicked over the dead bike and immediately regretted it. Now her foot hurt almost as much as her hands.

When she looked up, the blood in her veins turned to ice. The shimmery haze of the desert horizon had resolved into a line of dark shapes. Not magebikes—her brain automatically made the calculations. Based on the size of those shapes, it had to be a herd of chandru. Fully grown, massive, bone-crushing chandru . . . and they were headed this way.

If she had a working bike, she wouldn't give a toss. She'd be long gone before the herd reached her. But on foot, she was in real trouble. Even if chandru weren't predatory, they were unpredictable in herds and leery of smaller creatures. A stampede would kill her.

But what could she do? Nothing.

Screech was still circling above her. Yes, he'd definitely grown since the wastelanders had fixed his wing. It had been only a single day, but he looked twice as large as before, closer in size to the adult pteropters Jin had seen flying high above the wastes. She felt a prick of doubt that he really was the same pteropter—but then he screeched again, that earsplitting familiar call, and took wing toward the distant herd. She watched him fly away.

Limping, a sob caught in her throat, she started walking down the highway.

It was anyone's guess what would fail first: the mana or Yi-Nereen's strength.

She knelt on the ground, forearms crossed over her chest, hands flared. Thin streams of blue connected her fingertips to the dome that surrounded her. Faolin knelt before her, his forehead nearly touching hers. He still clutched the last bottle of mana from the satchel, as if holding on to the empty glass could make a difference. One by one, he'd tipped the bottles into Yi-Nereen's mouth, giving her the power to hold out another hour, another two hours.

Now they were gone. Faolin had spoken to her, his voice strained, but Yi-Nereen had nothing to say. She didn't understand him; they couldn't come up with a plan together. Talking would only drain her energy faster. Besides, there were no plans to discuss. She'd been casting for so long that if she tried to move from this spot, her concentration would fail and she'd lose her shield entirely.

Only one option remained, and she was trying not to think of it until she had to.

Her vision was fading slowly, the blue of her shield turning dull gray. She felt the sick tremble in her gut that heralded the last dregs of her mana. Yi-Nereen, First Daughter of the Tower of Arrested Stars and unquestionably the strongest shieldcaster of her generation, was at the very limit of her endurance.

"There's no point, you know."

Yi-Nereen opened her eyes. Falka sat on the other side of the shield, legs crossed. Her face was colorless beneath her tan, but her hands were red-brown with dried blood.

Yi-Nereen hadn't seen her in hours. She had taken the body of the dead raider away somewhere, leaving a pair of guards behind to watch Yi-Nereen.

"That shield won't last long enough for a rescue." Falka's smile reminded Yi-Nereen of a door ripped halfway off its hinges by a windstorm. "If a rescue is on its way. Which, if you know Jin-Lu at all, is quite the bold assumption."

Yi-Nereen said nothing. She wished she could close her ears to Falka's voice, take refuge in silence. Unfortunately she had little practice shutting out distractions. Yi-Nereen had once witnessed a guard hurl a messenger off the Wall for informing a shieldcaster that his wife had gone into labor. No one was allowed to disturb a shieldcaster during a storm.

"It isn't hard to win her over." Falka laid her hand against the shield, and Yi-Nereen resisted a shudder; she felt the woman's touch as if it were against her own skin. "But whether you use sweet words or cruelty, keeping her is another story."

*Shut up*, Yi-Nereen thought. *Stop talking.* Thoughts of Jin were a distraction she couldn't afford. Every part of her ached, not just from exhaustion but from regret. How long had she been telling herself that was all Jin was—first a diversion, then a way out of the Tower, but never anything more?

She kept silent. Perhaps that was all Falka wanted from her.

"She's one of the few with any freedom in this damned world. And that attracts parasites." Falka stroked a finger down the shield, smirking as if she knew exactly how it felt to Yi-Nereen. "I was one of them. Made a mess of things, though, and in the end she left me. Just like she's left you."

The pain in Yi-Nereen's stomach worsened. "Faolin," she whispered, hoping Falka couldn't hear her voice through the distortion of the shield. The boy's head snapped up, and his dark eyes found hers. He looked frightened, but as Yi-Nereen searched his face, his jaw tightened and he gave a small, determined nod—like he was ready to help, whatever she needed. Her heart twisted.

She'd known from the start there was only one way out. Going back to Kerina Rut would mean her death, one way or another. Surrendering wasn't an option.

The bottles had been a glimmer of hope, but they hadn't lasted long enough. She needed to either reduce the size of her shield or infuse more mana. If she abandoned Faolin outside the shield, Falka would probably torture him in front of Yi-Nereen to force her surrender. *She doesn't know I won't last much longer anyway.*

She'd told Jin there was mana in her blood—that she'd die without it. What she hadn't mentioned was that the last drop of mana in a Talented person's blood was the purest of them all. It was the spark of life, a single drop that contained more energy than a full infusion straight from a spring. The books in the Tower archives called it the Last Breath, and Yi-Nereen's grandfather had used it to almost singlehandedly shield the entire city during the Storm of Centuries. In the thirtieth hour of the storm, when the last conscious shieldcasters were nearing the point of collapse, he had summoned a dozen elders of the Low Talents—metalcrafters, stoneshapers, those the royals treated as labor and considered only slightly more valuable than the Talentless—and used them as human sacrifices. Drained them of their Last Breath and used it to wield a power so immense no one had equaled it since.

"Time's running out," Falka said softly. "Soon we'll be off to our next destination. I'll give you a hint—it isn't Kerina Rut. I may have taken your fiancé's coin, but I have no intention of bringing you back to him."

Yi-Nereen flinched. "What are you talking about?"

Falka pressed a finger to her curved lips. "Drop that shield of yours before you pass out, and I'll answer your questions."

Yi-Nereen's mind spun. Why would Falka double-cross Sou-Zell? She must intend Yi-Nereen for another buyer, someone who considered her more valuable than a runaway bride.

That didn't bode well. But would it be a fate worse than death?

Faolin was still looking at her, wide-eyed. He hadn't understood what Falka said or its implications. But he sensed Yi-Nereen's desperation and her waning strength. He put his hand on her knee and squeezed reassuringly. Yi-Nereen's breath caught.

"You don't know," she whispered, staring into his earnest eyes. "You don't know what I mean to do."

A memory struck her. Faolin hadn't been surprised by what she had done to Jin, had he? And now he was leaning slightly forward, chin tilted toward her, his posture open and innocent and willing—even though the faint tremble of his hand on Yi-Nereen's knee betrayed his fear.

For a split second, in the haze of her exhaustion, she saw a different face in place of his. A boy in a solarium at the top of a tower, pointing through the glass at a streak of light blazing across the sky. *Make a wish, Reena.*

*Kadrin.* An indescribable ache began in her chest and spread outward. If she failed here, she would never see him again, never know the man he'd become.

Faolin trusted her. Perhaps he would die either way, as soon as she lowered the shield. She could make it quick and gentle. Painless. There was no need to draw out the process of taking someone else's Last Breath. She had never done it before, never killed someone with her kiss and drawn forth the very essence of their life, but she had watched her father do it to a servant. *It is not a cost to be taken lightly,* he had told her afterward, *but it is fair. They could not live without us, and so we are only receiving our due. Remember that.*

Her vision swam so she could hardly see Faolin's face. She was losing feeling in her hands and feet, and her shield flickered around her, almost insubstantial. It was time. It was now or never.

Then she knew. In the final moment, she knew suddenly, with absolute certainty, that she couldn't do it. Never would. She could have sobbed from sheer relief.

*I am not a monster.*

Her shield faded, and the world dissolved into shadow.

# PART THREE

## CHAPTER SEVENTEEN

# GAMBLER'S FOLLY

*Second Age of Storms, 51st Summer, Day 23*

Sou-Zell stood on a bluff outside Kerina Rut, sweating under the midday sun. The city's walls were a glimmering metallic haze in the distance. A fabric canopy had been erected at the bluff's edge, and several servants stood beneath it, holding covered platters and urns of wine. A man in blue robes sat under the canopy, his chin pillowed in one palm, gazing out over the wastes.

The messenger who had brought Sou-Zell to the bluff bowed. "Shield Lord Lai-Dan," he announced, "Sou-Zell has arrived."

"Good, good," the royal said, without looking around. "Come and sit beside me, Sou-Zell. I arranged these seats to give us privacy, but we still have an excellent view."

Sou-Zell silently took a seat beside Lai-Dan, glad to enter the shade. Now he could see what lay below the bluff: a large oval-shaped dirt track. Shining metal shapes glistened in the sun, arrayed in a line along one short end of the oval. He should have guessed where he was being taken when Lai-Dan's messenger had led him outside the city; the Shield Lord had a well-known predilection for watching the magebike races. It was even rumored that the royal liked to place bets.

Sou-Zell had once imagined growing up to be one of the young knight hopefuls down below, racing for a chance to win riches and glory and the adulation of their peers. That was before he had learned his sparktalent was too weak to sustain a knight's duties: long patrols in the wasteland and maneuvers on armored warbikes. Before he had resigned himself to a career of blackmail and manipulation.

"Who do you favor this season?" Lai-Dan turned to Sou-Zell, smiling broadly. He had the same curiously light brown eyes and slanted cheekbones as his eldest daughter. While Yi-Nereen always seemed cold and remote, like a distant star, Lai-Dan had a way of seeming uncomfortably close. "Care to place a small wager?"

"I'm not familiar with this season's recruits. It would be foolish of me to stake coin on an outcome I have no means of predicting."

"Spoken like a mindreader." Lai-Dan chuckled. "There's no need to be nervous, my boy. I don't mean you any harm. You can even verify that for yourself, with that useful Talent of yours."

That was a trap if Sou-Zell had ever heard one. "I trust you implicitly, my lord."

"Good! The feeling is mutual, I assure you. That's why I was so comforted when I heard you hired someone to retrieve my daughter. I was sure you would only choose the best, which is why I saw no need to bring my own resources to bear. Until now, that is." The royal's eyes hungrily combed the ranks of assembled sparkriders below. The recruits had mounted their magebikes; standards fluttered from their handlebars, a different color for each competitor. "Well, though we haven't made any bets between ourselves, I'd like you to know I favor Green. I have an excellent feeling about him."

"Shield Lord," Sou-Zell said. "The . . . agent I hired may not have returned yet, but that doesn't mean they've failed. A storm passed between here and Kerina Sol shortly after your daughter left the city. She and the sparkrider who kidnapped her could have been forced to follow a different, longer route. It would explain the delay."

The royal waved his hand. "Many things are possible, Sou-Zell. Just as in gambling. It is left to a resourceful man to cover several possible outcomes, not only the one he favors most."

Sou-Zell forced a smile. "Have you bet on more than one rider?"

Lai-Dan chuckled. "I've bet on all of them. Just this morning I visited the knight-commander and brokered a deal. Ren-Vetaar shall dispatch a platoon of knights to fetch that troublesome daughter of mine from Kerina Sol."

A chill passed down Sou-Zell's spine. Below, the riders had begun their first circuit. Plumes of dust bloomed in their wake. Even from a distance, he heard the faint rumble of their engines and the roar of the assembled crowd.

"You'll risk war with the Sol-bloods, my lord." He swallowed his next words. *I did not think your daughter was so valuable to you. Will you truly go so far just to punish her?*

"The Sol-bloods would never be so foolish. They are cowards at heart. The Knights of Rut will persuade them it is in their best interest to return Kerina Rut's property, so we may all continue to enjoy the peace of these last few decades."

"I hope you are right."

There was nothing else Sou-Zell could say. It was Lai-Dan's right to do whatever he wished to bring back his daughter; she was still legally his property.

Lai-Dan leaned forward in his seat. The sparkrider flying the green standard had completed the first lap, a mere bike-length behind the leader of the pack, Orange. Sou-Zell hoped Orange would maintain his lead. It would be satisfying to see Lai-Dan's disappointment; he had never liked the man. Sou-Zell had spent his life immersed in the rumors that flowed through Kerina Rut like flood-water, and the currents surrounding the Lord of the Tower were dark indeed.

"Is there something else, my lord?" Sou-Zell prompted after the pause grew uncomfortably long.

Lai-Dan didn't take his eyes off the track. "There is no easy way to say this, my boy, but you will have to find yourself a new bride. Once I have recovered my daughter, I cannot in good conscience turn her over to you. I fear she would only bring your family shame."

Sou-Zell clenched his teeth. He didn't trust himself to respond right away.

None of this made any sense. Sou-Zell had expected Yi-Nereen's family to condemn her. He had prepared himself to fight for her life when she returned to Kerina Rut. He had planned to rely on her *difficulty*; surely pawning her off on Sou-Zell would be convenient for her family. But her father was claiming it as a reason to cancel their betrothal. Why? How could he possibly benefit?

Sou-Zell had been drawn to Yi-Nereen by the strength of her Talent. For the children she would bear, the last hope for his fam-ily's failing bloodline. Now he realized some small part of him had hoped for more. Though he had spoken to Yi-Nereen only on a handful of occasions, he had sensed her keen intelligence. She could have been more than his wife; she could have been a confidante and an ally.

Sou-Zell finally calmed enough to speak. "You are thoughtful and compassionate, my lord. But I remain willing to execute the marriage contract. Yi-Nereen can be brought back to Rasvel; my House and I will help her atone for her mistakes."

"A respectable statement." Lai-Dan clicked his tongue. "If I had anticipated your fortitude, perhaps I would have stayed the course. But I have made other arrangements for my daughter. Forgive me."

What did this blasted man *want*? Did he want Sou-Zell to beg? Surely these so-called other arrangements were a lie. No one else would take a disgraced runaway as a bride, unless they were as desperate as Sou-Zell.

Sou-Zell had never dared use his Talent on the Shield Lord. The consequences of being caught mindreading one of the most powerful men in Kerina Rut were too terrible to risk. But Lai-Dan was clearly distracted by the race going on below, especially with the green rider lagging behind his competitors. The Shield Lord had leaned forward, eyes fixed on the track.

Sou-Zell would never have an opportunity like this again.

He burned mana and brushed against Lai-Dan's mind. *Useless boy*, seethed the royal's thoughts. *I put twice as much coin on you as the other competitors, and why not? The odds were excellent. Your magebike is the latest in design, and you are twenty pounds lighter than any other rider.*

Damn it all, the man was a little *too* distracted. Sou-Zell would have to prod, as carefully as he could, and hope Lai-Dan didn't turn toward him; the color of his eyes would give him away. "Surely I deserve to know the name of my rival, my lord."

*Ah, if only I could tell him. How amusing his expression would be.* "So you can challenge him to a duel and kill him, or perish yourself? I think not, my boy. I know what young men are like—I used to be one myself."

*Yi-Nereen shall remain with her House, for good or ill. It was foolish to ever consider giving her away. After all, there is only one way to ensure a shieldtalented child, and that is for both parents to be shieldcasters. The stronger the better.*

Below, the green rider inched ahead of his competitors and roared across the finish line, victorious. Lai-Dan sighed in relief and turned to Sou-Zell, who swiftly extinguished his Talent, his heart thudding in his chest.

"In truth, you have no rival," Lai-Dan said. "Yi-Nereen will live in seclusion until the shame of her recent transgressions has been washed away by prayer and fasting. It may be years, even decades, and I cannot deny it will prove a drain on the Tower's resources—not to mention the matter of her lost bride price. But it is my responsibility as her father to repair her spiritual health and restore her grace in the eyes of Rasvel."

Lai-Dan was lying through his teeth. A moment ago, his thoughts had been consumed by Yi-Nereen's progeny—and now he claimed he wouldn't have her married for years?

It came to Sou-Zell in a frigid rush. Lai-Dan wasn't planning another marriage for Yi-Nereen. If her only suitable partner was another shieldtalented, generations of such matches had ensured there was only one place in Kerina Rut to find such a man.

The Tower itself. The ranks of Yi-Nereen's own family: her cousins, her brothers, her uncles . . . and her father.

"Such a pity," Lai-Dan exclaimed, oblivious to the nauseated grimace that no doubt twisted Sou-Zell's face. He was looking down at the track again. "If only the boy's odds had been worse, or I more decisive. I could have turned a far greater profit. But that's gambling for you, eh, Sou-Zell? The only way to know the outcome is to rig the game."

Sou-Zell stood. "If that's all, my lord, I must take my leave."

"Go and drown your sorrows however you must: wine, women, gambling. You have my blessing. And fear not—I won't spread news of your canceled betrothal to my daughter until her return to Kerina Rut. That should give you time to handle your affairs, which I trust you shall do with utmost aplomb."

Sou-Zell bowed stiffly. "Thank you."

He made it halfway down the bluff before he had to bend over and retch into the dirt. In the distance, the unseen crowd roared a mixture of delight and dismay. The game was finished, its winner decided. Shield Lord Lai-Dan had won his bet.

*Second Age of Storms, 50th Fall*

*Dear Kadrin,*

*I've been feeling much better lately. Thank you for continuing to ask after my health. In truth, I feel silly about how I behaved last year. There are times when all the world seems dark, with no way out, and I cannot recall what I know to be true: the shadow will pass.*

*Sometimes I take comfort in the stories my nursemaid used to tell me about a land beyond the mana wastes. The Green Kingdom, she called it. Do you have these tales in Kerina Sol? The funny thing is, the stories weren't all happy. Many of them were sad, like the tale of Queen Kevelyan's exile from the Green Kingdom and the thirty days she spent wandering the mana wastes until she died, alone but still proud. Yet somehow, remembering them comforts me; I cannot say why. Perhaps because they were beautiful, and beauty has always mattered more to me than joy.*

*If you recall any stories from your childhood, I would like nothing more than to hear them. I have already asked our courier, but getting her to talk about herself is like pulling fingernails. (Guilty.)*

*Wistfully,*
*Reena*

# CHAPTER EIGHTEEN

# THE THIRD SON

*Second Age of Storms, 51st Summer, Day 23*

Kadrin leaped backward, dodging the blade that swept within inches of his chest. The near miss sent a thrill pumping through his blood. He retreated another body length, giving himself some room, and flicked his blade from side to side, looking for an opening. There was none, of course. Old Merkla had gone back on the defensive, and her guard was nigh impenetrable. He'd have to create his own opportunity with a feint.

The moment he shifted his weight forward, Merkla moved. The tip of her blade met Kadrin's shoulder. Kadrin yelped, from surprise rather than pain—the thick jacket he wore dulled the blow—and abandoned his lunge with a disappointed groan. There was no point following through; Merkla had won the bout.

"That's match," Merkla said. Her rasping voice was dispassionate and perfectly level, as if she'd expended no energy at all whipping Kadrin into shape. In fact, as she removed her fencing mask, Kadrin saw that not a single strand of hair had escaped from her gray bun. *Show-off.*

"You could at least . . . pretend I'm making . . . progress," Kadrin wheezed, yanking off his own mask and wiping an embarrassing amount of sweat from his forehead. "My ego could use a break from these beatings. So could my body."

"You complained your previous instructors were too easy on you." Merkla stalked away from Kadrin and placed her weapon on a bench across the courtyard. "I thought you wanted a beating every now and then. Was I wrong?"

"No," Kadrin admitted, unbuckling his gauntlet. "I need the distraction."

His mind, undisciplined as always, wandered to the very person he needed distraction from. He could still smell the perfume that clung to each of Yi-Nereen's letters, rosewater and sandalwood. No matter how much sweating he did, he couldn't rid himself of that maddening bouquet. Normal days were difficult enough; Kadrin sometimes felt like he spent most of his existence in hibernation, a snake waiting for glimpses of the sun. But the days leading up to a new letter were the worst of all. Anticipation consumed his every waking moment. He kept glancing restlessly at doors and down hallways, as if he might be able to call forth a servant with news of Jin's arrival by the force of his will. Only bouts with Merkla forced him to focus on something else entirely—until she tired of thrashing him and called the session to an end.

Kadrin twisted the ring on his left hand and took a deep breath, trying to stave off the familiar anxiety. *Just a little longer.*

"I suppose your letter hasn't arrived yet," Merkla said. She was dabbing her face with a handkerchief, drying invisible drops of sweat. Like always, Kadrin's gaze was drawn to the scar that marred the right side of her face; it crossed directly over her eye and left her with one pupil permanently constricted. To Merkla's credit, the old injury never interfered with her ability to give the most judgmental stares Kadrin had ever seen, one of which was aimed at him now.

"No." Kadrin sighed and sank onto the bench beside his doffed jacket. Eliesen would have called it a theatrical flop, and Jin would have agreed. "My courier was due back yesterday. She must be delayed. Or perhaps she's working up the courage to deliver the news that Yi-Nereen never wants to hear from me again."

Merkla scoffed loudly. "Spare me the dramatics, Highness. I'm too old to nod sympathetically and feign interest." She stomped past him, pausing only to deliver a half-hearted pat to Kadrin's damp shoulder. "See you tomorrow."

Then she walked through an archway and out of sight, leaving Kadrin alone in the courtyard. Vines wound around the pillars above his head, rustling in the breeze. Somewhere nearby, a bird cooed. Kadrin rubbed the growing bruise on his shoulder. Suddenly all he could think of was the seconds rushing by like leaves on a strong wind, refusing to slow down.

The passage of time was a sword with two edges. Every moment drew him nearer to the next letter, the only spark in his tedious existence, but every moment was one less he might spend with Yi-Nereen if they ever met.

*Once* they met.

At least Jin would be here soon. Perhaps he could convince her to stay awhile. She would never agree to dine with Kadrin's family, had always flatly turned down the barest hint of an invitation, but on occasion he'd managed to wheedle her into staying for tea. Kadrin brightened at the thought. Yes, tea would be perfect. He could show Jin the new tea set he had commissioned from a potter in the Jade District. The saucers were painted to look like magebike gears, which might even coax a smile out of his stone-faced courier.

Kadrin made his way into the cool, shaded interior of the House. A servant hurried toward him; Kadrin's heart leaped into his throat.

"Has Jin arrived?" he demanded before the boy could speak. Then he winced. "Sorry, Wexler, how are you? Is your hand better?"

The boy held up a bandaged hand, a rueful smile on his face. "It's healing, Highness. Thanks for asking. Sorry to disappoint, but your courier hasn't arrived yet. It's your father. He wants to see you in his study."

"Oh." Kadrin forced a smile. "I'll be there as soon as I've washed up. Thanks, Wexler."

Half an hour later, he stood before the door to his father's study, bracing himself to knock. He wasn't *afraid* to see his father. Fear implied that his father had done something to provoke it, and the blame for Kadrin's inadequacies lay squarely on his own shoulders.

Kadrin knocked.

"Come in," came his father's voice from inside.

In his earliest memories, Kadrin was a child clinging to the edge of his father's desk, surrounded by bookcases so tall they might as well have been lofty trees heavy with the fruit of knowledge. Now he stood among bookcases and trophy cabinets that still dwarfed him, though he'd grown taller than his own father. It was the sheer weight of everything on those shelves that made Kadrin feel so small. All those words, containing the entire history of his House. All of it inaccessible to him.

Somewhere in his hazy boyhood lurked a memory of his father scolding him for misplacing a book of fairy tales from these very shelves. Kadrin hadn't lost the book. He had borrowed it, slipped it under his pillow, and was reading as much as he could every night. But admitting how much he struggled to understand a text for children felt worse than falsely confessing to losing track of the book. So confess he had. He'd assumed it would be easier to bear his father's anger than the shame of everyone knowing the truth: that Kadrin was incurably stupid.

He'd been right, but that didn't make the punishment easier to swallow. His father had banned him from ever borrowing books from the study again.

"Good afternoon, Father."

Rain Lord Matrios, Ruler of the House of Steel Heavens, glanced up from the scroll lying open across his desk. He was not a large man, but he moved like he was: slow and ponderous, every gesture filled with gravitas.

"Kadrin. There you are. You'll be coming with me to the Council meeting tomorrow."

Kadrin blinked. That was his father's way: to get straight to the point, without context or social niceties. Some time ago, Kadrin had realized his father's bluntness was a political tactic, meant to throw his rivals off their guard. It worked just as well on his own family.

"I will?"

He'd never been to a Council meeting before. Nor had he expected that to change. When one was the Talentless third son of a royal, with two older brothers jousting for influence and clout, one became accustomed to being overlooked.

"Tomorrow morning," his father said. "We'll leave for the Council chambers after breakfast."

"I . . . see."

Kadrin did not see. If any hints of this development had been dangled before him recently, he'd missed them. Why should he have paid attention? Usually the gears of Kerina Sol's political machinery, including the Rain Lord's affairs, were perfectly happy to keep turning without Kadrin's input.

He cleared his throat tentatively. "What do you need me at the Council meeting for, Father?"

Rain Lord Matrios's eyes flicked up to meet his. "It's time you took on more responsibilities to this House, Kadrin. Devros and Satriu have been attending Council meetings for several years now. Their contributions have even been valuable, on occasion."

*Several years?* Sometimes Kadrin's father could be uncharacteristically oblique. Kadrin was certain his oldest brother, Devros, had been around fifteen when he first attended a Council meeting. Devros was thirty now and had children of his own. Until today, it wouldn't have surprised Kadrin if his baby niece attended her first Council meeting before Kadrin did.

He chose his next question carefully. "What contributions do you expect from me, specifically?"

His father frowned at the scroll on his desk. "At the moment? The stenographer is on leave, and I've been asked to supply a replacement. It occurred to me that this would be a prime opportunity to introduce you to Council affairs."

The bottom fell out of Kadrin's stomach. *Stenographer.* The word replayed over and over in his head, like one of those talking birds at the street fair. He imagined himself sitting in the Council chambers, sweating over a blank page as the royals chattered all around him, their words fading into obscurity as Kadrin's trembling hand refused to pen a single character.

It couldn't be real; his father had to be pulling a prank on him. Never mind Kadrin would sooner expect Yi-Nereen to come crashing through the wall on a magebike than his father to crack a joke.

As Kadrin stood rooted to the spot, Rain Lord Matrios crossed his arms over his chest and sighed. "No need to look so distraught. Be thankful I haven't asked you to collate and present storm patterns from the last twenty years. That was Satriu's first Council assignment."

"I don't think I'm suited to taking notes, Father." Kadrin's mouth was dry. He couldn't shake the feeling of being a boy again, scolded for losing track of a book.

"I'm surprised to hear you say that," his father said, one eyebrow ever so slightly tilted upward. "You've written so many letters to that Rut-blood princess over the past three years, I assumed this assignment would be perfect. Do you think it's beneath you?"

"I—" Kadrin struggled to form words. His thoughts were all in competition, clamoring to come out first. *Jin writes those letters, not me. I didn't know you'd even noticed I was sending them. Is that why some have gone missing? Her name is Yi-Nereen, not "that Rut-blood princess." I don't think any sort of work is beneath anyone, especially me.*

His father waited for several agonizing seconds before sighing and picking up his brush. "I hadn't realized this would be a point of contention. I'll take Eliesen to the meeting tomorrow, and you can join your siblings on the Council sometime in the future. When you're ready."

It was a clear dismissal. Kadrin swallowed back a lump in his throat. His voice, when it came, was little more than a whisper. "Thank you, Father. I'll let you know."

He turned and left the study. Only in the safety of the corridor, with the thick wooden door shut behind him, did he press a fist to his mouth and take a long, shuddering breath.

If by some miracle Yi-Nereen ever came to Kerina Sol, how long would it take her to grow tired of him? Perhaps she could look past his Talentlessness, but not his idiocy. He was forever a child, the same boy who'd lied about losing a book. It would never change until he found a way to make himself useful.

Kadrin forced himself to move. He walked down the corridor,

quickening his steps until he was nearly jogging. If only Merkla hadn't left for the day. He needed to get his blood pumping, exhaust himself enough to fall into a deep sleep. He'd have to go for a run along the Wall to clear his head.

He wouldn't think about the Council or his father. He definitely wouldn't compare himself to Devros and Satriu for the ten-thousandth time and wonder what in the heavens had gone wrong. Under no circumstances would he consider, even fleetingly, that the only reason Yi-Nereen replied to his letters was because she pitied him.

*Empty your thoughts. This shouldn't be hard for you.*

Kadrin flung open the front door to the House and nearly barreled over someone standing outside, their hand raised to knock. "Sorry!" he said out of reflex. He was four steps past the threshold when he heard a familiar voice from behind him.

"Kadrin?"

Kadrin whirled around. All the thoughts he'd been struggling in vain to silence vanished abruptly from his head. "Jin?"

His courier stood there, swaying on the spot. Her short dark hair was caked with road dust; her eyes were hollow and exhausted. The front of her jacket was stained with something that looked suspiciously like blood. As Kadrin stared in horror, she opened her mouth to speak, but no sound emerged.

He took a step toward her and, without thinking, reached for her hands. She yanked away from him with a dull hiss. Stupid, stupid—he'd never touched her before; what was he doing now? Something caught his eye as she cradled the hand he'd touched: raised blisters in angry red across her palm, like she'd been gripping a scalding-hot teacup.

Jin's mouth worked. "Yi-Nereen," she said. "She needs our help, Kadrin. But we're too late. I—"

Her eyelashes fluttered, and this time Kadrin *really* didn't think. He stepped forward just in time to catch Jin as she crumpled into his arms. He hooked an arm under Jin's knees and cradled her. She was lighter than he'd imagined. The sharp musk of sweat, mixed with blood and the faint, sickening stench of burnt flesh, overwhelmed him—then the words she had just spoken sank in.

Yi-Nereen needed them.

And they were already too late.

*Second Age of Storms, 50th Fall*

*Dearest Reena,*
*I have always considered joy and beauty to be inseparable companions.*
*Everything beautiful brings me joy, and whatever brings me joy is*
*unfailingly beautiful. Then again, I never liked listening to sad stories.*
*What's the point of a tale where the hero doesn't triumph in the end?*
*It's just as you said, Reena. Everything is a temporary darkness. We*
*shall all get our happy ending with time.*

*My favorite childhood tale was the story of the Lost Highway. Do*
*they tell that one in Kerina Rut? Anyone who is born in the mana*
*wastes can never leave, except by the Lost Highway. It's a secret road a*
*person can only discover if they aren't looking for it, and they can only*
*travel to its end if they are pure of heart. Along the way, all the sins of*
*their ancestors will be washed away, allowing them to reach heaven.*

*When I was little, I vowed that I would someday find the Lost*
*Highway and take everyone I loved with me to heaven. You see the*
*problem, don't you? By making that vow, I nixed my chances of ever*
*stumbling across the Lost Highway. Ah well. Asking everyone I know*
*to remain pure of heart just in case I find a magical lost road to heaven*
*would make me a nuisance, I'm sure.*

*Besides, the tales aren't clear on what it means to be pure of heart.*
*If it means one cannot have ever stolen into the kitchens after curfew*
*and pocketed a custard bun to eat under the covers, I'm out of luck*
*several times over.*

*At your service, now and always,*
*Kadrin*

## CHAPTER NINETEEN

# A MOMENT TO BREATHE

*Second Age of Storms, 51st Summer, Day 23*

Moments ago, Jin had stood before the beautifully engraved doors to the House of Steel Heavens, struggling against a wave of fatigue to raise her arm and knock. Then the door had opened as if by magic—and there was Kadrin, like a hero out of a fairy tale, damp curly hair flouncing over one eye and a fresh bruise blooming on one exposed shoulder. He'd promptly spoiled that impression by rushing past Jin without a glance.

After that, she remembered nothing. Now she was weightless, gliding through the air as the blurred walls of the House's foyer flew past. Someone was carrying her. Normally this would be cause for concern, but all she felt was an overwhelming and unfamiliar sense of safety.

Soon she was lying on a divan amid a chorus of surprised voices. One was familiar; any tranquility Jin had felt vanished. She summoned all her strength to croak, "Eomma?"

The room swam into focus. It was a small parlor Jin recognized; she liked this room for its lack of grandeur, compared with the rest of the House. Her gaze focused on the painting above the sofa: a wasteland landscape. In a fit of surreal optimism, the artist had painted flowers growing along the highway.

Eomma stepped in front of the painting. She was dressed in her best: a long, beaded blue dress, a sunshine-yellow sash, and gold-plated earrings that flashed when she turned her head. Jin remembered wrapping those earrings carefully in a scarf and tucking them into her saddlebags the night she and Eomma had fled Kerina Tez. She hadn't seen her mother wear them in over a decade. Not since her father died.

"I'm sure she isn't badly hurt, Mistress Evemi," Kadrin was saying. "She managed to walk here, didn't she?"

"But what happened?" Eomma sounded near tears. "Jin, sweetheart, talk to me."

"A strong drink might revive her," spoke another crisp male voice.

Renfir, the House's majordomo. At least *his* presence made sense, though it was hardly comforting. He'd made his distaste for Jin and her profession plain since the day she'd first stepped into the House and accidentally flicked mana-cig ash onto the foyer tiles.

"Something for you as well, my dear?" Renfir went on.

*My dear?*

"Please," said Eomma. "Absinthe, if you have it. Thank you, Renfir."

*I'm definitely dreaming.* Jin let her eyes drift closed as she felt Eomma's soft palm against her forehead. She was loath to admit it, but being fussed over wasn't altogether unpleasant. A courier's life was lonely and thankless: long days in the saddle and the harshness of wind and sand. The last time she'd felt someone else's soothing touch was in Kerina Rut, when—

*Yi-Nereen.* Jin raised herself, groaning, into a half-sitting position. "Reena's in trouble."

Reena. The name rolled off her tongue like she'd been saying it all her life. Had Kadrin noticed? He leaned forward, eyes wide.

"What kind of trouble? Can't the Knights of Rut help?"

"She isn't in Kerina Rut anymore. She—" Damn it, she didn't have time to explain everything. "We were on our way here, together. But raiders cornered us. They were sent by Yi-Nereen's fiancé, Sou-Zell."

"Her fiancé?" Kadrin looked as if she'd struck him in the face. "I—I didn't know she was betrothed."

Jin barked out a laugh. "That's the least of our troubles." *Our.* There she went again. "Yi-Nereen bought me enough time to get away. But . . . the bike broke down, and I had to come the rest of the way on foot."

When she'd seen that chandru herd approaching, she'd been sure that was the end. But after Screech had flown off, the herd had changed direction—almost as if the pteropter had warned them away, as far-fetched as that sounded. She hadn't seen him or the chandru again.

After that, it had been a long, long walk to Kerina Sol. Dizzy and dry-mouthed from the heat, with no breath to spare, she'd silently brought down a thousand curses on her own head.

It was her fault the bike had broken down. If she hadn't ridden it like a fiend, roaring desperately away from Falka and her past mistakes . . .

*If I'd kept my promise in Kerina Tez, if I hadn't left Falka behind, none of this would have happened.* Sou-Zell might have sent another hunter after her, but no one except Falka would have been stubborn enough to track them through a storm. Fate had thrown them back together, to make Jin atone for her greatest failure.

"On foot? You could have been killed." Eomma collapsed next to Jin on the divan and threw her arms around her. Jin let herself relax into her mother's embrace, just for a moment. Eomma smelled like warm dough and confectioner's sugar, a scent at odds with the rest of Jin's life: leather and smoke and wasteland grit.

Jin pulled away. "Eomma, what are you doing here?"

Eomma smiled nervously and darted a glance at Kadrin. Jin stared at the prince, who averted his eyes. A slow suspicion wormed through her belly.

"Kadrin, this isn't the first time you've met my mother, is it?"

Kadrin gave a small, strained chuckle. "Is that important?"

"Have you—have you been *meeting* with her? To talk about me?" The guilty glance the two exchanged was confirmation enough. Jin's fingers curled reflexively. "What gives you the right?"

Kadrin raised his hands as if to shield himself. "I can see how it might strike you as improper—"

"*Improper?* How about a complete violation of privacy—"

"—but you never want to talk about yourself, Jin, or tell me anything about your life, and we've been friends for three years now—"

"We aren't friends," Jin snapped. "I work for you. That's all."

In the frosty silence that followed, she despised herself. She couldn't look at Kadrin. Instead she looked at her mother, who was wringing her hands in her lap.

Eomma hesitated, then said softly, "Jin, this isn't Kerina Tez."

She must have thought Jin was punishing Kadrin for what another charming, smooth-tongued prince had once done to her father, in another city hundreds of miles away. A few years ago, Eomma would have been right. Jin had spent her adolescence loathing royals and their offspring. She'd feared Kadrin, hated him for making her fear him—but only at first.

She'd quickly realized he was different. A Talentless prince whose family treated him like a vase placed carefully on a shelf and never touched for fear he might break. An impossibly gentle man whose every emotion shone like candlelight through paper, who so little understood cruelty that when he dropped a teacup and apologized, Jin wasn't sure if he was addressing her or the broken shards of ceramic.

Then Jin had kept her distance for a new, more frightening reason. It was easy to conceal her affection for Yi-Nereen, but Kadrin had a way of bringing down her guard. The more she revealed of herself, the harder it would be to hide how she felt.

And she *must* hide it, at all costs. Kadrin belonged to another, as did Yi-Nereen, and they had trusted Jin with every intimacy of their relationship. She had no right to put herself between them.

Jin risked a glance at Kadrin. He was staring at his hands, clearly trying to remain composed—and failing. Everything he felt always showed plainly on his face. Pain. Surprise. Regret.

Jin rose unsteadily to her feet. The beaded curtain hanging in the doorway clinked, and Renfir stepped into the parlor, bearing a tray. Jin took the cup he offered with uncommon gratitude. The absinthe stung her chapped lips, slid down her throat like a fiery snake, and coiled in her belly.

She lowered the cup and thought she saw Renfir smile at Eomma—then the smile was gone, replaced by the majordomo's usual expression of calm disapproval. *Must be imagining things.*

The absinthe did revive her. The numb hollowness of despair retreated, and Jin's pulse picked up again. There had to be some way to save Yi-Nereen.

"Kadrin, listen to me. As powerful as Yi-Nereen is, she couldn't have kept up a shield for this long. The raiders must have taken her back to Kerina Rut."

Kadrin raised his gaze from his hands. His eyes were duller than Jin had ever seen them. "Then she's lost to us," he said. "Her family will lock her away until she's married. And they'll certainly never let her send another letter."

"It's worse than that." Jin wanted to grab Kadrin and shake him back into his usual self. "When she decided to escape, it meant she couldn't ever go back. Or her family would kill her."

Eomma let out a small, pained cry. "That poor girl."

Jin almost moved to comfort her but stopped short when Renfir—*Renfir*, of all people—carefully placed the tray he was holding on a side table and put his hand on Eomma's shoulder.

*What in Rasvel's name is going on with those two?*

"Kill her?" Kadrin's voice was raw. "I can't imagine—I know the traditions in Kerina Rut are harsh, but her own *family*?"

Jin drained the rest of her absinthe in a scalding rush and slammed the glass down on the table, where it promptly shattered. She hardly felt the ceramic shards bite into her flesh; the burns had numbed her. Eomma gasped.

"Don't." Jin's voice throbbed with anger. "You have no idea what Kerina Rut is like. What her life is like. All you have is whatever fantasy you've spun for yourself—that she's a princess locked in a tower by her strict but well-meaning relatives. With all due respect, Your Highness, *grow up*. The world isn't a fairy tale."

She knew her words would cut deeper than the fragments of the broken cup. But she had to make Kadrin understand.

"If you care about her—if you love her—then you'll keep your promises and do everything in your power to save her. If you won't, at least give me a magebike so I can go back to Kerina Rut myself."

"Don't be absurd," Kadrin said, his face pale. "You'll be killed on sight."

Jin let out what could best be described as a snarl. Sparks flew from her blistered fingers and scattered over the tiled floor. "Do I look like I care?"

"Madam!" Renfir adjusted his spectacles and glared at Jin. "You will kindly refrain from setting fire to this House and frightening your poor mother. You will address Prince Kadrin in a manner befitting—"

"Never mind that, Renfir," Kadrin said. He rose from the sofa, shoulders squared. "Go ahead and set fire to the furniture, Jin; I'm sure there's someone down the hallway who can put it out. Anyway, you're right. I've been useless. But that ends now. I'm going to talk to my father and secure aid from the Knights of Sol."

Jin sucked in a breath. She wanted nothing more than to hop on her magebike and scatter her regrets in the wasteland. Instead she said curtly, "Well, good."

"I'll go now." Kadrin shifted his weight uncomfortably. He clearly didn't relish the prospect of asking his father for a favor. "Wait here, please, ladies. Renfir, would you fetch them more refreshments? This could be a while."

Renfir bowed and left the room. So did Kadrin, after casting a last glance at Jin over his shoulder. Jin collapsed on the sofa and let her eyes flutter shut. The thrill of shouting in a prince's face had faded; now she felt like the discarded skin of a snake. At least, she thought bitterly, she had managed to hide her feelings for Kadrin just now. In fact, she might have convinced him she didn't even *like* him.

The couch shifted as her mother sat beside her. "Oh, Jin," Eomma sighed. "Your poor hands. What happened to your gloves?"

Jin opened one eye. "Is Renfir courting you?"

To her credit, Eomma didn't blush. She looked down at her lap with a small, melancholy smile. "I'm courting *him*, dear. Prince Kadrin only asked to meet with me a few times, over a year ago. I met Renfir on one of those visits and found myself utterly charmed."

Jin let out a scoff before she could stop herself. She cleared her throat and avoided Eomma's gaze. "It's been going on for a year, and you didn't tell me?"

She'd solved an old mystery: about a year ago, when Renfir must have met her mother, the frequency of his judgmental stares had plummeted. He'd even stopped following Jin around with an ashtray whenever she visited the House. Mostly.

"I'm sorry, sweetheart. I would have told you eventually. Prince Kadrin asked me not to mention our meetings, which made matters difficult. He's such a nice boy. I didn't want to cause him any trouble." Eomma's tone was patient and reasonable, which only made Jin feel worse. "Renfir is quite a different man from your father. But I think that's exactly what I need. I'm too old for any more dashing outlaws."

Jin peeked at her mother. "I'm sort of a dashing outlaw myself now, you know."

Eomma's laugh was warm and musical. "You're Gao-Jin's daughter, make no mistake. But you're my daughter, too." She took Jin's hand gently and stroked her knuckles. "I know you're content out there, risking your life every day, but . . ." Tears welled in Eomma's eyes. "You can't be alone all the time, Jin-Lu. I would sleep soundly at night if you found someone to look after you."

"Don't worry about me." Jin grasped her mother's hand and squeezed, ignoring the pain that seared across her palm. "We can't worry about each other all the time. One of us has to be happy."

Eomma sighed. "Don't you think you deserve happiness, Jin?"

Jin didn't answer.

Renfir came and went with a platter of steamed buns stuffed

with chicken, which Jin readily devoured; her hunger almost equaled her impatience. Eomma got up and held a quiet conversation with the majordomo in the corridor. Jin was nearly restless enough to eavesdrop, but she felt a headache coming on and dug through her pockets for a mana-cig before remembering she'd left them in her saddlebags. It was a full hour before the beaded curtain twitched and Kadrin stepped back into the room.

The prince's eyes were shadowed, and he wore his displeasure plainly in the purse of his lips. Jin's stomach swooped.

"What did your father say?"

"He won't petition the Council on my behalf." Kadrin's voice was flat and slightly hoarse. *Like he's been shouting.* "There's a Council meeting tomorrow morning. I wasn't going to attend, but plans change."

"You think the Council can save Reena?"

"I don't know." Kadrin pressed a hand to his eyes. "But they're all we have."

*Second Age of Storms, 50th Fall*

*Dear Kadrin,*
*How different our childhoods must have been. My nursemaid had tales of*
*the Lost Highway, but hers were far more practical than yours. No heroes*
*pure of heart, just an ancient highway hidden by the Road Builders, which*
*led to a treasure trove full of riches both material and technological. She*
*never mentioned how one could find this highway. I suppose it wasn't*
*relevant, since as far as she was concerned, I would never leave Kerina Rut.*

*Truth be told, I have always resented hearing those stories, because*
*they made me ache so keenly for what I would never have—what has*
*been lost to us all. The time before there was a wasteland, when all the*
*world was green.*

*I'm growing melancholy again, aren't I? Let's see . . . I've been*
*thinking about what you said, about beautiful things bringing you joy.*
*I've tried making a list of things that are beautiful about my life. Here's*
*what I have so far:*

mist on the spring at dawn
distant harpsichord music floating through the Tower windows
the way a pot of fresh ink smells when you mix in a little dried rose petal
a smile on a friendly face

*I've come to realize the things I find beautiful are never things of my*
*own making. They are wrought by others' hands or the work of nature*
*itself. Perhaps that is a sign I should invest more effort into creating*
*beauty, instead of relying on others to show it to me.*

*With sincere affection,*
*Reena*

# CHAPTER TWENTY

# THE NATURE OF TALENT

*Second Age of Storms, 51st Summer, Day 23*

Yi-Nereen awoke to a chemical stench and the sensation of movement. She opened her eyes, nausea roiling in her stomach, and cringed; a bright light was shining into her face.

*Where am I?*

Engines rumbled ahead and behind. The stench was magebike exhaust, she realized, and the light came from a bike's headlamp. She was doubled over, stuffed inside an iron cage—a livestock trailer pulled behind a bike through a dark tunnel. A livestock trailer! As if she were a chicken or a calf.

Her first thought was for her satchel and the precious research within it. After a moment of panic, she found it with her in the trailer, wedged against her side. Then—to her shame—she thought of Faolin. Where was he? She could hardly see a thing. But she didn't have long to wonder; the cavalcade was slowing to a halt. Yi-Nereen closed her eyes and feigned unconsciousness as the magebikes' idling engines chugged and growled. Then something jabbed her side between the bars of the cage. Yi-Nereen yelped, her eyes flying open.

Falka grinned at her. "I hope the accommodations are to your liking, Highness. It's no perfumed bower, but those are in short supply in the wastes. Care to join me on a stroll?"

Yi-Nereen steeled herself. "I'll do nothing of the sort. Not until you tell me where we are."

"Do you think I'm afraid to lay a finger on you? You already know I'm not bringing you back to your fiancé, so there's no need to keep the goods intact." Falka cocked her head. "Perhaps I should leave you down here, alone in the pitch dark, until you come to your senses. Time is no object; no one is coming to your rescue. I've sealed the way behind us."

Before she could stop herself, Yi-Nereen envisioned Falka's threat: sitting helpless and alone in a cage in the dark, unable to straighten her legs or her spine, listening to the drip of moisture and the skitter of small clawed feet. The child within her quailed. *Not the cellar. Anywhere but there. I'll obey, Father.*

Falka unlocked the cage and swung open the door. Yi-Nereen paused only to sling her satchel over her shoulder before she crawled out and stood, stretching her stiff muscles. Her involuntary nap had restored some of her energy, but she still felt light-headed and weak. If she didn't infuse soon, she would likely pass out again.

Farther down the line of parked magebikes, she saw another raider freeing Faolin from a second trailer. The boy had only a moment to stretch before the raider forced his hands behind his back.

"He's just a child," Yi-Nereen said.

"And a sparkrider," Falka said. "Can't risk him stealing a bike and riding off, can we?"

Yi-Nereen ground her teeth. "He won't run."

Falka laughed, harsh and brittle. "You think he won't leave you? Still think Jin is coming back, too? You're too trusting, Highness. These aren't your subjects; they owe you no fealty."

*No,* Yi-Nereen corrected her silently. *He won't leave because you're the one who kidnapped his sister.*

The tunnel around them was clearly man-made. The floor was cracked in places but perfectly level, and black as tar. Ahead, the tunnel ended in a large, round door; instead of a handle, an odd wheel-shaped mechanism protruded from the center. Yi-Nereen watched two raiders sweat and strain to turn the wheel, until the entire door rolled away into the wall with a grinding *clunk-clunk*. Beyond lay a small empty chamber.

Yi-Nereen caught Faolin's eye. The boy looked exhausted and grubby; a bruise darkened his cheek, yet he smiled at her when their eyes met. She wondered if he'd fought back against their captors. It would have been a foolhardy, pointless thing to do, but Yi-Nereen couldn't fault him for it. She returned a smile imbued with all the confidence she could muster. *I'll find us a way out of here.*

Where *were* they? Yi-Nereen had been unconscious, so she had no idea how far they'd come, or if the entire journey had been underground. Part of her longed for the safe, familiar walls of the Tower, but she tamped down the feeling. There was no going home—only death or worse awaited her in Kerina Rut.

"I'll take you up first," Falka said. "It's quite a view."

Yi-Nereen had no choice but to follow Falka into the small chamber beyond the rolling door. It wasn't a chamber, she realized, but a shaft extending upward into the darkness. How would they ascend? She saw no ladder, only another metallic sconce on the wall, like the ones Faolin had used to light the temple.

Falka reached out, and blue sparks jumped from her hand to the sconce. It glowed, and Yi-Nereen felt the floor shift beneath them. She yelped and pressed herself against the wall, only to find it moving as well, grinding downward toward the floor.

No, the wall wasn't moving. *She* was. The sconce rose with the platform, illuminating the shaft above in blue light.

"Impossible," Yi-Nereen said.

"A question for you, Highness." Falka kept her hand pressed against the sconce, though her glowing orange eyes remained fixed on Yi-Nereen. "Magebikes were only invented forty years ago, yet sparkriders have been born with the Talent for as long as anyone can remember. Except they weren't called sparkriders before the creation of those machines. Do you know what people called them?"

"Lamplighters." The answer sprang from Yi-Nereen's lips before she could stop it, a habit formed from years of tutors quizzing her.

"That's right. Lamplighters. Good for little else but lighting torches and candles. You can do that with a flint and tinder—no need for Talent. So they were mostly useless." Falka had taken on an annoyingly didactic tone, like a priest delivering a sermon. "But that never made sense, did it? All our other Talents are useful. The priests say Rasvel gave every child a gift to help humanity flourish. Yet until a clever inventor thought of combining two wheels and an engine powered by sparks and mana, it seemed the Giver of Blessings had snubbed more than just the Talentless."

How long was this platform going to keep rising? Yi-Nereen could still see nothing but darkness above them. It was difficult to tell how fast they were ascending, but surely they should have reached the surface of the wastes by now.

"Here's what I've learned, Highness: Sparktalent is useful for far more than riding magebikes. It is the original Talent, the ancestor and precursor to all others. What survives of the Road Builders' technology seems to rely on it completely."

"How could you possibly know all of this?" Yi-Nereen hated giving Falka the satisfaction of engaging with her, but always she thirsted for knowledge. Was it possible Falka had discovered something Yi-Nereen hadn't managed to hear whispers of in all her years of research?

"Do I not strike you as a scholar?" Falka laughed. "No, you're right. I've never been one for the books. Instead, years ago, I found myself a patron: someone who's studied the Road Builders and what remains of them for longer than you or I have been alive. Ancient history doesn't really interest me, but it turns out there are advantages to knowing things no one else does."

So Falka had a patron. Did that mean they were on their way to see this mysterious scholar, whoever it was? Yi-Nereen longed to ask, but Falka had already refused to answer a similar question once. She couldn't risk Falka shutting down on her completely.

"Back at the temple," Yi-Nereen said slowly, "you and Jin were saying things that didn't make sense. About her Talent, and yours."

She had pieced some of it together. Falka was clearly an important figure from Jin's past—an ex-lover, it seemed. Jin had never mentioned her, and they had obviously parted on bitter terms. But why had Falka spoken as if her Talent were a newly laid curse?

"Yes. You're quicker on the uptake than Jin ever was." Falka's voice was quieter now. "Have you realized by now I was born Talentless?"

Yi-Nereen flinched. *Impossible,* she almost said. *You're lying.*

It went against everything she'd ever been taught. Talent was a gift bestowed at birth, the mark of Rasvel's favor—and the Talentless, cursed by Makela, could never become otherwise. Perhaps Falka was mad; it was a more likely explanation than any other.

But she couldn't argue with Falka openly. If she wanted to escape, she had to get the raider to lower her guard.

"We all were," Falka went on. "Me and my freebooters. But I was the first to become Talented. Do you want to hear how it happened, Highness? I can tell you're dying to call me a liar." She smiled knowingly. "I was born in Kerina Tez. A shit place to be born Talentless, doubly so a Talentless girl. I did cruel things to survive. Ugly things. Jin saw everything and kept her mouth shut. I thought it meant she didn't mind." Falka scoffed quietly. "I thought it meant she cared about me anyway."

*That's Jin.* The woman who held her tongue until she could no longer restrain herself, whose face rarely expressed emotion, except for the way her dark eyes sparkled when she was amused. Often Yi-Nereen had wondered what went through Jin's head when she was reading Kadrin's letters aloud or taking down Yi-Nereen's dictations. Did she think them ridiculous, two royals making flowery promises they couldn't possibly keep? Jin had carried letters and the occasional parcel between them for three years, privier to both of their deepest, most passionate thoughts than anyone else in the world. Yet that intimacy extended only one way. Yi-Nereen hadn't known much of Jin's heart until they'd become fugitives together.

Until Jin had become a fugitive *for her.*

"After she left," Falka said, her tongue curling around the words as if they were embers, "I answered a notice from a man looking for Talentless volunteers for an experiment. I didn't care about the coin, but I knew a few other Talentless who had answered the advertisement and vanished afterward. I was looking for a fight, I suppose. I wanted to kill whoever was behind the disappearances.

"Then I met him. Instead of killing him right away, I let him talk. I realized he wasn't a remorseless killer or even just a crazy old man. He was a genius. He'd discovered a way to transplant Talent into those who weren't born with it, but it wasn't perfected. The procedure had proven deadly to all who'd undergone it so far." Falka smiled. "So I asked him, *What will happen to me if it succeeds?* And he said, *You'll be free.*"

"You believed him?" Yi-Nereen asked. "You let him perform this procedure on you, even though it killed everyone who underwent it before you?"

Falka's eyes flashed. "Tell me you wouldn't risk everything for a chance to be free, Princess. At least I only gambled with my own life, not anyone else's."

Yi-Nereen felt her cheeks heat. "Jin helped me of her own volition. I didn't coerce her."

"No? You're saying you didn't know about her feelings for you? I find that hard to believe."

*I could never be certain. That's why I gave her the coin.*

Guilt twisted in her stomach, just as it had countless times before. Ever since the beginning, since Kadrin's very first letter, all she had seen was a way out. She'd told Kadrin whatever he needed to hear, cultivated his feelings for her until he was hers.

It had stunned her to realize, almost from the first letter, that the task was already done. The man had been in love with her since they were children. And Yi-Nereen was almost certain she'd loved him, too: that boy she remembered from gardens and courtyards, the glowing halo in the dark tomb of her memory. But that was long ago, when she'd still imagined she had the luxury of love. Now she didn't know what she felt, and she had forbidden herself from delving too deeply into her own heart—out of fear she'd lose the stomach for what she had to do.

It was harder to tell where Jin's loyalties lay. But with her time running out, Yi-Nereen had taken a chance, and her gamble had paid off. She'd used the courier, just as she would have used Kadrin if everything had gone to plan. It was for everyone's good, not just hers. The kerinas depended on her making it to a place of safety.

"At least *I* cared about her," Falka said softly. "That was real."

Yi-Nereen looked away. *It doesn't matter how I feel. Only that I survive.*

The shaft around her rumbled. The platform was slowing. It came to a rest at the top of the shaft, before a door identical to the one below. Falka took her hand off the sconce, her eyes dimming, and jerked her chin toward the wheel. "If you don't mind, Highness."

Yi-Nereen considered fighting back. The platform had stopped, which meant she wouldn't risk getting stuck in the shaft without Falka to operate the sconce. It was just the two of them in this small space. Falka wouldn't be able to effectively use that long cutlass hanging at her hip. The raider would still have the advantage in a brawl; though shorter than Yi-Nereen, she was muscular and obviously had fighting experience. But a slim shot was better than none.

But if she did manage to subdue Falka, what then? She'd have to take her chances with whatever lay outside that door, probably the wild wastes.

And Faolin would remain with the raiders. He'd been captured because of her; she'd almost killed him to secure her own safety, and now she was contemplating leaving him to his fate?

Yi-Nereen bit her lip. *I deserve whatever's coming.*

"In your own time," Falka said with a knowing sneer.

Yi-Nereen let her thoughts of resistance dissolve. She stepped up next to Falka, and together they slowly rotated the wheel. The door rolled away, and a gust of wind rushed in to fill the chamber, ruffling the sleeves of Yi-Nereen's caftan. The air was frigid and smelled like nothing she'd ever known before, wild and fresh and intoxicating.

Outside lay nothing but the night sky, dotted with stars. The moon was huge and full, white as polished bone. Yi-Nereen, who had spent her whole life in a tower, knew at once they were very high up. Higher than she'd ever been before, higher than should be possible.

"Mount Vetelu," Falka said. "A secret lost to time, but for one man."

Yi-Nereen stared at her. The name Mount Vetelu rang a faint bell in her memory, like she'd read it in a dusty text long ago without comprehending what it meant. She was racking her brain, trying to remember, when Falka reached out and plucked the strap of her satchel from her shoulder.

"No!" Her first instinct was to cast a shield, burning mana that wasn't there. The air flickered around her, but no translucent bubble took form. A moment later, pain sliced through her temples, worse than any headache she'd ever felt. Yi-Nereen gasped and stumbled, vaguely aware that she was only a few steps away from the edge of the abyss.

"I've been dying to know what you've got in here," Falka said. Tongue between her teeth, she rooted inside the pack and came up with a handful of parchment. "Paper? That's all? I'd hoped to find a princess's dowry."

She let the wind snatch the parchment from her hand; the sheets fluttered away like freed birds. Yi-Nereen's stomach plummeted.

"Please." She was alarmed to hear herself begging, pleading with Falka to stop. *My notes. My research.* They *were* her dowry—more than that, they were her penance. Without her findings on the population crisis, how could she prove her theories to the royals of Kerina Sol? How could she save the kerinas and wash out the stain of her grandfather's legacy?

Falka smirked, openly delighted to have found a way to hurt her. In her eyes, Yi-Nereen again glimpsed the madness that had overcome the woman after Jin had killed the raider in the ruins. For a moment, she was certain the person behind those eyes wasn't Falka at all.

"Another lesson, Princess," Falka said. "Jin's heart wasn't yours to take."

And she flung the satchel into the void.

*Second Age of Storms, 50th Fall*

*Dear Reena,*
*How dearly I long for a poet's soul, so I could write an ode to all I find*
*beautiful in this world. I know just where I would start.*

*Fortunately, I have something better to offer you. Ta-da! Jin, please*
*reveal the parcel at this point, with as much flair as you can muster.*
*(Lower your expectations.)*

*Yes, I have finally managed to get my hands on a volume of Kerina*
*Sol's Scrolls of Talent. It was much more difficult to get hold of than*
*I expected. I know it's been a year and you've probably moved on to*
*another project, but I harbor the foolish hope that this will be useful to*
*you nonetheless.*

*I won't get into the details of how I procured the Scroll, but suf-*
*fice to say it's an original copy and I will need to, ahem, return it. As*
*you know, I'm rubbish with the written word, so I decided the fastest*
*way would be to send the original along, let you make your own copy,*
*and then have you send it back with Jin. Everything should work out*
*perfectly as long as no one notices the Scroll is missing in the meantime.*
*(He's unhinged.)*

*Should you ever require anything, Reena, you have but to mention*
*it. I am, without exaggeration, entirely at your disposal.*

*Your faithful retainer,*
*Kadrin*

## CHAPTER TWENTY-TWO

# THE PRINCE'S GAMBIT

*Second Age of Storms, 51st Summer, Day 24*

Kadrin lay awake in bed. Occasionally he got up to pace the length of his darkened bedchamber. Damn it all, why hadn't he been born a sparkrider? Terrible things could be happening to Reena *right now*. If Jin was right, he was already too late.

He flung open the doors to his balcony. Leaning against the rail, he breathed deep of the night air. The fragrance of the garden below drifted upward, damp and sweet. *Think of anything but Reena.*

A memory floated toward him, hazy on the midnight breeze: Jin's weight in his arms, her head lolling against his shoulder. Kadrin grimaced. She'd reminded him yesterday of something he'd been selfish enough to forget: he was Jin's employer, not her friend. If she ever knew what he felt . . .

No, he would never put her in that position. He would never risk making her feel that she had to either jeopardize her income or reciprocate his affections.

*As if she would!* It was proof of his idiocy that such thoughts endured in the echoing cavern of his skull. Jin plainly disdained the life he lived, the luxurious trappings of the House and everyone within. If only she knew how stifled he felt—how much he longed to follow her onto the open road, where the divisions of society ceased to be of consequence.

And—Kadrin groaned internally—none of it mattered. He couldn't court two women at once. He'd made his choice long ago.

Perhaps he would forget his feelings for Jin when he and Reena were reunited at last. Yes, it was only natural that, separated from the woman he loved, his affections would misplace themselves onto the person who symbolized their connection. As long as Jin never had an inkling, no harm would be done.

Kadrin let out a shaky sigh and shook his head. *Why don't I believe that?*

He went inside, cast himself down on the bed, and fell into an uneasy sleep. Distant temple bells roused him at dawn. He dressed in his smartest robe, scrutinized his hair in the mirror, and went to breakfast like a prisoner going to his last meal. He'd just slumped into his chair and reached for his coffee when someone across the table cleared their throat.

Kadrin raised his head and met Jin's cool brown gaze. She sat with her arms crossed, dressed in a man's tunic much cleaner than yesterday's bloodstained leather jacket. A cup of coffee sat steaming on the table in front of her. Her hands were bandaged and her face was pink with sunburn.

"Jin? What in Rasvel's name are you doing here?"

"Drinking coffee," she said, "and waiting for you."

"I meant *what are you doing in my family's banquet hall.*"

"Banquet hall," Jin repeated, glancing disinterestedly over the long sandstone table, the paintings of fruit on the walls, and the alcoves where servants lurked during feasts. "So that's what this room is called. I'm here because your father saw me on his way to the

Council chambers and asked me—well, *told* me—to see that you didn't dawdle over breakfast."

No wonder Jin seemed disgruntled. "Sorry. I—"

"What's this?" inquired a breezy voice from the doorway. Eliesen, Kadrin's sister, floated toward him and draped herself over the back of his chair. She wore her dressing gown and silk slippers, her thick dark curls forming a bouncy halo. "My brother's mysterious courier, taking coffee in our House instead of sneaking in and out like a wraith in a leather jacket?"

Jin flushed and pushed back her chair. "Meet you at the Council chambers, Kadrin."

"Oh, stay!" Eliesen flounced into a seat and snatched a bun from the platter in the center of the table, dusting powdered sugar across the tablecloth. "I've been dying to meet you officially—a *courier*. I've spent plenty of time around knights, but they're beginning to bore me. You know, I'm surprised Kadrin has never asked for a ride on your magebike. Unless he has, and he's just kept it a secret from the family?"

"Elie," Kadrin said, "leave Jin alone. Now isn't the time." He tried to catch Jin's eye and failed; she was staring at his sister warily, as if she were a wild animal. This was his fault. He hadn't had a chance to tell Eliesen about the trouble with Yi-Nereen last night.

Anxiety gripped his stomach. Reena was depending on him to persuade the Council. What if his mouth went dry and he couldn't form words? Gods, he was truly the most useless of all his siblings.

"So you're Kadrin's sister," Jin said. "I've heard a lot about you."

Eliesen beamed. "Have you? I wish that was mutual. Will you be taking breakfast with us more often from now on? If my brother isn't interested, I'm *always* in the mood to go for a ride."

His sister's voice had taken on a silky tone Kadrin didn't care for at all. He reached over and swiped her half-eaten bun from her plate, ignoring her yelp of protest. "I *said* now isn't the time. Let's go, Jin. I want to get to the Council chambers early and practice my speech."

Eliesen's pout followed the two of them out of the banquet hall. Once he and Jin were alone in the corridor, Kadrin cleared his throat and mumbled, "Sorry." He wasn't certain what he was apologizing for. His embarrassing flirt of a sister? Whatever his father had said to Jin earlier? His own missteps and overreaches, a clumsy pattern going back years?

All he knew was he had to apologize for something. The air between him and Jin felt charged. If he didn't know better, he would think *she* was the one holding something back. But no—Kadrin was the one with a shameful secret. Jin had nothing to hide. She was just capable, honest Jin, like always.

"Come on," Jin said, avoiding his eyes. "Reena needs us."

Shield Lord Tethris stared at Kadrin down the length of her thin, bony nose, then looked past him at his father. "Matrios, what do you think of your son's proposal?"

The Council chambers were stiflingly hot. All the windows in the long, oval-shaped hall were open, but Kadrin's robe still stuck to his back; sweat ran freely down his sides. The meeting chamber was arranged like a gallery with several tiers of seating. Each royal had their own section, marked by a piece of slate painted with their House's sigil. Kadrin sat beside his father. Jin—to Kadrin's dismay—had been relegated to the highest tier, among the servants and courtiers who had accompanied their royals to Council.

Despite everything, Kadrin couldn't look at Jin without smiling. She stuck out like a pteropter in a chicken coop. Jin didn't need to be tall or broad to intimidate. It was her stony expression, the way she kept her arms crossed over her chest, the dark cast to her eyes that said, *None of you have seen what I have.*

At the sound of his father's voice, Kadrin snapped back to attention.

"I recuse myself from the discussion," his father was saying. "Let Kadrin's proposal stand on its own merits."

"But you must have an opinion," Shield Lord Tethris said. She made an impatient hand signal, and one of the servants brought her a small basin. Kadrin watched wisps of turquoise smoke curl up from the basin's surface and dissipate into the air—liquid mana. The other royals were tracking the basin's progress with thinly veiled interest. Infusing mana was an excellent way for the Talented to cool off in hot weather. Kadrin longed for water, but he hadn't seen any in the chamber.

Kadrin's father sighed and adjusted the collar of his robe. Kadrin stared at his father, silently hoping, pleading, but the Rain Lord didn't even glance at him.

"Relations between Kerina Sol and Kerina Rut have a fraught history, as we are all aware. Our priests rarely agree on matters of theology, and war darkens our past. Yet in recent decades, we have made progress at repairing that diplomatic relationship. Of all the Houses of High Talent in Kerina Rut, the Tower of Arrested Stars has been our most agreeable partner in this endeavor." Matrios's voice wavered slightly. "Lai-Dan, Lord of the Tower, has even been so gracious as to overlook certain ambassadorial missteps."

Over the rush of blood to his ears, Kadrin heard Shield Lord Tethris say, "You speak of the incident involving your son."

"Yes," Kadrin's father said. "An old matter, long since laid to rest. I mention it only to underscore the debt we owe the Tower."

Kadrin glanced over his shoulder to see Jin's dark eyes fixed on him from the high reaches of the gallery. She had shifted forward in her chair; her hands twitched. No one but a royal or a member of a royal's family could speak at Council without first being addressed. But it was clear she wanted Kadrin to intervene.

Kadrin cleared his throat, his heart pounding. "Let me remind the Council a woman's life is at stake here. Princess Yi-Nereen sought Rasvel's Sanctuary in Kerina Sol. She sought the protection of this Council. We owe it to her to—"

Shield Lord Tethris cut him off. Her voice, sonorous and smooth, drowned out Kadrin's with ease. "Matrios, I don't believe you finished making your point. Please continue." She cast a stern eye on Kadrin. "In this Council, we speak in turn."

Kadrin gripped his knees with white knuckles. His brother Satriu had once come storming home from Council, evicted after speaking out of turn. Kadrin couldn't risk being thrown out. He *had* to succeed here. It was the only thing he'd ever attempted that mattered.

His father still wasn't looking at him. "What my son says is true. If Princess Yi-Nereen seeks sanctuary in Kerina Sol, it is our duty to grant it, by sacred law. *If* she reaches our city. While she remains bodily in Kerina Rut, she remains its citizen—and by their law, her family's property. It is unfair. It is regrettable. But it is what it is."

Kadrin rose from his chair, and every gaze in the room came to rest on him. "Are you finished now, Father?"

Now Rain Lord Matrios looked at him, his brow furrowed. "I am."

*This is my chance.* So far their plan had played out as he'd envisioned; Kadrin had invited Jin to tell the royals of the fate Yi-

Nereen faced in Kerina Rut, and she had done so with her typical blunt edge. Many of the royals had seemed disturbed, even angry. Now it was time for Kadrin's final speech.

He'd feared his mouth would dry up and he'd be unable to utter a sound. But in that moment, everything he felt for Reena and Jin bloomed in his chest, and he found his voice.

"This is my first time at Council," he said. "Yet I have spent my life proud to call myself Sol-blood. Our kerina is like no other. We live by Rasvel's truth, and we do not let fear influence our ethics. I believe in Rasvel's Sanctuary, not merely as a local tradition, but as holy doctrine."

He looked past all the faces in the room at the only one that mattered. Jin wasn't smiling, but she didn't need to. Her steady gaze was enough.

"No person can be property. Not here, and not in Kerina Rut. Yi-Nereen is not her father's possession; she does not belong to the Tower. She is a woman free under Rasvel's gaze, like any other. We cannot call ourselves Rasvel's servants if we sit idle while she is held against her will. I implore you all: we must send aid."

His voice died away into stillness. Finally he looked around the room—and his heart sank.

No one looked outraged or called to action; they looked *bored*. Bloom Lord Feyrin was bathing his swollen knuckles in mana and didn't even appear to be listening.

Kadrin's skin prickled with something unfamiliar: anger. It stung like sweat in a cut. How dare these royals remain so unmoved? They had muttered furiously among themselves at Jin's earlier statement, but perhaps they weren't angry at Kerina Rut. Perhaps their anger was with Jin for discussing a problem they would rather pretend didn't exist.

He'd grown up listening to temple priests sing of shelter for the weak and liberty for all. His father and brothers had repeated those prayers like they meant every word.

*Hypocrites.*

This must be exactly how Jin had felt yesterday. No wonder she'd smashed a cup and shouted at him. He must have looked to her as the royals appeared to him now: enthroned in their grand chambers, dripping with false sympathy and hollow righteousness.

"Enough, Kadrin." His father eyed him with pity. "You've made your argument. We'll put it to a vote. My lords, the proposal is to dispatch a company of sparkrider knights to the walls of Kerina Rut, bearing a demand for Princess Yi-Nereen to be relinquished into Kerina Sol's custody. Who is in favor?"

Kadrin knew it was over, yet he couldn't stop himself from glancing desperately about the room, looking at each royal in turn, willing them to raise their slate in support. Not a single one moved. The entire chamber was silent as a graveyard.

"Then it is done," Shield Lord Tethris said. "This Council's decision is final, and no member present may act in defiance of its wishes."

Sick with despair, Kadrin turned to look for Jin, but her seat was empty. When had she left? He flinched at the weight of his father's hand on his arm and shook himself free before his father could speak.

"I see," he said hoarsely. "I see what this Council is. What *you* are. I can't believe I ever worried about disappointing you."

He rose through the gallery tiers and left the room without another word.

Jin hadn't gone far. Kadrin found her on the Marble Palace's steps, a stone's throw from the double doors into the Council chambers. She was staring down at the crowded square below, which bustled with spice merchants and cloth vendors and Talented artisans plying their trade.

"So the Knights of Sol aren't going to Yi-Nereen's rescue," she said, her voice flat. "And did I hear that Shield Lord correctly—Tethris, or whatever her name was? No one who was in that room can try to help Yi-Nereen on their own?"

Kadrin took a deep breath, his body humming with tension. "Yes, but I don't care. Damn the Council and my spineless father. I'm going with you to save Reena."

For a dizzying moment he thought Jin might smile and embrace him. Instead, she turned away and said, "No, you aren't."

His breath caught. "What?"

"Just . . . go home, Kadrin. Let me take care of it. Please."

The world had slipped, like a mirror turned askew on the wall. Jin, pleading with him? Something was profoundly wrong.

He knew how gravely he'd disappointed her. He'd failed to leverage his influence as a royal's son, the only advantage he had to offer. The Council might as well have laughed in his face. Of course she didn't want his help anymore.

"Jin." He couldn't catch his breath; his chest was tight. "You can't go alone. You'll be killed."

"And if I take you with me?" she asked. "What then?"

"The two of us can figure something out—"

"*Two* of us," she said. "That's the problem."

The breath surged back into Kadrin's lungs as he understood. If he went with Jin, and by some deific miracle they rescued Reena, Jin couldn't bring two passengers out of Kerina Rut on her magebike. That *was* a problem, but it could be solved.

"You can come back for me," he said. "Get Reena to safety and come back. Or I'll hitch a ride with another courier. It's still better than you going alone."

"It's too much of a risk."

"Well, it's *my* life we'd be risking, and I say it's worthwhile."

"No." She turned to face him, eyes blazing. "You've done what you could, Kadrin. I won't put you in danger when I'm the one who—"

"Who what?" Kadrin asked, but Jin pressed her lips together and stared at him like she wanted to light him on fire. Well, if she wouldn't talk, he would fill the silence. He was used to doing that. "I know what you think of me. Trust me, I understand now, better than I ever have. But I'm finished with sitting around while someone else does my dirty work. If I don't do this . . ." He swallowed. "I'm not the man Reena deserves."

Jin glared at him a moment longer, but then something passed across her face, like a cloud against the sun, and her mouth relaxed. "Well," she said softly, "that's the most idiotic thing I've heard all morning."

Kadrin's heart beat faster. "You *did* hear Bloom Lord Feyrin's complaint about the public baths using too much water, didn't you? And his suggestion to put up flyers telling everyone to bathe no more than once a week?"

Jin cracked a smile, and the world slid back into place. But her eyes remained dark and somber. "If I left you here, you'd only get yourself thrown in a prison cell for trying to disobey the Council, wouldn't you?"

"Absolutely. So you're taking me with you?"

Jin only grunted in response.

"Then we'll need a bike," Kadrin said.

*Second Age of Storms, 50th Fall*

*Dear Kadrin,*
*I truly don't know what I have done to deserve your kindness. I'm*
*ashamed to admit that I had all but abandoned my research. I've*
*found it difficult to concentrate this past year, and without any new*
*material to cross-reference, drawing conclusions from what little I had*
*seemed pointless.*

*Even a single volume of the Scrolls of Talent is a godsend. I shall*
*resume my work as soon as this letter is penned. Rasvel's mercy, Kadrin,*
*I can't believe you stole from the temple. I will redouble my prayers to*
*the Giver for the next year, in hopes he will overlook this matter.*

*I enclose a small token of my appreciation for your efforts. I don't*
*know whether it is fashionable for the men in Kerina Sol to wear*
*jewelry, but here it is the custom for men to go about festooned in rings.*
*I could perhaps have bought a ring without attracting undue suspi-*
*cion, but in honor of your recent exploits, I decided to steal one of my*
*brother's instead. He must have a hundred he never wears, so I'm sure*
*he won't miss it. Besides, if you knew him, you would agree he deserves*
*to be the victim of more crimes.*

*I hope you wear it. Across all the distance between us, I want some*
*small part of me with you. It already was, but the sensation of metal*
*around one's finger—its smoothness, its weight—makes the intangible*
*feel real.*

*With undying gratitude,*
*Reena*

# IN THE SHADOW OF THE WALL

*Second Age of Storms, 51st Summer, Day 24*

"Couriers have used this place for years," Jin said. "The best place to stash undelivered goods is somewhere no one wants to go."

She'd led Kadrin into the bowels of the Curing District, past rows of tannery vats redolent of gore and excrement. Jin was used to the smell, but Kadrin clearly had never frequented this part of town. He nodded, his face a bit green, as Jin stepped toward the shack at the end of the alley. With half the roof caved in, the shack looked like it might fall down on their heads, but Jin knew the effect was just for show. After a brief glance down the alley, she opened the shack's side door to reveal the gleaming form of a magebike hidden within.

Kadrin gaped. "Is that yours?"

"No. I told you, I left mine at the ruins. This one belongs to a knight your sister is courting. She was gracious enough to arrange for me to borrow it."

Kadrin's expression was priceless; Jin wished she could bottle it. "You planned this with *Elie*? But you two only met this morning!"

"Actually, that isn't true. We've met before." Jin dragged the magebike out of the shed. It was a damned heavy beast, built to seat a knight in full plate. Hopefully that meant the tank would last the journey across the wastes, with Jin and Kadrin riding double.

"But you've always avoided meeting my family." Kadrin sounded completely bewildered. "I thought you wouldn't get along with Elie in particular. Because she's—well, so *different* from you. When? And why didn't you tell me?"

Jin had hoped this conversation would never take place. Even now, perhaps, she could come up with some explanation for how she'd convinced Eliesen to acquire the bike. But that would be a direct lie, and she'd never told Kadrin one of those before. The only option left was the truth.

"Eliesen and I *are* different. But that doesn't always stop people from—from getting along." She made a helpless gesture with her hands. "Rasvel's mercy, Kadrin. You must know your sister isn't shy about pursuing anyone who interests her. I do mean *anyone*."

"Oh," Kadrin said, a flush immediately rising to his cheeks.

Jin dragged a hand over her face and quickly regretted it; her burned palm stung like hellfire. "It wasn't only my secret to keep."

She wished she could sink into the mud and never resurface. Part of her wanted to go on explaining, give more context—it had been only one time, and she hadn't known Eliesen was a noblewoman until later. She'd been a mess over Falka, and Elie had been so kind . . . but hearing more details was probably the last thing Kadrin wanted. *Jin* didn't even want to dwell on the specifics. She hadn't realized until a long time afterward why she'd been so receptive to Eliesen's advances: the siblings bore an uncanny resemblance, especially in the dark.

She cleared her throat. "We've wasted enough time. Yi-Nereen needs us, remember?"

Kadrin blinked slowly, looking at her like he'd never seen her before. "Ah, yes. Are we—should we ride now?"

"No, the streets are too crowded. We'll need to take the bike outside the walls."

They set off toward the gate, with Jin walking the magebike and casting about for a change of topic. The streets of Kerina Sol were full of their usual clamor: merchants hawking wares, children laughing as they kicked balls into gutters, chickens clucking. Yet all Jin could hear was the silence between her and Kadrin. She was about to start a desperate discussion about the weather when Kadrin finally spoke up.

"I've been thinking about what happens when we reach Kerina Rut," he said. "They'll have Reena under guard, won't they? You won't just be able to ride off with her like you did before."

"No, definitely not."

"I've done a little reading." Kadrin sounded almost bashful. "Courting in Kerina Rut has its own set of sacred traditions. The oldest law of courtship is the Law of Prior Claim. If a woman—or more likely, her family—spurns her betrothed and selects a new match, the wronged man can challenge her new fiancé to a duel by the sword. The winner gets final claim to the woman's hand."

Jin sighed. "I've heard of that law. It's barbaric. How do you expect to get Sou-Zell to issue the challenge?"

"He isn't the wronged man," Kadrin said. "I am."

"Come again?"

"Reena can declare that *I* was her original betrothed. She never sought her family's permission for it, but according to the Law of Prior Claim, that doesn't actually matter. A man is allowed to defend his claim even if it was never made official. A promise from the woman herself is all that's needed."

*You've obviously put a lot of thought into this.* Yi-Nereen wasn't the only one who had planned for their future together, it seemed.

Jin felt a flash of bitterness chased by guilt; she had no right to feel betrayed. "There's one problem with that, Kadrin. I've read all of your letters—hell, I put them to paper—and Yi-Nereen never made such a promise."

"Here's where it gets tricky."

Kadrin lifted his hand. Sunlight caught on his ring, a heavy obsidian band studded with silver skulls. Kadrin wore a different assortment of earrings, bangles, and necklaces every time Jin saw him, most of them gold or copper to complement his warm brown skin, but there was only one piece of jewelry he never took off; Jin knew exactly where it had come from. She'd carried it across the wastes in her breast pocket.

"Kerina Sol has its own traditions around jewelry," Kadrin said. "After all the letters we've exchanged—proof of courtship—the ring she sent me was tantamount to a marriage proposal."

Now Jin couldn't help but smile, though her fondness was fighting a pitched battle with the beast of longing inside her. "Yi-Nereen is cleverer than both of us combined. Do you think she realized what she was doing?"

"I—I considered that." Kadrin looked down at the cobblestone road, blushing. "I hardly dared hope, but I considered it."

How she hated to cut his dreams short. But now wasn't the time for fantasies. "I don't think it will work, Kadrin. Her fiancé could simply laugh in your face and shut the door—and there wouldn't be anything we could do to stop him."

"A last resort, then. If subterfuge fails."

Jin frowned as another thought occurred to her. "What makes you so sure you would win the duel?"

"You said Yi-Nereen's fiancé is a mindreader." Kadrin grinned. "It's a huge advantage in swordplay—knowing where your opponent's next strike will land, whether they've anticipated yours. Well, his Talent won't work on me. He'll have lost his greatest asset."

How did he sound so sure, so unafraid? And why did Jin feel almost the same? Like she could just ride out there, rescue a princess, and take on the world.

They met no trouble at the gate; the guards merely glanced over Jin's bike and waved them through. Jin didn't miss Kadrin's quiet intake of breath as they stepped out from the shadow of the Wall. Beneath their feet lay the cracked asphalt of the highway; before them stretched the wild wastes.

"We're going out there." Kadrin's eyes were fixed on the horizon.

Jin straddled her magebike. "Last chance to turn back."

Kadrin's response was to climb onto the bike behind her. "Where am I supposed to hold on?"

Jin swallowed. She hadn't felt nearly this awkward when she'd ridden with Yi-Nereen. Of course, there had been plenty to distract her then, like guards shooting at them or a violent storm chasing them down. *I could use a distraction or two now.*

"You'll have to hold on to me." She touched her waist. "Hands here."

Kadrin hesitated, then tentatively put his arms around Jin. "Like this?"

Jin forgot how to breathe. Rasvel's mercy, but he was *warm.* Her chest was tight and fluttering. His embrace was torture, and it was frightening how much she wanted to sink into it and never resurface.

*Why not enjoy yourself?* a traitorous voice asked. *This won't last. Once they're reunited, you'll have all the time in the world to be alone. Just like you deserve.*

"Closer." Jin's voice was strained. She cleared her throat. "The closer you are, the easier it will be to balance." Kadrin shifted until his front was pressed against Jin's back and she felt his breath on her neck. *It's going to be a long ride.* "Ready?"

"Yes," Kadrin said. "Jin, I wanted to say—thank you. For letting me come with you. I promise I won't let you or Reena down." She heard his smile in his voice, warm and golden.

Jin restrained a shiver. She didn't want or deserve his thanks—not when she'd been helpless to make any decision other than to help him and Yi-Nereen, for reasons both simple and painfully complicated. They had to do with her father's mistakes; promises she'd whispered into Falka's hair long ago; Jin's own secret wishes, too fragile to exist in reality; and always, the undeserved gift of her sparktalent.

She loved too easily, and promises were hard to keep.

They'd been on the road for a few hours when Jin saw a plume of smoke and dust in the distance, chrome flashing under the sun. Another rider, approaching from the opposite direction—alone. Jin relaxed. Raiders never traveled alone.

The unspoken custom of the wastes dictated she slow down and pull alongside the other rider to exchange tidings. It was always useful to hear news of nearby chandru herds, or sightings of territorial rovex. Some couriers used these road meetings to shorten a journey by exchanging goods.

Jin didn't want to stop. Every moment mattered. But what if the rider had news of Kerina Rut? Yi-Nereen's return to the city in disgrace would have caused a stir. Any information could be worth spending a few minutes.

She raised her hand in the sign of meeting, and the other rider mirrored the gesture. Kadrin's weight pressed into her as the bike slowed. If he wondered why they were stopping, he didn't ask.

Finally the two bikes pulled side by side and Jin hit the brakes. The other rider was slim, clad in full leather and a pteropter bonehelm. Dark glass shone in the bonehelm's orbital openings, obscuring the rider's eyes from view. Disquiet stirred in Jin's stomach. There was something familiar about the set of those shoulders, the crisp lines of the bone-plated vest.

"Hail, sparkrider," she said cautiously.

In response, the rider raised his gloved hands to remove his helm. Off came the saurian skull, and Jin found herself staring into the slanted, dark eyes of a man who had once offered to light her mana-cig in a shaded gazebo by the spring.

Yi-Nereen's betrothed, Sou-Zell.

# PART FOUR

# CHAPTER TWENTY-THREE

# A CHANCE ENCOUNTER

*Second Age of Storms, 51st Summer, Day 24*

"You," Jin said. "What are *you* doing here?"

"I could ask you the same," Sou-Zell said, "but fortunately I don't need to."

His eyes flared violet. A moment too late, Jin remembered his second Talent. Her restraint evaporated. With a furious growl, she swung out of the saddle and launched herself at Sou-Zell. His hand flew up to catch her fist an inch from his jaw, but Jin had followed through; her weight took him bodily off his bike. They crashed to the ground in a tangled, piping-hot mess of metal and elbows.

She'd had no plan other than to injure him as grievously as she could. For one glorious moment, she had her hands around Sou-Zell's neck, and he was sputtering and turning red.

"Don't you read my fucking mind." Her spittle dotted his contorted face. "That's goddamn private."

"Jin!" Kadrin was behind her somewhere, shouting. "What are you doing? Who *is* that?"

Taken aback, Jin loosened her grip—and in a flash, Sou-Zell had a knife at her throat. Jin glared, and he bared his teeth at her; they were both panting too hard to speak.

Then Sou-Zell said in a seething voice, "Get—get *off* me, you beast. I—am not—your enemy."

"Get your fucking knife away from me!"

"I'll second that," Kadrin said. A sword tip appeared, gleaming, at the hollow of Sou-Zell's neck. "Two of us and one of you, whoever you are. So why don't we all settle down and talk this out?"

Sou-Zell curled his lip. "Gladly, once you order this feral woman of yours to stand down."

"Choke on a cactus," Jin said.

"I don't command her." Kadrin's voice turned cold. "Now, I may not be the smartest man in the wasteland, but given your frankly astonishing lack of manners, I'll wager you're Sou-Zell."

Sou-Zell's expression changed. It was subtle, no more than a flaring of the nostrils, but Jin didn't have to be a mindreader to recognize disgust when she saw it.

"Ah," he said softly. "And you're Kadrin."

"That's *Prince* Kadrin to you," Jin said.

The cool pressure against her neck became a sting. Sou-Zell's eyes were black with anger, and a frisson of fear snaked down Jin's spine, but she held his gaze. The pressure vanished. Jin scrambled backward, heart pounding, and flinched when Kadrin touched her arm.

"Are you okay?"

At her terse nod, Kadrin lowered his sword, though he didn't sheathe it. Sou-Zell remained sprawled on the ground. Jin realized he wasn't going anywhere soon; his magebike had toppled across his legs. That was going to leave an awful set of bruises, if he hadn't broken anything. *Good.*

"Use your Talent on me again, and I'll kill you with my bare hands," she said.

"I welcome the attempt," Sou-Zell said, managing to sound haughty despite being flat on his back. "First, tell me what you've done with my fiancée."

Jin stiffened and glanced at Kadrin. His face mirrored her own bewilderment. "What *we've* done? Aren't you the one who took her?"

Could Yi-Nereen have possibly maintained her shield for this long, keeping Falka and her raiders at bay? No—not even Reena could accomplish such a feat. Jin had never heard of a shieldcaster able to stand against a storm for longer than five hours before needing replacement. It had been two days since she had left Yi-Nereen at the ruins.

Falka must have Reena. But if she hadn't brought the princess back to Kerina Rut, they could be anywhere.

"You gain nothing by these lies." Sou-Zell propped himself up on his elbows and pushed gingerly at his magebike. The machine didn't budge. Jin was too panicked to appreciate the sight of him wincing. "I meant it when I said I wasn't your enemy."

"Are we supposed to believe you came all this way just to offer Reena and me your blessings?" Kadrin asked.

Sou-Zell's lips thinned. "Rasvel save me from fools. It isn't me you should fear. It's Shield Lord Lai-Dan. He's sending the Knights of Rut to Kerina Sol to demand his daughter's return."

Jin collected herself. "And what are you supposed to be, the advance guard?"

"A messenger with a warning," Sou-Zell said. "You must not allow Lai-Dan to claim his daughter. A fate worse than death awaits her if you do."

A moment of silence passed. Then Jin grabbed Kadrin's arm. "I need to talk to you. Privately."

They withdrew a few yards away from Sou-Zell and his magebike. Jin allowed herself a moment of fierce pleasure at the thought of the man's helplessness. She despised mindreaders, and Sou-Zell especially. He'd invaded her mind twice, ordered the guards of Kerina Rut to shoot them down, and sent a bounty hunter to steal Yi-Nereen—and to kill Jin. Oddly enough, the last part bothered her the least.

"I don't think he's lying," she said reluctantly. "He would've had no reason to ride all this way if Yi-Nereen were in Kerina Rut. I'm not saying we can trust him, but it sounds like he isn't our biggest problem anymore."

Kadrin chewed his lip. Wasteland dust speckled his cheek, and Jin resisted the urge to brush it away.

"What happened out here, Jin?" he asked. "You said raiders ambushed you and Yi-Nereen. How did you know they were working for that pompous lizard over there?"

Jin hesitated. Her shame, her secret guilt, none of it mattered anymore. She had to lay all her cards on the table to give them the best chance possible of saving Yi-Nereen's life.

Well, not *all* the cards. She saw no earthly reason he ever needed to know about the kiss.

She heaved a sigh. "Okay. Here's what happened. I was on my way to Kerina Rut when a storm hit . . ."

The story took only a few minutes to tell, but to Jin it felt like hours. Kadrin's face shifted through cycles of fear and awe, his mouth only opening on occasion as if to ask a question, then snapping shut as he gestured for her to continue whenever she paused for him. Finally she reached the skirmish in the ruins.

"The two raiders with me were distracted—that gave me the chance. I got the upper hand on one, so I grabbed her weapon and—"

A wave of horror crashed over her. Somehow she'd simply refused to let herself remember what had happened next. Now it came surging back, vivid and bloody. She'd *killed* someone.

"And what?"

Jin's head spun. She opened and closed her mouth, her throat hot and tight. "I . . . I . . ."

Kadrin's expression shifted. Perhaps he'd recalled how she looked when she showed up at his doorstep: trembling, covered in blood. "Oh," he said quietly.

The enormity of what Jin had done weighed on her—not just her confession to murder, but everything else. She couldn't explain what Falka might be capable of without touching on the life they'd lived in Kerina Tez. Every word barely held back the weight of all those fraught, wretched years. Until she'd finally turned her back on everyone—not just Falka, but Lorne and his apprentices and the street kids who'd depended on her for food and protection.

In this moment, Kadrin would realize she was far from the immovable, self-possessed courier she'd pretended to be all this time. He'd see her for what she was: a house of cards constantly on the brink of collapse. An eternal fuckup staggering from one mistake to the next.

Kadrin said nothing. Instead, he did the unthinkable: he took a step toward her, put his arms around her, and drew her close.

The breath left Jin's body in a startled gasp. She'd spent years avoiding the inevitability of Kadrin's pity. But now a small, broken part of her shattered into pieces. She let herself go limp even as she choked back a sob.

Kadrin tightened his hold. "Fucking hell, Jin," he said, "none of that should have happened to you." And she felt—or perhaps imagined?—the light press of a kiss on the crown of her head.

"You can't—you can't say *fuck*," she protested into his jacket. "You're a prince."

"And look who I've been spending time with lately."

They pulled apart. Jin swiped a hand across her eyes and realized she'd forgotten about Sou-Zell. "Shit." She whirled around; Sou-Zell was still lying beneath his bike, propped up on his elbow. He gave her a sardonic little wave when he noticed her looking. *Bastard.*

Kadrin rubbed his temples. "Okay. So this raider, Falka, has Reena, but we don't know where they are, only where they're *not*. Sounds like the only lead we have is to go back to the ruins."

Jin nodded tightly. She had a selfish reason to return to the ruins; her bike was still there. If a raider had so much as left a fingerprint on it, she'd choose violence.

"We need to decide what to do with *him*," she said.

The words had hardly left her mouth when she heard Sou-Zell call out, "I couldn't agree more. In fact, I have several opinions on the matter. Care to hear them?"

Jin stalked over to the fallen magebike. "I told you if you used your Talent on me again—"

"If you don't wish to be overheard, then keep your voice down," Sou-Zell said. "More importantly, I'm losing feeling in my feet. I hate to ask for your assistance, but no other option presents itself."

"Why should we help you? You read my mind constantly without permission, and you tried to kill me and Yi-Nereen when we escaped." Jin scowled. "Furthermore, you're an asshole."

"Firstly, Rasvel gave me a Talent, so I use it. Secondly, I punished the watch captain who gave the order to shoot at you. He won't be using his hands to load a crossbow anytime soon. Perhaps his teeth." Sou-Zell smiled thinly, though his face had lost its color. "As for your final accusation, I cannot refute it."

"Come on, Jin." Kadrin stepped up beside her. "Let's get the bike off him. Then he'll owe us a favor."

"Ever the optimist," Jin grumbled, but she moved to help. She and Kadrin lifted Sou-Zell's magebike back onto its kickstand. It was a handsome model, Jin noted grudgingly, with a custom steel-form frame. Lean but powerful, like hers—though hers needed its seat replaced, and its fenders were more grime than steel.

Sou-Zell sat up and rubbed his shins. The knife he'd held to Jin's throat was nowhere in sight. She eyed the many pockets on his vest and realized she'd forgotten to bring a weapon of her own. Hopefully Kadrin's confidence in his swordsmanship was warranted; he and Sou-Zell might be coming to that duel sooner rather than later.

"Now we can have a civil discussion," Sou-Zell said. "The bounty hunter I hired deceived me; I admit it. She's made off with Princess Yi-Nereen, and the two of you have no idea where they've gone. But you know where to start looking. Am I right so far?"

"We're wasting time," Jin said.

"Then I'll be clear—I intend to follow you. It will save everyone's time and energy if we travel together."

Jin crossed her arms. "Absolutely not."

Sou-Zell sighed. "I should have known a woman wouldn't be reasonable." He turned to Kadrin, and again Jin saw his expression change—that subtle look of disgust. She knew that look well, had seen it leveled at her mother countless times. People like Sou-Zell believed the Talentless were less than human. An absurd, ridiculous belief. It made her want to punch him again.

Kadrin didn't seem to have noticed Sou-Zell's expression—or if he did, he didn't react. "I agree with Jin," he said. "We won't let you *or* the Knights of Rut take Reena back to your city."

"Haven't I made myself clear?" Sou-Zell's voice was soft but cutting. "I don't care where you take the princess, as long as you don't give her to her father. What I *do* care about is tracking down a woman who cheated me. I'll recover the coin she stole and ensure she never crosses me again. In this, I believe, our interests align."

"Fine," Kadrin said.

Jin, who had been on the verge of saying *The answer is still no, and fuck you* with great satisfaction, turned to Kadrin in disbelief. "What? He'll steal Reena away at the first opportunity. You're being naive—"

"That isn't going to happen," Kadrin said. He'd flinched when the word *naive* left Jin's mouth, and she regretted saying it. But his brown eyes were clear, and his voice was steady with resolve. "He won't lay a hand on her, not with both of us around. And the fact is, Jin, we need another sparkrider."

Jin looked away and cursed under her breath. He was right. It was too much of an advantage to pass up. She didn't know if Faolin and Yi-Nereen were still together, but even if they were, what condition would Faolin be in?

Her skin crawled at the thought of keeping a mindreader nearby, but at least Twinblessed couldn't use both their Talents at the same time. As long as Sou-Zell was on a magebike, her mind was her own.

Sou-Zell glanced between her and Kadrin. He probably couldn't decide which of them was worse: a woman or a Talentless. "Then we have an accord? Good. I left the city as soon as I could, but the Knights of Rut are surely close behind."

"The knights think she's in Kerina Sol," Jin said. "They don't worry me. There's only one person who does."

Kadrin touched her arm. "Would Falka hurt her?" he asked quietly. "You know her best."

Jin sighed and turned her gaze toward the horizon, where the highway met the pale blue sky in a delirious shimmer. "I don't think I do. Not anymore."

*Second Age of Storms, 51st Spring*

*Dear Kadrin,*

*Yet again I must apologize for a long delay since my last letter. You must tire of my excuses. I did receive your letters inquiring after my health, and I am happy to report that I am, indeed, well. The darkness—if we shall call it that—has not come upon me for almost a year now. It is a small victory to rise from one's bed every morning, but I celebrate it nonetheless.*

*No, I fear my recent silence has been for a perfectly mundane reason. I have been subject to all manner of social engagements. Dinners, balls, ceremonies . . . Since Mother went to Rasvel last winter, I have taken on her responsibilities as Lady of the Tower in addition to my own. It has been difficult to find time to meet with our courier without attracting my father's suspicion; he has been far more attentive to me lately. I hope it is not too callous of me to say the sooner he remarries, the better.*

*In your last letter, you asked if I was grieving for Mother. I have struggled to answer that question, even for myself. My brothers wept when she breathed her last, and again when we gave her body to the spring, but I did not. I am convinced I loved her, at least when I was a child. So what, then, is this hollowness within me now I am grown? It is like a seed that should have bloomed but never did. Perhaps because the earth in which it was planted was sour.*

*I don't expect you to give me answers, Kadrin. But thank you for listening.*

*Still enduring,*
*Reena*

## CHAPTER TWENTY-FOUR

# TESTAMENT

*Second Age of Storms, 51st Summer, Day 24*

Wind whistled through the ruined temple and over the courtyard where Jin knelt before the statue of Makela. She pressed her hand to the ground, as if she might be able to sense where Falka and Yi-Nereen were now. Beside her was a patch of dust stained dark with blood. When Jin closed her eyes, she saw the trident in her hands sinking into a woman's chest, parting flesh and grinding against bone. So she tried not to blink.

"I can't tell where these tracks lead," Kadrin said. He squatted a few paces away, squinting at the marks the raiders' magebikes had left in the dust, and gestured vaguely. "Here's one set going that way. I think."

"Probably mine," Jin said. *When I left her.*

She raised her face toward the weathered stone statue. It must have taken great skill to sculpt the veil draped over the statue's head and shoulders; the folds of fabric looked so real and soft, she felt they might deform if she touched them. Only the eyes of the Talent Thief, hidden beneath the stone veil, knew where Falka had gone. Jin wished she could pray for answers, but in truth, she'd never had much use for the gods. It wasn't likely they'd answer her now.

Kadrin's footsteps crunched over silt behind her. "Jin—"

"I've found something." Sou-Zell's voice, echoing through the courtyard. "Come and see."

Jin glared at Sou-Zell, who stood at the bottom of a crumbling staircase leading to a different part of the ruins. She hadn't meant to lose track of him, but hell if the fucker wasn't slippery as an oiled cat.

"Don't tell me what to do," she said, but she followed him anyway, Kadrin in tow.

They went up the stairs, through a shadowy arcade lined with cracked pillars that led to another, smaller courtyard, and there, at the top of the steps leading down into it, Jin's blood turned to ice. At the courtyard's center was a wide square of bare earth. Perhaps a tree had once grown there, but there was no tree now.

The butt of a trident had been thrust into the earth like a stake, its prongs pointed at the sky. Impaled on the trident's tines was the body of the raider Jin had stabbed. Her head was thrown back, sightless eyes fixed on the sky, jaw hanging slack.

Jin felt Kadrin's hand on her arm; she tore herself away and turned her back on him, on the body in the courtyard, on everything. Bile rose in her throat.

*Why?* Why had Falka done this?

"Rasvel have mercy," she heard Kadrin mutter.

"She hasn't been dead long." From the sound of Sou-Zell's voice, he was down in the courtyard with the body. He didn't sound horrified, merely curious. "Perhaps a day or two. Hmm. There's a note here." Though Jin refused to look, her traitorous imagination showed her Sou-Zell reaching toward the corpse, his fingers brushing against her bloody chest. "It's addressed to Jin-Lu. I suppose that's you, Courier?"

"Read it." Jin kept her back turned. "What does it say?"

"Are you sure?" Sou-Zell's indolent drawl made her want to drive a tire iron through his skull. "That sounds to me like an invasion of privacy."

"Give it here," Kadrin said. Jin heard his footsteps descending into the courtyard and the rasp of parchment as he presumably snatched the note from Sou-Zell's hands.

"*Dearest Jin-Lu. This is goodbye. You won't see me again, nor your princess. Her Highness is going to help me change everything. With her death—*"

Kadrin's voice broke. Jin almost turned around, almost went to him. But the horror of what she'd seen in the courtyard stayed her. After a moment, he went on.

"*With her death, I'll have the power to take my—my vengeance.* That's all it says." Kadrin sounded as lost as a child. "Jin, what does that mean? Is she going to kill Reena?"

Jin couldn't speak. Her chest throbbed. *Falka, what have you done? What have I done?* Though the ruins were still, she heard a scream in her ears, shrill and full of blame.

She'd wished so many times for Falka to return from the dead. But this wasn't Falka. The girl Jin had known in Kerina Rut had been feral and filled with bitterness, but still human: vulnerable, capable of love. Now that girl was truly gone. It was like losing her all over again, with interest.

*And Faolin is caught up somewhere in this mess.* Instead of saving his sister, Jin had led him to his doom.

Through the ringing in her ears, she heard Sou-Zell's scathing tone. "That's what it says, isn't it? Can't you read, boy?"

Kadrin's voice, shaken but hard. "Don't call me that."

"I'm certainly not going to call you Highness. I've seen mongrel dogs with stronger claim to royalty. A pity you weren't drowned at birth; we wouldn't be here looking for Princess Yi-Nereen then, would we? She would be safe at home."

The rasp of a sword unsheathed. "One more *word*—"

Jin turned. Down in the courtyard, Sou-Zell and Kadrin faced each other from opposite sides of the impaled corpse. Kadrin's rapier shivered in the air, a line of silver. Sou-Zell stood weaponless, but he looked like a cat flexed to spring, his lip drawn back in a silent snarl.

"Stop," Jin whispered. Then, louder—"Stop!"

Though every step toward the corpse filled her with horror, she forced herself forward until she stood between Kadrin and Sou-Zell. The ringing in her ears hadn't stopped. Her body was shaking from fear and disgust. But she made herself stoop to pick up the bloody scrap of parchment that lay discarded at Kadrin's feet.

While Kadrin and Sou-Zell glared at each other, Jin reread the note. The slant of the script tore at her heart—the faint body memory of Falka tracing the word *Mine* on her skin in the dark—but she pushed the pain away as she read. She had to understand what this meant.

*Her Highness is going to help me change everything.* Falka had said something similar earlier, hadn't she? *I'm here for the shieldcaster princess. The kid will make a nice bonus. He's sparktalented, isn't he?*

"Why did she care about Faolin?"

Out of the corner of her eye, she saw Sou-Zell shrug. "Who's Faolin?"

"The missing posters," Jin said slowly. "At the spring. All those sparkriders. Sou-Zell, you said it was probably raiders. Raiders kill couriers to steal our bikes and our supplies. But they don't live long, and there aren't hordes of them out in the wastes. Not enough to take that many people."

"You think it was Falka?" Sou-Zell sounded genuinely thoughtful. He seemed to have forgotten Kadrin's sword, still drawn and leveled at his heart. "Even if she's targeting sparkriders, Princess Yi-Nereen isn't one."

Jin groaned and dug her thumbs into her temples. She felt herself teetering on the edge of a vast abyss of revelation. "I don't know what Falka's doing. But this isn't about me—if it were, she wouldn't have gone through the trouble of taking Reena. What she always hated most . . ."

Kadrin blew out a huff of air. "Don't hold out on us, Jin. It's Reena's life at stake here."

Jin couldn't look him in the eye, not while they both stood in the shadow of a woman whose life she'd taken.

"Kerina Tez," she said. "I suppose leaving wasn't enough for her. She always talked about wanting to raze it to the ground."

"So is that where they've gone?" Kadrin asked. "Kerina Tez?"

"Yes. Maybe. I don't know." Jin raised her trembling hands to her face. "I still don't know how she plans for Yi-Nereen to help her. Or why she's rounded up a bunch of sparkriders."

She almost mentioned what she'd managed to keep to herself thus far: that Falka had been born Talentless. It still didn't make sense. The only possible explanation—even though Jin knew it was wrong—was that Falka had concealed her sparktalent from Jin for years. But what if there was another possibility?

Sou-Zell ambled away from Jin and Kadrin to stand on the other side of the corpse. He sucked in a breath. "Now, that's interesting."

Jin forced herself to join him. There on the back of the raider's neck was a Talentless brand, raised and white. Jin bit her lip in shock. "But . . . she was a sparkrider. I saw her on a bike."

"Another one," Sou-Zell said. "Talentless, yet somehow spark-talented. What does it mean?"

So he already knew about Falka. Jin didn't ask how; it didn't matter. Here was proof Falka hadn't lied to her. She truly *had* been Talentless, and so had at least one of her raiders. That meant—

"Wait." Kadrin had followed Jin; she was glad to have his steady presence nearby, even though she still couldn't look at him. "Missing sparkriders and Talentless who've somehow gained sparktalent? That's no coincidence. And here we are, in a temple dedicated to the Talent Thief." His voice was hushed, like someone might overhear him and accuse him of blasphemy. "Could they be stealing another's Talent for themselves?"

Sou-Zell scoffed. "Talent is not some shiny bauble to be snatched by a thief. It is a person's soul; it is part of what they are. You cannot steal it any more than you can pilfer the blood from someone's veins, or the breath from their lungs."

The memory of Yi-Nereen's lips on hers in the storm—her veins burning, alight with electricity—made the hairs on Jin's arms stand on end.

"You can steal a person's mana," she said. "Why not their Talent?"

Sou-Zell glared at her. "What are you talking about, woman?"

Jin sensed Kadrin bristle beside her; this time she put a hand on *his* arm. "Some shieldcasters can take a person's mana. Siphon it right out of their body. Maybe Talent works the same way."

"What you speak of isn't possible."

"I've seen it done," Jin said. "So I don't care what you think."

"I believe you," Kadrin said. The warm rush of gratitude this brought Jin dissipated instantly with his next words: "So how do they do it?"

Jin opened her mouth but could think of nothing to say.

Against all odds, Sou-Zell came to her rescue with a dismissive

"What does it matter? All of this is conjecture, and we are no closer to finding the princess. If the bounty hunter's plan involves killing Yi-Nereen, we are certainly too late to stop her." He brushed road dust from his jacket. "There is nothing more to learn here. I will leave this place and rendezvous with the Knights of Rut. The princess is beyond their reach now, so I might as well join forces with them to find her killer."

"You'll give up so easily?" Jin rounded on him, her hands in tight fists. "Leave Yi-Nereen for dead, just like that?"

Sou-Zell lifted his chin, looking down at her with unveiled disdain. "I . . . regret her loss," he said. "But I do not believe in miracles, or children's stories, or clinging fast to a hopeless cause. I am responsible for my family alone. If Princess Yi-Nereen is no longer my intended bride, I owe her nothing."

"You came to warn her," Jin said. "*At great personal risk*, you said. Forget owing her something or getting your money back—you must care about her, at least a little."

Something in Sou-Zell's dark eyes shifted; it reminded Jin of the games she'd played on feast days as a child, puzzles where a piece moved or a lever rose when you took a step toward the right solution.

"You know nothing," he said. "All this foolish posturing is just a way of staving off reality. You cannot save her. Cast me as the villain if you like; I do not care."

Jin burned with anger. She wanted to fly at Sou-Zell again, but it would solve nothing. She wanted to tell him all the reasons he was a bastard and deserved to die alone, but that was a mindreader's game: playing with people, turning them into weapons against themselves.

*But you don't need to be a mindreader to play that game.* Jin's anger cooled as she realized Falka had manipulated her, too. When they were young and Jin had been helpless but to love her, she'd kept Jin starved for her affection, always longing for more. Now she'd left Jin the corpse of a woman she'd killed on display with a note pinned to her ruined chest. The note wasn't a goodbye, nor was it a gloating celebration of triumph.

"It's misdirection," Jin said. "The only reason she would go to all this trouble is if we *do* know where she's going. Because I've already been shown the way."

She turned to Kadrin. As she did, she saw a muscle in Sou-Zell's jaw twitch, as if he were annoyed she hadn't risen to his insults. Well, screw him. If his way of gaining the upper hand was to provoke people, then simply ignoring him would drive him mad.

Kadrin was looking at her with new light in his eyes. "Well, Jin?" He sounded breathless and eager. "Don't keep us in suspense."

"There's a chamber full of bones," she said. "Under the ruins. Faolin showed me when we were looking for his sister. I don't know what's down there, but that has to be it."

"And if it isn't?" Sou-Zell asked.

Jin shrugged and kept her back turned on him. "Then it won't be your problem," she said. "You're leaving, aren't you?"

She waited. Every second ticking past brought a fresh wave of satisfaction; silence meant she'd cornered him. To give an answer either way would admit defeat. Quite honestly, she hoped he *would* leave.

"You won't be rid of me that easily," Sou-Zell said at last.

*Well, you can't win 'em all.*

Jin placed her hands in the outstretched palms of the statue. The stone at Makela's feet slid aside, revealing the passage. At the same time, she heard the rush of wings overhead. With a triumphant warble, Screech dropped out of the air and landed on the statue's head, his talons gripping the veil where Makela's eyes would be. The pteropter's feathers, gold along his back and iridescent purple in the crest that fanned out behind his head, shone brilliantly under the sun. Now, up close, Jin estimated he was the size of a small child. He cocked his head at her.

"Good gods," Sou-Zell said. "Is that a saurian?"

Kadrin laughed, his eyes shining with delight. "It's your saurian, isn't it, Jin? But he's so big! Didn't you say he fit inside your helm?"

"He's grown. Don't ask how." Jin sighed. "Hold on."

She dug through her pack until she found some dried meat wrapped in cloth. *This beast is just going to follow me around until I die, isn't he?* She tossed the meat up to the pteropter, who snapped it out of the air without leaving his perch. He didn't budge as Jin and the other two filed down the passage beneath the statue; she sensed his beady eyes on her back.

Jin had never been superstitious. But she desperately hoped, though she refused to admit it, that the pteropter's appearance was a sign they were going the right way.

Because if they weren't, Yi-Nereen and Faolin were doomed.

*Second Age of Storms, 51st Spring*

*Dearest Reena,*
*I'm always glad to hear from you, no matter how long you keep me waiting. If I could, I would trade you some of my responsibilities. How would you like to care for a whole passel of squirming kittens? One of the palace cats was ill after she gave birth, so I had to feed her little ones and keep them clean while she recovered. I rigged a water clock to drop a pebble on a gong every two hours so they wouldn't starve. They're so delicate when they're small.*

*My condolences, once more, for your lady mother. The hollowness of which you speak—I think it's pain, only in a different form. Everyone feels pain differently. It doesn't make you less human if you can't weep. It must hurt even more if you can't, I should think—all that grief walled up inside with nowhere to go.*

*One of the kittens didn't make it. Eliesen said I should have waited to name them until after I was sure they would all survive, but I don't think anyone deserves to pass on nameless. She was Zafyra. It's nothing compared to losing a mother, but I have to tell you, I bawled my eyes out over the poor little thing. I felt like I failed her. But you didn't fail your mother, Reena. I'm sure you've made her proud as a mother can be of her daughter.*

*I'm not sure I should even ask, but have you had any time to continue your research lately? You seemed close to a breakthrough the last time you spoke of the Scroll. No pressure from my side; I just know how much it matters to you.*

*All of my love,*
*Kadrin*

## CHAPTER TWENTY-FIVE

# NO HEAVEN

*Second Age of Storms, 51st Summer, Day 24*

Yi-Nereen was counting hours. In the darkness, she saw and heard nothing aside from Faolin's slow breathing in the adjoining cell and water dripping steadily somewhere nearby. She estimated each drip of water was three seconds apart, so every twenty drips was a minute. One thousand and two hundred drips meant the passage of an hour. But counting to one thousand without losing her place was a challenge, so every time she reached a hundred and twenty, she marked the count on her fingers. Ten fingers to an hour; then she started over.

She had to count, or the darkness would drive her mad.

If her count was right, four hours had passed since Falka had brought them to these lightless cells. And before that, it had taken perhaps an hour—Yi-Nereen hadn't been counting then—to reach Mount Vetelu's peak and the ancient castle perched there, a lurking silhouette Yi-Nereen had only glimpsed against the starry sky before Falka had dragged her inside. Another creation of the Road Builders, though it could hardly be called a ruin.

Nothing made sense now. From the mountainside, Yi-Nereen had seen the entire wasteland. She had looked in ignorance upon the land where she was born, recognizing none of it—the silver roads glistening in moonlight, the glowing torches of the kerinas, the flickering mass of storms moving slowly across the cracked expanse—until Falka pointed at a distant cluster of light and said, "That's Kerina Rut, Princess. Say your farewells, if you wish."

Then Yi-Nereen had oriented herself at last. She was far west of Kerina Rut, deep into the Barrens—a part of the wastes no courier dared explore, according to Jin. A secret underground road had led her here, from the ruined Temple of Makela into the very heart of Mount Vetelu. A road that bypassed the massive territorial saurians who roamed the surface.

The Lost Highway. Yi-Nereen shuddered at the thought—her childhood stories come to life.

What was Kadrin's version of the tale? *A secret road a person can only discover if they aren't looking for it, and they can only travel to its end if they are pure of heart. Somewhere along the way, all the sins of their ancestors will be washed away, allowing them to reach heaven.*

This couldn't be heaven. Yi-Nereen was the furthest a person could be from pure of heart, and her ancestors' sins—especially the unspeakable crime her grandfather had visited upon those twelve sacrifices during the Storm of Centuries—could never be washed away. Not while Yi-Nereen still carried the same parasitic ability her grandfather had discovered. Not when she had used it herself, considered wielding it as he had.

In the adjoining cell, Faolin shifted and whimpered in his sleep. Yi-Nereen lost count. "Damn," she said quietly. She had only moments to resume, or she'd lose track of time completely.

But the boy's voice softened her heart. She felt her way to the iron bars and put her hand through. Faolin had fallen asleep with his back pressed against the bars. Yi-Nereen stroked his sweaty, rumpled hair.

"Sleep," she whispered.

He'd fought again when they'd put him in the cell. At the sight of the tiny, lightless room, the boy had flown into such a spitting fury of fists and teeth that for a terrifying moment, Yi-Nereen thought the raiders would kill him. She'd cried out his name, and only at the sound of her voice did he stop struggling. After the raiders had left, he'd clung to her hands through the bars, and she'd felt the trembling of his body, his barely disguised panic.

Yi-Nereen had talked to him, even though he couldn't understand her. She told him stories of home, of Kadrin as a boy, of her sisters. From time to time he'd speak back in his own tongue, his voice soft and hesitant. In the end, she didn't know who was comforting whom. But Faolin's ragged breathing had eventually slowed and he'd fallen asleep.

Stroking his hair brought back confused memories of her younger sisters. She hadn't been permitted to spend much time with them after their mother's death; duty kept them apart. But even before then, she hadn't been close to them. She had felt a kind of resentment for them that made her feel hot and embarrassed now. They'd never raised their voices to the Shield Lord like she did; they faded into the background and let Yi-Nereen take her punishments alone. She shouldn't have expected anything else. It was survival, a game they played better than she did.

Somehow Faolin felt more like kin to her than her own siblings, despite the short time they'd known each other. She couldn't explain it, but she felt it: an unspoken bond curled around both their hearts like a sleeping serpent. It was quiet and uncomplicated, unlike everything else she cared about.

For all she'd suffered in Kerina Rut, Yi-Nereen had loved her city: the melancholy sound of the temple bells, the landscape of tiled rooftops she saw from her window each morning, the fragrant orchards tended by bloomweavers in green robes. She had loved her people and sworn to save them.

Now her city would fall as Kerina Tez had, lost to fear and lightning, because Yi-Nereen had failed in her duty. Falka had thrown her research to the winds; the only remaining copy lived in Yi-Nereen's head, and soon that would be lost, too.

She mouthed the words silently in the darkness, just as she'd written them down.

*We thought we knew better than the gods. We believed Talent was our claim to divinity. We excised the Talentless from our bloodlines like we were carving out a disease, but we were wrong. A tree is more than just its flowers.*

Kerina Rut would perish without ever knowing the truth. The simple, blasphemous truth.

*We were wrong. We* are *the cursed ones.*

Yi-Nereen's hair stood on end. Were those footsteps? Yes—someone was approaching the cell block. She scrambled to her feet and nearly lost her balance. She was still dangerously light-headed from mana thirst. Deprived of her Talent, she was helpless. Anyone could do whatever they liked to her—kick her, strike her, lay stripes over her knuckles with a birch rod until she played the hymns without a mistake—

The stone door opened. Light spilled across the cell block. Yi-Nereen shielded her eyes. When she lowered her hand, Falka was standing outside her cell in unnerving silence. Yi-Nereen opened her mouth to speak when she heard another sound, distant but chilling. She'd heard it before, muffled by stone, but with the door open she knew it for what it was. A rovex's roar.

"What is that?" Yi-Nereen breathed.

Falka shrugged. She resembled a ghost, pale and still stained in blood. "When the Road Builders abandoned this place, they left some things behind. Prototypes, apparently." Her voice was hoarse. "Don't ask."

Yi-Nereen shivered. *That* raised even more questions, but a different mystery still burned in her mind. "You stole a sparkrider's Talent." Saying the words aloud felt like heresy, but that was nothing new to her, not anymore. "What happens to the victim? Do they die? Is that what happened to Faolin's sister?"

"Yes," Falka said simply.

A chill settled into Yi-Nereen's bones. Hardly a surprise after everything she'd learned, but still, here it was in stark black and white: the reason why Falka had brought her to this place. This was her fate, to have her Talent ripped away, to die incomplete.

She'd tried for years to convince herself the beliefs she'd been raised with were a lie. She'd told herself, over and over, that Talentless were real people with the same hopes and dreams as the Talented. They weren't born without souls—they were just different. Kadrin was proof, wasn't he? He was the purest man she'd ever met; surely some reward awaited him after death, something more than oblivion. She wanted to cling to those convictions.

But the priests' words still echoed in her head, and she could not silence them.

*Without a soul, one cannot be reborn in paradise.*

Yi-Nereen had no illusions about her own soul. It was sour, bruised, a shattered rind with all the goodness sucked out of it—but it was hers, and without it she was nothing.

If she had the strength, perhaps she would break down and beg. But sapped of mana, alone and helpless, confronted with her worst fear, Yi-Nereen could not even summon the wherewithal to plead for her life. Instead she asked, "Does it hurt?"

Falka looked at her for a long while before answering. Though the darkness made it hard to discern the other woman's features, Yi-Nereen fancied she saw something other than impatience on Falka's face. Was it regret? Hesitation? But when Falka spoke, her voice was perfectly level.

"It's painful for the recipient. Like coals beneath your skin, smoldering for days. As for the donor? What does it matter? Death is worse than any pain."

*Spoken like someone who has never longed to die*, Yi-Nereen thought, but she said nothing.

In the face of her silence, Falka shrugged. "You'll find out soon. But not just yet."

In the cell beside Yi-Nereen's, Faolin had awoken. He was sitting up, wary gaze fixed on Falka. He couldn't have understood their conversation, but perhaps he sensed something was about to happen. Now Falka turned toward him and fit a key into the lock on his cell door.

Yi-Nereen had prepared herself to die. But it had never occurred to her that she might not be first.

"No," she said. "Not him. What are you doing?"

The cell door opened, and Faolin moved. He leaped to his feet and cast a shower of sparks at Falka, so bright Yi-Nereen shut her eyes on instinct. But Falka was unfazed, even as the sparks hissed against her skin. Squinting past the white-hot impressions the sparks had left on her retinas, Yi-Nereen saw Falka hurl the boy against the wall and draw her saber.

The hilt struck Faolin's temple with a sickening thud. The boy slumped, senseless and bleeding. Falka dragged him from the cell, his legs trailing over the stone floor.

Yi-Nereen forgot her exhaustion. She hardly felt the bruising chill of metal against her skin as she threw herself at the bars, rattling her cell door on its hinges. "*Stop*, please." Her voice was alien to her, desperate in a way she didn't recognize. "Take me; I'm ready to die, *please*—"

Falka ignored her as she stepped into the open doorway, still dragging the boy behind her. In the light spilling from the hallway, Yi-Nereen saw Faolin stir, his eyes fluttering open. He whispered something, weak and confused. "Amrys . . ."

Then the door ground shut, and Yi-Nereen heard nothing but her own ragged breathing.

Alone. She was alone in the pitch black.

Slowly her heartbeat calmed, but the pressure in her chest wouldn't go away. It built to a crescendo—she wished it would squeeze her heart until it burst. Yi-Nereen did the only thing she could: she pressed her face against the bars and screamed.

In the raw sound of her voice, she heard years of unspoken grief: for her mother, for the love and hatred she bore her father and brothers, for the twisted, hollow creature she had become. It erupted from her in a deafening, endless torrent.

Then all was silent, and she wept.

*Second Age of Storms, 51st Spring*

*Dear Kadrin,*

*You mention the pride a mother has for a daughter. I cannot recall ever wondering if Mother was proud of me. Here in Kerina Rut, pride is not a feminine virtue. Women strive to be humble, graceful, skilled, even intelligent, and we either succeed or fail to satisfy these requirements. But success is not accompanied by fanfare. It is merely what is expected. I believe my competences satisfied Mother while she was alive, but the problem with being First Daughter of one's House is there are no achievements to obtain and be done with. There is only lifelong service.*

*You ask about my research? The Scroll was extremely useful, but it turns out time spent away from my studies has been the most valuable of all. I have a theory, Kadrin. I'm almost afraid to tell you for fear of disproving it later, but you deserve to know.*

*What if the Talentless aren't a mistake? (I know in my heart they are not. You, especially, are not a mistake. But this is what the priests have told us, and this is what I seek to disprove.) The harder we try— by one barbaric measure or another—to reduce the number of Talentless children born, the more appear, as if to spite us. What if it isn't spite? What if the gods are trying to make us understand something?*

*Rasvel and Makela aren't enemies. One gives and one takes, but taking isn't always stealing. Sometimes things have to be taken away for the good of the bereft. I know that probably makes no sense. But there's something here; I feel it. I'm close to a discovery. And it will all be thanks to you.*

*I'm sorry about your kitten. Zafyra got to know you and what it was like to be cared for while she was still in this world. Take solace in that; I know I do.*

*Ever yours,*
*Reena*

## CHAPTER TWENTY-SIX

# THE LOST HIGHWAY

*Second Age of Storms, 51st Summer, Day 24*

In the chamber behind the temple mural, choked with the ancient musk of death, Jin knelt among skeletons. Sou-Zell had already gone ahead to investigate the next passage, and though she knew time was short, this was something she had to do.

"I'm here," she said to the bones of a child nestled between two adults who had died propped up against the wall: "I see you. When this is done, you'll get a proper funeral."

When she'd sent sparks into the first sconce inside the temple to light the way as Faolin had done, something unexpected had happened. She'd *felt* something: the same way she sensed how fast the pistons in her engine were firing when she sent sparks down the intake, she felt her sparks traveling through the wall and spreading through the temple like spiderwebbing cracks in a pane of glass. As she stood there, hand pressed to the sconce, she felt the whole place come alive around her. She became a part of it: one moment she'd been Jin-Lu the courier, human shaped, and now she was a vast structure with lonely ruined wings, fallen columns, and archways that moaned as the wind came through, a place whose caretakers had long since gone away—

Then she'd snatched her hand back. The foreign sensations

faded instantly, though the lights stayed on. She'd broken out in a cold sweat. And Kadrin, looking concerned, had asked why she was crying.

The temple had whispered to her about these bones. There had been a calamity—some deadly threat outside. Everyone in the temple had taken shelter here, inside the secret vault. But when the danger passed, they'd been trapped. Unable to open the mural from the inside, they'd starved to death.

Jin straightened.

"Wedge something in the door," she told Kadrin, who stood watching her. "Trust me."

Sou-Zell came back into the chamber. "It's a road."

Jin and Kadrin stared at him and said simultaneously, "What?"

"A highway," Sou-Zell said impatiently. "Underground. It doesn't lead to another part of the temple; it goes much farther than that. We'll need our bikes."

Sou-Zell was right. Past the chamber of bones, the hallway veered downward and became a tunnel. Standing on cracked black cement, Jin breathed deep; under the mildew, she smelled exhaust fumes.

"Here," Kadrin said, handing her a sack. "What you asked for from the other chamber."

Jin glanced in the sack. Mana bottles glowed inside. "Thanks. We might need them." Who knew how far the tunnel went? It could even lead them out of the wasteland.

"Bottled mana?" Sou-Zell grumbled. "May well be poison."

"I wasn't offering *you* any," Jin said.

She straddled her bike and worked her hands over the grips.

Kadrin climbed on behind her. He rested his chin on her shoulder for a brief moment that left Jin's heart in shambles.

"We're going to find her," he said.

Jin could only nod thickly.

Against all expectations, the tunnel turned out to be rather dull. Jin soon grew sick of staring at the same stretch of black cement illuminated by her headlights. The walls were marked here and there with hieroglyphs, but it wasn't worth slowing down to stare at them; they flashed by, mere blurs. The tunnel seemed to follow an irregular curve that twisted and looped back on itself, like the highways on the surface above. Jin wondered why it wasn't just a straight shot from the ruined temple to wherever the road ended. There were no forks, no exits, seemingly nowhere to go but onward.

As the hours went by, Jin's mind drifted. She could devote only so much attention to navigating the curves, and she'd even grown used to the sensation of Kadrin's arms around her waist. She thought of what lay at the end of this tunnel: Falka, Yi-Nereen, and Faolin.

*What am I going to do about Falka?*

Jin was already a murderer. But she'd killed that raider in a moment of desperation, with no time to think her options through. Falka was a different story. They'd once been closer than anything—they'd been in love. Now whatever bond existed between them was stretched to its thinnest point. If Jin tugged on it, she had a feeling it would snap.

Sou-Zell wanted revenge on Falka for cheating him. Kadrin probably didn't care what happened to her, as long as he saved Yi-Nereen. But what about Jin? What did *she* want?

She wanted answers. Why had Falka disappeared? Why hadn't she come to find Jin after becoming Talented? Why had she set out on this vengeful path? Was there any way Jin could save her? Even after all this time, after everything Falka had done . . .

Kadrin loosed his arm from Jin's waist and gestured vigorously. Jin snapped to attention and eased off the engine.

Ahead, the darkness gave way to an orange glow the color of firelight. It seemed to ripple and shift, reflective like liquid. It was just around a bend. She took the corner at a crawl, her skin tingling.

Before them lay a lake of molten orange, a liquid metal that gave off no heat. Thick sunset-colored mist formed eddies and currents above its surface in a pattern both strange and familiar. Because it was mana. It had to be, though it was the wrong color. Nothing else had that quality of being half smoke and half liquid, and though mana had no smell, Jin had smoked enough mana-cigs to recognize the way it cooled the air.

She fed the engine just enough sparks to keep it idling. Sou-Zell pulled up beside her.

"How unusual," he said, in what Jin thought was the understatement of the century.

"Is *this* what mana looks like in its true form?" Kadrin's voice in Jin's ear sounded far less perturbed than she felt. "Before the storms bring it to the surface?"

"I don't know." Jin exchanged a glance with Sou-Zell. For a single breath, she felt a grudging kinship with him; mana was as food or air to both of them, but this was a sobering reminder of how little they knew about its origins. "We'll either have to turn back or cross."

The road led onward into the orange mist. It formed a narrow bridge over the mana lake. No telling how far it might stretch to the other side—if there was another side.

Jin rumbled forward at a cautious pace. Mist closed over the road behind her. Now she was exposed, surrounded by glowing orange.

Something broke through the mana to her left—the immense

curve of a smooth back, many times the length of Jin's magebike and patterned with glowing stripes. Its skin gleamed wetly, like feathers fused by moisture. It moved through the smoke swirling above the spring's surface and slipped under again, vanishing from sight.

Jin's throat closed in terror. "Fuck." Only a handspan of concrete separated her from the mana on either side. She couldn't see the beginning or the end of the road. She was out in the middle of a void, and there was a fucking *monster* swimming around beneath her.

Fear took over. Sparks surged from her hands and hit the engine like water on flames—but instead of a hiss, the bike replied with a roar. They flew forward so quickly, Jin couldn't even see the road through the mist before she was plowing across it. Blood thundered in her ears; if Kadrin was shouting at her, she couldn't hear. She only felt his death grip on her waist.

There was the mana beast again, breaking the surface to her right this time—so close she caught a glimpse of a flat black eye the size of a magebike wheel, revealed by a whitish membrane that rolled back over the eye before the beast slipped underneath—

A tunnel! They'd reached the other side. Jin shot down the tunnel's mouth and into the darkness, leaving the orange glow of the spring behind. She had to force herself to slow down. A voice in her head still gibbered in terror. *What was that thing?* It was like a saurian, if saurians swam in mana like pteropters flew in the sky.

"Jin?" Now she could hear Kadrin's panicked voice in her ear. "What happened? You just took off."

"I—didn't you see?"

"See what?" Sou-Zell had stopped just behind her bike. Jin twisted around to stare at him and Kadrin both. How could they have missed the beast? It had surfaced twice, the second time so close she could have reached out and touched it.

She looked past Kadrin's confused frown at Sou-Zell. Over the glare of his headlights, she could see him only as a silhouette. If the mana vapors had given her visions, perhaps it wouldn't have affected Kadrin, but Sou-Zell was every bit as Talented as she was. Jin ground her teeth. Well, if he wasn't going to admit to hallucinating a saurian swimming in the mana, neither was she.

"Forget it," she said. "Let's keep going."

Yi-Nereen had lost track of time after Faolin had been taken away, leaving her in the dark. Time wasn't all she had lost. Gone, too, was her fear. She had faced all the horror and grief a silent prison cell could contain, and her ghosts lay quietly now. Something had crept in to replace them.

For the first time in years, Yi-Nereen burned with an unholy rage.

When Falka returned, Yi-Nereen lowered her veil over her face and stood at the bars of her cage, waiting. Light spilled from the door as it opened, but the veil shielded Yi-Nereen's eyes. She made out Falka's silhouette as the other woman stepped into the cell block.

For a moment, neither of them spoke. Then Yi-Nereen said, "I gather it's time."

"Vann wants to meet you first." Falka's voice was oddly flat. "Save your questions for him. He adores the sound of his own voice."

Yi-Nereen swallowed her shock. *Vann?* As in Tibius Vann, the disappeared inventor of the magebike? Was that Falka's mysterious patron? It made some sense; the man had been a genius. If anyone could unlock the secret of transferring Talent, it would be the same person who'd invented a way to cross the wastes. The truly laughable part of all this was that Yi-Nereen had always longed to meet him.

Now she would get her chance.

She allowed herself a moment of cold resolve. She would find out what Faolin had died for before she set it aflame—even if she burned along with it. If Jin ever came, at least she would find the ashes of Yi-Nereen's vengeance.

At the thought of Jin, Yi-Nereen's heart throbbed. If the circumstances had been different . . .

No. It didn't bear lamenting now.

Falka led Yi-Nereen out of the prison block and through a maze of passages. This castle was like some union between the ruined temple in the wastes and the Tower of Arrested Stars. The walls were hewn stone and smelled faintly of decay; scraps of rotting tapestries still hung here and there. Voices echoed from some of the chambers they passed. Yi-Nereen shivered, wondering if the voices belonged to Falka's raiders or the ghosts of the ancients who must have built this place.

A month ago, she would have been breathless with excitement at the prospect of exploring one of the Road Builders' creations. Here were the treasures of technology at the end of the Lost Highway, arrayed beneath her fingertips. But someone had gotten here first.

At the top of a spiral staircase, Falka opened a door and thrust Yi-Nereen inside. "Here she is," she said as Yi-Nereen struggled to rise from her knees and survey her surroundings.

Her first impression was of light. An entire wall of the room had been replaced with glass that admitted the crimson glow of the rising sun. Dawn washed over the mountain and the wasteland below. Yi-Nereen thought of something she'd once written to Kadrin: *I've been thinking about what you said, about beautiful things bringing you joy.*

Pain stabbed at her heart. How unfair it was she would never see him in the flesh, the man he'd grown into. He must have changed so much. Was his smile the same as it had been when they were children playing together in sun-drenched gardens—the smile that stole her breath every time she looked at him? She would never know, just as she'd never know if she could fall in love with him all over again. If she was even capable of love.

Tables filled the parlor, strewn with loose parchment covered in calligraphy and labeled drawings, as well as instruments: some Yi-Nereen recognized, including a set of scales and a water clock, and others whose function she could only guess, like the long metal tube mounted on a stand above a thin sheet of glass. Standing amid the chaos was an elderly man wearing spectacles. The smile he gave Yi-Nereen was inoffensive, almost meek. Her stomach twisted. Didn't he look familiar?

"Hello, Princess Yi-Nereen. We finally have the chance to meet. How wonderful!"

His voice was warm, and he was still smiling at her. Yi-Nereen's confusion deepened. She put a hand on the nearest table to steady herself, almost upsetting a pot of ink. Was *this* Tibius Vann? This harmless-looking old man who would've looked perfectly at home poring over scrolls in the Tower's archives? He seemed too frail to have any crossover with a band of murderous raiders.

"Who are you?" she asked.

*Second Age of Storms, 51st Spring*

*Dear Reena,*

*Sometimes I fear we will never meet. Don't laugh, but I have these night-mares from time to time. In them, I'll be on my way to Kerina Rut to see you, but when I arrive, something awful has happened. Sometimes you've died of plague or fallen into the spring; others, you've simply decided you don't want to see me anymore. Jin says it's my mind playing tricks on me, that dreams don't mean anything. I hope she's right.*

*Forgive me. I'm feeling out of sorts today. Yesterday evening at dinner, Father and Devros were discussing a recent Council meeting. Some of the royals want to end Rasvel's Sanctuary, closing our gates to refugees. It's against our faith, of course, but they say too many Talent-less are entering the city. The news from Kerina Tez has everyone fright-ened. A whole kerina descending into anarchy, with hundreds dead or injured every time a storm hits . . . I understand why the royals are concerned, though I don't agree with their proposal. Anyway, Father and Devros were talking, and I accidentally spilled my wine. The way they looked at me—like they were both just remembering my existence, remembering a Talentless was sitting at their dinner table with them, listening to everything they said.*

*When people look at me like that, I don't feel human.*

*I don't want people to fear their children being born Talentless. There must be a reason we exist, a real reason, not just a cruel joke played by the gods. Rasvel is kind; he looks after us all. He wouldn't have allowed thousands to be born just to cause trouble for everyone else. Would he?*

*Devotedly yours,*
*Kadrin*

## CHAPTER TWENTY-SEVEN

# REVELATIONS

*Second Age of Storms, 51st Summer, Day 25*

"My name is Tibius Vann. At least, it has been for the past forty years." The old man limped around a table and drew nearer to Yi-Nereen. He carried a cane with a metal tip that rang a clear, hollow note whenever it struck the stone floor. "Before that . . . ah, but we'll get there soon. First I want to see you. You'll forgive me for standing so close—my eyesight isn't what it was."

Bewildered, Yi-Nereen looked at Falka. The raider woman leaned against the wall near a display case filled with glowing bottles of mana. Her arms were crossed over her bloodstained white shirt, and she watched the old man's movements with a frown.

Where was Faolin's body? Yi-Nereen had expected to be brought to the place where the boy had died. Part of her stubbornly insisted that if she didn't see his body, he might still be alive.

Tibius stood an arm's length from Yi-Nereen, peering at her through his spectacles. Even in her weakened state, she realized she was stronger than the old man. She could snatch his cane away and bludgeon him to death before Falka could even cross the room.

In the dark of her cell, she'd decided she would stop at nothing to get her revenge. Mercy had failed to save Faolin's life; she'd given up her chance of rescue by sparing the boy, only for him to be murdered anyway. Vann, nodding and mumbling to himself as he examined her, was as complicit in Faolin's death as the rest of them. Yet something in Yi-Nereen quailed at the thought of striking down a helpless old man.

"Yes," Tibius said suddenly. He pushed up his spectacles and flashed her a distracted smile. "Just as I thought. A fine woman, like your mother, and very strong in the Talent, from what I hear."

Yi-Nereen stepped back. "You knew my mother?"

It wasn't the question she'd meant to ask, but it had slipped out. She couldn't shake the nagging feeling she *knew* him. She studied his face. He looked classically Tez-blood, like Falka herself: fair skin, thin-lipped mouth, prominent jawline. Few Tez-blood lived in Kerina Rut; she should not find his features familiar. Yet somehow they were.

Tibius hadn't answered her question. He was fiddling with the handle of his cane. After a pause, he turned and limped toward the glass wall, where a door led onto a balcony. "Shall we speak outside? It's stuffy in here."

"Stop wasting time, Vann," Falka growled from the corner. "I told you, Jin-Lu might show up. Don't underestimate her ability to fuck with your plans. She's got the spark, too."

"Forgive Falka her poor manners. Though I suppose she's correct; I do have a tendency to natter on at times. Still, important conversations are always better with a view, aren't they?"

Tibius opened the balcony door wide. Cool air blew inside, rustling the papers on the tables. Yi-Nereen followed. Vertigo gripped her by the throat as she stared over the railing. Below, the mountainside dropped sharply away to reveal the vastness of the wastes, tinged bloody by the rising sun. Scattered dark shapes moved in the distance: the rovex who guarded the Barrens, she guessed. Leading away from the mountain's base was a highway, like a black snake stretched across the gray-brown wasteland.

*So there is a highway that leads here.*

Yi-Nereen squinted, hoping to spot a magebike riding down that highway. But she saw nothing. Cold certainty settled into her heart. The roads in the Barrens weren't marked on courier maps, and Jin had no reason to search for her in the wastes. There would be no rescue.

"An awful place," Tibius said. "Dry and dead, like a mummified corpse. Nothing green and living, except for what the bloomweavers create—constructs of Talent, kept alive only by magic. There is so little here that is beautiful. Wouldn't you agree, Highness?"

"No," Yi-Nereen said, remembering the flowers Kadrin had sent her years ago and the dried petals she'd kept pressed in the pages of a book. "Enough of this." She squared her shoulders and faced the old man. "Who are you? I don't mean your name. I want to know where you come from and why you're doing this. Murdering people to steal their Talent—it isn't just wrong, it's unnatural. You brought me out here to talk, so explain yourself."

"Yes." Tibius was smiling again. "You do take after your mother, but I see a great deal of Zon-Lai in you as well. He used to make demands in that exact tone—as if to argue with him wasn't only a waste, but a sin."

"You knew my grandfather." It wasn't a question.

Tibius exhaled, tapping his chin. "He was my brother."

Yi-Nereen caught her breath. It wasn't possible. The man standing before her was clearly Tez-blood, with no traces of Rut to speak of. But . . . hadn't she studied this phenomenon in the children of people who had migrated between kerinas? The children looked like their parents at first, but after years of infusing from a kerina's spring, they began to resemble the people around them. Every mana spring left its own subtle signature on a person over time: shifting the color of their hair, the slant of their cheekbones, the density of their freckles. That was how you could tell a Lav-blood from a Rut-blood, and why couriers who had infused from several springs seemed to belong nowhere at all.

No wonder Tibius looked so mystifyingly familiar to her. Those dark, knowing eyes—she had seen them staring back at her from a portrait in her bower for as long as she could remember. They were her grandfather's eyes. He had died before she was born, but Yi-Nereen had never been permitted to forget his face.

No one in the Tower had ever breathed a word about Yi-Nereen having a great-uncle. She had assumed her grandfather had no siblings—that they had all been stillborn, or killed soon after birth if they were Talentless. People didn't speak about such things, and they certainly weren't recorded.

"Yes," Tibius said. "I've been conspiring to bring about this family reunion for many years. First with your mother, though I never succeeded before her untimely death, and now with you. It was no easy task, since I have been exiled from Kerina Rut—our home— for almost three-quarters of a century."

Yi-Nereen let out a shaky breath. "Are you . . . Talentless?"

It was the only explanation she could think of for Tibius's continued survival. Her grandfather had died the way all Talented who lived long enough did: the mana in his veins had betrayed him. That had been over twenty years ago.

"Not quite, but a good guess."

Tibius's eyes flared orange, and sparks danced across his wizened knuckles. Yi-Nereen's heart skipped. She'd studied her own family's genealogical records to near obsession; there was no trace of sparktalent recorded in her bloodline. She thought of the murals in the ruined Temple of Makela—of the shieldcaster child born to a bloomweaver and a Talentless. Rasvel's miracle, and unless this was all an elaborate trick, it had happened in her own family. What if it wasn't uncommon at all?

When one ceased to mindlessly accept everything the temple preached, all manner of things became possible. That was the truth she desperately wanted to tell the kerinas. A chance to *show* them— she'd sell her soul for that chance.

"In those days," Tibius said, "sparktalent was considered next to useless. You know this, I presume? I was older than Zon-Lai by minutes, but it simply wouldn't do to have our proud family line squandered by a lamplighter heir. So they left me in the wastes to die of exposure and cede the lordship to my twin brother. Fortunately, I lived long enough for the saurian herders to find me instead."

Yi-Nereen's mind spun with questions. She seized on one almost at random. "Saurian herders?"

"You've met them. That boy who came here with you, the sparkrider."

Yi-Nereen's stomach swooped. Faolin. She had never expected to be standing here, having a civil conversation with her kidnapper, but this was her chance for answers.

"Where is he?" she asked.

Something like annoyance flashed across Tibius's face—then his genial, sympathetic smile returned. "I'm sorry, child. His people are precious to me, for more reasons than one. But the boy and his sister were unfortunate enough to be born with Talent. I promise you this: his end was swift."

Anger swept through Yi-Nereen like a burning tide. She closed her eyes, choking on it. *Faolin, I'm sorry.* It wasn't enough, would never be enough.

"Show me," she said. "I want to see his body."

Her mind was at war with her heart. She'd come to this confrontation with nothing but certainty of her fate and a burning desire for vengeance. But the revelations Tibius was laying before her, one by one, in an enticing banquet of forbidden knowledge, were grinding against her resolve. A treacherous part of her was starting to believe she could reason with him. If she saw Faolin's body, she could reignite her rage, and the mist would clear. She would know what to do.

"I cannot." Was that remorse in Tibius's voice, or Yi-Nereen's wishful thinking at work?

"You cannot, or you will not?"

"The defuser I engineered from what remains of Road Builder technology is grievously crude. It breaks down all traces of the flesh so it can extract what remains." Tibius sighed, the most human sound Yi-Nereen had heard from him yet. "I'm working on a better machine, one with a much lower mortality rate. Regrettably, it isn't ready."

Was he regretful because Faolin was dead, or because his machine was imperfect? This line of questioning had done nothing to solidify Yi-Nereen's resolve. She couldn't even picture Faolin's corpse, just a vague, frightening image of him dissolving away into thin air. The defuser—that was a word she hadn't heard before. *De*fuse, the opposite of *in*fuse. Infusing mana was a natural process, as simple as physical contact. What would a machine that could do the opposite even look like?

"Why?" she whispered. "I understand Falka, a little. But what do you stand to gain from this? You invented the magebike. You could have been wealthy and powerful, never mind what our family did to you."

"I learned much among the herders," Tibius said. "Most of us have forgotten the ancient ways. We cling so closely to our Talents—our mutations—so we can pretend this wasteland is natural and compatible with human life." Tibius scowled at the horizon. "You say stealing Talent is unnatural, but understand this: there is nothing natural about the way you have lived. Mana isn't a gift from the gods; it's a drug we take out of desperation. The more we use, the more dependent we grow. Only the Talentless are free, but they won't remain so for long."

Yi-Nereen stared at him. He could have been reading her treatise aloud. Every word that fell from his lips was blasphemy, but blasphemy she had embraced by candlelight, poring over stolen records for years and coming to inescapable conclusions. *We are the cursed ones.*

In pruning the High Houses of their Talentless, the priests of Rasvel had doomed them all. The bloodlines had weakened, and the damage was perhaps irreversible. The only chance the kerinas had was to dismantle the High Houses altogether, end the practice of wedding Talent to Talent, and grant the Talentless the freedoms and prestige of which they had been robbed for so long. Yi-Nereen had known the priests and royals of Rut would sacrifice the world before they gave up their power, but nothing else would do; it was already too late.

"Great-Uncle," she asked, "do you know how to save the kerinas?"

She'd abandoned hope in the dark of her prison cell and given herself over to revenge. But if there was still a way . . .

Tibius put his hand over hers on the balcony rail. "Indeed I do, my child," he said. "I intend to undo the Road Builders' destruction of their own empire. I will restore the land to what it once was: a fertile cradle of civilization. The storms will be no more; the kerinas will be no more. Those who survive will awaken to a world where the boundaries of Talent no longer divide them."

Yi-Nereen looked at him sharply. "Those who survive?"

"It's simple." Tibius's face brightened, and not just from the light of dawn. The pressure of his hand on hers was surprisingly strong, considering his appearance. "The Talented need mana to survive. The only way to restore the wasteland is to drain its mana, like pus from a wound. So the Talented, who have used their power to subjugate those under their care instead of protecting them, will all die. Their sacrifice will lead us into a new age."

Silence reigned over the balcony. Yi-Nereen wanted to laugh. Drain the mana from the wastes? Kill all the Talented? It was the plan of a child with an overactive imagination. But the man standing before her was far from a child. He knew the secrets all the scholars of the kerinas had barely begun to guess existed. He could transfer Talent from one person to another; the proof was standing in the next room. What if he could truly accomplish what he was describing?

If the kerinas went on trying to purge their Talentless, the storms would kill them all. Yi-Nereen had banked on what she believed was their only hope: to cure the bloodlines and restore balance before it was too late. She had never once considered it might be possible to stop the storms.

"Great-Uncle—" she began.

"You're fucking kidding me." Falka stepped onto the balcony, the orange light of dawn falling over her. "That's your plan, Vann? You told me we were going to take out the High Houses and let the

Talentless rule the kerinas. You didn't mention they'd rule because we were going to *kill everyone else*."

"I hoped it wouldn't come to that." Tibius seemed unfazed by Falka's anger. "I wanted to find another way. But you made a mistake letting that courier escape, Falka. I told you to kill her. Now it's only a matter of time before she brings the knights here and our plans all crumble to dust—the careful work of a lifetime, in my case. No, I won't risk it. We have what we need, and this may be our last chance."

Falka scoffed. "Are you crazy? We're Talented, all three of us. We'll die along with the rest."

"Of course not." Tibius spoke with the impatience of a man explaining himself to a child. "The Road Builders destroyed themselves in their hubris, but at least a few of them were cautious enough to plan for the future. There is enough mana stored in the castle to last several Talented the rest of their lives, provided they use it prudently. We will survive—as we must, for all great change is followed by great upheaval. The inheritors of our new kingdom will need leaders."

Falka chewed her lip. "The High Houses can screw themselves, for all I care. But *all* the Talented?"

"It must be done!" Tibius's voice cracked like a whip. "We already killed the world. Now we haunt its grave. How long will the kerinas survive if nothing changes? Another generation, two? What good are those lives if it all comes to destruction in the end? We have a chance, here and now, to start fresh. Not only opportunity, but power—power that may never come again."

Falka eyed him and muttered, "How fortunate you were here to arrange all of this."

Tibius ignored her. "Only one question remains." He turned to

Yi-Nereen, his face softening. "Will you help me, my child? I need your gifts, but I need not take them by force. You can live, and we can work together."

Yi-Nereen could hardly breathe. So she had been right, and Falka wrong. Tibius Vann hadn't planned to kill her. And the future he promised—the land restored, the kerinas united, the Talentless freed—held its own bloody allure. Thousands would die, an unforgivable cost, but thousands more would live. And she and Kadrin would be among them. But what about . . .

*Jin.* An icy hand clenched Yi-Nereen's heart. She couldn't condemn Jin to die. But there would be time, surely, to find the courier and explain everything? To save her, induct her into their small group of surviving Talented.

Yi-Nereen squeezed her eyes shut. Visions of her own future flickered across the darkness of her eyelids. No father or brothers, no betrothed to keep her in a gilded cage and force her to bear his children. No one to stop her from going wherever she wanted, being with whomever she loved. Oh Rasvel, she would be *able* to love at last.

Could she really do this?

"My dear, this isn't a choice between right and wrong," Tibius said, his voice still paternal and kind. "It's a choice between our current suffering and living to see the world reborn. Live to see it with me, Yi-Nereen."

Her visions faded, replaced by a single face: Faolin, looking at her with sadness in his dark eyes. *Amrys.* What would he want her to do? His kin would all survive in Tibius's grand future. Would he have willingly paid his own life and his sister's in exchange? Yi-Nereen could still feel his damp hair between her fingers. Her chest ached.

She could ensure his death had not been in vain. Later, when the dust settled, she could see justice done to his murderers. The world was neither simple nor fair; she had always known this. Sometimes the guilty had to be spared for the greater good, at least for a while, despite what they'd done to the innocent.

As for the royals of the kerinas, hadn't she always known they would rather die than listen to her? Now they would have their wish.

Yi-Nereen opened her eyes and looked upon her great-uncle's smiling, wrinkled face.

"Very well," she said, and something shivered deep inside her. "How do we begin?"

*Second Age of Storms, 51st Spring*

*Dear Kadrin,*

*I wish I could reassure you, as you have so often done for me. Alas, my faith has never been blind. Do the gods have the best of intentions for us? I cannot say. What I do know is, you cannot rely on the goodwill of others if you want to survive. We must make our own destinies.*

*Yet even as I speak these words, I know they are unworthy of you, Kadrin. I fear it's selfish of me to ask you this, but please: don't let your light grow dim like mine.*

*I can't promise all will be well, but I can promise I will never turn away from you. Whatever truths I discover, be they good or evil, as long as you go on shining, I will find my way to you. Listen to Jin, not your nightmares. As infuriatingly stiff-lipped as our courier can be at times, she is wise. (And older than both of you. Don't forget that.)*

*You were born for a reason, Kadrin. Perhaps that reason was to remind the wastes that kindness and beauty don't require Talent to flourish. You must do more than survive; you must hold fast to yourself. Do this for me, if no one else.*

*I can only have faith in this world as long as you are in it.*

*The moon to your sun,*
*Reena*

# CHAPTER TWENTY-EIGHT

# HAND OF THE GODS

*Second Age of Storms, 51st Summer, Day 25*

"Incredible," Kadrin said. He was staring, mesmerized, at the walls sliding past the circular platform as it rose. The sconce's gently pulsing light illuminated his wide eyes and parted lips. "You can actually control the Road Builders' technology. I never imagined anything like this could exist."

Jin breathed through her nose and concentrated on quelling her nausea. She kept her hand pressed against the sconce, though she wanted nothing more than to rip it away so the platform would stop ascending. She had the sickening feeling they were already far above any height where it was reasonable for a human to exist. Why hadn't the Road Builders confined themselves to building things at ground level? No one but pteropters belonged in the sky.

"I need to tell you something," Kadrin said quietly. Now he was looking at Jin, which was a problem; if Jin were to puke, she would really prefer to do it when he wasn't staring at her. "Now that we have a minute alone, without that insufferable rogue breathing down our necks."

The insufferable rogue had agreed to stay below with the mage-bikes while Jin and Kadrin scouted the bizarre moving chamber at the end of the tunnel. At the moment, Jin envied him. She wrestled back a wave of nausea. "What is it?"

Kadrin took a deep breath. His expression was uncharacteristically serious. *That can't be good.*

"I want you to know . . . Damn it all, Jin, I want you to know how much I admire you. I know you don't consider me a friend, but—" His voice broke, and Jin's heart clenched. "I have a feeling we're walking into deadly peril, and I can't think of anyone I'd rather have by my side."

"Kadrin—"

"No, I'm sorry, I'm not finished." He sounded close to tears, and he looked it, too. Jin couldn't pull her gaze from his face—his dear, earnest face, which never could conceal his feelings. "I'm glad we met three years ago. That it was you and not any other courier."

Jin swallowed hard. Her stomach was churning. What would kill her first, her nausea or her guilt? Kadrin wouldn't be saying these things to her if he knew—about her and Reena, the way she felt about them both. She wasn't the friend he deserved.

"Please don't," she said. "Don't thank me."

Kadrin was silent for a moment, just looking at her in the dim blue light. Then he spoke in a hoarse voice: "I've never wanted to overstep or put you in an awkward position. But it will simply kill me if I never get the chance to tell you I—"

"I kissed Reena."

Jin's heart was beating so quickly she could hardly breathe. Now it was out in the open—the secret she'd planned to take to her grave. If she'd only waited a little longer, if he'd said nothing, she might have been successful. Who knew what awaited them at the top of this shaft?

"You . . ." Kadrin blinked and cleared his throat. For once, Jin found it impossible to tell what he was thinking. Was he angry? Hurt?

She wanted to explain the circumstances—that she and Yi-Nereen had been about to die, that the kiss had literally saved their lives—but an explanation would just be a lie in a different form. The truth was, Jin was in love with Yi-Nereen.

Of course, that wasn't the *whole* truth. But it was all she could justify letting on.

Kadrin put his hand over his face and coughed. No—that wasn't a cough. He was *laughing*. "By the gods, Jin. First my sister, and now Reena? Is there anyone else I know who you haven't kissed, or am I the only one on that list?"

Jin gaped at him. She had the distinct sensation that the platform had dropped away and she was rising through the air unassisted, completely weightless. "You aren't angry?"

For some reason, her question only made Kadrin laugh harder. Wiping a tear from his eye, he stifled a snort and said, "A little. But only because I'm feeling—well, left out, I suppose. To think, all these years I've been sending Reena love letters, and you've been having your way with her behind my back. It puts some things into perspective."

"Wait," Jin said in horror. "It isn't like that. Not at all."

The platform ground to a stop. In her distraction, Jin hadn't noticed it slowing down. They came to rest before a wheel-operated door like the one they'd found down below. Kadrin stepped forward and heaved at the wheel. It had taken Jin and Sou-Zell's combined effort to open the first one, but Kadrin made two full rotations before Jin could gather herself to speak.

"Kadrin, stop. I—"

The door rolled away. Wind swirled violently into the chamber.

Jin recognized the sharp taste of the air at once. Every courier knew that faintly chemical tang.

Kadrin had opened the door into a storm.

Falka's blood burned. She stood upon the castle ramparts, arms open to the heavens, and called the storm. Wasteland wisdom held that the storms came from elsewhere, were sent rolling across the land by the hand of the gods, but Falka knew the truth. The storm was everywhere, always, waiting to be brought to life. All it needed was the spark.

If Tibius was right—if the old man hadn't finally leaped off the precipice into full-blown madness—this would be the last storm she ever called.

"Better make it a good one," Falka muttered.

Her skin tingled as the tempest formed above her, a roiling spiral of dark clouds that began at a single point and spread rapidly outward. The clouds' underbelly flickered with violet light.

In her old life, Falka would have trembled with fear. It was every kerina dweller's nightmare to stand unprotected in the heart of a storm. But Tibius had taught her to control the storms as she had the Road Builders' loci, and Falka took fierce pleasure in the task. What had once been a source of terror had become the only way she felt alive.

But now . . . this would be the last storm. She would never be able to conjure this feeling again. Once Tibius and Yi-Nereen finished their preparations below, the wasteland would be changed forever. Death would sweep across the wastes, destroying everything and everyone Falka hated. It was victory, vengeance, freedom all in one. It was all she'd ever wanted.

So why did she feel so hollow? She saw Ziyal's impaled corpse whenever she closed her eyes. Whenever her hands were empty, she felt the warmth of the sparkrider boy's blood as she dragged him, still struggling feebly, toward the steel bed of the defuser. Even with the voice of the storm bellowing in her ear, she heard Jin's voice desperately telling her, *I came back, but you were gone. I looked for you.*

"Too late," Falka shouted into the howling wind. She bared her teeth and laughed at the sky: a shrill, desolate sound, even to her own ears.

Soon it would end. Everyone she despised would be gone—and she would have only herself to live with, for as long as she could bear it.

"Drink this," Tibius Vann said.

He and Yi-Nereen were in his parlor cramped with tables and equipment, and he held up a vial that shone so brightly Yi-Nereen couldn't look straight at it. The mana inside was blue, or something like it—a new hue she didn't have a name for.

"What is it?"

"I call it ambrosia." Tibius gazed hungrily at the vial; the light didn't seem to bother him. The old man's arm trembled as he held the vessel aloft, but his voice remained level and strong. "Your grandfather called it the Last Breath. This is why the boy who came with you had to die, child. His death is your gift."

A chill washed over Yi-Nereen. She had spared Faolin at the temple ruins, and both of them had been captured. Now he was dead, and she was about to consume his soul for its power. Had it all meant nothing? Had fate left her only the illusion of choice?

"I thought Falka wanted to steal his Talent," she said. Her voice came out uncannily flat, as if someone else were speaking, someone who felt nothing.

"The process is one and the same, but the effects—those depend upon the recipient. Falka was Talentless, so when she drank ambrosia brewed from a sparkrider's Last Breath and mana distilled by the Road Builders, it imbued her with the spark. You won't gain a new Talent, Yi-Nereen—your existing power will be amplified, many times over, but only for a short time." Tibius paused to take a breath; it seemed his speeches were beginning to tax him. "When Falka's storm touches the wasteland, you must be ready."

Outside the tower, the wind began to moan. The sky above the balcony darkened. Yi-Nereen shuddered. She remembered the tempest that had chased her and Jin from Kerina Rut, how bewildered Jin had been by a storm that could change direction. It must have been Falka's doing.

Yi-Nereen remembered believing the gods had sent that storm, to drive them into the right place to save the wastelander child. How naive she had been. Now she knew the truth: if there were gods in the wastes, they were Falka and Tibius Vann.

What was divinity but knowledge and the power to use it? With Falka as his right hand, Tibius would change the destinies of everyone in the known world.

And hadn't that always been her secret desire? She and Tibius had both been betrayed by the same House, the same system. His rejection had been sudden and violent, but Yi-Nereen's had been insidious: a lifetime of preparation for her fate as a sacrificial womb. And still they both loved their people enough to do what must be done.

In that moment, she thought no one loved them more.

"Ready for what?" she asked. "You still haven't explained what I am to do."

Tibius lowered the vial and sighed. "My brother discovered a rare ability locked away in our bloodline. Something only a powerful shieldcaster can use, for reasons even I don't understand. This ability is the same as the process I use to defuse Talented individuals, but while my process was discovered through extensive trial and error, yours is innate. This is what I need from you, child. Except you won't be draining a person of their mana. You'll be draining the entire wasteland."

Yi-Nereen took a step backward, stunned. "I can't—it doesn't work that way."

"It will, once you infuse this." Tibius shook the vial gently. A few brilliant bubbles popped at its surface. "Just as infusing distilled mana enhances a person's sparktalent, allowing them to operate the loci as if they were a Road Builder—you didn't know that, did you?—this ambrosia shall grant you a Road Builder's powers of creation and destruction. Just as they created the wasteland, so shall you destroy it."

"And the storm?" Yi-Nereen's voice was barely more than a whisper. "Why does Falka need to summon a storm?"

Tibius's smile faltered. "Not just a storm, my dear. The Storm of Centuries, though it hasn't been quite a century since the last one—a little more than half, by my count." His face darkened like the skies outside the glass window. "What a spectacular failure that was. I almost killed myself doing it, and for what? I had no idea what I was doing. I could have destroyed the entire wasteland without anything to show for it."

"You haven't answered my question, Great-Uncle."

"Of course. Such good fortune to have you here with me now,

child. A clever young mind to anchor a confused old man's thoughts. The storm is needed to stir up the land, to bring forth the mana pooled below. Only a sparkrider and shieldcaster, both immensely strong in the Talent and working together, can pull this off."

*I wish it were Jin.* The thought sprang unbidden into Yi-Nereen's mind. *I wish she were here with me, she and Kadrin both, so I could explain to them what I'm doing and why. It's for both of them. For Kadrin, so he doesn't feel alone and unwanted ever again. For Jin, so she never has to worry about her mother.*

"You needed me," she realized aloud. "You were waiting for me to escape Kerina Rut and come to you. All of this—you've been planning it for years."

"Decades," Tibius said. "Since before you were born. This is our family's legacy." He smiled at her, a smile so warm and paternal it jolted her with its unfamiliarity. "*Your* legacy, Yi-Nereen."

Her legacy. Not a life of servitude, not children with a man she despised.

*For good or ill, I will leave my mark on the world.*

Her head still ached fiercely from mana thirst. Truly, it was a miracle she'd gone this long without passing out at Tibius's feet. Yi-Nereen held out her trembling hand.

"Very well. I'm ready."

The vial was so cold it numbed her palm as soon as Tibius placed it there. The old man was wearing gloves, but Yi-Nereen's skin was bare. She pried the cork free with her teeth, as she had seen Jin do before, and gulped down its contents.

Her muscles went rigid. The vial fell and shattered on the floor. The cold hit her all at once, soaking into every inch of her body. Then, like a cloth soaked in oil and lit with a spark, she went up in flames. A small logical part of her knew she wasn't truly burning, because Tibius's bony hands were clenched on her arms, holding her in place as she seized and whimpered.

*Reena.* A voice cut through the roaring in her nerves, the muffled screams trapped inside her chest. *Reena, what's happening? I can hear you again. Have they killed you, too?*

Yi-Nereen's vision swam; blue washed over Tibius's study, the vibrant blue of mana. The agony setting her blood afire made it almost impossible to think. But she knew that voice, though she had never heard it speak in a language she fully understood.

It was Faolin.

# PART FIVE

## CHAPTER TWENTY-NINE

# INTO THE STORM

*Second Age of Storms, 51st Summer, Day 25*

"This is madness!" Huddled in the doorway to the lift, Sou-Zell stared at the sky outside with fear and loathing. "Storms are deadly enough on the ground. We must be miles above the earth. No shieldcaster, no shelter. If you go out there, you'll die."

"I didn't bring you up here to whine," Jin said through gritted teeth. "Now listen. This isn't a natural storm. Falka's controlling it somehow. And if one sparkrider can call down a storm, two of us might have a chance of getting through it intact."

Minutes ago, she'd ventured onto the narrow, rocky path leading away from the lift. The wind had battered her so violently she'd thought it would sweep her off the dizzying drop to her right, but she had to *see*. She couldn't just give up and wait out the storm. What if Yi-Nereen was being held captive just around the corner?

What she'd witnessed was impossible. Around the mountain's shoulder was a ruined castle perched above the void, like a gray-feathered saurian overlooking the wastes. The growing storm swirled around a single point atop the ruin where a distant figure stood, so tiny Jin could barely identify them as human.

But she knew in her gut who it was. Just like the first time she'd seen Falka command a storm: the day she'd crashed her magebike on the road to Kerina Rut.

"How?" Sou-Zell demanded. "Convince me you aren't insane."

Jin let out a frustrated growl. She'd forgotten—Sou-Zell might have sparktalent, but he wasn't a true sparkrider. *He* had certainly never fled down a highway with a storm licking at his heels before.

"Look, if a sparkrider gets caught in a storm, it's bad. But you can survive for a little while. You have to anticipate where the next bolt is going to strike. If you're quick enough with your Talent, you can redirect it. Like swerving your bike around a hole." You didn't need to be strong to redirect mana lightning, just fast and lucky.

Sou-Zell's eyes flared violet. Jin's skin crawled; she couldn't *feel* him digging into her mind, but knowing he was doing it was sickening enough. After a moment that felt like hours, the glow faded from Sou-Zell's eyes and he said brusquely, "You aren't lying. Or at least, you believe your own words."

"Why would I lie? To get both of us killed? Fuck, you really don't trust anyone, do you?"

"It's still the plan of an imbecile."

Jin wanted to snatch Sou-Zell by the collar of his bone-studded vest and fling him over the drop. She hoped he was reading that thought. But even if his sparktalent was weak, his help would drastically increase her chances of getting through this storm alive.

In theory, anyway. Jin had never done it before. All she had were Lorne's stories, and if she was honest, he'd been known to exaggerate.

She turned to Kadrin. "You stay here. It's going to be hard enough getting the two of us through, and you're . . ."

"Deadweight?" She'd never seen him wear such a bitter smile. It didn't suit him at all. "Forget it. I'll stick close, and if a bolt hits me, well, it hits me. Just make sure you keep going if it does."

His tone made Jin's blood run cold. "Stop saying shit like that!" She shook out her hands, trying to quell the terror building inside her. "There's no reason to be an idiot. *Stay. Here.*"

"I won't do that, Jin." His voice was calm. But instead of lifting her spirits, that only frightened her more. "Once you get to the castle, who knows what'll happen? You'll need backup, someone who can swing a sword, even if he is an idiot. And I'm not about to let you go with only *him* for company." He looked at Sou-Zell with palpable contempt. "I once told Reena I wouldn't hesitate to walk through a storm for her. Well, not in those exact words, but I'll be damned if I don't live up to that."

Jin's eyes stung with angry tears. "And when you die, am I supposed to tell her you threw your life away for no good reason?"

"As touching as this is," Sou-Zell said, "if we're going to go, let's not dawdle. The storm's only going to get worse. Let the prince come if he wants."

Jin bit the inside of her cheek hard enough to taste blood. As much as she despised it, Sou-Zell was right. Gods, why couldn't he be wrong? She should never have given in to Kadrin after the Council meeting. She could've left him in the safety of Kerina Sol. How unforgivably selfish she'd been.

"Stay close to me," she said. "Fuck, just—hold on to me, okay? And you." She jabbed a finger at Sou-Zell. "Don't you dare fucking touch me, but stay as close as you can."

Sou-Zell's only response was to curl his lip. Well, she'd have to take that as agreement. Jin turned to face the storm outside the lift, her heart pounding. The path leading up the slope to the castle had looked impossibly narrow. Swirling debris darkened the air, masking the drop to the wasteland below, but Jin knew it was there. The void was calling her name.

Kadrin's hands settled onto her waist from behind.

"Thank you," he said in her ear. "And I'm sorry for earlier. What's between you and Reena isn't any of my concern."

Jin turned her head and choked out, "There isn't anything between me and Reena." It wasn't entirely true, but it would have to do. Louder, she said, "Ready? Good. Let's go."

She stepped out of the lift and into the howling winds.

Everything else faded away. There was no world but this one, no reality but the storm's brutal embrace. Dust and darkness. She couldn't afford to think of anything, not even what awaited them at the end. Her feet shuffled mechanically along the path. Every ounce of her attention had to be focused on one thing and one thing only: the next lightning strike.

What had Lorne told her all those years ago, when she was just a grease-stained kid sitting in his garage, handing him tools while he worked on a bike?

*You know how your bike feels alive when you're sitting on it, pushing sparks down the wire? Imagine you're in a storm, and the air is alive all around you. Burn a little mana, and you'll hear a hundred voices whispering in your ear, so faint you can hardly make out what they're saying. No other feeling like that in the world, but it's playing with fire. If you don't listen, you're dead.*

She burned mana, but instead of letting it loose as sparks, she kept the energy simmering under her skin. The moment she did, she heard them. Just like Lorne had said. For once, he hadn't been spinning tall tales.

The storm was alive and whispering her name. *Jin.* Just as the ruined temple had poured its loneliness into her soul, the storm spoke to her of hatred and longing and regret. *Jin, where are you? How could you leave me? Jin. Jin, I'll kill you.*

A bolt came streaking down from the boiling heavens. Jin didn't see it—she felt it, a manifestation of the storm's hatred. She threw out Talent and grasped the bolt, flung it sideways. It stabbed down into the void, and the sky howled its displeasure in great crackling booms.

*Jin-Lu. Liar, traitor, heartbreaker. Your love is so easily given, but it means nothing.* You *mean nothing.*

Jin hurled another bolt into the void below. She couldn't afford to respond, though she sensed she had the power to do so. All she had to do was reach back through the voice of the storm to its source, all the way to that tiny figure atop the ruins.

The wind snatched at her like Makela's grasping fingers, trying to rip her off the path, trying to tear her in two. She kept trudging forward and deflecting bolts, always just a hair short of too late. Exhaustion and adrenaline fought for control of her body. Sweat drenched her clothes. How far had they come? How much was left? She saw nothing, felt nothing but the path climbing steeply beneath her feet and Kadrin's grip on her waist. Sou-Zell might have been reduced to ashes already, for all she knew. She couldn't spare a glance over her shoulder.

*Jin*, the storm screamed. *It's too late. I'm not waiting for you, not any longer. Die. Die!*

Jin stumbled. At that precise moment, a bolt slashed down. She couldn't react in time, but the bolt wasn't aimed at her—it struck the rock wall above and beside her. Sharp fragments of stone exploded outward, slicing her jacket and her exposed cheek.

Then the ground lurched. The narrow path was giving way to the storm's fury. The pressure around her waist vanished.

*Kadrin!* She was part of the storm, and her terrified scream came not from her flesh-and-blood lips, but from her soul, carried on the wind by the conduit of her Talent. All her wits, her resolve to keep going no matter what happened, blew away like dust. Jin turned.

The rockfall had shattered the path, leaving a gap behind them. Kadrin lay flat against the surviving section, hands reaching down into the abyss, grasping for—for what?

Sou-Zell had fallen. He dangled above the dizzying void, his face stark white with terror. Kadrin's fist was clenched under the collar of Sou-Zell's jacket, anchoring him above the drop. All his muscles strained against gravity. Jin threw herself down beside Kadrin, but his arms were longer than hers—she couldn't reach.

Rolling onto her back, she screamed in frustration and sent a bolt skittering sideways. The sky above had turned pure black, and the bolts were coming down faster than ever. Grit stung her eyes.

*Oh, Jin*, purred the storm. *I have you now.*

No. She wouldn't die here, and neither would Kadrin. Not for a scoundrel like Sou-Zell.

"Let him go!" she shouted at Kadrin. "We'll all die!"

She caught a glimpse of Sou-Zell's face swaying in the emptiness, his teeth bared in a rictus of pain and hatred—but fear most of all. Jin looked away and sent another bolt flying. She couldn't let herself care. Kadrin had to live, at all costs.

But Kadrin wasn't listening. "I've got you," he called down to Sou-Zell, his voice strained. "I'm not letting go."

Jin screamed at the heavens, a wordless howl. In her soul she called out to Falka, to the gods, to anyone who was listening. *Please don't let him die. I'll give anything. Please, save us.*

And she waited for the next lightning strike, the next attack to parry, knowing it was useless. Her nerves were frayed to ribbons, and the storm spoke in too many voices for her to listen to them all.

If she and Kadrin had just kept going, perhaps they would have made it. Perhaps.

Against the flickering darkness of the clouds, something moved. She recognized that shape, the wheeling pattern it made in the sky.

A pteropter.

The clouds' dark underbelly lit up in a glowing violet spiderweb. Then a dozen bolts all stabbed down at once, streaking toward Jin, Kadrin, and Sou-Zell as if drawn by magnetism. Jin braced herself to be vaporized. But midair the bolts collided with that wheeling dark shape—the pteropter glowed so brilliantly Jin's eyes ached. Yet she went on staring, because what she saw made no sense.

Halfway between heaven and earth, Screech drank in the lightning and didn't burn—instead, he *grew*. The dark shape swelled, wings spreading to a massive length, horned head stretching outward.

Then a great screech pierced the storm. The pteropter wheeled and glided over Jin as if celebrating its triumph. More lightning stabbed down from the sky, but it split and arced out to either side of the flying saurian, as if afraid to strike it again.

Jin drew breath. The gods had heard her plea. She was alive. All three of them were alive.

# CHAPTER THIRTY

# DESPERATE MEASURES

*Second Age of Storms, 51st Summer, Day 25*

The castle appeared from the swirling dust like a phantom, its door flung wide open as if it were waiting for them. Holding on to each other, skin scraped bloody and clothes in tatters, the three of them stumbled inside. When they were all in, Jin broke away and yanked on the heavy stone door, trying to shut out the storm. Kadrin came to help. By their combined efforts, the door ground into place, and the wind's howl died to a distant moan.

Panting, Jin leaned against the stone. Before her lay a wide, gloomy hall whose function had been lost to time and ruin. Chandeliers hung from lengths of rusted chain; storm dust covered the floor and the moldering shapes of furniture in a thick, glittering blanket.

Sou-Zell stood beneath one of the cobweb-swathed chandeliers, gazing up at the vaulted ceiling. He hadn't spoken since Jin and Kadrin had hauled him back onto the path, and he had the look of a man who wasn't sure whether he was dreaming.

"We made it." Kadrin grinned at Jin, then pulled her into a hug. Jin let herself sag against his broad chest. Navigating the lightning storm had drained both her mana and her energy, leaving her an exhausted shell of a person.

In the end, her abilities alone hadn't been enough to get them through. Screech had. Somehow the annoying little pteropter who'd almost killed her once had just saved them all.

And now she knew how he'd grown—by absorbing mana lightning. Could all saurians do that, or was he unique?

"Not done yet." Jin patted Kadrin's arm and pulled away. They still had to make it to Yi-Nereen and Faolin.

Kadrin nodded, pushing back sweaty hair from his forehead. "How are we going to find Reena? This place is massive."

"I have an idea," Jin said. "Look around—see if you can find one of those sconces from the temple."

It didn't take long to find a sconce tucked in an alcove, next to a door that looked rusted into its frame. Jin took a deep breath and laid her hand against the exposed metal. She didn't have much mana left, but fortunately the sconces required little. This time she was prepared for the sensation of her sparks spreading outward, questing into every corner of the ruined castle and feeding back echoes of what they discovered.

The castle wasn't as lonely as the temple had been. It had stood empty for a long time, yes; the children who'd once scampered, laughing, through its many corridors were no more. But someone else had come recently. In the slow way a castle tells time, the new-comer had arrived only moments ago, but his coming had changed everything in the blink of an eye. Rooms were emptied and dusted, objects carried back and forth, more people came and went—or sometimes they never left. The castle had gruesome stories to tell, and Jin couldn't bear to hear them.

*I don't care what happened before. Show me who's here now, and where they are.* She poured more sparks into the sconce. *Show me.*

The castle was stubborn. It refused to show her anything clearly;

it gave her only sensations and memories, silhouettes through frosted glass. She sensed Talent moving through the castle's corridors, like pockets of infection traveling along its veins. Four bright clusters of sparktalent here, another five there. A single spark at the top of the ruins; that was Falka, had to be. But where were Yi-Nereen and Faolin?

*There!* Above her, deeper into the castle: two lights pulsing side by side, one orange and one blue. A sparkrider and a shieldcaster. Relief crashed over Jin like a wave. They were both still alive. She wasn't too late.

She severed her connection to the castle and staggered away from the wall. Kadrin took her arm and held her upright.

"What happened?" he asked.

"They're here. Reena and Faolin. Falka, too. But not just them—other sparkriders, a dozen of them. Must be Falka's raiders. And they're headed for us. They know we're here somehow." Probably the same way Jin had sensed them—if Falka could use the sconces, her raiders could too.

Kadrin didn't ask how she knew. By now, he must be getting used to her pulling new sparktalent tricks from under her hat. "Reena's here? Are you sure? Is she all right?"

"I can't tell," Jin said. "She's alive—that's all I know. Kadrin, I need to—"

Only Kadrin's grip kept her from collapsing. Fatigue had caught up to her; she could hardly stand. Black spots danced before her eyes. *Come on, Jin.* She was so close now. She couldn't fail. Not again.

"Here, drink," Kadrin said, and the cool rim of a bottle found her dry lips. Jin gulped down bitter, smoky mana, even though she knew it wouldn't help. She wasn't weakened by mana thirst, but by the sheer effort of getting them through the storm. Let Kadrin believe he was making a difference—he *was*, just by holding her, but she couldn't tell him that.

"You said there are raiders on their way." Sou-Zell had broken his silence. Jin hadn't noticed him approaching, but he stood at Kadrin's shoulder now. He was bleeding from a cut on his cheek. "Then we need to move. Which direction?"

Jin reached for the sconce again, ignoring Kadrin's sounds of protest. She fed it sparks and concentrated, fending off the pressure of the castle's memories and searching for what she needed.

"They're almost here. They've cut off the way to Reena. No—there's a way around. Through some kind of gallery."

She tore her hand away, panting, and looked up into Kadrin's wide brown eyes. He was supporting almost all her weight now, one arm wrapped tightly around her back. With his other hand, he brushed a strand of hair from her cheek and tucked it behind her ear. Was she imagining the tenderness of that touch, the way his fingers lingered on her skin?

"Take the way around," he said. "I'll stay here and make sure no one follows you."

"No." Jin turned her head, seeking his hand with her lips. Delirium and exhaustion crept over her, loosening her resolve. All she wanted was to close her eyes and drift away. "I can't. She needs *you*, Kadrin."

"You're the only one who can find her." All she saw was his face: the broad ridge of his nose, long lashes shadowing his eyes. His voice was low, edged with desperation and something else she couldn't place. "Rasvel forgive me, but if this is what it takes . . ."

He bent down and kissed her. The fatigue that shrouded her blew away at once, like clinging cobwebs caught by a strong wind.

Before she could stop herself, she was kissing him back. Her arms snaked around his neck and pulled him closer. Then someone nearby cleared their throat and Jin jerked away. What was she doing? What was *Kadrin* doing?

It was Sou-Zell who'd cleared his throat, of course. Mercifully he said nothing as Jin and Kadrin shuffled apart.

After a moment's painful silence, Kadrin said, "Give Reena my best, will you? Tell her I'll see her soon."

Jin bit her lip. She wasn't going to try reading into that, or anything that had happened in the last minute. Definitely a problem for Future Jin to solve, if she lived long enough. She looked at Sou-Zell, daring him to make a comment. But he only said, "Go."

"You're not coming?" Didn't he want revenge on Falka? Wasn't that why he'd suffered the company of a Talentless and a woman for this long?

Sou-Zell glanced sidelong at Kadrin. The tension in his jaw and his furrowed brow screamed of bitter resolve—like he was forcing himself down an untraveled road and finding it unpleasant.

"You need time to find Princess Yi-Nereen. These raiders will make short work of one pampered Talentless armed with a sword fit for the stage and little else. I will stay and give you more time."

Kadrin drew his sword from its sleek leather scabbard. Jin didn't know much about swords, but she was inclined to agree with Sou-Zell: the blade was pretty but delicate looking, a pin-straight sliver of steel with a jeweled basket hilt.

"I think you'll be surprised by the performance I can put on with this," he said with a smirk. "Stage or no stage."

Sou-Zell shot him a withering look. "Don't make me regret this."

"They'll come from there." Jin pointed at a door across the hall;

now that the room was filled with blue light, she saw the door was the only one clear of cobwebs. "There's an adjoining hallway—if I go now, I can slip through before they see me."

Her voice trembled. Seeing the sword in Kadrin's hand made it all real; soon he and Sou-Zell would be fighting for their lives. Her traitorous mind pictured Kadrin on the floor, brown eyes staring at the dusty ceiling while a red flower bloomed on his breast. On her way to the door, she exchanged a look with Sou-Zell, a look saying what her voice could not.

*Don't you let him die.*

All she got in response was a steady glare and the barest hint of a nod.

She opened the door and crept down the hallway until she found the side passage the castle had shown her. As she slipped into the shadows, she heard a shout from the corridor she'd just left.

Jin moved faster. The clamor faded into the distance as she hurried along. Before it was silenced completely, she thought she heard clashing steel and Kadrin's raised voice—but perhaps it was her imagination.

Then she was alone, stealing through a ruined castle with her heart in her throat, stopping now and then to check her path by a sconce on the wall. Every time she did, the sconce bloomed with light; she couldn't figure out how to make it stop. Each one was like a signal fire marking her route.

She stopped at a heavy, iron-studded door. The gallery wasn't far now. She just had to cross through it and a small room on the other side to find the place where she'd sensed Yi-Nereen and Faolin.

She opened the door. Beyond lay the gallery, an enormous hall transformed into a maze. Freestanding walls cut the room into twisting passages and switchbacks. Some of the walls were bare, with only faint grease marks to betray what had once hung there, but most still displayed paintings or sculptures on plinths. The paintings were so thick with dust it was impossible to tell their subjects; the sculptures were draped in rotting cloth that threatened to crumble at a touch. All this Jin noted offhand as she moved haltingly through the room. It should have been simple, a straight shot to the other side—but she kept finding herself in dead ends, confronted by hollow-eyed busts peeking through moth-eaten funeral shrouds. She wanted to howl with rage and knock down the walls, cobwebbed paintings and all.

Something fell and crashed to the floor. Not behind her, but somewhere else in the maze. Jin stopped in her tracks. Was someone else in here with her?

She looked around in the gloom for a sconce. Nothing. Her heart was already pounding, but now her skin prickled. There was a sound, a low and steady *whoosh* like the breathing of a large animal. She hadn't noticed it over her own echoing footsteps, but now it filled the room. A memory flashed into her head: waking up in the canyon to find the chandru looming over her, bathed in its breath.

Jin glanced up. The gallery's vaulted ceiling was lost to darkness. Were her eyes playing tricks on her, or was part of the darkness deeper than the rest? Now she felt it on her face: a warm breeze that smelled of carrion.

She couldn't bear it. Raising her trembling hand, she burned mana. Sparks flew from her fingers into the gloom, flaring and vanishing—but not before she *saw*.

Hunched, armored shoulders, two bony protrusions above the eyes like stunted horns, and a dripping jaw filled with sharp teeth.

*Oh*, thought Jin before the panic hit, *that looks just like my helmet.*

The rovex swung its head, glared straight at Jin, and roared.

# CHAPTER THIRTY-ONE

# MY MARK UPON THE WORLD

*Second Age of Storms, 51st Summer, Day 25*

Yi-Nereen flinched. "What was that noise?"

"Don't worry, my child. It was nothing." Tibius's voice was soothing, but the old man couldn't hide his excitement as he limped ahead of Yi-Nereen, cane tapping against the stone. "This is the place. Come, come."

Falka had spoken true about the pain; Yi-Nereen could hardly walk. Her vision swam, and her body burned from the ambrosia's icy touch. Stumbling along, she'd caught glimpses of her surroundings; now they were in some kind of theater. Two grand staircases on either side of the room led up to a balcony overlooking the stage. Perhaps the castle's royals had watched performances from there—though the Road Builders probably didn't have royals, did they? This all felt like a dream.

*Focus, Reena. Don't let Tibius distract you. You didn't imagine that noise. It was a rovex's roar.*

The voice in her head sounded just like Faolin's, another sign she was going mad. Had the ambrosia broken her mind? It couldn't have truly contained his consciousness—could it?

*He's probably controlling the rovex. Some sparkriders can, though it's difficult. It's easier if you know how to speak to them. Saurians are living creatures with minds of their own, just like you or me. They don't like to be leashed.* A pause, then a self-conscious laugh. *I meant living creatures like you. I keep forgetting.*

If by some arcane power it *was* Faolin, how could she understand him? They'd spoken different tongues in life. When they had sheltered beneath her shield, facing a terrible fate side by side, she had felt a bond forming with him—something deeper than words. But that didn't explain how she could hear him after death.

"Come, come!" Tibius waved her on.

Yi-Nereen followed, staggering up the left-hand staircase and onto the balcony.

Tibius threw open a door. Wind howled into the theater. The door led outside to yet another balcony, just large enough for Yi-Nereen and Tibius to stand abreast. Falka's storm raged around them, seething darkness slashed through with lightning. Yi-Nereen knew storm dust and debris torn from the wastes were lashing her exposed skin, drawing blood, but she felt nothing except the ambrosia's freezing flames.

"Look down there." Tibius pointed.

Yi-Nereen leaned over the cast-iron railing. This vantage point offered a different view than the one from his laboratory. She could see down the mountain's exposed flank, steep granite bare of vegetation and streaked in white and gray. But as the storm pounded against the stone, veins brightened the rock: a spiderweb of liquid orange. Yi-Nereen stared, mesmerized.

*He said the storm would draw mana from below the earth*, Faolin said. *There must be a well inside the mountain. If that well breaks, the entire mountain will collapse beneath us.*

Tibius patted Yi-Nereen's shoulder. "We'll leave that one for last," he said. "Don't worry, you'll be able to shield us all. You're about to become more powerful than any Talented in hundreds of years."

*Don't do this, Reena.* Doubt streaked Faolin's voice. *There must be a reason he's using you instead of taking your power for himself. You heard him—he wants to lead the survivors. Become a god in the new kingdom he wants to create. So why would he let you be the one to reshape the world?*

"I can hear him," Yi-Nereen said desperately, clutching her temples. "The boy. He's speaking to me, Great-Uncle. How can that be?"

"I'm sorry, child." Tibius smiled a sad, sympathetic smile. "There will be time to grieve later. But he is gone. What you hear is an echo, nothing more."

"But you—you used his soul—"

"The Rasvelites tell many lies, but the existence of the soul is the greatest lie of all. It is the lie that gives them leave to treat the Talentless like animals. It is the key to the grand deception that made you a servant to your own father. It is why he beat you and locked you away when you dared protest his treatment of his Talentless servants."

*So what? Just because the priests are liars, just because your father is a cruel man who brought up your brothers in his likeness, it doesn't mean every Talented in the wastes is a lost cause.*

Yi-Nereen wavered. How could she do this—decide whether to listen to her great-uncle or the voice of a dead boy in her head? Where was her own resolve? Before she had infused the ambrosia, she'd agreed that the kerinas were doomed; they would never be able to course-correct in time, even if the High Houses could be convinced to give up their power. But how could she know that for certain?

311

And why did Tibius care? The kerinas had rejected him, so who was he trying to save?

"It's time," Tibius said. "Use the power I've given you, Yi-Nereen. Can you feel it—the pain tearing this land apart? It was green once. Rolling hills covered in grass and tall, lovely trees. Herds of animals drinking from clear springs. You must have seen their like in your storybooks: beasts of all sizes and shapes, their bones lost to the ages. Now this land is dead, rotting away, but you can bring it back to life. Only you can do this."

She could hear the longing in his voice. It was sincere—it had to be. And he had studied the Road Builders since before she was born. What good were her fleeting doubts against the heft of his knowledge?

Yi-Nereen burned ambrosia. The relief was sudden and immense, like a cold cloth pressed to her feverish forehead.

Her shield bloomed, swelling outward. Instead of holding back the storm, it broke through and kept growing. She felt everything her shield touched: the castle's ancient stones, the heat of mana pooling under the mountainside, and finally the wasteland.

Tibius was right. The land was riddled with infection. She sensed the mana springs like pus-filled boils, crusted with plaque: the kerinas. Cities filled with people who fed on the land's corruption like blood-bloated flies.

She had the power to lance the boils and starve the flies. It was the only way for the wasteland to heal.

And who were the flies, but the very same people who had controlled and abused her since before she could speak? People who had threatened the life of an ambassador's son when they realized he was Talentless, painted his door in blood, and stolen him from Yi-Nereen's life for nine desolate years. People who would kill her for desiring freedom.

The father who'd burned her books when he'd found the dried petals of a long-dead flower pressed inside their pages.

She wouldn't hesitate any longer. If Tibius was a god, she would be his destroying angel. It was time to create something beautiful, with her own two hands.

Jin screamed, which was the only reasonable reply to the deafening roar of a ten-foot-tall rovex. The last of her sparks lit up the saurian's knifelike teeth as it swung its head down toward her. There was a wall in the way, but the rovex simply crashed through it. Wood splinters and chips of paint flew everywhere, slicing through Jin's storm-ravaged clothes. She felt a sharp sting on her cheek.

She ran. Her instincts wailed at her to get on her bike and *ride*. But she didn't have a bike, just her useless two feet, and none of Lorne's lessons had prepared her to face a rovex at close quarters, *indoors*. Jin charged down a narrow aisle lined with moldy paintings, the rovex snarling behind and above her, only to find herself at a dead end. "Oh, fuck—"

*Crash.* The dead end wasn't a dead end anymore. She was staring at the rovex's flared nostrils and glistening teeth as it shook bits of sculpture off its muzzle. Jin scrambled away.

The gods were laughing at her. They'd sent a pteropter to save her from a storm, and now a rovex to kill her. She was dead, dead meat on two legs, and her sparktalent was useless—

Wait. Was that a *door*?

Somehow she'd made it to the other side of the gallery. The rovex thundered behind her, crashing through walls and shattering sculptures. Jin threw herself against the door, sobbing in terror. It wasn't locked, thank Rasvel, just fucking *heavy*. At last it ground open, hinges screeching, and she flung herself through the gap. Her fumbling hand found a sconce on the wall.

It was a small room. The only furnishing was a stone pedestal in the center, topped with a sculpture of a crouching figure. The sculpture was so lifelike Jin could swear it was breathing. Then it shifted and turned.

Covered from head to toe in glittering storm dust, Falka smiled at her.

"You came back," she said softly. "I didn't really believe you would, not until I felt you walk into my storm."

Jin stood there, breathing hard. Behind her came the frustrated roar of the rovex, and more clattering and crashing. She hardly noticed. Until now, her mind had stubbornly refused to picture this moment: the moment when she faced Falka again.

What could she say? What magic words could she use to turn back time, to bring back the girl she'd loved and lost in place of the bitter woman standing before her now?

"You're too late." Falka jumped down from the pedestal and began circling it in slow, lazy steps, dragging her finger across the plinth. "Tibius and his silver-tongue have finished their work. Your princess is going to destroy the kerinas. Actually, I believe she's already started."

"Why did you take her?" All of Jin's exhaustion had come rushing back with interest. She slumped against the wall, numb and cold. "Just to get revenge on me?"

"She surprised me." Falka licked her lips. "I took her for a meek little thing, but she's *angry*. Tibius didn't have to work hard to convince her. I guess you have a type, don't you, Jin? Girls who want to burn down the world and dance in the ashes."

In the space of a heartbeat, she was right in front of Jin. There was a blade in her hand, and her smile had vanished. Now, at last, Jin saw someone she recognized: the girl Falka used to be was looking out from those cold green-flecked eyes.

Jin swallowed back a lump in her throat. "Falka, where have you been?"

How often she had asked Falka that question when they were together in Kerina Tez. *Where were you last week? What have you been doing?* Jin had felt like a girl in love with a summer storm: there one day, gone the next. She'd lived in fear that Falka would slip away and never come back.

But storms always, *always* returned, for better or worse. Jin had realized that too late.

"I've been everywhere," Falka said, "but I haven't been myself. And I can't blame it on you, much as I'd like to." She stood unnaturally still, as if she were afraid to disturb the air around her. "I wanted to blame everything on you for a long time. I kept running away and coming back, to see if you'd still be there. Then one day you weren't. I should have gone on with my life, realized you didn't love me."

"I did," Jin said.

She reached out and took Falka by the shoulders. Falka didn't resist; she shuddered, still clutching her knife. Jin's heart throbbed painfully. She didn't know what she felt anymore. There were no magic words, but it didn't matter; she was too tired to use them. She let the last of her reason fade and pulled Falka closer, closer, until her arms were wrapped around Falka's neck and her nose was buried in Falka's dusty hair.

"I did. I do. It would be easier if I didn't."

She felt Falka's body trembling against hers. "It's too late."

"Yeah." Jin closed her eyes, felt hot tears slide down her cheeks. "I know."

She wasn't surprised by the pain as Falka's knife slid between her ribs. No, she'd been expecting that. What did surprise her was Falka's breathless sob as the knife went in, like she was the one who'd been stabbed.

"You left me," Falka said. "I was alone—and I screwed up."

The knife went in a second time. Jin grunted and swayed. Now Falka was holding her up, even as her tears soaked Jin's neck.

"I killed him. Demond. I brought him to Tibius, and he ripped his soul out in front of me. Fed it to me in a vial. Then he was with me, all the time. Talking in my head, driving me mad. You have no idea—you have no idea what I had to do just to get him to *shut up*—"

"Falka . . ."

"There were others. Ziyal. She made me feel alive sometimes, but she wasn't *you*. She couldn't hold me like you used to. I wouldn't have believed her promises, but I still wanted to hear them. I wanted *your* promises, from her mouth. Because I'm weak—I'm nothing, I'm less than nothing, I never deserved . . . Oh gods, Jin. You're bleeding."

Falka let her go. Jin fell back against the wall. Her head slammed into the stone; she slid to the floor. Her hand went to her side, where Falka had stabbed her. Warm and wet, but somehow cold, too.

"Who hurt you, Jin? I'll kill them."

Falka dropped to her knees, her knife clattering on the stone tiles. Her face was white under her freckles and sunburn, her eyes so dilated they were almost completely black.

"You're *mine*. I watched over you, kept the storms away—it was me. I'm your hound, your shadow. Don't you dare leave me behind. Not again."

She collapsed, racked with violent sobs, utterly senseless. Jin heaved herself to her feet. She had the vague, drunken sense that if she kept her hand pressed against her wound, she wouldn't die. At least not yet. Which was good, because she still had work to do.

"I'll come back," she said. "Promise."

She stepped carefully around Falka and limped toward the door, dripping blood as she went. Falka never noticed her leave. She lay huddled on the floor in a broken heap, weeping and whimpering as if Jin were already dead.

*Second Age of Storms, 51st Summer*

*Dear Kadrin,*
*You may find this letter peculiar to look at, for it is the first I have penned in my own hand. Such exhilaration washes over me as I write these words: by dawn, I shall either be free or dead.*

*I have decided to leave this prison with the help of my steadfast bodyguard, Teul-Kim, and our friend, Courier Jin. If I am caught tonight, it will end in my death, one way or another . . . but if that happens, I shall use the last of my power to ensure this letter reaches you.*

*I love you. With all my hollow, worthless heart, I love you. I loved you when we were children, and for all the years I was alone, and every day of my godforsaken life. When my lifeless body is given to the spring, I shall dissolve into a thousand invisible pieces and every single one shall love you still. This love is all I had in life and I shall surrender it to no one, not even death.*

*Please look after Jin. Make sure her riding gloves aren't torn and a warm hearth and friendly face await her at the end of every journey. Somehow I am sure she will never abandon you, and if I must leave this world, it is my dearest wish for the two people I treasure most to look after each other.*

*We will meet again, Kadrin, when the storm has passed.*

*Reena*

*Honeythorn: bittersweetness, the fleeting nature of things*
*Cloud-of-heaven: salvation, rescue, gratitude*
*Erasmuth: a vow never broken, true love*

# CHAPTER THIRTY-TWO

# HOMECOMING

*Second Age of Storms, 51st Summer, Day 25*

Jin pushed the door open and stepped onto a stage. The curtain had rotted into trailing strips that danced in an invisible breeze. Beyond the stage stretched endless rows of empty seats, an audience of ghosts. The theater was dark save for flashes of cobalt light. Every flash cast shadows across the stage: the silhouettes of two people standing on a balcony, just outside an open door.

With one hand, Jin held her side. She shaded her eyes with the other, squinting through the strobing light.

"Reena? Faolin?"

Her voice was lost to the storm. Somehow she would have to make it up those stairs to the balcony.

Every step sent fresh agony lancing through her side, like another stab from Falka's knife. The wound hurt, but in a way, the pain was a comfort. It meant she still had time. Once she became numb, she'd worry.

She dragged herself up the stairs, willing her body not to quit just yet.

❋

*Did you hear that? Someone's calling for us.*

Yi-Nereen reached across the wasteland. Her grasp felt infinite, bounded only by the limits of Falka's storm. She wasn't in control of the storm, but she rode it like a feather on the wind. It spread quickly, swelling outward from the mountain to encompass the entire wasteland. In every kerina, stormwatchers were no doubt watching the skies blacken and sounding the alarm. Bells would ring, and shieldcasters would be roused from sleep and summoned to the walls, still exhausted from the last storm—for there was never enough time to recover, not completely—but ready to serve. Always ready to serve.

Yi-Nereen felt Falka's storm touch the first kerina. The city had already raised its dome. Yi-Nereen pushed against it with her own shield and found it held. She pushed harder. The mana spring lay beneath the dome, and she wouldn't be able to drain it until she broke down the combined efforts of the city's shieldcasters, stripped away their defenses. The thought sickened her, but she pushed the nausea away. It was too late to turn back.

She clung to the image Tibius had painted for her: a land covered in green, blooming with flowers. Beauty. Peace.

Her shield was stronger than the kerina's defenders—she could sense it—but she struggled nonetheless. Back in her physical body, she felt blood trickling from her nose. The ambrosia had strengthened her Talent, but not her body to match.

*That's it.* Faolin's voice was hushed. *That's why he didn't take your Talent for himself. No single person was meant to wield this much power. It's going to kill you.*

"Good," Yi-Nereen whispered. She didn't know whether she was speaking the words with her flesh-and-blood tongue, or if everyone in the wastes could hear her voice in the thunder. "I've always wanted to die."

*Don't say that. What about Jin and Kadrin? Jin will die along with all of the other Talented if you aren't around to save her.*

What was the point of saving anyone? They had been born to die, all of them. Born and raised in their own tomb, locked from the inside. The only way to save the world was to burn it down and start again.

But the new world wasn't for her anyway. She didn't deserve to see it.

She pushed. The kerina's defenders broke, and suddenly Yi-Nereen was inside. She—or the storm; who knew which was which—reached hungrily for the spring. All that mana, hideous and beautiful, corrupted blue blood. Soon it would be gone.

*Stop! Reena, just listen!*

She hesitated, though the storm never stopped moving: it tore through the kerina in restless circles, pummeling buildings and shaking the earth. Back in the ruins, someone was calling her name. Faintly, weakly—but now she was listening, and it was all she could hear.

*It's Jin.*

Jin clung to the back of a chair, staring at the balcony. Yi-Nereen stood there, facing outward into the swirling storm, arms spread wide as if she wanted to embrace the very wind. But the figure standing beside her wasn't Faolin. It was a white-haired man stooped with age, leaning on a cane. He had turned at Jin's hoarse call, and now he stared at her with an annoyed expression, as if she'd interrupted his breakfast.

Jin had no idea who he was, but she didn't care. "Reena. It's me."

A shudder ran through Yi-Nereen's body. She turned, arms collapsing to her sides. Her eyes blazed with blue light, and she stared through Jin as if she couldn't see her. Her lips moved soundlessly for several moments, like she couldn't remember how to speak. "Jin?"

Jin's strength was draining away. It was the moment she'd feared; the pain was beginning to recede. Her hand was slippery with blood; it dripped between her fingers and fell in damning drops to the floor.

But she pushed herself upright and took a few hesitant steps toward Yi-Nereen. "Where's Faolin?"

The old man stepped in the way. Though he had perhaps been taller than Yi-Nereen once, age had bowed him so his eyes were level with Jin's. He pointed his cane at her; his sneering frown reminded Jin of the way Sou-Zell looked at Kadrin.

"So you're the courier. Falka was meant to ensure you wouldn't make it this far." His eyes lingered on Jin's bloody side. "Well, it looks like she did her best."

Yi-Nereen groped blindly until her hand found the old man's shoulder. "Is she hurt?"

"Never mind that," Jin said. She heard her voice as if through water, distant and warped. The theater flickered around her, dark to light to dark again. "I'm here to take you home, Reena. Home to Kadrin."

Something was terribly wrong. She knew it from Faolin's absence, from Yi-Nereen's sluggish movements, from the old man's contemptuous glare—like he'd already won whatever game he was playing, and Jin was spoiling his victory celebration. Falka's words echoed in her head. *It's too late.*

But it didn't matter. Whatever Yi-Nereen was doing, it didn't matter. Only one thing mattered, and that was doing what Jin had set out to do from the start. She would bring Reena and Kadrin together if it killed her. That was the only way to make it all right. Everything—her father, Lorne, Falka, Ziyal, Faolin. All the death, all the suffering, everything and everyone she'd lost.

There had to be a happy ending. Even if it wasn't hers.

Jin sank to her knees. Her hand fell away from her side. It probably hadn't done much good where it had been, so that was fine.

"Please, Reena. Come home."

*I knew she'd come back*, Faolin said. *She found us.*

Yi-Nereen trembled. She still couldn't see; her mind was far away, riding the storm as it raged through the kerina. But at the same time, she was in the ruins with Jin and Faolin's voice in her head.

*I can't take this,* she cried out soundlessly.

She heard Tibius scoff. "Don't let her distract you, my child. We have no time to waste. You must finish your work before the storm fades, or all will have been in vain."

*I remember now,* Faolin said. *He was there when Falka killed me. He . . . he called me his grandson. And he watched me die.*

*No,* Yi-Nereen said. *Impossible.*

Tibius had lived among the wastelanders. They were all Talentless, except for two: Faolin and his sister. Could it be the truth? But then . . .

*You and I are kin.* Faolin's voice was veiled in sadness. *I wish I'd known when I was alive.*

Yi-Nereen wanted to deny it. Blood was what bound her to her father and brothers, to Tibius himself. It had brought her nothing but misery until now. Until Faolin.

Could it be true, that her bloodline was more than sin and ambition? How badly she wanted to believe that. She longed to believe in so many things, like the possibility of a future for herself, Jin, and Kadrin. That longing had destroyed her, because everything she wanted seemed so far beyond her grasp. It was easier to turn her back on it altogether and embrace destruction.

*We're still together, for now. I can't save Amrys. But I can help you save yourself.*

"Yi-Nereen." Tibius's voice was sharp now. "Are you listening?"

"Please, Reena." That was Jin. "Come home."

*Don't you see, Reena?* Faolin asked, his voice sure and strong. *She's your family. Not this man. He sacrificed me because I wasn't useful— he'll throw you away when he's done. Forget his speeches about peace and a new world. Can't you see he's a selfish, power-hungry man just like the ones he claims to hate? Just like your grandfather.*

If it was truly Jin, if she had truly come, then the knowledge that lived in Yi-Nereen's head could reach the kerinas. There was still a chance to save everyone, not only the Talentless—with her life, not her death. It was a tiny hope, a candle flame flickering at the heart of a vast darkness. But someone had taught her to trust in the coming dawn.

Yi-Nereen drew herself back from the storm. It was like pulling away from an immense spiderweb clinging to her skin and hair— but she drew back, weeping. How foolish she'd been, to walk from one jailer straight into the arms of another. No more would she serve. She was finished.

She just hoped it wasn't too late.

Something thudded below the balcony. Jin looked hazily down into the theater. Two figures were advancing down the wide central aisle: Kadrin and Sou-Zell.

Jin's heart soared. Both men looked considerably worse for wear; Sou-Zell was wearing so much blood he might have painted himself in it, and Kadrin had lost an entire sleeve from his leather jacket. But they were alive.

Jin rose halfway from the floor, borne by a sudden surge of strength. "Kadrin!"

Kadrin looked up. Jin caught a glimpse of his blood-streaked face before she had to sink back down again. Through the rushing in her ears, she heard him shout her name.

Then, much closer at hand, the old man hissed through his teeth. "More interruptions. How tiresome."

He loomed over Jin, who found herself suddenly reevaluating the threat he posed. But he wasn't paying attention to her. His eyes smoldered orange. A sparkrider? She realized then that she'd been mistaken—the castle had never shown her Faolin. He must not have made it. A hollow ache filled her chest.

The old man shouted a word she didn't know, in a language that sounded eerily like Faolin's. Then Jin heard a chilling sound: the rovex's thundering roar.

When Sou-Zell was a boy, he'd stood atop the Wall for hours, watching the wastes in the hopes of spotting a rovex. All he'd seen were distant herds of chandru or wheeling specks of pteropters high in the sky. He'd pored over illustrations and begged his father's oldest friend, a knight named Ell-Tuin, to describe a rovex's roar. The lean, rugged man had laughed, tousled his hair, and said, *I couldn't begin to do it justice. And if I did, you'd wet your trousers.*

He'd forgotten that old desire, along with Ell-Tuin's face. Now the memory came rushing back. Except Sou-Zell wasn't six years old anymore, and he wasn't shielding his eyes against the sun on top of the Wall. He was a man, bloody, beaten, and burned.

The rovex burst onto the stage, crashing straight through the wall behind the shredded curtain, small clawed arms curled in front of its massive chest. It swung its head back and forth, illuminated in flashes of lightning. Its glowing eyes settled on Sou-Zell and Kadrin, who were standing frozen in the aisle. Steam puffed from its nostrils.

"Holy Rasvel," breathed Kadrin. "Is that a *rovex*?"

His voice broke Sou-Zell's trance. Not because of what he'd said—of course it was a rovex; it didn't need to be *stated*—but because of the awe in his voice. Sou-Zell's skin crawled. He despised the notion that this was something he and this Talentless oaf might have once shared: the childish desire to see a real, live rovex.

The rovex took a single lazy step across the stage. The theater shook with its weight.

Sou-Zell grabbed Kadrin's arm, none too gently. "Move. Now."

For a moment he thought the idiot prince wouldn't listen. During the skirmish against the raiders, he'd eschewed tactics and brandished his sword like he was in a dueling tournament, showing off for a crowd. It had taken all of Sou-Zell's skill to keep him alive.

Somehow they'd made it through. Several of the raiders had fallen before Sou-Zell's knife or Kadrin's sword, and the rest had scattered into the castle's depths. Then he and Kadrin had found their way here, almost completely by accident.

Now Kadrin seemed amenable to Sou-Zell's direction. He nodded quickly, his throat working as he stared at the rovex. "The stairs."

Sou-Zell meant to tell Kadrin to take the left-hand staircase, while he made for the right. The rovex wouldn't be able to chase them both. But he didn't have the chance. The rovex roared again—and Sou-Zell's mind went blank. Kadrin stumbled down a row of seats toward the right-hand staircase; Sou-Zell scrambled after him.

The rovex was faster. Out of the corner of his eye, Sou-Zell saw it crouch, flexing its muscular hindquarters—then it leaped. With an impact that shook the entire castle, it landed at the base of the staircase, crushing the first four steps into rubble. They were cut off. Sou-Zell pulled Kadrin back, away from the saurian's scything jaws.

No time for words. He dragged the prince toward the other staircase.

*Slam. Crunch.*

Now there was no second staircase. Only the rovex, looming over them with an orange spark dancing deep inside each of its black eyes.

Above the saurian's massive head, Sou-Zell glimpsed the courier. Jin-Lu had dragged herself to the edge of the balcony and was half draped over the railing; Sou-Zell saw blood gleaming on her fingers. She was looking at Kadrin with her emotions written all over her face, terror and love. Then her eyes fell on Sou-Zell, who felt something within him surge up in response. *I know*, he wanted to snarl. *I know. Don't remind me.*

He shouldered in front of Kadrin, shoving the hapless prince backward. Empty-handed, he glowered up at the rovex. He'd run out of blackpowder, and his knife was gone. His Talents, both of them, were useless. This would all be over quickly.

Sou-Zell always paid his debts.

Jin tore her eyes away from the scene below—Sou-Zell standing between Kadrin and the rovex, looking bitter and scornful as ever—and saw the old man before the door leading to the storm. His eyes still glowed orange as he chanted in Faolin's tongue, his voice booming like thunder.

Beside him, slumped on the floor, was Yi-Nereen. Her hand was pressed to her sweat-soaked forehead.

"Jin!" Her voice was faint but still audible. "Tibius is controlling the rovex. Jin, I—"

The rest of her words were lost to the rovex's roar. The saurian's voice carried a new note, a note of triumph. It had its quarry cornered and none could stand against it. Not Sou-Zell, bare-handed and bloody. Not Kadrin and his beautiful sword. Certainly not half-dead, eternal failure Jin-Lu.

She knew with utter clarity she had exactly one shot left. These were her final moments. She longed to spend them looking at Yi-Nereen, brilliant and breathtaking, or perhaps cradled in Kadrin's strong arms. She ached for both of them, together and at once. For three years she had swallowed this forbidden desire, knowing she wasn't worthy of either of them. Not when she loved like her heart was a promise: made to be broken.

*This is a promise I'm going to keep.*

Jin summoned the last of her strength and charged. She staggered like a misshapen, rolling boulder toward the old man standing on the balcony. At the last moment, her leg gave out and she fell—but it was enough. Tibius didn't have the chance to step aside before Jin's shoulder took him in the chest.

She wasn't big, but she didn't need to be. The wasteland didn't care how strong you were, only that you were stubborn enough to survive—or choose exactly the right moment to die.

They went over the balcony together into the churning black of the storm.

# CHAPTER THIRTY-THREE

# SURVIVORS

*Second Age of Storms, 51st Summer, Day 25*

Jin fell. She spun through dark, gritty clouds as lightning flashed around her. Below her she caught glimpses of the gray slope— but it had changed. Veins of orange pulsed in the rock, a glowing web.

She'd lost Tibius. That didn't matter. She'd made certain he would fall to his death, and if there was any goddamn justice in the world, that would break his control over the rovex and Kadrin would be safe. Sou-Zell could take him and Reena home to Kerina Sol. They'd be together, at long last.

Below her, the mountain groaned and shuddered. The orange veins pulsed brighter—then, with a mighty tremor, the stone split. It cracked open along the glowing lines, and smoke hissed from fresh vents, smoke that bled from orange to blue as it tasted air. Jin fell toward the heaving stone.

It was a mana spring, welling up before her eyes. She was going to fall right into it. But who cared what happened to her? What mattered were Kadrin and Reena, up in the castle. The castle that was about to split apart and be swallowed by the newly forming spring.

It had all been for nothing.

The rovex shook its head and snarled—a broken noise, almost a whimper, completely unlike the confident roar of moments ago. Kadrin didn't stop to wonder why it seemed distracted.

"Now!"

He sprinted for the crushed remains of the staircase on the right. The steps at the bottom had collapsed, but just out of Kadrin's reach was a still-intact railing. There wasn't time to sheathe his sword, so he dropped it—then he turned and put out his hands. Sou-Zell was right at his heel. He hesitated only a moment before stepping onto Kadrin's interlaced fingers.

Kadrin swung his arms upward with all his might. As it turned out, he'd slightly overestimated Sou-Zell's weight. *Damn the man, doesn't he get enough to eat?* Sou-Zell sailed over the railing and recovered in time to land lightly on his feet, like a cat. He turned at once to reach down and pull Kadrin up.

"Jin!" Kadrin called. "Reena!"

He took the stairs two at a time, heedless of the rovex's bewildered snorting behind him. When he reached the top, his heart sprang into his throat and stayed there, like a stuck pit.

A woman stood in a doorway, framed by the flickering storm. She wore a black caftan and a veil over her dark hair. Her back was turned. Kadrin couldn't tell if he was trembling or if it was the floor beneath his feet. A muffled curse from Sou-Zell told him it was probably the castle. But he wasn't thinking of that now.

"Reena," he said, his voice hesitant and thick with questions: *Is it you? Are you real?*

The woman turned. Dark eyes stared from a lovely, exhausted

face. Blood had run freely from one nostril over the curve of her lip and down her dimpled chin.

"She jumped." Her voice was horrified. "It's all coming apart. I didn't mean for this to—Rasvel, what have I done?"

Kadrin barely heard what she was saying. He was too busy staring at her. Here she was: the girl he remembered from his youth, fully grown. He'd tried to imagine her so many times; he'd sketched her portrait repeatedly and even made one disastrous attempt at a painting. But all his fantasies were faint and colorless, cobbled together from descriptions he'd wrung out of an impatient Jin. They couldn't measure up to reality.

Jin. For a moment he forgot how to breathe. Then he said, "She *jumped*?"

Reena let out a choked sob. Kadrin moved past her to the balcony. The castle groaned and shook so violently it nearly took him off his feet. He grabbed the railing, snared Reena's waist with his other arm, and drew her close until the trembling stopped. Then he looked down.

"Oh," he said. "When did that get there?"

Below the castle churned the electric blue of a freshly formed mana spring. It grew wider before his eyes, bubbling and hissing, eating away at the rocky slope. That was why the castle was shaking; its foundation was being dissolved, as easily as sugar in tea.

And Jin had fallen in there. Even if the fall hadn't killed her, the mana would. Kadrin had seen a man die of mana poisoning once. He had managed to drag his way out of the spring, but he'd died in agony all the same. Spending even a few seconds completely immersed in mana was fatal.

To the Talented, anyway.

He turned to Reena. His hands found her face, pushed back her veil, and wiped the tears from her cheeks. She looked up at him, stricken, and Kadrin pressed a kiss to her forehead. It felt natural, easy as breathing. Like the twelve years had been nothing and they'd never been apart.

"I don't know if you figured this out from my letters," Kadrin said, "but sometimes I do things without thinking them through. Stealing a Scroll of Talent. Growing flowers on a whim. Writing to a woman I haven't seen in years, who might be married to someone else and has probably forgotten all about me."

Reena's brow furrowed. "What?"

"I'm just reminding you. Because I want to make sure you know this is different." His words came out in a hurried rush. There wasn't much time, after all. "I've spent the last ten seconds thinking through everything that could possibly go wrong. What I might lose. And I've decided it's a damned stupid idea." He sucked in a breath. "But I'm doing it anyway."

Realization snapped into place in Yi-Nereen's eyes. She clutched at his torn jacket. "Kadrin, no, *don't*—"

He kissed her again, on the lips this time. Then he pulled away with the taste of her blood on his tongue and said huskily, "Be right back."

He dove over the railing.

Jin plunged through the smoke and into the mana's icy clutches. At once, all sensation fled; she was completely weightless, suspended in nothing. Time stopped. Pain vanished. A thin line of red trailed through the opaque blue. Her blood, marking the way back to the surface.

But there was no need to do anything about it. Jin let her eyes drift shut. She felt drowsy and tranquil. Drowning in mana had always sounded like a painful death, so she was glad to find it wasn't.

*Oh, Jin.*

The sigh rustled through the mana. Jin opened her eyes. Fear lanced through her, but only for a moment before the mana's chilling touch sapped it away once more.

The enormous saurian she'd seen in the underground spring was swimming around her in slow, silent circles. Stripes along its flank flashed in the pulsating glow. Its flat black eye surveyed her calmly.

Jin reached out and touched the creature. She didn't burn mana; there was no need. Instead of her sparks questing through stone, part of her moved through the creature. She glimpsed millennia, a consciousness older than the wasteland, older than the Road Builders. *You're the original saurian, aren't you? The rest were created in your image.*

How ancient it was, how unknowable. And yet, it felt familiar.

She drew back her hand. The saurian swam gracefully away. And there was her father where it had been, floating in the mana, his fingers entwined with hers. Gao-Jin smiled at her.

"Little pteropter," he said. "You always wanted to learn how to fly. But jumping from a cliff?"

Jin wasn't surprised to see her father. Not here on the hazy edge of death—exactly where spirits belonged. But she was surprised by the sudden punch of how much she'd fucking missed him.

"Sorry, Appa," she whispered. "I guess I had to learn somehow. Sparkriders just aren't meant to fly."

"Don't count yourself out just yet." Her father squeezed her hand. "I tried to show you: the wasteland is full of strange, terrible, lovely things. It isn't the world where I wanted to leave you, but it's the world that made you who you are."

"And who is that?"

"A wanderer who sees beauty in every twisted corner of the world. A survivor who isn't afraid to die when it counts. Someone who loves with all her heart, no matter how many times it breaks."

The mana stirred. A dark shape appeared above Jin, where her blood trail led away into the blue. The figure slowly grew larger. She looked at her father, suddenly terrified of losing him all over again. "I don't want to leave you."

"Everyone leaves," he said. "You can't stop that from happening. But this is the truth, Jin: if you can pick yourself up from a fall, if you can go on loving even when it breaks you, if you can follow the stars when you're lost, you'll never be alone."

Arms closed around her waist. She clutched her father's hand, trying to hold on even as a powerful force pulled her away—but her father let her go with a smile still on his lips, and vanished. Then she was drawn upward, out of the depths.

As the mountain crumbled and the castle shook itself to pieces around her, Yi-Nereen turned away from the railing and saw Sou-Zell. He was clinging to a banister and covered in blood, though none of it seemed to be his. Their eyes met.

She had only ever spoken to him once, at her mother's funeral. He'd approached her and offered his condolences in a voice that made her question whether they were sincere. But he had broken the protocols of courtship to do it, though she hadn't known that until later. She had been the last to learn of their engagement.

She had no idea what he was doing here. Had he come to drag her back to Kerina Rut? Old anger flared in her chest, but it quickly settled. Sou-Zell didn't look like he was in a position to drag anyone anywhere. He looked drained, helpless, and afraid, though he was obviously trying not to show it.

The shieldcasters of the kerina she'd almost destroyed must have been terrified, too. Yi-Nereen's stomach churned. It had seemed like the right thing to do, the only thing. Men like her father would never change. They would have to die, all of them, for the world to recover from the evils they'd wrought. But . . . here was Sou-Zell. He'd obviously accompanied Kadrin and Jin. And *they* wouldn't have brought him if they thought he couldn't change.

*No one else needs to die*, Faolin said. *You can save them all. Everyone in this castle. Even Falka.*

Yi-Nereen was too exhausted to argue. If Faolin wanted his murderer to live, Yi-Nereen would use the last of her power to grant his wish.

She burned ambrosia for the final time. Her shield bloomed and spread, sweeping through the castle. She touched everyone who still lived within the ruin: Sou-Zell, Falka, the raiders. She wrapped herself around them and held them tightly in a web of her Talent as the castle trembled and fell apart, joining its architects in death. Until all that remained of the ruin at the mountain's peak was her shield and the precious lives within, interconnected bubbles suspended by Yi-Nereen's will alone.

The storm had moved away without an anchor; it would pass over the wasteland as an ordinary storm, eventually diminishing to a mere breeze. The sky was radiant with sunlight.

*Now that's beauty*, Faolin said. *Don't you think?*

Kadrin burst from the spring and dragged Jin onto the stony bank. He sprawled beside her, greedily sucking down air. He didn't know if they were safe yet, but the world had stopped shaking, and that was good enough for him.

He crawled to Jin and pushed her hair away from her face. She wasn't even wet—that was one of the more bizarre things about mana, in Kadrin's opinion. But she wasn't breathing.

"Jin," he said, shaking her. "Come back. Don't do this."

Her side was covered in blood, sticky and dark, but when he pulled up her shirt, he couldn't find any wound. Her pulse still beat, though it was slow and sluggish. Then she coughed and opened her eyes.

Kadrin's relief crystallized instantly to dread. Jin's eyes burned like molten pools of flame. A little moan of pain escaped her lips. Kadrin put his hand to her cheek and withdrew it with a hiss: her skin was scalding hot.

He'd been too late. Of course, he'd known he would be. It took only seconds for mana poisoning to set in. But damn it, he'd seen Jin pull off so many miracles. If anyone could survive this, it was her.

"Come on, Jin," he said, hands hovering uselessly over her body. "You got us through the storm. You saved Reena. You're the toughest person I know. Please." His voice broke, but he stumbled on. "We were so close to going home. And I never got to tell you . . ."

The last few words died in his throat. What was the point in saying them now?

Kadrin had been under the surface for less than a minute, or so he thought—but perhaps time passed differently in mana. Everything had changed since he'd leaped from the ruined castle's balcony. A miniature wasteland surrounded him. Great chunks of rock and masonry were everywhere, as if they'd rained down from the heavens; the air was choked with dust. Kadrin couldn't see farther than ten paces. He didn't know what had happened to the castle. Fear gripped his heart, fear for Reena—but he couldn't leave Jin to die alone on the banks of the spring.

Her back arched, her face contorted in agony. Now her skin was glowing faintly, as if fire were trapped in her blood. Kadrin tore off his ruined jacket and wrapped it around his arms. Then he pulled Jin into his lap. He could feel the blazing heat of her flesh even through the leather, but he *had* to hold her. "One more miracle, Jin. Please."

"Kadrin?"

He looked up. Through the thick dust hanging in the air, Reena stepped into view, holding her sleeve over her nose and mouth. Her eyes widened at the sight of Jin. She crossed the distance in a few long strides and sank to her knees beside Kadrin. Behind her came Sou-Zell.

"Thank Rasvel you're all right." Reena reached out as if she was going to touch Kadrin's face; then she drew back her hand. For a few moments, neither of them moved or spoke. All they did was stare at Jin as she shook and burned in Kadrin's arms. Dust drifted slowly around them, peacefully, as if the wasteland didn't care Jin was suffering.

Finally Reena raised her face to Kadrin. Her eyes were reddened and her cheeks shone with tears. "Kadrin, we can't let this go on."

"What are you saying?"

He didn't want to hear her answer. He didn't want to hear anything that wasn't *Kadrin, we can fix this. We can save her.*

"I'm saying . . ." Reena took in a shuddering breath. "Damn it, Kadrin. I can't—I can't watch her suffer." Her voice came out strangled with pain.

*No. This can't be real.* He pulled Jin closer, ignoring her scalding heat, his throat so tight he couldn't speak or even cry.

"Wait." Sou-Zell's voice rang out from behind them, strained but still somehow imperious. He dropped to one knee beside Reena. His jaw was tight and he didn't look at Jin; he fixed Reena with his dark stare instead. "The courier said some shieldcasters could siphon mana from a person's body. Is it true?"

Reena froze. The muscles in her throat tightened. "Yes. It's true." Kadrin's heart skipped a beat. "Then try, Reena. Please."

The dust was settling. Above, the sky burned clear, brilliant blue. Sou-Zell drew back, a haggard shadow in the wreckage. In the distance, Kadrin thought he heard something: a faint rumble, like a stampede. But he gave it little thought.

Reena lifted her veil, wiped dried blood from her mouth with the back of her wrist, and bent over Jin. One hand stroked Jin's hair, the only part of her that was cool to the touch. The other hand crept into Kadrin's. Then she leaned down and pressed her mouth to Jin's.

Kadrin watched. He could do nothing but watch, his pulse stuttering in his chest, as Reena winced and trembled. Jin must be burning her, but she didn't pull away. The air crackled; Kadrin could *feel* the flow of energy between the two women. A sudden fear gripped him: Wouldn't the mana Reena drew from Jin poison her as well?

He almost pulled her back—he couldn't lose them both. Then Reena's grip on his hand tightened to the point of pain, and a shield shimmered around them, a translucent half dome pulsing with energy. *That* was where the excess was going, Kadrin realized. She'd bleed it off with a shield. His clever, beautiful Yi-Nereen.

Then it was over. Reena pulled back, eyes blazing blue for a brief moment before they faded back to brown. Kadrin looked at her in awe. He touched Jin's face with a trembling hand. Her skin was cool, and she'd stopped seizing. Her eyes fluttered open, and focused briefly on Kadrin and Reena in turn. Then they closed as she lost consciousness once more.

Kadrin laid her gently on the ground and took Reena by the hands, grinning fiercely. "You saved her."

The distant rumble was growing louder. Kadrin looked around, hackles rising, but he could see little past the rubble and fallen rocks surrounding them. What was it? Thunder? No, the sky was clear.

Magebike engines.

## CHAPTER THIRTY-FOUR

# A DUEL FOR HER HAND

*Second Age of Storms, 51st Summer, Day 25*

Eight magebikes roared through the rubble, sending up fresh clouds of dust. Astride each one sat a rider in full plate that gleamed bright under the wasteland sun. Silver standards fluttered from their handlebars, emblazoned with an arc of stars. Yi-Nereen sprang to her feet and turned in a circle.

*The Knights of Rut. It's over now.*

They would drag her back home. Home to her father, to her brothers, to the kerina she hadn't destroyed when she had the chance. Horror suffused Yi-Nereen's body, ice-cold as the mana she'd just drained from Jin's blood.

The knights halted in a circle surrounding Yi-Nereen, Kadrin, and Jin, who still lay senseless on the ground. One by one the engines fell silent. The riders dismounted in a clamor of clanking plate. They stood at attention, lances held at their sides, except one: the leader, who moved toward Yi-Nereen with heavy, purposeful steps.

Kadrin's voice rang out. "Not a step closer." He shielded Yi-Nereen with his body, which made her want to laugh and cry at the same time. What could he do? Her brave Kadrin, Talentless and weaponless against a full platoon of knights. It was already over.

The knight removed his helm. Yi-Nereen knew him at once by

341

Hana Lee

the broad scar across the bridge of his nose and his heavily sloped brow: Captain Dev-Larai. He had been among the honor guard at her mother's funeral. What else did she know about him? Was he a compassionate man, a cowardly one, susceptible to bribes? Damn it, she couldn't remember.

"Your Highness," Captain Dev-Larai said. "I expected to find you within the walls of Kerina Sol. Were you forced into the Barrens by the storm, as we were?" He glanced around, frowning. "It matters not. Here you are."

Yi-Nereen raised her chin. "Did my father send you?"

"Knight-Commander Ren-Vetaar sent me." He left out the obvious: *At your father's order.*

"I will not go back," Yi-Nereen said. She drew herself up, defiant. "I will die first."

The captain drummed his gloved fingers on the haft of his lance. "I can't allow that, Your Highness. You are to be returned, whole and unharmed, to Shield Lord Lai-Dan."

Yi-Nereen inched backward. Behind her hummed the freshly born mana spring, filled to the brim with death; her blood surged with the power she'd taken from Jin. If Captain Dev-Larai took another step toward her, she would take a step back. She was quick with her shield. He would be helpless to stop her.

The captain's gaze flickered between her and the spring—then to Jin's unconscious body.

"Anyone who aided in your escape faces a death sentence," he said.

*No.* Yi-Nereen trembled, fighting back a sob at the futility of it all. Why couldn't her life be hers alone, to take as she pleased?

"You can't do this." Kadrin's voice was thunder. He stood before Yi-Nereen in just his torn shirt, bare-handed and glaring at Captain Dev-Larai. "She's under the protection of Kerina Sol. I'm Third Heir to the House of Steel Heavens. It will be war if you touch either of us."

He was lying, and quite badly. Yi-Nereen almost laughed. He sounded just the same as he had when he was a boy, hiding hands covered in powdered sugar behind his back. Captain Dev-Larai wasn't fooled. She saw it in his unimpressed stare.

"Princess Yi-Nereen is no refugee," he said. "We are not in—"

"Pardon the interruption, Captain, but I need a word with you."

Sou-Zell stalked through the circle of magebikes. He looked a sight in his bloody clothes with his hair full of dust; at his sudden appearance, half the knights stiffened and leveled lances at him.

Captain Dev-Larai raised his hand, waving them down. "Lord Sou-Zell. What are you doing here?" His voice was guarded but respectful.

Sou-Zell ignored the question. "I have discovered information the knight-commander must hear without delay. Forget the courier and the Talentless prince. Forget even Princess Yi-Nereen. Her abandonment of Kerina Rut is no longer of any consequence. Crimes against the gods have been committed here, and not by her hand."

"I have my duty, Lord Sou-Zell." Captain Dev-Larai's voice dropped to a low growl. "As do you."

If Sou-Zell was stymied by the captain's resistance, he didn't show it. He waved a hand as if nothing made any difference. "We cannot know if the prince or this courier were involved in Princess Yi-Nereen's escape. It was a dark night, was it not? No one saw the courier's face. And the Sol-blood prince was certainly not present."

For a few heartbeats, no one moved or spoke. Captain Dev-Larai and Sou-Zell stared at each other: one frowning, the other perfectly placid. Then the captain sighed.

"If Princess Yi-Nereen comes of her own will, no one else need be harmed."

Yi-Nereen met the captain's dark eyes. Hatred burned within her. If she'd listened to Tibius, if she'd finished carrying out his plan, she would have had nothing to fear from Kerina Rut or her father. Not when he and all the knights assembled here would have died from mana thirst within days. But she'd heard Jin's voice, and she'd turned away from her work.

*It isn't fair.* Faolin's voice was hardly more than a defeated whisper. *I'm sorry, Reena. I think . . . I think sometimes you do the right thing and suffer for it.*

"Wait."

Kadrin stepped between Captain Dev-Larai and Sou-Zell. The former glared at him with the open disgust Yi-Nereen was used to seeing on the faces of knights confronted by Talentless beggars; the latter was wearing a small, mysterious smile, imperceptible to anyone who wasn't paying attention. Yi-Nereen's blood ran cold. What was Kadrin doing? Did Sou-Zell know?

Kadrin raised his hand. Something flashed in the sunlight: a ring on his finger. He pointed at Sou-Zell. "I don't know exactly the right words, but—Sou-Zell, I challenge you. I challenge your claim to Princess Yi-Nereen. She made a betrothal promise to me a year ago, and beneath the eyes of the gods, I accepted. I have worn her ring every day since then. By the Law of Prior Claim, I challenge you to a duel by blade to decide who she belongs to, once and for all."

Yi-Nereen closed her eyes. *Oh, Kadrin.*

Once, long ago, this had been her plan: a safeguard against any future proposals of marriage. But then she had learned of her engagement to Sou-Zell—a betrothal he and his father had planned for years, without her knowledge. Years before she'd ever thought of sending the ring to Kadrin. It was too late.

Captain Dev-Larai snorted. "Lord Sou-Zell has no obligation to accept—"

"I accept Prince Kadrin's challenge."

The smile had vanished from Sou-Zell's face, without any hint it had ever existed. He was glowering at Kadrin, looking for all the world like a man insulted beyond description. His fists curled by his sides. But Yi-Nereen's mind spun. Sou-Zell must know the Law of Prior Claim as well as she did, if not better. His claim was the prior by years. Kadrin's challenge had no standing.

"We require arms," Sou-Zell said to Captain Dev-Larai. The captain looked taken aback for a moment before shaking his head and gesturing to his men. Two knights came forward and offered their lances to Sou-Zell and Kadrin. None of them carried swords.

Kadrin took the offered weapon and stared down at its gleaming tip. Then he raised his head. Yi-Nereen caught his eye, her heart pounding. She didn't know what was going to happen next—and neither did he, by his expression. But he smiled all the same. It was a warm, radiant smile, the exact smile that had lived in her memory for twelve years, through all the storms and desolate nights. It was a smile that said, *It's going to be all right. We are the heroes of this story.*

Something inside Yi-Nereen fractured, like a jar shattered so all the brightly colored beetles within could fly free. She knew she would never be able to piece it together again. All her resolve, her stubborn insistence that love was a childhood luxury she'd moved beyond, slipped through her fingers at the sight of that smile. She was undone.

One of the knights lifted Jin's unconscious body and carried her to the side. Yi-Nereen went with her. She sank to the ground, pulled Jin halfway into her lap, and stroked her hair. It was the only way she could keep herself calm. And it couldn't hurt anyone; Jin wouldn't remember.

She'd told herself she felt nothing true for Jin or Kadrin, that she was only using them to serve her own ends. But it was a lie, had always been a lie.

"You came back for me," Yi-Nereen whispered, her hand lingering over a tiny scar on Jin's cheek. How wrong it felt to see Jin lying still and quiet, when in Yi-Nereen's dreams she was always flying across the wastes on her magebike, the wind in her hair, fierce and free. "What have I done to deserve you?"

Sou-Zell and Kadrin faced each other in the middle of a ring of watching knights. Kadrin hefted the lance in his hand, looking uncertain; Sou-Zell stood as calmly as a pillar carved from stone. No one in the wreckage of the fallen mountain breathed. Yi-Nereen's heart was beating so quickly she thought it might burst.

Then Captain Dev-Larai said, "Begin."

Sou-Zell's lance clattered to the ground. He dropped to one knee before Kadrin, folded his wrists above his head, and said, "I give."

Yi-Nereen clutched Jin close. Kadrin stared at Sou-Zell in disbelief. Some of the knights muttered darkly behind their helms. Captain Dev-Larai's brow furrowed angrily, like he'd just discovered his opponent cheating at cards.

"Lord Sou-Zell, do you mock our traditions? Our gods?"

Sou-Zell raised his head, his face utterly blank, eyes smoldering violet. "Of course not, Captain. Our laws are sacred—every last one. Wouldn't you agree?"

Captain Dev-Larai blanched. He opened his mouth to reply but said nothing. That was when it dawned on Yi-Nereen: it was finally, truly over.

*Oh, good,* Faolin said drowsily. *You're free, Reena. That's good. Because whatever the ambrosia did to you, it's gone now, and . . . I thought I could stay with you, but I think I have to go.*

Yi-Nereen pressed her face into Jin's hair and said, "Thank you." She wasn't speaking to Faolin alone. The words were for Jin and Kadrin, too, and even Sou-Zell. But there would be time to thank them all properly later. Right now, she sensed Faolin slipping away. What would happen to his soul? She hoped he would find his way to the afterlife somehow, to be with Rasvel and Amrys. If the Lost Highway was real, why not heaven?

*Reena, would you do something for me? I wanted to ask Jin, but I don't think I'll get the chance.*

"Of course." Yi-Nereen felt tears running down her face again and falling into Jin's hair as the courier breathed slowly against her chest. "Anything."

She listened to Faolin's last words, straining to hear his soft, fading voice—and then there was only silence. The boy was gone.

# Hana Lee

*Second Age of Storms, 51st Summer*

*Dear Kadrin,*

*We've done it. Courier Jin and I have escaped Kerina Rut. You won't believe where I am now. I'm sitting in a canyon populated by a tribe of wastelanders who don't speak a word of Dirilish and keep a tame chandru as some kind of pet. It's a long story. I truly believed we were going to die, but somehow we survived.*

*I was in a state last night when I wrote you that letter. Thank Rasvel you won't ever read it now. Can you believe it? I forgot to include the most important thing for you to know. How foolish of me.*

*I've cracked it, Kadrin. I know why the High Talents are dwindling. When I finished cross-referencing the Scroll against Kerina Rut's birth records, it was clear as day. But now I can tell you in person! I'll give you this letter the moment I see you. Then we'll talk for hours, like I've been longing to do for so many years. I can't wait for all my words to be free from their prison of ink and parchment, free to fill the room like a flock of birds. I'll talk so much you'll be sick of it.*

*For now, there's a reason I'm writing this letter. I have something I'm afraid to tell you, Kadrin. I don't know what you'll think of me, or if it will change things between us. I don't want anything to change. But I've been living a lie for so long, I can't bear the idea of escaping one only to fall into another. I shall cast away all my secrets, starting with this one.*

*I think I love*

# CHAPTER THIRTY-FIVE

# NO MORE PROMISES

*Second Age of Storms, 51st Summer, Day 27*

It was warm when Jin woke. Sunlight poured across the bed from a slatted window, dividing the room into brightness and shadow. Hanging on the wall directly in front of her was a familiar painting of the wasteland, dotted with wildflowers in white, yellow, and purple. She stared at it, blinking slowly.

"Welcome back!"

The voice came from the deepest shadow in the room, right beneath the window. Jin jerked upright and immediately regretted it. Her whole body ached and her head spun, like she'd spent the last several days burning with fever. She squinted into the shadow. The voice had been familiar.

"Eliesen?"

Kadrin's sister leaned forward, snapping the book in her lap shut. Her eyes were ringed in galena, lending credence to the theory that this was all a dream; Jin had never seen a Sol-blood woman wearing makeup before.

"How much do you remember?" Eliesen asked. "I had Kadrin tell me everything, in case I was the one here when you woke up. Oh, he's going to be inconsolable when he finds out. He wanted so badly to be the first face you saw."

Jin sank carefully back into her cushions. She touched her ribs, recalling the wetness of her own blood. "I think I remember most of it." How could she forget the agony of the mana burning her from the inside out, even as it healed her fatal wound? Kadrin's desperate voice, begging her for a miracle? Or the icy relief of Yi-Nereen's kiss? "Are they both—"

"Alive and well? Yes." Eliesen hopped onto Jin's bed and leaned back, swinging her legs. "Safe in the House? Also yes. It's been a couple of days since you all came back. Escorted by the Knights of Rut, no less." She tossed Jin a wicked grin. "*And* someone else. A courier, I think. Handsome, dark-haired, and a complete asshole. What's his name?"

"What am I doing in your parlor?"

"Kadrin said it was the only room in the House you liked. He had a bed moved in here, the dolt. Even though I told him he could just put the painting on a bedchamber wall and you wouldn't know the difference."

Jin sighed. "I meant—why aren't I at home? Where's my mother?"

"Oh, that." Eliesen frowned. "Let's see, how do I break this news? Your house was destroyed in a storm two days ago. The worst one we've had in fifty years. They're already calling it the Second Storm of Centuries. It broke through the dome in minutes and then it blew over, just like that. But not before it took out two whole districts."

Jin shot up again, heedless of her aching bones. "Which two?"

Eliesen's lip quivered. "Curing and Forge."

Eomma's house was in Curing District. A heavy weight pressed down on Jin's chest. She couldn't breathe.

"My mother?"

Eliesen inched closer. She reached out to stroke Jin's cheek, her eyes bright. Then she collapsed against Jin's chest, giggling. "Absolutely fine. She was here at the House, with Renfir. She only just stepped out of this room five minutes ago."

Air rushed out of Jin in a painful exhale. "I hate you." But she wrapped her arms around Eliesen and pressed her chin against the other woman's head, dizzy with relief.

Eomma's bakery, the little two-room shack she'd scrubbed, painted, and filled with sacks of flour and sugar tins, their new home in Kerina Sol—gone. Her mother must be inconsolable.

Footsteps thumped down the hallway outside. Eliesen pulled away. "That'll be Kadrin. He stomps around like a rovex."

Sure enough, when the door creaked open moments later, Kadrin's face peered inside.

"Jin!"

The door flew open. The next thing Jin heard was Eliesen's squawk as she was pushed aside, and the next thing she felt was Kadrin's arms around her. Over his broad shoulder, she saw Yi-Nereen lingering in the doorway. The princess smiled faintly when she caught Jin's gaze. The galena around her eyes was a little smeared, as if she'd been crying.

Jin freed one arm from Kadrin's crushing embrace and reached out wordlessly. Yi-Nereen hesitated for a moment. Then she came slowly over to the bed and stood there, wringing her hands, until Jin caught her by one trailing sleeve and dragged her down. It was an awkward three-way hug, with Kadrin's chin digging into Jin's neck and Yi-Nereen's veil snagged on the bedpost, and Jin was sure she had the worst morning breath known to man. But they were all there, and it was perfect. Jin never wanted it to end.

"The Council wasn't pleased with me for running off against their wishes," Kadrin said with a sheepish grin. "I'm actually on house arrest. Which isn't so bad, since everyone I care about is here in the House. There was talk of sending Reena to stay with Shield Lord Tethris and her family—distant relations, apparently."

"Very distant," Yi-Nereen said.

"But Father argued for her to remain here, as his guest. I think he regrets how things went between us at the last Council meeting." A shadow flitted across Kadrin's face, but it was gone almost as quickly as it came. "That was only decided this morning. You haven't missed much, Jin."

Jin nodded slowly. She almost let her next question go unasked. Did she truly want to know? It had been hard enough hearing about what had happened to Faolin. The thought that if she'd arrived just hours earlier, she could have saved him . . . but instead, he'd met the same lonely end as his sister, a guilt Jin would carry with her the rest of her life.

But she had to know. "Falka?" she asked quietly.

Kadrin and Yi-Nereen exchanged slow glances.

"She's alive," Yi-Nereen said. Her voice was careful, as if she were treading across a floor of broken glass. "The rest of the raiders scattered when the castle fell. But not her. She seemed—unwell."

Jin swallowed. She held the memories of Falka sobbing on the floor at arm's length, to confront later. "Where is she now?"

A longer pause than before. Then Kadrin said, "Sou-Zell and the Knights of Rut took her. She's their prisoner now. There wasn't much we could do; the captain seemed determined not to leave empty-handed. And Sou-Zell didn't argue. Actually, I thought he seemed rather keen on bringing her back to Kerina Rut."

"Of course he was." Bitterness colored Yi-Nereen's voice. "She knows the secret of transplanting Talent from one person to another. Sou-Zell's House is withering from lack of Talent in their bloodline. Now he doesn't have to trouble himself with a marriage contract to solve that problem. He has everything he wanted, and if anyone is willing to pay the cost of what Falka and Tibius Vann discovered, it's him."

Kadrin scratched the back of his neck. "I don't know, Reena. After our duel, I'd like to believe the man's on his way to turning over a new leaf."

"If you ask me, he's just spotted the leaf on the ground, and he's considering giving it a poke to see if there's a scorpion under it."

Jin took little notice of Kadrin's snickering, or Yi-Nereen's hesitant yet satisfied smile. She stared at the wall, her exhaustion and soreness creeping back. *Oh, Falka. It was your worst nightmare to be anyone's prisoner.*

Yi-Nereen touched her arm. "Are you feeling ill, Jin? Kadrin's physician examined you and said you were healthy, but he admitted no one knows the long-term effects of acute mana poisoning. Since you're the first to survive it."

"I'm fine." Jin put her hand over Yi-Nereen's without thinking. Then she froze. Her gaze crept up to Yi-Nereen's face—to her soft, light brown eyes and her parted lips, still blistered and peeling. A lump formed in her throat. She pushed back her blanket and slid out of bed, ignoring her protesting bones. "Excuse me."

Then she fled. Well, more accurately, she hobbled out of the converted parlor and down the hallway, stiff legs groaning with every step. Her mind was filled with images of Kadrin and Yi-Nereen laughing on her bed, holding hands, stealing glances at each other when they thought Jin wasn't looking. How sweet the two of them looked together—as if the whole world had been built just for them.

She had to be alone. The first door she opened led into the garden. Standing there in the shade of the ivy-wrapped columns, breathing in the fragrance of the bloomwoven flowers growing in their beds, she felt her brief burst of energy fade.

A dark suspicion had taken hold of her in the parlor. Now it pressed closely against her chest. She wouldn't be able to breathe until she knew.

Faolin, in the canyon when she'd awoken from Reena's first kiss. *Jin se imbyr?* He'd wanted to know if she still had the spark. Why had he wanted to know?

Jin closed her eyes and burned mana. But there was nothing to burn. Jin gripped her own throat as if she were drowning—but this wasn't dying for lack of air. It was the realization she didn't need air anymore, would never breathe it again.

She was Talentless.

She'd just collapsed onto a stone bench, trembling and spent, when she heard Kadrin's voice calling her name from inside the House.

He came into the garden alone. Jin stared past him at the red-and-white flowers in the nearest garden bed. No flowers grew in the wasteland, but she'd never missed them. Jin's world didn't have flowers.

"Where's my bike?"

Kadrin sighed. "I hoped you wouldn't ask."

That meant it was gone. Crushed beneath the mountain as it

fell, most likely. Or buried beneath the rubble, still at the bottom of the lift. Either way, it was a moot point.

Jin sucked in a breath and let the air slowly escape. It was time to stop thinking about all she'd lost. She had to think about the future. About finding a new place for her and Eomma. Taking odd jobs to tide them over while she hunted for someone to teach her a new trade.

Moving on from this House and everyone in it.

Kadrin sank onto the bench beside her, and Jin abruptly realized it was the first time they'd been alone together since he'd kissed her in the castle.

"It's crossed my mind," he said finally, "that I can't possibly repay you."

"Don't try," Jin said. The force of her sentiment surprised her. The last thing she wanted was for either Kadrin or Yi-Nereen to acknowledge what she'd done. Because she knew she hadn't done it out of some honorable obligation. She wasn't their hero.

Kadrin didn't seem to have heard her. He was twisting the ring on his finger; the small silver skulls caught the sunlight as they went round and round. "When we thought you were—when we thought you might not wake up . . ." He shook his head, cleared his throat. "I want to give you everything. I'm serious. My family's wealth, the stars in the sky, the blessings of heaven. Of course I can't actually do any of that, but it's still less than I owe you for bringing Reena home and saving both our lives." He met her eyes, smiling ruefully. "If you could ask for anything, Jin, what would it be?"

*To turn back time*, she thought.

She imagined a version of herself who had never fallen in love. A Jin made of steel, who gave nothing away for less than a fair price, let alone her heart. Would that Jin still have ended up here? Or would she have taken Yi-Nereen's coin purse at the Tower of Arrested Stars and walked away without a shred of guilt?

She wasn't made of steel. She wanted too much—*needed* too much. And if Yi-Nereen and Kadrin found out the true price Jin had paid to save their lives, all their gratitude would turn into guilt.

Jin had already known the three of them could never be equals. It surprised her how much it hurt to finally accept that truth.

"There's only one thing you can do for me."

The look in Kadrin's eyes stilled her. "Anything, Jin."

It seemed a lifetime ago that she'd stood in a dark harbor in Kerina Rut, with the scent of plums heavy in the night air and Teul-Kim's low voice in her ear.

"Reena's in your hands now," Jin said. "Watch over her."

Kadrin caught her arm as she stood. "Why does that sound like a goodbye?"

"I can watch over myself," a new voice said. Yi-Nereen stepped out of the shadows between the pillars. How long had she been there? She came to stand beside the bench with her hand on Kadrin's shoulder. "I don't need any more handlers." The words were pointed, but her voice was gentle. "So, Jin, I'm afraid we'll have to find some other way to make things right between us."

Jin clenched her fists. Why were they making this so difficult? She had tortured herself for years with thoughts of what she could never have. Now the job was over, and she could leave. This wasn't supposed to be like leaving Falka—a dagger twisting in her ribs forevermore. Kadrin and Yi-Nereen had each other. They were happy. They didn't need her.

"I'm sorry," she said, "but there's no way you could."

Yi-Nereen and Kadrin exchanged glances.

"You're right," Yi-Nereen said. "It's an impossible situation. And it's your fault for being impossible not to love."

There was no sound in the garden besides the sigh of wind through the flower beds and water trickling down the gabled roofs. Jin stood like a statue in the midst of it all. She had misheard Yi-Nereen, simple as that.

"We've talked," Kadrin said. "For hours and hours, until one thing was clear. None of it feels right without you." He took Yi-Nereen's hand, but his gaze was fixed on Jin. "What if we found a way to make it work?"

Jin couldn't breathe. A thousand thoughts whirled through her head at once. But the traitorous voice that spoke to her often in Kadrin's or Yi-Nereen's presence, cajoling her to hoard the time she had with them, was silent.

*Don't ever leave me*, said a different voice, and she nearly choked. Everything she wanted, and she couldn't reach out and take it. Not with Falka's shadow in the corners of her mind and her lost Talent a hollow in her core. She felt like her hands were stained with engine grease; anything she touched would be ruined. But if she left to heal, to become clean again somehow, she couldn't expect them to wait for her.

If she left, she'd be letting them go.

"Jin?" The breeze had picked up, and Yi-Nereen's brow was creased in concern beneath her fluttering veil. "Are you all right?"

Jin looked away from the two royals, up at the sky. Her chest ached fiercely. Her stupid, stupid heart. How she loved them both. How desperately she wanted to be part of their beautiful world. To live behind a Wall, safe and content. To forget the taste of being alone.

"I don't know."

She spoke the words into the heavens, because she couldn't look at either of them. A cloud was drifting past, a pale wisp hardly visible against the blue of the sky. She remembered jumping from a castle atop a mountain, plummeting through the storm. Soaring over dunes on her magebike. Flying. Free.

Whatever freedom still existed for her, she wouldn't find it here. Not now. But perhaps someday.

"I can't make any more promises," she said, her voice little more than a whisper. "I'm sorry."

This time Kadrin and Reena didn't follow her. They remained in the garden, staring after her in stunned silence, and Jin left them with the flowers. She limped through the House until she found the front door, just as tall and imposing as the day she'd first walked through it, scattering ashes on the tile. Her throat itched as she stared at it. For a single, fragile moment, she thought about turning around.

Then she opened the door and stepped through. Wind brushed her hair back from her face like the gentle touch of a lover. The avenue outside was quiet; the cherry blossom trees were in riotous bloom. Jin left the House of Steel Heavens behind, and she didn't look back.

# ACKNOWLEDGMENTS

You can write a novel on your own, but it takes the help of countless others to bring it to life. This is the part where I try to name as many of those people as I can. And to all the people I'm about to accidentally leave out, a huge *thank you so much and whoops, my bad!*

My agent, Paul Lucas, who has been a steadfast champion of my work from the start. My agent's assistant, Eloy Bleifuss, for his thoughtful feedback and taking care of all the little details. The rest of the folks at Janklow & Nesbit US.

My editor, Amara Hoshijo, for loving my book and my characters the way I do. The rest of Saga's editorial team, Joe Monti and Jéla Lewter. And all the rest of Saga/Gallery Press, most of whom I've never met but who have already been working hard to help my book succeed. Thank you so much!

My loyal critique partners and first readers: Virginia Fox, Xander Wade, and Julie Voh. You're the ones who give me the strength to keep writing even when it all feels pointless. For all the late-night commiseration over Discord and the pep talks with too many exclamation points and emojis . . . Thank you!

My beta readers and cheerleaders for *Road to Ruin* (in no particular order): Mia, Raidah, SJ, Nemo, Chloe, Carissa, Frances. Stay awesome!

# Acknowledgments

Everyone involved in the making of the film *Mad Max: Fury Road*.

My writer group chats, for keeping me sane. There's a lot of them now (too many for me to stay on top of all the notifications), but WMC was the first and I'll always be grateful.

My Bay Area writer friends, who drag my introverted self out to places and force me to have a good time: Victoria Shi and Julia Vee.

My D&D group, whose exploits inspired me to get back into writing books during the pandemic: Shalin, Greg, Jyu, John, Arthur, and Jeff.

My friends Daniel and Jane, for always being there.

My parents, for providing me with all the books I could devour as a child, and my four brothers, all of whom I love dearly: 오빠, Jason, RJ, and Jake.

My partner's family, for reading my books even if fantasy isn't their favorite genre, and endlessly supporting me in my publishing career: Rajiv, Rupal, Anjali, Kavi, and Sarah.

My partner, Shalin. It'll be ten years together by the time this book is released into the wild. Thank you for being there through all the ups and downs, and for always being my number one fan, even when you think I should have written a different ending. And our cats, Saskia and Calcifer, for being soft and adorable and the best creatures on earth.

And finally, thank you for reading this book!

## ABOUT THE AUTHOR

Hana Lee is a biracial Korean American writer who also builds software for a living. She has an undying love for fantastical stories in all their forms, especially video games, and a habit of writing to moody indie rock playlists. Her short writing has appeared in *Fantasy Magazine* and *Uncanny Magazine*. She lives in California with her partner and two beloved cats.